Alexander Pope

Works. With his last corrections, additions, and improvements;
carefully collated and compared with former editions, together with
notes from the various critics and commentators

Vol. 4

Alexander Pope

Works. With his last corrections, additions, and improvements; carefully collated and compared with former editions, together with notes from the various critics and commentators
Vol. 4

ISBN/EAN: 9783337115005

Printed in Europe, USA, Canada, Australia, Japan

Cover: Foto ©Andreas Hilbeck / pixelio.de

More available books at **www.hansebooks.com**

THE

WORKS

OF

Alexander Pope, Efq.

IN FOUR VOLUMES COMPLETE.

WITH HIS LAST

CORRECTIONS, ADDITIONS,

AND

IMPROVEMENTS.

Carefully collated and compared with former EDITIONS :

TOGETHER WITH

NOTES from the various CRITICS and COMMENTATORS.

VOL. IV.

LONDON:

Printed for the EDITOR, and fold by J. WENMAN, No. 144, Fleet-ftreet, and all other Bookfellers in Great Britain and Ireland.

MDCCLXXVIII,

CONTENTS of the FOURTH VOLUME.

A 2   25. Dr.

9. To

CONTENTS.

From

vi CONTENTS.

CONTENTS

vii

LET-

LETTERS

OF

Mr. POPE,

AND

Several of his FRIENDS.

Quo Defiderio veteres revocamus Amores.
Atque olim amiffas flemus Amicitias!

CATULL.

VCL. IV.   B

L E T T E R S

TO AND FROM

SEVERAL PERSONS,

From the Year 1711 to 1714.

L E T T E R I.

To the Hon. J. C. Efq;

June 15, 1711.

I Send you Dennis's remarks on the * Eſſay ; which equally abound in juſt criticiſms and fine railleries. The few obſervations in my hand in the margins, are what a morning's leiſure permitted me to make purely for your peruſal. For I am of opinion that ſuch a critic, as you will find him by the latter part of his book, is but one way to be properly anſwered, and that way I would not take after what he informs me in his preface, that he is at this time perſecuted by fortune. This I knew not before ; if I had, his name had been ſpared in the Eſſay, for that only reaſon. I can't conceive what ground he has for ſo exceſſive a reſentment : nor imagine how theſe † three lines can be called a reflection on his perſon, which only

---

* On Criticiſm

† But Appius reddens at each word you ſpeak,
And ſtares tremendous with a threa:'ning eye,
Like ſome fierce tyrant in old tapeſtry.

deſcribe

describe him subject a little to anger on some occasions. I have heard of combatants so very furious, as to fall down themselves with that very blow which they design'd to lay heavy on their antagonists. But if Mr. Dennis's rage proceeds only from a zeal to discourage young and unexperienced writers from scribling, he should frighten us with his verse, not prose: for I have often known, that, when all the precepts in the world would not reclaim a sinner, some very sad example has done the business. Yet, to give this man his due, he has objected to one or two lines with reason, and I will alter them in case of another edition; I will make my enemy do me a kindness where he meant an injury, and so serve instead of a friend. What he observes at the bottom of page 20 of his reflec- tions, was objected to by yourself, and had been mended but for the haste of the press: I confess it what the Eng- lish call a Bull, in the expression, though the sense be manifest enough: Mr. Dennis's Bulls are seldom in the expression, they are generally in the sense.

I shall certainly never make the least reply to him; not only because you advise me, but because I have ever been of opinion, that, if a book can't answer for itself to the public, 'tis to no sort of purpose for its author to do it. If I am wrong in any sentiment of that essay, I pro- test sincerely, I don't desire all the world should be de- ceived (which would be of very ill consequence) merely that I myself may be thought right (which is of very little consequence.) I would be the first to recant, for the benefit of others, and the glory of myself; for (as I take it) when a man own's himself to have been in an er- ror, he does but tell you in other words, that he is wiser than he was. But I have had an advantage by the pub- lishing that book, which otherwise I should never have known; it has been the occasion of making me friends and open abettors, of several gentlemen of known sense and wit; and of proving to me what I have till now doubted, that my writings are taken some notice of by the world, or I should never be attacked thus in particular. I have

read

read that 'twas a cuftom among the *Romans*, while a general rode in triumph, to have the common foldiers in the ftreets, that railed at him and reproached him, to put him in mind, that though his fervices were in the main approved and rewarded, yet he had faults enough to keep him humble.

You will fee by this, that whoever fets up for wit in thefe days ought to have the conftancy of a primitive Chriftian, and be prepared to fuffer martyrdom in the caufe of it. But fure this is the firft time that a Wit was attacked for his *Religion*, as you'll find, I am moft zealoufly in this treatife; and you know, Sir, what alarms I have had from the * oppofite fide on this account. Have I not reafon to cry out with the poor fellow in *Virgil*,

Quid jam mifero mihi denique reftat ?
Cui neque apud *Danaos* ufquam locus, et fuper ipfi
Dardanidæ infenfi pœnas cum fanguine pofcunt !

'Tis however my happinefs that you, Sir, are impartial.

Jove was alike to *Latian* and to *Phrygian*,
For you well know, that Wit's of no Religion.

The manner in which Mr. D. takes to pieces feveral particular lines, detached from their natural places, may fhew how eafy it is to a caviller to give a new fenfe, or a new nonfenfe to any thing. And indeed his conftructions are not more wrefted from the genuine meaning, than theirs who objected to the heterodox parts, as they called them.

Our friend the Abbe is not of that fort, who with the utmoft candour and freedom has modeftly told me what others thought, and fhewn himfelf one (as he very well expreffes it) rather of a number than a party. The only difference between us in relation to the Monks, is that he thinks moft forts of learning flourifhed among them, and

* See the enfuing Letter.

I am

I am of opinion, that only fome fort of learning was barely kept alive by them: he believes that in the moft natural and obvious fenfe, that line (A fecond deluge learning over-run) will be underftood of learning in general; and
I fancy 'twill be underftood only (as 'tis meant) of polite
learning, criticifm, poetry, &c. which is the only learning
concerned in the fubjcft of the effay. It is true, that the
monks did preferve what learning there was, about Nicholas the fifth's time; but thofe who fucceeded fell into
the depth of barbarifm, or at leaft ftood at a ftay while
others arofe from thence, in fo much that even Erafmus
and Reuchlin could hardly laugh them out of it. I am
highly obliged to the Abbe's zeal in my commendation,
and goodnefs in not concealing what he thinks my
error. And his teftifying fome efteem for the book juft
at a time when his brethren rais'd a clamour againft it,
is an inftance of great generofity and candour, which I
fhall ever acknowledge.

                                           Your, &c.

LETTER II.

To the fame.

                                      June 18, 1711.
IN your laft you informed me of the miftaken zeal of
fome people, who feem to make it no lefs their bufinefs
to perfuade men they are erroneous, than doctors do that
they are fick; only that they may magnify their own cure,
and triumph over an imaginary diftemper. The fimile
objected to in my Effay,

        (Thus wit, like faith, by each man is apply'd
        To one fmall fect, and all are damn'd befide.)

plainly concludes at this fecond line, where ftands a
full ftop: and what follows (*Meanly they feek, &c.*) fpeaks
only of wit (which is meant by that bleffing, and that
                                                     fun

fun) for how can the fun of faith be faid to fublime the fouthern wits, and to ripen the geniufes of northern cli-, mates ? I fear, thefe gentlemen underftand grammar as little as they do criticifm : and, perhaps, out of good na-ture to the monks, are willing to take from them the cenfure of ignorance, and to have it to themfelves. The word *they* refers (as I am fure, I meant, and as I thought every one muft have known) to thofe Critics there fpoken of, who are partial to fome particular fet of writers, to the prejudice of all others. And the very fimile itfelf, if twice read, may convince them, that the cenfure here of damning, lies not on our church at all, unlefs they call our church *one fmall fect* : and the cautious words *(by each man)* manifeftly fhew it a general reflection on fuch (whoever they are) who entertain thofe narrow and limited notions of the mercy of the Almighty ; which the reformed mi-nifters and prefbyterians are as guilty of as any people living.

Yet after all, I promife you, Sir, if the alteration of a word or two will gratify any man of found faith though weak underftanding, I will (though it were from no other principle than that of common good nature) comply with it. And if you pleafe but to particularize the fpot where their objection lies (for it is in a very narrow compafs) that ftumbling block, tho' it be but a little pebble, fhall be removed out of their way. If the heat of thefe good difputants (who, I am affraid, being bred up to wrangle in the fchools, cannot get rid of the humour all their lives) fhould proceed fo far as to' perfonal reflections upon me, I affure you, notwithftanding, I will do or fay nothing however provok'd (for fome people can no more provoke than oblige) that is unbecoming the true character of a catholic. I will fet before me the example of that great man, and great faint, Erafmus ; who in the midft of ca-lumny proceeded with all the calmnefs of innocence, and the unrevenging fpirit of primitive chriftianity. Howe-ver, I would advife them to fuffer the mention of him to

pafs

pafs unregarded, left I fhould be forced to do that for his
reputjon which I would never do for my own; I mean,
to vindicate fo great a light of our church from the malice of paft times, and the ignorance of the prefent, in a
language which may extend farther than that in which
the trifle about criticifm is written. I wifh thefe gentlemen would be contented with finding fault with me only, who will fubmit to them right or wrong, as far as I only am concerned ; I have a greater regard to the quiet of
mankind, than to difturb it for things of fo little confequence as my credit and my fenfe. A little humility
can do a poet no hurt, and a little charity would do a
prieft none : for, as St. Auftin finely fays, *Ubi charitas, ibi
humilitas, ubi humilitas, ibi pax.*

Your, etc.

LETTER III.

To the fame.

July 19, 1711.

THE concern which you more than feem to be
affected with for my reputation, by the feveral accounts you have fo obligingly given of what reports and
cenfures the holy Vandals have thought fit to pafs upon
me, makes me defirous of telling fo good a friend my
whole thoughts of this matter : and of fetting before you
in a clear light, the true ftate of it.

I have ever believed the beft piece of fervice one could
do to our religion, was openly to exprefs our deteftation
and fcorn of all thofe mean artifices and *pia fraudes,* which
it ftands fo little in need of, and which have laid it under
fo great a fcandal among its enemies.

Nothing has been fo much a fcarecrow to them, as that
too peremptory and uncharitable affertion of an utter impoffibility of falvation to all but ourfelves ; invincible ignorance excepted, which indeed fome people define under

fo

ſo great limitations, and with ſuch excluſions, that it ſeems, as if that word were rather invented as a ſalvo, or expedient not to be thought too bold with the thunderbolts of God, (which are hurled about ſo freely on almoſt all mankind by the hands of eccleſiaſtics) than as a real exception to almoſt univerſal damnation. For beſides the ſmall number of the truly faithful in our church, we muſt again ſubdivide ; the Janſeniſt is damned by the Jeſuit, the Jeſuit by the Janſeniſt, the Scotiſt by the Thomiſt, and ſo forth.

There may be errors, I grant, but I can't think them of ſuch conſequence as to deſtroy utterly the charity of mankind ; the very greateſt bond in which we are ingaged by God to one another : therefore, I own to you, I was glad of any opportunity to expreſs my diſlike of ſo ſhocking a ſentiment as thoſe of the religion I profeſs are commonly charged with ; and I hoped, a ſlight inſinuation, introduced ſo eaſily by a caſual ſimilitude only, could never have given offence ; but on the contrary muſt needs have done good ; in a nation and time, wherein we are the ſmaller party, and conſequently moſt miſrepreſented, and moſt in need of vindication.

For the ſame reaſon I took occaſion to mention the ſuperſtition of ſome ages after the ſubverſion of the Roman Empire, which is too manifeſt a truth to be denied, and does in no ſort reflect upon the preſent profeſſors of our faith, who are free from it. Our ſilence in theſe points may, with ſome reaſon, make our adverſaries think we allow and perſiſt in thoſe bigotries ; which yet in reality all good and ſenſible men deſpiſe, though they are perſuaded not to ſpeak againſt them, I can't tell why, ſince now it is no way the intereſt even of the worſt of our prieſthood (as it might have been then) to have them ſmothered in ſilence : for, as the oppoſite ſects are now prevailing, 'tis too late to hinder our church from being ſlander'd ; 'tis our buſineſs now to vindicate ourſelves, from being thought abettors of what they charge us with. This can't fo well be brought about with ferious faces; we muft laugh with them at what deferves it, or be content to be laughed at, with fuch as deferve it.

As to particulars: you cannot but have obferved, that at firft the whole objection againft the fimile of Wit and Faith lay to the word They: when that was beyond contradiction removed (the very grammar ferving to confute them) then the objection was againft the fimile itfelf ; or if that fimile will not be objected to (fenfe and common reafon being indeed a little ftubborn, and not apt to give way to every body) next the mention of Superftition muft become a crime ; as if religion and fhe were fifters, or that it were fcandal upon the family of Chrift, to fay a word againft the devil's baftard. Afterwards more mifchief is difcover'd in a place that feemed innocent at firft, the two lines about *Schifmatics*. An ordinary man would imagine the author plainly declared againft thofe fchiftics for quitting the true faith out of a contempt of the underftanding of fome few of its believers : but thefe believers are called *dull*, and becaufe I fay that thofe fchifmatics think fome believers dull, therefore thefe charitable interpreters of my meaning will have it that I think all believers dull. I was lately telling Mr. *** thefe objections: who affured me I had faid nothing which a catholic need to difown; and I have caufe to know that gentleman's fault (if he has any) is not want of zeal : he put a notion into my head, which, I confefs, I can't but acquiefce in; that when a fet of people are piqued at any truth which they think to their own difadvantage, their method of revenge on the truth-fpeaker is to attack his reputation a by-way, and not openly to object to the place they are really galled by : what thefe therefore (in his opinion) are in earneft angry at, is that Erafmus, whom their tribe oppreffed and perfecuted, fhould be vindicated after an age of obloquy by one of their own people, willing to utter an honeft truth in behalf of the dead, whom no man fure will flatter, and to whom few will do juftice.

Others,

Others, you know, were as angry that I mentioned Mr. Walfh with honour; who, as he never refufed to any.one of merit of any party the praife due to him, fo honeftly deferved it from all others, tho' of ever fo different intere-refts or fentiments. May I be ever guilty of this fort of liberty, and latitude of principle! which gives us the hardinefs of fpeaking well of thofe whom envy oppreffes even after death. As I would always fpeak well of my living friends when they are abfent, nay becaufe they are abfent, fo would I much more of the dead, in that eternal abfence; and the rather, becaufe I expect no thanks for it.

Thus, Sir, you fee I do in my confcience perfift in what I have written; yet in my friendfhip I will recant and alter whatever you pleafe, in cafe of a fecond edition (which I think the book will not fo foon arrive at, for Tonfon's printer told me he drew off a thoufand copies in this firft impreffion, and, I fancy, a treatife of this nature, which not one gentleman in threefcore, even of a liberal education, can underftand, can hardly exceed the vent of that number.) You fhall find me a true Trojan in my faith and friendfhip, in both which I will perfevere to the end. Your, &c.

LETTER IV.

To my Lord LANSDOWN.

Binfield, Jan. 10, 1712.

I Thank you for having given my poem of Windfor Foreft its greateft ornament, that of bearing your name in the front of it. 'Tis one thing when a perfon of true merit permits us to have the honour of drawing him as like as we can; and another, when we make a fine thing at random, and perfuade the next vain creature we can find that 'tis his own likenefs; which is the cafe every day of my fellow fcriblers. Yet, my Lord, this honour

has

has given me no more pride than your honours have given you; but it affords me a great deal of pleasure, which is much better than a great deal of pride; and it indeed would give me some pain, if I was not sure of one advantage; that whereas others are offended if they have not more than justice done them, you would be displeased if you had so much: therefore I may safely do you as much injury in my word, as you do yourself in your own thoughts. I am so vain as to think I have shewn you a favour, in sparing your modesty, and you cannot but make me some return for prejudicing the truth to gratify you: This I beg may be the free correction of these verses, which will have few beauties, but what may be made by your blots. I am in the circumstance of an ordinary painter drawing Sir Godfrey Kneller, who by a few touches of his own could make the piece very valuable. I might then hope, that many years hence the world might read, in conjunction with your name, that of

Your Lordship's, &c.

LETTER V.

The Hon. J. C. to Mr. POPE.

May 23, 1712.

I AM very glad for the sake of the widow, and for the credit of the deceased, that * Betterton's remains are fallen into such hands as may render them reputable to the one, and beneficial to the other. Besides the public acquaintance I long had with that poor man, I also had a slender knowledge of his parts and capacity by private conversation, and ever thought it pity he was necessitated by the straitness of his fortune, to act (and especially to his latest hours) an imaginary and fictitious part, who

---

* A Translation of some part of Chaucer's Canterbury Tales, the Prologues, etc. printed in a Miscellany with some works of Mr. Pope, in 2 vol. 12mo, by B. Lintot.

was

was capable of exhibiting a real one, with credit to himfelf, and advantage to his neighbour.

I hope your health permitted you to execute your defign of giving us an imitation of Pollio; I am fatisfy'd
'twill be doubly divine, and I fhall long to fee it. I ever
thought church-mufic the moft ravifhing of all harmo-
nious compofitions, and muft alfo believe facred fubjects,
well-handled, the moft infpiring of all poetry.

But where hangs the *Lock* now? (tho' I know, that
rather than draw any juft reflection upon yourfelf of the
leaft fhadow of ill-nature, you would freely have fupprefs'd one of the beft of poems.) I hear no more of it—
will it come out in Lintot's Mifcellany or not? I wrote
to Lord Petre upon the fubject of the Lock, fome time
fince, but have as yet had no anfwer, nor indeed do I
know when he'll be in London. I have, fince I faw you,
correfponded with Mrs. W. I hope fhe is now with her
Aunt, and that her journey thither was fomething facili-
tated by my writing to that lady as preffingly as poffible,
not to let any thing whatfoever obftruct it. I fent her
obliging anfwer to the party it moft concern'd; and when
I hear Mrs. W. is certainly there, I will write again to
my Lady, to urge as much as poffible the effecting the
only thing that in my opinion can make her niece eafy.
I have run out my extent of paper, and am

Your, &c.

LETTER VI.

The Anfwer.

May 28, 1712.

IT is not only the difpofition I always have of converfing
with you, that makes me fo fpeedily anfwer your
obliging letter, but the apprehenfion left your charitable
intent of writing to my Lady A. on Mrs. W.'s affair
fhould be fruftrated, by the fhort ftay fhe makes there.
She went thither on the 25th with that mixture of expectation

tation and anxiety, with which people ufually go into
unknown or half-difcover'd countries, utterly ignorant of
the difpofitions of the inhabitants, and the treatment they
are to meet with. The unfortunate of all people are the
moft unfit to be left alone ; yet, we fee, the world generally takes care they fhall be fo : whereas, if we took a
confiderate profpect of the world, the bufinefs and ftudy
of the happy and eafy fhould be to divert and humour,
as well as comfort and pity, the diftreffed. I cannot
therefore excufe fome near Allies of mine for their conduct of late towards this Lady, which has given me a
great deal of anger as well as forrow : all I fhall fay to
you of them at prefent is, that they have not been my
Relations thefe two months. The confent of opinions in
our minds, is certainly a nearer tye than can be contracted by all the blood in our bodies ; and I am proud of
finding I have fomething congenial with you. Will you
permit me to confefs to you, that all the favours and
kind offices you have fhewn towards me, have not fo
ftrongly cemented me yours, as the difcovery of that generous and manly compaffion you manifefted in the cafe
of this unhappy Lady ? I am afraid to infinuate to you
how much I efteem you : Flatterers have taken up the
ftyle which was once peculiar to friends, and an honeft
man has now no way left to exprefs himfelf befides the
common one of knaves ; fo that true friends now-a-days
differ in their addrefs from flatterers, much as right maf-
tiffs do from fpaniels, and fhow themfelves by a dumb,
furly fort of fidelity, rather than by a complaifant and
open kindnefs.—Will you never leave commending my
poetry ? In fair truth, Sir, I like it but too well myfelf
already : expofe me no more, I beg you, to the great
danger of vanity, (the rock of all men, but moft of
young men) and be kindly content for the future, when
you would pleafe me thoroughly, to fay only you like
what I write.

Your, &c.

LETTER

LETTER VII.

Dec. 5, 1712.

Y OU have at length complied with the requeſt I have often made you, for you have ſhown me, I muſt confeſs, ſeveral of my faults in the ſight of thoſe letters. Upon a review of them, I find many things that would give me ſhame, if I were not more deſirous to be thought honeſt than prudent; ſo many things freely thrown out, ſuch lengths of unreſerved friendſhip, thoughts juſt warm from the brain without any poliſhing or dreſs, the very diſhabille of the underſtanding. You have proved your-ſelf more tender of another's embryos than the fondeſt mothers are of their own, for you have preſerved every thing that I miſcarried of. Since I know this, I ſhall in one reſpect be more afraid of writing to you than ever, at this careleſs rate, becauſe I ſee my evil works may again riſe in judgment againſt me; yet in another reſpect I ſhall be leſs afraid, ſince this has given me ſuch a proof of the extreme indulgence you afford to my ſlighteſt thoughts. The reviſal of theſe letters has been a kind of examina-tion of conſcience to me; ſo fairly and faithfully have I ſet down in them, from time to time, the true and un-diſguiſed ſtate of my mind. But I find, that theſe which were intended as ſketches of my friendſhip, give as imper-feƈ images of it, as the little landſcapes we commonly ſee in black and white do of a beautiful country; they can repreſent but a very ſmall part of it, and that deprived of the life and luſtre of nature. I perceive, that the more I endeavoured to render manifeſt the real affeƈtion and value I ever had for you, I did but injure it by repre-ſenting leſs and leſs of it : as glaſſes which are deſign'd to make an objeƈt very clear, generally contraƈt it. Yet as when people have a full idea of a thing firſt upon their own knowledge, the leaſt traces of it ſerve to refreſh the remembrance, and are not diſpleaſing on that ſcore; ſo, I

hope,

hope; the foreknowledge you had of my esteem for you, is the reason that you do not dislike my letters.

They will not be of any great service (I find) in the design I mentioned to you: I believe I had better steal from a richer man, and plunder your letters (which I have kept as carefully as I would Letters Patent, since they intitle me to what I more value than titles of honour.) You have some cause to apprehend this usage from me, if what some say be true, that I am a great borrower; however, I have hitherto had the luck that none of my creditors have challenged me for it: and those who say it are such, whose writings no man ever borrow'd from, so have the least reason to complain; and whose works are granted on all hands to be but too much their own. Another has been pleased to declare, that my verses are corrected by other men: I verily believe theirs were never corrected by any man: but indeed if mine have not, 'twas not my fault; I have endeavour'd my utmost that they should. But these things are only whisper'd, and I will not encroach upon Bays's province and *pen whispers*, so hasten to conclude

Your, &c.

LETTER VIII.

From my Lord LANSDOWN.

Oct. 21, 1713.

I AM pleased beyond measure with your design of translating Homer. The trials which you have already made and published on some parts of that author, have shewn that you are equal to so great a task: and you may therefore depend upon the utmost services I can do you in promoting this work, or any thing that may be for your service.

I hope Mr. Stafford, for whom you was pleased to concern yourself, has had the good effects of the Queen's

grace

grace to him. I had notice, the night before I began my journey, that her Majefty had not only directed his pardon, but order'd a writ for reverfing his outlawry.

Your, &c.

LETTER IX.

To General ANTHONY HAMILTON *.

Upon his having tranflated into French Verfe the *Effay on Criticifm*.

Oct. 10, 1713.

IF I could as well exprefs, or (if you will allow me to fay it) tranflate the fentiments of my heart as you have done thofe of my head, in your excellent verfion of my Effay; I fhould not only appear the beft writer in the world, but, what I much more defire to be thought, the moft your fervant of any man living. 'Tis an advantage very rarely known, to receive at once a great honour and a great improvement. This, Sir, you have afforded me, having at the fame time made others take my fenfe, and taught me to underftand my own; if I may call that my own which is indeed more properly yours. Your verfes are no more a tranflation of mine, than Virgil's are of Homer's; but are, like his, the jufteft imitation, and the nobleft Commentary.

In putting me into a French drefs, you have not only adorned my outfide, but mended my fhape; and, if I am now a good figure, I muft confider you have naturaliz'd me into a country which is famous for making every man a fine gentleman. It is by your means that (contrary to moft young travellers) I am come back much better than I went out.

I cannot but wifh we had a bill of commerce for tranflation eftablifhed the next parliament; we could not fail

* Author of the Memoirs of the *Count de Grammont*, *Cæfar*, and other pieces of note in French.

of being gainers by that, nor of making ourſelves amends for any thing we have loſt by the war. Nay, tho' we ſhould inſiſt upon the demoliſhing of Boileau's works, the French, as long as they have writers of your form, might have as good an equivalent.

Upon the whole, I am really as proud, as our miniſters ought to be, of the terms I have gain'd from abroad; and I deſign, like them, to publiſh ſpeedily to the world the benefits accruing from them; for I cannot reſiſt the temptation of printing your admirable tranſlation here *; to which, if you will be ſo obliging to give me leave to prefix your name, it will be the only addition you can make to the honour already done me. I am

Your, &c.

* This was never done, for the two printed French verſions are neithe of this hand. The one was done by Monſieur Roboton, private ſecretary to King George the firſt, printed in quarto at Amſterdam, and at London 1717. The other by the Abbé Reſnel, in octavo, with a large preface and notes, at Paris, 1730.

LETTERS

LETTERS

TO AND FROM

Mr. STEELE, Mr. ADDISON, Mr. CONGREVE, &c.

From the Year 1712 to 1715.

LETTER I.

Mr. STEELE to Mr. POPE.

June 1, 1712.

I AM at a folitude, an houfe between Hampftead and London, wherein Sir Charles Sedley died. This circumftance fet me a thinking and ruminating upon the employments in which men of, wit exercife themfelves. It was faid of Sir Charles, who breath'd his laft in this room,

> Sedley has that prevailing gentle art,
> Which can with a refiftlefs charm impart
> The loofeft wifhes to the chafteft heart;
> Raife fuch a conflict, kindle fuch a fire
> Between declining Virtue and Defire,
> Till the poor vanquifh'd Maid diffolves away
> In dreams all night, in fighs and tears all day.

This was a happy talent to a man of the town, but, I dare fay, without prefuming to make uncharitable conjectures on the author's prefent condition, he would rather have had it faid of him that he had pray'd,

D 2

.   .   Oh thou my voice infpire,
.   ..Who tcuch'd Ifaiah's hallow'd lips with fire !

I have turn'd to every verfe and chapter, and think you
have preferv'd the fublime heavenly fpirit throughout the
whole, efpecially at—*Hark a glad voice*—and—*The lamb
with wolves fhall graze.*—There is but one line which I
think below the original,

He wipes the tears for ever from our eyes.

You have exprefs'd it with a good and pious, but not fo
exalted and poetical a fpirit as the prophet, *The Lord
will wipe away tears from off all faces.* If you agree with
me in this, alter it by way of paraphrafe, or otherwife
that when it comes into a volume it may be amended.
Your poem is already better than the Pollio. I am

Your, &c.

L E T T E R II.

The Anfwer.

June 18, 1712.

YOU have obliged me with a very kind letter, by
which I find you fhift the fcene of your life from
the town to the country, and enjoy that mix'd ftate which
wife men doth delight in, and are qualified for. Methinks the moralifts and philofophers have generally run too
much into extremes in commending entirely either folitude,
or public life. In the former, men for the moft part grow
ufelefs by too much reft, and in the latter are deftroy'd by
too much precipitation ; as waters lying ftill, putrify, and
are good for nothing, and running violently on do but
the more mifchief in their paffage to others, and are
fwallow'd up and loft the fooner themfelves. Thofe indeed who can be ufeful to all ftates, fhould be like gentle ftreams, that not only glide thro' lonely valleys, and
forefts amidft the flocks and fhepherds, but vifit populous
towns in their courfe, and are at once of ornament and
                                                    fervice

fervice to them. But there are another fort of people who feem defign'd for folitude, fuch I mean, as have more to hide than to fhow. As for my own part, I am one of thofe whom Seneca fays, *Tam umbratiles funt, ut putent in turbido effe quicquid in luce eft.* Some men, like fome pictures, are fitter for a corner than a full light; and, I believe, fuch as have a natural bent to folitude (to carry on the former fimilitude) are like waters, which may be forced into fountains, and exalted into a great height, may make a noble figure and a louder noife, but after all they would run more fmoothly, quietly, and plentifully, in their own natural courfe upon the ground *. The confideration of this would make me very well contented with the poffeffion only of that quiet which Cowley calls the companion of obfcurity. But whoever has the mufes too for his companions, can never be idle enough, to be uneafy. Thus, Sir, you fee, I would flatter myfelf into a good opinion of my own way of living. Plutarch juft now told me, that 'tis in human life as in a game at tables, where a man may wifh for the higheft caft, but, if his chance be otherwife, he is e'en to play it as well as he can, and to make the beft of it. I am

Your, &c.

LETTER III.

To Mr. STEELE.

July 15, 1712.

YOU formerly obferved to me, that nothing made a more rediculous figure in a man's life, than the difparity we often find in him fick and well: thus one of an unfortunate conftitution is perpetually exhibiting a miferable example of the weaknefs of his mind, and of his

* The foregoing fimilitudes our Author had put into verfe fome years before, and inferted in o Mr. Wycherly's poem on *Mix'd Life.* We find them in the verfification very d ftinct from the reft of that poem. See his pofthumous works, octavo, page 3 and 4.

4

body,

body, in their turns. I have had frequent opportunities of late to confider myfelf in thefe different views, and, I hope, have received fome advantage by it, if what Waller fays be true, that

> The foul's dark cottage, batter'd and decay'd,
> Lets in new light thro' chinks that time has made.

Then furely ficknefs, contributing no lefs than old age to the fhaking down this fcaffolding of the body, may difco-ver the inward ftructure more plainly. Sicknefs is a fort of early old age : it teaches us a diffidence in our earthly ftate, and infpires us with the thoughts of a future, bet-ter than a thoufand volumes of philofophers and divines. It gives fo warning a concuffion to thofe props of our va-nity, our ftrength and youth, that we think of fortifying ourfelves within, when there is fo little dependance upon our outworks. Youth at the very beft is but a betrayer of human life in a gentler and fmoother manner than age : 'tis like a ftream that nourifhes a plant upon a bank, and caufes it to flourifh and bloffom to the fight, but at the fame time is undermining it at the root in fecret. My youth has dealt more fairly and openly with me, it has afforded feveral profpects of my danger, and given me an advantage not very common to young men, that the attractions of the world have not daz-zled me very much; and I begin, where moft people end, with a full conviction of the emptinefs of all forts of ambition, and the unfatisfactory nature of all human pleafures. When a fmart fit of ficknefs tells me this fcur-vy tenement of my body will fall in a little time, I am e'en as unconcern'd as was that honeft Hibernian, who being in bed in the great ftorm fome years ago, and told the houfe would tumble over his head, made anfwer, what care I for the houfe ? I am only a lodger. I fancy 'tis the beft time to die when one is in the beft humour; and fo exceffively weak as I now am, I may fay with con-fcience, that I am not at all uneafy at the thought, that ma-

ny

ny men, whom I never had any efteem for, are likely to enjoy this world after me.   When I reflect what an inconfi-
derable little atom every fingle man is, with refpect to the
whole creation, methinks 'tis fhame to be concern'd at
the removal of fuch a trivial animal as I am.   The morning after my exit, the fun will rife as bright as ever, the
flowers fmell as fweet, the plants fpring as green, the
world will proceed in its old courfe, people will laugh as
heartily, and marry as faft, as they were us'd to do.
The memory of man (as it is elegantly exprefs'd in the
Book of Wifdom) paffeth away as the remembrance of a
gueft that tarrieth but one day.   There are reafons
enough, in the fourth chapter of the fame book, to make
any young man contented with the profpect of death.
" For honourable age is not that which ftandeth in
" length of time, or is meafur'd by number of years.
" But wifdom is the grey hair to men, and an unfpotted
" life is old age.   He was taken away fpeedily, left
" wickednefs fhould alter his undarftanding, or deceit be-
" guile his foul," &c.   I am

Your, &c.

LETTER IV.

To Mr. STEELE.

Nov. 7, 1712.

I Was the other day in company with five or fix men
of fome learning; where chancing to mention the famous verfes which the Emperor Adrian fpoke on his death
bed, they were all agreed that 'twas a piece of gaiety unworthy of that prince in thofe circumftances.   I could not
but differ from this opinion: methinks it was by no means a
gay, but a very ferious foliloquy to his foul at the point
of its departure; in which fenfe I naturally took the verfes
at my firft reading them, when I was very young, and
before I knew what interpretation the world generally
put upon them.

Animula

Animula vagula, blandula,
Hofpes comefque corporis,
Quæ nunc abibis in loca?
Pallidula, rigida, nudula,
Nec (ut foles) dabis joca !

" Alas, my foul ! thou pleafing companion of this body,
" thou fleeting thing that art now deferting it ! whither
" art thou flying? to what unknown fcene ? all tremb-
" ling, fearful, and penfive ! what now is become of thy
" former wit and humour? thou fhalt jeft and be gay
" no more."

I confefs I cannot apprehend where lies the trifling in
all this : 'tis the moft natural and obvious reflection imaginable to a dying man : and if we confider the Emperor
was a heathen, that doubt concerning the future fate of
his foul will feem fo far from being the effect of want of·
thought, that 'twas fcarce reafonable he fhould think
otherwife ; not to mention that here is a plain confeffion
included of his belief in its immortality. The diminutive
epithets of *vagula blandula*, and the reft appear not to me
as expreffions of levity, but rather of endearment and
concern; fuch as we find in Catullus, and the authors
of *Hendeca-fyllabi* after him, where they are ufed to exprefs the utmoft love and tendernefs for their miftreffes.—
If you think me right in my notion of the laft words of
Adrian, be pleas'd to infert it in the Spectator : if not to
fupprefs it.   I am. &c.

Adriani morientis ad ANIMAM,

TRANSLATED.

Ah fleeting fpirit ! wand'ring fire,
    That long haft warm'd my tender breaft,
Muft thou no more this frame infpire ?
    No more a pleafing chearful gueft ?
Whither, ah whither art thou flying !
    To what dark undifcover'd fhore ?
Thou feem'ft all trembling, fhiv'ring, dying,
    And wit and humour are no more.

LET-

LETTER V.

Mr. STEELE to Mr. POPE,

Nov. 12, 1712.,

I HAVE read over your Temple of Fame twice, and cannot find any thing amifs, of weight enough to call a fault, but fee in it a thoufand thoufand beauties, Mr. Addifon fhall fee it to-morrow : after his perufal of it, I will let you know his thoughts. I defire you would let me know whether you are at leifure or not ? I have a defign which I fhall open a month or two hence, with the affiftance of the few like yourfelf. If your thoughts are unengaged, I fhall explain myfelf further. I am

Your, &c,

LETTER VI,

The Anfwer,

Nov, 16, 1712.

YOU oblige me by the indulgence you have fhewn to the poem I fent you, but will oblige me much more by the kind feverity I hope for from you. No errors are fo trivial but they deferve to be mended. Bnt fince you fay you fee nothing that may be call'd a fault, can you but think it fo, that I have confin'd the attendance of * Guardian fpirits to heaven's favourites only ? I could point you to feveral, but it is my bufinefs to be informed of thofe faults I do not know ; and as for thofe I do, not to talk of them but to correct them. You fpeak of that poem in a ftyle I neither merit, nor expect ; but, I affure you, if you freely mark or dafh out, I fhall look upon your blots to be its greateft beauties : I mean, if Mr. Addifon and yourfelf fhould like it in the whole ; otherwife the trouble of correction is what I would not take, for I was

* This is not now to be found in the *Temple of Fame*, which was the Poem here fpoken of.

really fo diffident of it as to let it lie by me thefe † two‑ years, juft as you now fee it. I am afraid of nothing fo‑ much as to impofe any thing on the world which is unwor‑ thy of its acceptance.

As to the laft‑period of your letter, I fhall be very ready and glad to contribute to any defign that tends to the ad‑ vantage of mankind, which, I am fure, all yours do. I wifh I had but as much capacity as leifure, for I am per‑ fectly idle : (a fign I have not much capacity.)

If you will entertain the beft opinion of me, be pleas'd to think me your friend. Affure Mr. Addifon of my moft faithful fervice, of every one's efteem he muft be affured already. I am

Your, &c.

LETTER VII.

To Mr. STEELE.

Nov. 29, 1712.

I AM forry you publifhed that notion about Adrian's verfes as mine : had I imagined you would ufe my name, I fhould have exprefs'd my fentiments with more modefty and diffidence. I only fent it to have your opi‑ nion, and not to publifh my own, which I diftrufted. But I think the fuppofition you draw from the notion of Adrian's being addicted to magic, is a little uncharitable, (" that he might fear no fort of deity, good or bad") fince in the third verfe he plainly teftifies his apprehen‑ fion of a future ftate, by being folicitous whither his foul was going. As to what you mention of his ufing gay and ludicrous exprefſions, I have own'd my opinion to be that the exprefſions are not fo, but that diminutives are as often in the Latin tongue, ufed as marks of tendernefs and concern.

Anima is no more than my foul, *animula* has the force of my dear foul. To fay *virgo bella* is not half fo endearing

† Hence it appears th's Poem was writ when the Author was twenty‑two years old.

as *virguncula bellula*; and had Auguftus only called Horace *lepidum hominem*, it had amounted to no more than
that he thought him a pleafant fellow : 'twas the *homunci-
olum* that exprefs'd the love and tendernefs that great Emperor had for him.   And perhaps I fhould myfelf be much
better pleas'd, if I were told you call'd me your little
friend, than if you complimented me with the title of a
great genius, or an eminent hand, as Jacob does all his
authors.   I am

Your, &c.

LETTER VIII.

From Mr. STEELE.

Dec. 4, 1712.

THIS is to defire of you that you would pleafe to make
an ode as of a chearful dying fpirit, that is to fay,
the Emperor *Adrian's Animula vagula* put into two or three
ftanza's for mufic. If you comply with this, and fend me
word fo, you will very particularly oblige   Your, &c.

LETTER IX.

The Anfwer.

I Do not fend you word I will do, but have already
done the thing you defire of me. You have it (as
Cowley calls it) juft warm from the brain. It came to
me the firft moment I waked this morning : Yet you'll
fee, it was not fo abfolutely infpiration, but that I had in
my head not only the verfes of Adrian, but the fine frag-
ment of Sappho, &c.

The dying Chriftian to his SOUL

O D E.

I.

Vital fpark of heav'nly flame !
Quit, oh quit this mortal frame :

E 2

Trem-

Trembling, hoping, ling'ring, flying,
Oh the pain, the blifs of dying!
Ceafe, fond Nature, ceafe thy ftrife,
And let me languifh into life.

II.

Hark! they whifper; Angels fay,
Sifter Spirit, come away!
What is this abforbs me quite,
Steals my fenfes, fhuts my fight,
Drowns my fpirits, draws my breath?
Tell me, my Soul, can this be Death?

III.

The world recedes; it difappears!
Heav'n opens on my eyes! my ears
    With founds feraphic ring:
Lend, lend your wings! I mount! I fly!
O Grave! where is thy victory?
O Death where is thy fting?

LETTER X.

To Mr. ADDISON.

July 20, 1713.

I Am more joy'd at your return than I fhould be at that
of the fun, fo much as I wifh for him this melancholy
wet feafon; but 'tis his fate too, like yours, to be difpleafing to Owls and obfcene animals, who cannot bear
his luftre. What put me in mind of thefe night-birds
was John Dennis, whom, I think, you are beft revenged
upon, as the Sun was in the fable upon thefe bats and
beaftly birds above-mentioned, only by *fhining on*. I am
fo far from efteeming it any misfortune, that I congratulate you upon having your fhare in that, which all the
great men and all the good men that ever lived have had
their part of, Envy and Calumny. To be uncenfured
                                                    and

and to be obfcure, is the fame thing. You may conclude, from what I here fay, that 'twas never in my thoughts to have offered you my pen in any direct reply to fuch a Critic, but only in fome little raillery; not in defence of you, but in contempt of him †. But indeed your opinion, that 'tis entirely to be neglected, would have been my own, had it been my own cafe; but I felt more warmth here, than I did when firft I faw his book againft myfelf (tho' indeed in two minutes it made me heartily merry.) He has written againft every thing the world has approv'd thefe many years. 1 apprehend but one danger from Dennis's difliking our fenfe, that it may make us think fo very well of it, as to become proud and conceited, upon his difapprobation.

I muft not here omit to do juftice to Mr. Gay, whofe zeal in your concern is worthy a friend and honourer of you. He writ to me in the moft preffing terms about it, though with that juft contempt of the Critic that he deferves. 1 think in thefe days one honeft man is obliged to acquaint another who are his friends; when fo many mifchievous infects are daily at work to make people of merit fufpicious of each other; that they may have the fatisfaction of feeing them look'd upon no better than themfelves. I am

Your, &c.

LETTER XI.

Mr. ADDISON to Mr. POPE.

Oct. 26, 1713.

I Was extremely glad to receive a letter from you, but more fo upon reading the contents of it. The * Work you mention, will, I dare fay, very fufficiently recommend itfelf when your name appears with the Propofals : and if you think I can any way contribute to the forwarding of them, you cannot lay a greater obligation upon

---

† This relates to the paper occafion'd by Dennis's Remarks upon Cato, call'd Dr. Norris's *Narrative of the Frenzy of John Dennis.*
* The Tranflation of the Iliad.

me,

me, than by employing me in fuch an office. As I have an ambition of having it known that you are my friend, I fhall be very proud of fhewing it by this, or any other inftance. I queftion not but your Tranflation will enrich our Tongue, and do honour to our Country; for I conclude of it already from thofe performances with which you have obliged the public. I would only have you confider how it may moft turn to your advantage. Excufe my impertinence in this particular, which proceeds from my zeal for your eafe and happinefs. The work would coft you a great deal of time, and, unlefs you undertake it, will, I am afraid, never be executed by any other; at leaft I know none of this age that is equal to it befide yourfelf.

I am at prefent wholly immerfed in country bufinefs, and begin to take delight in it. I wifh I might hope to fee you here fome time, and will not defpair of it, when you engage in a work that will require folitude and retirement. I am

Your, &c.

LETTER XII.

Mr. ADDISON to Mr. POPE.

Nov. 2, 1713.

I Have receiv'd your letter, and am glad to find that you have laid fo good a fcheme for your great undertaking. I queftion not but the Profe * will require as much care as the Poetry, but the variety will give yourfelf fome relief, and more pleafure to your readers.

You gave me leave once to take the liberty of a friend, in advifing you not to content yourfelf with one half of the nation for your admirers, when you might command them all. If I might take the freedom to repeat it, I would on this occafion. I think you are very happy that you are out of the fray, and I hope all your undertakings will turn to the better account for it.

---

* The Notes to his Tranflation of Homer.

You

You fee how I prefume on your friendfhip in taking all this freedom with you : but I already fancy, that we have lived many years together in an unreferved conver- fation, and that we may do fo many more, is the fincere wifh of

Your, &c.

LETTER XIII.

To Mr. ADDISON.

YOUR laft is the more obliging, as it hints at fome little niceties in my conduct, which your candour and affection prompts you to recommend to me, and which (fo trivial as things of this nature feem) are yet of no flight confequence, to people whom every body talks of, and every body as he pleafes. 'Tis a fort of tax that attends an eftate in Parnaffus, which is often rated much higher than in proportion to the fmall poffeffion an author holds. For indeed an author, who is once come upon the town, is enjoy'd without being thanked for the plea- fure, and fometimes ill-treated by thofe very perfons who firft debauched him. Yet, to tell you the bottom of my heart, I am no way difpleafed that I have offended the violent of all parties already ; and at the fame time I af- fure you confcientioufly, I feel not the leaft malevolence or refentment againft any of thofe who mifreprefent me, or are diffatisfied with me. This frame of mind is fo eafy, that I am perfectly content with my condition.

As I hope, and would flatter myfelf, that you know me and my thoughts fo entirely, as never to be miftaken in either, fo 'tis a pleafure to me that you guefs'd fo right in regard to the author of that Guardian you mentioned. But I am forry to find it has taken air, that I have fome hand in thofe papers, becaufe I writ fo very few as nei- ther to deferve the credit of fuch a report with fome peo- ple, nor the difrepute of it with others. An honeft Jaco- bite fpoke to me the fenfe or nonfenfe of the weak part of his party very fairly, that the good people took it ill of me, that I writ with Steele, tho' upon never fo indifferent fubjects. This, I know, you will laugh at as well as I do; yet I doubt not but many little calumniators and perfons of four difpofitions will take occafion hence to be-fpatter me. I confefs I fcorn narrow fouls of all parties; and if I renounce my reafon in religious matters, I'll hardly do it in any other.

I can't imagine whence it comes to pafs, that the few Guardians I have written are fo generally known for mine; that in particular which you mention I never dif-covered to any man but the publifher, till very lately; yet almoft every body told me of it.

As to his taking a more politic turn, I cannot any way enter into that fecret, nor have I been let into it any more than into the reft of his politics. Tho' 'tis faid, he will take into thefe papers alfo feveral fubjects of the po-liter kind, as before : but I affure you, as to myfelf, I have quite done with them for the future. The little I have done, and the great refpect I bear Mr. Steele as a man of wit, has render'd me a fufpected Whig to fome of the violent; but (as old Dryden faid before me) 'tis not the violent I defign to pleafe.

I generally employ the mornings in painting with Mr. Jervas *, and the evenings in the converfation of fuch as I think can moft improve my mind, of whatever deno-mination they are. I ever muft fet the higheft value upon men of truly great, that is, honeft principles, with equal capacities. The beft way I know of overcoming calumny and mifconftruction, is by a vigorous perfeverance in eve-ry thing we know to be right, and a total neglect of all that can enfue from it. 'Tis partly from this maxim that I depend upon your friendfhip, becaufe I believe it will do juftice to my intention in every thing; and give me leave to tell you, that (as the world goes) this is no fmall affurance I repofe in you. I am

Your, &c.

* See the Epiftle to him in verfe, writ about this time.

LETTER

LETTER XIV.

To Mr. Addison.

Dec. 14, 1713.

I Have been lying in wait for my own imagination, this week and more, and watching what thoughts came up in the whirl of the fancy, that were worth communicating to you in a letter. But I am at length convinced that my rambling head can produce nothing of that sort; so I muft e'en be contented with telling you the old ftory, that I love you heartily. I have often found by experience, that nature and truth, tho' never fo low or vulgar, are yet pleafing when openly and artlefsly reprefented: it would be diverting to me to read the very letters of an infant, could it write its innocent inconfiftencies and tautologies juft as it thought them. This makes me hope a letter from me will not be unwelcome to you, when I am confcious I write it with more unrefervednefs than ever man wrote, or perhaps talk'd to another. I truft your good-nature with the whole range of my follies, and really love you fo well, that I would rather you fhould pardon me than efteem me; fince one is an act of goodnefs and benevolence, the other a kind of conftrained deference.

You can't wonder my thoughts are fcarce confiftent, when I tell you how they are diftracted. Every hour of my life my mind is ftrangely divided; this minute perhaps I am above the ftars, with a thoufand fyftems round about me, looking forward into a vaft abyfs, and lofing my whole comprehenfion in the boundlefs fpace of Creation, in dialogues with Whifton and the Aftronomers; the next moment I am below all trifles groveling with T * in the very centre of nonfenfe: now I am recreated with the brifk fallies and quick turns of wit, which Mr. Steele in his livelieft and freeft humours darts about him; and now levelling my application to the infignificant obfervations and quirks of Grammar of C* and D*.

Good God! what an incongruous animal is man! how

unfettled in his beft part, his foul ; and how changing and
variable in his frame of body ? the conftancy of the one
fhook by every notion, the temperament of the other
affected by every blaft of wind! What is he altogether
but one mighty inconfiftency : ficknefs and pain is the
lot of one half of him, doubt and fear the portion of the
other! What a buftle we make about paffing our time,
when all our fpace is but a point ? what aims and ambitions are crowded into this little inftant of our life, which
(as Shakefpear finely words it) is rounded with a fleep ?
Our whole extent of being is no more, in the eye of him
who gave it, than a fcarce perceptible moment of duration. Thofe animals whofe circle of living is limited to
three or four hours, as the Naturalifts tell us, are yet as
long-lived, and poffefs as wide a fcene of action as man,
if we confider him with a view to all Space, and all Eternity. Who knows what plots, what atchievements a
mite may perform in his kingdom of a grain of duft,
within his life of fome minutes ; and of how much lefs
confideration than even this, is the life of man in the fight
of God, who is from ever, and for ever ?

Who that thinks in this train, but muft fee the world
and its contemptible grandeurs, leffen before him at every thought ? 'Tis enough to make one remain ftupify'd
in a poize of inaction, void of all defires, of all defigns,
of all friendfhips.

But we muft return (thro' our very condition of being)
to our narrow felves, and thofe things that affect ourfelves : our paffions, our interefts flow in upon us, and
unphilofophize us into mere mortals. For my part, I never return fo much into myfelf, as when I think of you,
whofe friendfhip is one of the beft comforts I have for the
infignificancy of myfelf. I am

Your, &c.

LETTER XV.

To Mr. Addison.

Jan. 30, 1713-14.

YOUR letter found me very bufy in my grand under-taking, to which I muft wholly give up myfelf for fome time, unlefs when I fnatch an hour to pleafe myfelf with a diftant converfation with you and a few others, by writing. 'Tis no comfortable profpect to be reflect-ing, that fo long a fiege as that of Troy lies upon my hands, and the campaign above 'half over, before I have made any progrefs. Indeed the Greek fortification, upon a nearer approach, does not appear fo formidable as it did; and I am almoft apt to flatter myfelf, that Homer fecretly feems inclined to a correfpondence with me, in letting me into a good part of his intentions. There are indeed a fort of underling auxiliars to the difficulty of a work, called Commentators and Critics, who would frighten many people by their number and bulk, and per-plex our progrefs under pretence of fortifying their au-thor. Thefe lie very low in the trenches and ditches they themfelves have digged, encompaffed with dirt of their own heaping up: but I think there may be found a me-thod of coming at the main works by a more fpeedy and gallant way than by mining under ground, that is, by ufing the poetical engines, wings, and flying over their heads.

While I am engaged in the fight, I find you are con-cerned how I fhall be paid, and are folicitous that I may not have the ill fate of many difcarded Generals, to be firft envied and malign'd, then perhaps prais'd, and laftly neg-lected. The former (the conftant attendant upon all great and laudable enterprizes) I have already experienced. Some have faid I am not a mafter in the Greek, who either are fo themfelves or are not: if they are not, they can't tell; and if they are, they can't without having catechiz'd me. But if they can read (for I know fome critics can, and others cannot) there are fairly lying before them fome fpecimens of my tranflation from this Author in the Mifcellanies, which they are heartily welcome to. I have met with as much malignity another way, fome calling me a Tory, becaufe the heads of that party have been diftinguifhingly favourable to me; fome a Whig, becaufe I have been favoured with yours, Mr. Congreve's, and Mr. Craggs's friendfhip, and of late with my Lord Halifax's patronage. How much more natural a conclufion might be formed, by any good-natured man, that a perfon who has been well ufed by all fides, has been offenfive to none. This miferable age is fo funk between animofities of Party and thofe of Religion, that I begin to fear moft men have Politics enough to make (thro' violence) the beft fcheme of government a bad one; and Belief enough to hinder their own falvation. I hope for my own part never to have more of either than what is confiftent with common Juftice and Charity, and always as much as becomes a Chriftian and an honeft man. Tho' I find it an unfortunate thing to be bred a Papift here, where one is obnoxious to four parts in five, as being fo too much or too little; I fhall yet be eafy under both their miftakes, and be what I more than feem to be, for I fuffer for it. God is my witnefs, that I no more envy you Proteftants your places and poffeffions, than I do our Priefts their charity or learning. I am ambitious of nothing but the good opinion of good men, on both fides; for I know that one virtue of a free fpirit is worth more than all the virtues put together of all the narrow-foul'd people in the world. I am

Your, &c.

LETTER

LETTER XVI.

To Mr. Addison.

Oct. 10, 1714.

I Have been acquainted by * one of my friends, who
omits no opportunities of gratifying me, that you
have lately been pleas'd to fpeak of me in a manner which
nothing but the real refpect I have for you can deferve.
May I hope that fome late malevolencies have loft their
effect? Indeed it is neither for me, nor my enemies, to
pretend to tell you whether I am your friend or not; but
if you would judge by probabilities, I beg to know which
of your poetical acquaintance has fo little intereft in pretending to be fo? Methinks no man fhould queftion the
real friendfhip of one who defires no real fervice. I am
only to get as much from the Whigs, as I got from the
Tories, that is to fay, Civility; being neither fo proud
as to be infenfible of any good office, nor fo humble, as
not to dare heartily to defpife any man who does me an
injuftice.

I will not value myfelf upon having ever guarded all
the degrees of refpect for you; for (to fay the truth) all
the world fpeaks well of you, and I fhould be under a
neceffity of doing the fame, whether I car'd for you or
not.

As to what you have faid of me, I fhall never believe
that the author of Cato can fpeak one thing and think
another. As a proof that I account you fincere, I beg a
favour of you: it is, that you would look over the two
firft books of my tranflation of Homer, which are in the
hands of my Lord Hallifax. I am fenfible how much the
reputation of any poetical work will depend upon the character you give it: 'tis therefore fome evidence of the
truft I repofe in your good-will, when I give you this
opportunity of fpeaking ill of me with juftice; and yet

* See a Letter from Mr Jervas, and the Anfwer to it, N9 22, 23.

expect

expect you will tell me your trueft thoughts, at the fame
time that you tell others your moft favourable ones.

I have a farther requeft, which I muft prefs with earneftnefs. My bookfeller is re-printing the Effay on Criticifm, to which you have done too much honour in your
Spectator of N° 253. The period in that paper, where
you fay, " I have admitted fome ftrokes of ill-nature into
that Effay," is the only one I could wifh omitted of all
you have written ; but I would not defire it fhould be fo,
unlefs I had the merit of removing your objection. I beg
you but to point out thofe ftrokes to me, and, you may
be affured, they fhall be treated without mercy.

Since we are upon proofs of fincerity (which I am
pretty confident will turn to the advantage of us both in
each other's opinion) give me leave to name another paffage in the fame Spectator, which I wifh you would alter :
it is where you mention an obfervation upon Homer's
Verfes of Sifyphus's Stone, as * never having been made
before by any of the Critics : I happened to find the fame
in Dionyfius of Halicarnaffus's Treatife, Περὶ συνθέσεως
ὀνομάτων, who treats very largely upon thefe verfes. I
know you will think fit to foften your expreffion, when
you fee the paffage ; which you muft needs have read,
though it be fince flipt out of your memory. I am, with
the utmoft efteem,

                                  Your, &c.

LETTER XVII.

To the Honourable ⸺⸺

                                  June 8, 1714.

THE queftion you afk in relation to Mr. Addifon and
Philips, I fhall anfwer in a few words. Mr. Philips did exprefs himfelf with much indignation againft me
one evening at Button's Coffee-houfe (as I was told) fay-

* Thefe words are fi ce left out in Mr. Tickel's edition, but were extant
in all during Mr. Addifon's life.

                                  ing,

ing, that I was enter'd into a cabal with Dean Swift, and others, to write againſt the Whig-Intereſt, and in particular to undermine his own reputation, and that of his friends Steele and Addiſon : but Mr. Philips never opened his lips to my face, on this or any like occaſion, tho' I was almoſt every night in the ſame room with him, nor ever offer'd me any indecorum. Mr. Addiſon came to me a night or two after Philips had talk'd in this idle manner, and aſſured me of his diſbelief of what had been ſaid, of the friendſhip we ſhould always maintain, and deſir'd I would ſay nothing further of it. My Lord Hallifax did me the honour to ſtir in this matter, by ſpeaking to ſeveral people to obviate a falſe aſperſion, which might have done me no ſmall prejudice with one party. However, Philips did all he could ſecretly to continue the report with the Hanover Club, and kept in his hands the ſubſcriptions paid for me to him, as Secretary to that Club. The heads of it have ſince given him to underſtand, that they take it ill; but (upon the terms I ought to be with ſuch a man) I would not aſk him for this money, but commiſſion'd one of the Players, his equals, to receive it. This is the whole matter : but as to the ſecret grounds of this malignity, they will make a very pleaſant hiſtory when we meet. Mr. Congreve and ſome others have been much diverted with it, and moſt of the gentlemen of the Hanover Club have made it the ſubject of their ridicule on their Secretary. It is to this management of Philips, that the world owes Mr. Gay's Paſtorals. The ingenious author is extremely your ſervant, and would have complied with your kind invitation, but that he is juſt now appointed Secretary to my Lord Clarendon, in his embaſſy to Hanover.

I am ſenſible of the zeal and friendſhip with which, I am ſure, you will always defend your friend in his abſence, from all thoſe little tales and calumnies, which a man of any genius or merit is born to. I ſhall never complain while I am happy in ſuch noble defenders, and in ſuch contemptible opponents. May their envy and ill-

nature

nature ever increafe, to the glory and pleafure of thofe they would injure; may they reprefent me what they will, as long as you think me, what I am,

Your, &c.

LETTER XVIII.

July 13, 1714.

YOU mention the account I gave you fome time ago of the things which Philips faid in his foolifhnefs: but I can't tell, from any thing in your letter, whether you received a long one from me about a fortnight fince. It was principally intended to thank you for the laft obliging favour you did me; and perhaps for that reafon you pafs it in filence. I there launch'd into fome account of my temporal affairs, and intend now to give you fome hints of my fpiritual. The conclufion of your letter draws this upon you, where you tell me you prayed for me. Your proceeding, Sir, is contrary to that of moft other friends, who never talk of praying for a man after they have done him a fervice, but only when they will do him none. Nothing can be more kind than the hint you give me of the vanity of human fciences, which, I affure you, I am daily more convinced of; and indeed I have, for fome years paft, look'd upon all of them no better than amufements. To make them the ultimate end of our purfuit, is a miferable and fhort ambition, which will drop from us at every little difappointment here, and even, in cafe of no difappointments here, will infallibly defert us hereafter. The utmoft fame they are capable of beftowing, is never worth the pains they coft us, and the time they lofe us. If you attain the top of your defires that way, all thofe who envy you will do you harm; and of thofe who admire you, few will do you good. The unfuccefsful writers are your declared enemies, and probably the fuccefsful your fecret ones; for thofe hate not more to be excelled, than thefe to be rival'd: and at the upfhot, after a life of perpetual application, you reflect that you have been doing nothing for yourfelf, and that the fame or lefs induftry might have gain'd you a friendfhip that can never deceive ' end, a fatisfaction which praife cannot beftow, nor vanity feel; and a glory, which (tho' in one refpect like fame, not to be had till after death) yet fhall be felt and enjoy'd to eternity. Thefe, dear Sir, are unfeignedly my fentiments, whenever I think at all; for half the things that employ our heads deferve not the name of thoughts, they are only ftronger dreams of impreffions upon the imagination: our fchemes of government, our fyftems of philofophy, our golden worlds of poetry, are all but fo many fhadowy images and airy profpects, which arife to us but fo much the livelier and more frequent, as we are more overcaft with the darknefs, and difturbed with the fumes, of human vanity.

The fame thing that makes old men willing to leave this world, makes me willing to leave poetry, long habit and wearinefs of the fame track. Homer will work a cure upon me; fifteen thoufand verfes are equivalent to fourfcore years, to make one old in rhyme: and I fhould be forry and afhamed, to go on jingling to the laft ftep, like a waggoner's horfe, in the fame road, and fo leave my bells to the next filly animal that will be proud of them. That man makes a mean figure in the eyes of reafon, who is meafuring fyllables and coupling rhymes, when he fhould be mending his own foul, and fecuring his own immortality. If I had not this opinion, I fhould be unworthy even of thofe fmall and limited parts which God has given me; and unworthy of the friendfhip of fuch a man as you. I am

Your, &c.

LETTER XIX.

July 25, 1714.

I Have no better excufe to offer you, that I have omitted a tafk naturally fo pleafing to me as converfing 'upon paper with you, but that my time and eyes have been wholly employ'd upon Homer, whom, I almoft fear, I fhall find but one way of imitating, which is, in his blindnefs. I am perpetually afflicted with head-achs that very much affect my fight, and indeed fince my coming hither I have fcarce paft an hour agreeably, except that in which I read your letter. I would ferioufly have you think, you have no man who more truly knows to place a right value on your friendfhip, than he who leaft deferves it on all other accounts than his due fenfe of it. But, let me tell you, you can hardly guefs what a tafk you undertake, when you profefs yourfelf my friend: there are fome Tories who will take you for a Whig, fome Whigs who will take you for a Tory, fome Proteftants who will efteem you a rank Papift, and fome Papifts who will account you a Heretic.

I find, by dear experience, we live in an age, where it is criminal to be moderate; and where no one man can be allowed to be juft to all men. The notions of right and wrong are fo far ftrain'd, that perhaps to be in the right fo very violently, may be of worfe confequence than to be eafily and quietly in the wrong. I really wifh all men fo well, that, I am fatisfied, but few can wifh me fo; but if thofe few are fuch as tell me they do, I am content, for they are the beft people I know. While you believe me what I profefs as to religion, I can bear any thing the bigotted may fay: while Mr. Congreve likes my poetry, I can endure Dennis, and a thoufand more like him; while the moft honeft and moral of each party think me no ill man, I can eafily bear that the moft violent and mad of all parties rife up to throw dirt at me.

I muft expect an hundred attacks upon the publication of my Homer. Whoever in our times would be a profeffor of learning above his fellows, ought at the very firft to enter the world with the conftancy and refolution of a primitive Chriftian, and be prepared to fuffer all fort of public perfecution. It is certainly to be lamented, that if any man does but endeavour to diftinguifh himself, or

gratify

gratify others by his ftudies, he is immediately treated as a common enemy, inftead of being looked upon as a common friend; and affaulted as generally as if his whole defign were to prejudice the ftate, or ruin the public. I will venture to fay, no man ever rofe to any degree of perfection in writing, but thro' obftinacy, and an inveterate refolution againft the ftream of mankind; fo that if the world has received any benefit from the labours of the learned, it was in its own defpite: for when firft they effay their parts, all people in general are prejudiced againft new beginners; and when they have got a little above contempt, then fome particular perfons, who were before unfortunate in their own attempts, are fworn foes to them, only becaufe they fucceed.—Upon the whole, one may fay of the beft writers, that they pay a fevere fine for their fame, which it is always in the power of the moft worthlefs part of mankind to levy upon them when they pleafe.

I am, &c.

LETTER XX.

To Mr. JERVAS.

July 28, 1714.

I AM juft enter'd upon the old way of life again, fleep and mufing. It is my employment to revive the old of paft ages to the prefent, as it is yours to tranfmit the young of the prefent, to the future. I am copying the great mafter in one art, with the fame love and diligence with which the Painters hereafter will copy you in another.

Thus, I fhould begin my epiftle to you, if it were a Dedicatory one. But as it is a friendly letter, you are to find nothing mention'd in your own praife, but what only one in the world is witnefs to, your particular good-natur'd offices to me.

I am cut out from any thing but common acknowledgments, or common difcourfe: the firft you would take

G 2   ill,

ill, though I told but half what I ought; fo in fhort the laft only remains.

And as for the laft, what can you expect from a man who has not talk'd thefe five days? who is withdrawing his thoughts as far as he can, from all the prefent world, its cuftoms, and its manners, to be fully poffefs'd and abforpt in the paft? When people talk of going to Church, I think of facrifices and libations; when I fee the parfon, I addrefs him as Chryfes, prieft of Apollo; and inftead of the Lord's prayer, I begin,

> *God of the filver Bow*, &c.

While you in the world are concern'd about the Proteftant Succeffion, I confider only how Menelaus may recover Helen, and the Trojan war be put to a fpeedy conclufion. I never inquire if the queen be well or not, but heartily wifh to be at Hector's funeral. The only things I regard in this life, are, whether my friends are well? whether my Tranflation go well on? whether Dennis be writing criticifms? whether any body will anfwer him, fince I don't? and whether Lintot be not yet broke?

                                I am, &c.

LETTER XXI.

To the fame.

                                Aug 16, 1714.

I Thank you for your good offices, which are numberlefs. Homer advances fo faft, that he begins to look
bout for the ornaments he is to appear in, like a modifh
modern author,

> Picture in the front,
> With bays and wicked rhyme upon't.

I have the greateft proof in nature, at prefent, of the amufing power of Poetry, for it takes me up fo entirely, that I fcarce fee what paffes under my nofe, and hear nothing that is faid about me. To follow poetry as one

                    3   ought,

ought, one muſt forget father and mother, and cleave to it alone. My reverie has been ſo deep, that I have ſcarce had an interval to think myſelf uneaſy in the want of your company. I now and then juſt miſs you as I ſtep into bed; this minute, indeed, I want extremely to ſee you, the next I ſhall dream of nothing but the taking of Troy, or the recovery of Briſeis.

I fancy no friendſhip is ſo likely to prove laſting as ours, becauſe, I am pretty ſure, there never was a friend-ſhip of ſo eaſy a nature. We neither of us demand any mighty things from each other; what Vanity we have, expeɛts its gratification from other people. It is not I that am to tell you what an Artiſt you are, nor is it you that are to tell me what a Poet I am; but 'tis from the world abroad we hope (piouſly hope) to hear theſe things. At home we follow our buſineſs, when we have any; and think and talk moſt of each other when we have none. 'Tis not unlike the happy friendſhip of a ſtay'd man and his wife, who are ſeldom ſo fond as to hinder the buſineſs of the houſe from going on all day, or ſo indolent as not to find conſolation in each other every evening. Thus well-meaning couples hold in amity to the laſt, by not expeɛting too much from human nature; while romantic friendſhips, like violent loves, begin with diſquiets, pro-ceed to jealouſies, and conclude in animoſities. I have lived to ſee the fierce advancement, the ſudden turn, and the abrupt period, of three or four of theſe enormous friendſhips, and am perfeɛtly convinced of the truth of a maxim we once agreed in, that nothing hinders the con-ſtant agreement of people who live together, but merely vanity; a ſecret inſiſting upon what they think their dig-nity of merit, and an inward expeɛtation of ſuch an over-meaſure of deference and regard, as anſwers to their own extravagant falſe ſcale; and which no body can pay, be-cauſe none but themſelves can tell exaɛtly to what pitch it amounts.

I am, &c.

LETTER

LETTER XXII.

Mr. JERVAS to Mr. POPE.

Aug. 20, 1714.

I Have a particular to tell you at this time, which pleafes me fo much, that you muft expect a more than ordinary alacrity in every turn. You know I could keep you in fufpenfe for twenty lines, but I will tell you directly, that Mr. Addifon and I have had a converfation, that it would have been worth your while to have been placed behind the wainfcot, or behind fome half-length picture, to have heard. He affur'd me, that he would make ufe not only of his intereft, but of his art, to do you fome fervice; he did not mean his art of poetry, but his art at court; and he is fenfible that nothing can have a better air for himfelf than moving in your favour, efpecially fince infinuations were fpread, that he did not care you fhould profper too much as a poet. He protefts that it fhall not be his fault, if there is not the beft intelligence in the world, and the moft hearty friendfhip, &c. He owns, he was afraid Dr. Swift might have carried you too far among the enemy, during the heat of the animofity; but now all is fafe, and you are efcap'd even in his opinion. I promis'd in your name, like a good Godfather, not that you fhould renounce the devil and all his works, but that you would be delighted to find him your friend merely for his own fake; therefore prepare yourfelf for fome civilities.

I have done Homer's head, fhadow'd and heighten'd carefully; and I inclofe the out-line of the fame fize, that you may determine whether you would have it fo large, or reduced, to make room for feuillage or laurel round the oval, or about the fquare of the bufto? perhaps there is fomething more folemn in the image itfelf, if I can get it well perform'd.

If I have been inftrumental in bringing you and Mr. Addifon together with all fincerity, I value myfelf upon
it

it as an acceptable piece of fervice to fuch a one as I know you to be.

Your, &c.

LETTER XXIII.

Mr. POPE's Anfwer.

Aug. 27, 1714.

I AM juft arrived from Oxford, very well diverted and entertain'd there. Every one is much concern'd for the Queen's death. No panegyrics ready yet for the King.

I admire your Whig-principles of refiftance exceedingly, in the fpirit of the Barcelonians: I join in your wifh for them. Mr. Addifon's verfes on Liberty, in his letter from Italy, would be a good form of prayer in my opinion, *O Liberty! thou Goddefs heavenly bright!* &c.

What you mention of the friendly office you endeavour'd to do betwixt Mr. Addifon and me, deferves acknowledgments on my part. You thoroughly know my regard to his character, and my propenfity to teftify it by all ways in my power. You as thoroughly know the fcandalous meannefs of that proceeding which was ufed by Philips, to make a man I fo highly value, fufpect my difpofitions toward him. But as, after all, Mr. Addifon muft be the judge in what regards himfelf, and has feem'd to be no very juft one to me; fo, I muft own to you, I expect nothing but civility from him, how much foever I wifh for his friendfhip. As for any offices of real kindnefs or fervice which it is in his power to do me, I fhould be afhamed to receive them from any man who had no better opinion of my morals, than to think me a Partyman; nor of my temper, than to believe me capable of maligning, or envying another's reputation as a poet; fo I leave it to time to convince him as to both, to fhew him the fhallow depths of thofe half-witted creatures who misinformed him, and to prove that I am incapable of

endea-

endeavouring to leſſen a perſon whom I would be proud
to imitate, and therefore aſham'd to flatter. In a word,
Mr. Addiſon is ſure of my reſpeĉt at all times, and of
my real friendſhip whenever he ſhall think fit to know
me for what I am.

For all that paſs'd betwixt Dr. Swift and me, you
know the whole (without reſerve) of our correſpondence.
The engagements I had to him were ſuch as the aĉtual
ſervices he had done me, in relation to the ſubſcription
for Homer obliged me to. I muſt have leave to be grateful to him, and to any one who ſerves me, let him be
never ſo obnoxious to any party : nor did the Tory-
party ever put me to the hardſhip of aſking this leave,
which is the greateſt obligation I owe to it; and I expeĉt
no greater from the Whig-party than the ſame liberty.
—A curſe on the word Party, which I have been forc'd
to uſe ſo often in this period ! I wiſh the preſent reign
may put an end to the diſtinĉtion, that there may be no
other for the future than that of Honeſt and Knave, Fool
and Man of ſenſe; theſe two ſorts muſt always be enemies; but for the reſt, may all people do as you and I,
believe what they pleaſe, and be friends.

I am, &c.

LETTER XXIV.

To the Earl of HALLIFAX.

MY LORD,   Dec. 1, 1714.

I AM obliged to you both for the favours you have
done me, and for thoſe you intend me. I diſtruſt
neither your will nor your memory, when it is to do
good ; and if ever I become troubleſome or ſolicitous, it
muſt not be out of expeĉtation, but out of gratitude.
Your lordſhip may either cauſe me to live agreeably in
the town, or contentedly in the country, which is really
all the difference I ſet between an eaſy fortune and a ſmall
one. It is indeed a high ſtrain of generoſity in you, to
think

think of making me eafy all my life, only becaufe I have been fo happy as to divert you fome few hours: but if I may have leave to add, it is becaufe you think me no enemy to my native country, there will appear a better reafon; for I muft of confequence be very much (as I fincerely am)

Yours, &c.

---

*LETTER XXV.

Dr. PARNELLE to Mr. POPE.

I AM writing you a long letter; but all the tedioufnefs I feel in it is, that it makes me, during the time, think more intently of my being fo far from you. I fancy, if I were with you, I could remove fome of the uneafinefs which you may have felt from the oppofition of the world, and which you fhould be afhamed to feel, fince it is but the teftimony which one part of it gives you that your merit is unqueftionable. What would you have otherwife, from ignorance, envy, or thofe tempers which vie with you in your own way? I know this in mankind, that when our ambition is unable to attain its end, it is not only wearied, but exafperated too at the vanity of its labours; then we fpeak ill of happier ftudies, and, fighing, condemn the excellence which we find above our reach.——

My † Zoilus, which you us'd to write about, I finifh'd laft fpring, and left in town. I waited till I came up to fend it you; but not arriving here before your book was out, imagin'd it a loft piece of labour. If you will ftill have it, you need only write me word.

I have here feen the Firft Book of Homer ‡, which

* This, and the three Extracts following, concerning the Tranflation of the firft Iliad, fet on foot by Mr. Addifon, Mr. Pope has omitted in his firft Edition.
† Printed for B. Lintot, 1715, 8°, and afterwards added to the laft edition of his poems.
‡ Written by Mr. Addifon, and publifhed in the name of Mr. Tickell.

came out at a time when it could not but appear as a kind of fetting up againſt you. My opinion is, that you may, if you pleaſe, give them thanks who writ it. Neither the numbers, nor the ſpirit, have an equal maſtery with yours; but what ſurprizes me more is, that a ſcholar being concerned, there ſhould happen to be ſome miſtakes in the author's ſenſe; ſuch as putting the light of Pallas's eyes into the eyes of Achilles, making the taunt of Achilles to Agamemnon (that he ſhould have ſpoils when Troy ſhould be taken) to be a cool and ſerious propoſal; the tranſlating what·you call *Ablution* by the word *offals*, and ſo leaving Water out of the rite of luſtration, &c. but·you muſt have taken notice of all this before. I write not to inform you, but to ſhew I always have you at heart.

I am, &c.

Extraꞓt from a LETTER of the

Rev. Dr. BERKLEY, Dean of Londonderry.

July 7, 1715.

——Some days ago, three or four gentlemen and myſelf, exerting that right which all readers pretend to over authors, ſat in judgment upon the two new Tranſlations of the firſt Iliad. Without partiality to my countrymen, I aſſure you, they all gave the preference where it was due; being unanimouſly of opinion, that yours was equally juſt to the ſenſe with Mr. ——'s, and without compariſon, more eaſy, more poetical, and more ſublime. But I will ſay no more on ſuch a thread-bare ſubjeꞓt, as your late performance is at this time.

I am, &c.

Extraꞓt

Extract from a LETTER of

Mr. GAY to Mr. POPE.

July 8, 1715.

——I have juſt ſet down Sir Samuel Garth at the Opera.
He bid me tell you, that every body is pleas'd with your
tranſlation, but a few at Button's; and that Sir Richard
Steele told him, that Mr. Addiſon ſaid the other tranſlation was the beſt that ever was in any language *. He
treated me with extreme civility, and, out of kindneſs,
gave me a ſqueeze by the fore finger.—I am inform'd,
that at Button's your character is made very free with as
to Morals, &c. and Mr. Addiſon ſays, that your Tranſlation and Tickell's are both very well done, but that
the latter has more of Homer.

I am, &c.

Extract from a LETTER of

Dr. ARBUTHNOT to Mr. POPE.

July 9, 1715.

——I congratulate you upon Mr. T*'s firſt book. It
does not indeed want its merit; but I was ſtrangely diſappointed in my expectation of a tranſlation nicely true
to the Original; whereas in thoſe parts where the greateſt
exactneſs ſeems to be demanded, he has been the leaſt
careful, I mean the hiſtory of ancient ceremonies and
rites, &c. in which you have with great judgment been
exact.

I am, &c.

---

* Sir Richard Steele afterwards, in his Preface to an Edition of the
Drummer, a Comedy, by Mr. Addiſon, ſhews it to be his opinion, that
" Mr. Addiſon himſelf was the perſon who tranſlated this book."

LET-

LETTER XXVI.

Mr. Pope to the Hon. James Craggs, Esq;

July 15, 1715.

I Lay hold of the opportunity given me by my Lord Duke of Shrewsbury, to assure you of the continuance of that esteem and affection I have long borne you, and the memory of so many agreeable conversations as we have pass'd together. I wish it were a compliment to say, such conversations as are not to be found on this side of the water; for the Spirit of dissention is gone forth among us; nor is it a wonder that Button's is no longer Button's, when old England is no longer old England, that region of hospitality, society, and good humour. Party affects us all, even the wits, tho' they gain as little by politics, as they do by their wit. We talk much of fine sense, refin'd sense, and exalted sense; but for use and happiness, give me a little common sense. I say this in regard to some gentlemen, profess'd Wits of our acquaintance, who fancy they can make Poetry of consequence at this time of day, in the midst of this raging fit of Politicks. For they tell me, the busy part of the nation are not more divided about Whig and Tory, than these idle fellows of the feather about Mr. T*'s and my Translation. I (like the Tories) have the town in general; that is, the mob, on my side; but it is usual with the smaller party to make up in industry what they want in number, and that is the case with the little senate of Cato. However, if our principles be well considered, I must appear a brave Whig, and Mr. T. a rank Tory: I translated Homer for the public in general, he to gratify the inordinate desires of one man only. We have, it seems, a great Turk in poetry, who can never bear a brother on the throne; and has his mutes too, a set of nodders, winkers, and whisperers, whose business is to strangle all other offsprings of wit in their birth. The new translator of Homer is the humblest slave he has, that is to say, his first Minister;

ter; let him receive the honours he gives me, but receive them with fear and trembling; let him be proud of the approbation of his abfolute Lord, I appeal to the people, as my rightful judges and mafters; and if they are not inclined to condemn me, I fear no arbitrary high-flying proceeding from the fmall Court-faction at Button's. But after all I have faid of this great man, there is no rupture between us. We are each of us fo civil and obliging, that neither thinks he is obliged; and I, for my part, treat with him, as we do with the Grand Monarch, who has too many great qualities not to be refpected, though we know he watches any occafion to opprefs us.

When I talk of Homer, I muft not forget the early prefent you made me of Monfieur de la Motte's book: and I can't conclude this letter without telling you a melancholy piece of news, which affects our very entrails; L* is dead, and foupes are no more! You fee I write in the old familiar way. " This is not to the minifter, but " to the friend †." However, it is fome mark of uncommon regard to the minifter, that I fteal an expreffion from a Secretary of State.

I am, &c.

LETTER XXVII,

To Mr. CONGREVE.

Jan. 16, 1714-15.

MEthinks when I write to you, I am making a confeffion; I have got (I can't tell how) fuch a cuftom of throwing myfelf out upon paper without referve. You were not miftaken in what you judged of my temper of mind when I writ laft. My faults will not be hid from you, and perhaps it is no difpraife to me that they will not: the cleannefs and purity of one's mind is never better proved, than in difcovering its own fault at firft view;

† Alluding to St. John's Letter to Prior, publifhed in the *Report of the Secret Committee,*

as when a stream shews the dirt at its bottom, it shews also the transparency of the water.

My spleen was not occasioned, however, by any thing an abusive angry critic could write of me. I take very kindly your heroic manner of congratulation upon this scandal; for I think nothing more honourable, than to be involved in the same fate with all the great and the good that ever lived; that is, to be envied and censured by bad writers.

You do no more than answer my expectation of you, in declaring how well you take my freedom, in sometimes neglecting, as I do, to reply to your letters so soon as I ought. Those who have a right taste of the substantial part of friendship, can wave the ceremonial: a friend is the only one that will bear the omission; and one may find who is not so, by the very trial of it.

As to any anxiety I have concerning the fate of my Homer, the care is over with me: the world must be the judge, and I shall be the first to consent to the justice of its judgment, whatever it be. I am not so arrant an author as even to desire, that if I am in the wrong, all mankind should be so.

I am mightily pleased with a saying of Monsieur Tourreil: " When a man writes, he ought to animate him-
" self with the thoughts of pleasing all the world : but
" he is to renounce that desire or hope the very moment
" the book goes out of his hands."

I write this from Binfield, whither I came yesterday, having pass'd a few days in my way with my Lord Bolingbroke; I go to London in three days time, and will not fail to pay a visit to Mr. M——, whom I saw not long since at my Lord Hallifax's. I hoped from thence he had some hopes of advantage from the present administration; for few people (I think) but I, pay respects to great men without any prospects. I am in the fairest way in the world of being not worth a groat, being born both a Papist and a Poet. This puts me in mind of re-acknowledging your continued endeavours to enrich me.

But,

But, I can tell you, 'tis to no purpofe, for without the
Opes, æquum mi animum ipfe paralo.

LETTER XXVIII.

To Mr. CONGREVE.

March 19, 1714-15.

THE Farce of the What-d'ye-call-it * has occafioned
many different fpeculations in the town. Some
look'd upon it as a mere jeft upon the Tragic poets, others
as a fatire upon the late War. Mr. Cromwell hearing
none of the words, and feeing the action to be tragical,
was much aftonifhed to find the audience laugh; and
fays the Prince and Princefs muft doubtlefs be under no
lefs amazement on the fame account. Several Templars
and others of the more vociferous kind of critics, went
with a refolution to hifs, and confefs'd they were forced
to laugh fo much, that they forgot the defign they came
with. The court in general has in a very particular manner come into the jeft, and the three firft nights (notwithftanding two of them were court-nights) were diftin-
guifhed by very full audiences of the firft quality. The
common people of the pit and gallery received it at firft
with great gravity and fedatenefs, fome few with tears ;
but after the third day, they alfo took the hint, and have
ever fince been very loud in their claps. There are ftill
fome fober men who cannot be of the general opinion ;
but the laughers are fo much the majority, that one or two
critics feem determined to undeceive the town at their
proper coft, by writing grave differtations againft it : to
encourage them in which laudable defign, it is refolved a
preface fhall be prefix'd to the Farce, in vindication of
the nature and dignity of this new way of writing.

Yefterday Mr. Steele's affair was decided : I am forry
I can be of no other opinion than yours, as to his whole
carriage and writings of late. But certainly he has not

* Written by Gay.

only

only been punifhed by others, but fuffered much even
from his own party in the point of charaéter, nor (I believe) received any amends in that of intereft, as yet,
whatever may be his profpeéts for the future.

This gentleman, among a thoufand others, is a great
inftance of the fate of all who are carried away by party-
fpirit of any fide. I wifh all violence may fucceed as ill:
but am really amazed, that fo much of that four and pernicious quality fhould be joined with fo much natural
good humour as, I think, Mr. Steele is poffeffed of.

       I am, &c.

LETTER XXIX.

To Mr. CONGREVE.

       April 7, 1715.

M R. Pope is going to Mr. Jervas's, where Mr. Addifon is fitting for his piéture; in the mean time,
amidft clouds of tobacco at a coffee-houfe, I write this
letter. There is a grand revolution at Will's; Morrice
has quitted for a coffee-houfe in the city, and Titcomb
is reftored, to the great joy of Cromwell, who was at a
great lofs for a perfon to converfe with upon the fathers
and church hiftory : the knowledge I gain from him, is
entirely in painting and poetry; and Mr. Pope owes all
his fkill in aftronomy to him and Mr. Whifton, fo celebrated of late for his difcovery of the longitude in an extraordinary copy of verfes *. Mr. Rowe's Jane Gray is
to be play'd in Eafter-week, when Mrs. Oldfield is to
perfonate a charaéter direétly oppofite to female nature ;
for what woman ever defpifed Sovereignty ? You know
Chaucer has a tale where a knight faves his head by difcovering it was the thing which all women moft coveted.
Mr. Pope's Homer is retarded by the great rains that
have fallen of late, which caufes the fheets to be long a
drying: this. gives Mr. Lintot great uneafinefs, who is

* Call'd, *An Ode on the Longitude*, in Swift and Pope's Mifcellanies.

                 now

now endeavouring to corrupt the Curate of his parish to pray for fair weather, that his work may go on. There is a six-penny Criticism lately published upon the tragedy of the What-d'ye-call-it, wherein he with much judgment and learning calls me a blockhead, and Mr. Pope a knave. His grand charge is against the Pilgrim's Progress being read, which, he says, is directly levell'd at Cato's reading Plato: to back this censure, he goes on to tell you, that the Pilgrim's Progress being mentioned to be the eighth edition, makes the reflection evident, the Tragedy of Cato having just eight times (as he quaintly expresses it) visited the press. He has also endeavoured to show, that every particular passage of the play alludes to some fine part of tragedy, which, he says, I have injudiciously and profanely abused *. Sir Samuel Garth's poem upon my Lord Clare's house, I believe, will be publish'd in the Easter-week.

Thus far Mr. Gay, who has in his letter foreftall'd all the subjects of diversion, unless it should be one to you to say, that I sit up till two a clock over Burgundy and Champagne; and am become so much a rake, that I shall be ashamed, in a short time, to be thought to do any sort of business. I fear I must get the gout by drinking, purely for a fashionable pretence to sit still long enough to translate four books of Homer. I hope you'll by that time be up again, and I may succeed to the bed and couch of my predecessor; pray cause the stuffing to be repaired, and the crutches shorten'd for me. The calamity of your gout is what all your friends, that is to say, all that know you, must share in; we desire you, in your turn, to condole with us, who are under a persecution, and much afflicted with a distemper which proves mortal to many poets, a Criticism. We have indeed some relieving intervals of laughter (as you know there are in some diseases); and it is the opinion of divers good guessers, that the last fit will

---

* This curious piece was intitled, A compleat Key to the What-d'ye-call-it, writ en by one Griffin a Player, assisted by Lewis Theobald.

not be more violent than advantageous; for poet's af-
fail'd by critics, are like men bitten by Tarantulas, they
dance on so much the faster.

Mr. Thomas Burnet hath play'd the precursor to the
coming of Homer, in a treatise called Homerides. He
has since risen very much in his criticism, and after af-
faulting Homer, made a daring attack upon the * What-
d'ye-call-it. Yet there is not a Proclamation iſſued for
the burning of Homer and the Pope by the common hang-
man; nor is the What-d'ye-call-it yet silenced by the
Lord Chamberlain.

Your, &c.

LETTER XXX.

Mr. CONGREVE to Mr. POPE.

May 6.

I Have the pleasure of your very kind letter. I have
always been oblig'd to you for your friendſhip and
concern for me, and am more affeĉted with it, than I
will take upon me to expreſs in this letter. I do aſſure
you there is no return wanting on my part, and am very
sorry I had not the good luck to see the Dean before I left
the town : it is a great pleasure to me, and not a little
vanity to think that he misſes me. As. to my health,
which you are so kind to enquire after, it is not worse
than in London : I am almoſt afraid yet to say that it is
better, for I cannot reaſonably expeĉt much effeĉt from
these waters in so ſhort a time; but in the main they
seem to agree with me. Here is not one creature that I
know, which, next to the few I would chooſe, contributes
very much to my satisfaĉtion. At the same time that I
regret the want of your converſation, I pleaſe myſelf with
thinking that you are where you firſt ought to be, and engaged where you cannot do too much. Pray give my

---

* In one of his papers call'd *The Grumbler*.

humble

humble fervice and beft wifhes to your good mother. I am forry you don't tell me how Mr. Gay does in his health; I fhould have been glad to have heard he was better. My young Amanuenfis, as you call him, I am afraid, will prove but a wooden one: and you know *ex quovis ligno*, &c. You will pardon Mrs. R———'s pedantry, and believe me to be

Your, &c.

P. S. By the inclofed you will fee I am like to be imprefs'd, and enroll'd in the lift of Mr. Curll's Authors; but, I thank God! I fhall have your company. I believe it is high time you fhould think of adminiftering another Emetic.

L E T T E R S

TO AND FROM

SEVERAL PERSONS;

From the Year 1714 to 1721.

LETTER I.

The Rev. Dean BERKLEY to Mr. POPE.

Leghorn, May 1, 1714.

A S I take ingratitude to be a greater crime than impertinence, I chufe rather to run the rifque of being
thought guilty of the latter, than not to return you my
thanks for a very agreeable entertainment you juft now
gave me. I have accidentally met with your Rape of the
Lock here, having never feen it before. Style, painting;
judgment, fpirit, I had already admired in other of your
writings; but in this I am charm'd with the magic of your
invention, with all thofe images, allufions; and inexpli-
cable beauties, which you raife fo furprifingly, and at
the fame time fo naturally, out of a trifle. And yet I
cannot fay that I was more pleas'd with the reading of it,
than I am with the pretext it gives me to renew in your
thoughts, the remembrance of one who values no hap-
.pinefs beyond the friendfhip of men of wit, learning; and
good-nature.

I remember to have heard you mention fome hal
form'd defign of coming to Italy. What might we not
expect from a mufe that fings fo well in the bleak climate

of

of England, if fhe felt the fame warm fun, and breathed he fame air with Virgil and Horace ?

There are here an incredible number of poets, that have all the inclination, but want the genius, or perhaps the art of the Ancients. Some among them who under-ftand Englifh, begin to relifh our authors; and I am in-formed that at Florence they have tranflated Milton into Italian verfe. If one who knows fo well how to write like the old Latin poets, came among them, it would probably be a means to retrieve them from their cold, trivial con-ceits, to an imitation of their predeceffors.

As merchants, antiquaries, men of pleafure, &c. have all different views in travelling; I know not whether it might not be worth a poet's while to travel, in order to ftore his mind with ftrong images of nature.

Green fields and groves, flowery meadows and purling ftreams are no were in fuch perfection as in England : but if you would know lightfome days, warm funs, and blue fkies, you muft come to Italy; and to enable a man to defcribe rocks and precipices, it is abfolutely neceffary that he pafs the Alps.

You will eafily perceive that it is felf-intereft makes me fo fond of giving advice to one who has no need of it, If you came into thefe parts I fhould fly to fee you. I am here (by the favour of my good friend the Dean of St. Patrick's) in quality of Chaplain to the Earl of Peterbo-rough; who about three months fince left the greateft part of his family in this town. God knows how long we fhall ftay here. I am

Your, &c.

LETTER II.

Mr. POPE to Mr. JERVAS in Ireland,

July 9, 1716.

THO', as you rightly remark, I pay my tax but once in half a year, yet you fhall fee by this letter upon the neck of my laft, that I pay a double tax, as we non-jurors

jurors ought to do. Your acquaintance on this fide of the fea are under terrible apprehenfions from your long ftay in Ireland, that you may grow too polite for them; for we think (fince the great fuccefs of fuch a play as the Non-juror) that politenefs is gone over the water. But others are of opinion it has been longer among you, and was introduced much about the fame time with frogs, and with equal fuccefs. Poor Poetry! the little that is left of it here longs to crofs the feas, and leave Eufden in full and peaceable poffeffion of the Britifh laurel : and we begin to wifh you had the finging of our poets, as well as the croaking of our frogs to yourfelves, *in fæcula fæculorum.* It would be well in exchange if Parnelle, and two or three more of your fwans would come hither, efpecially that fwan, who like a true modern one, does not fing at all, Dr. Swift, I am (like the reft of the world) a fufferer by his idlenefs. Indeed I hate that any man fhould be idle, while I muft tranflate and comment; and I may the more fincerely wifh for good poetry from others, becaufe I am become a perfon out of the queftion; for a Tranflator is no more a poet, than a Taylor is a man.

You are, doubtlefs, perfuaded of the validity of that famous verfe,

> 'Tis Expectation makes a Bleffing dear :

but why would you make your friends fonder of you than they are ? There is no manner of need of it. We begin to expect you no more than Anti-chrift; a man that hath abfented himfelf fo long from his friends ought to be put into the Gazette.

Every body here has great need of you. Many faces have died for want of your pencil, and blooming ladies have wither'd in expecting your return. Even Frank and Betty (that conftant pair) cannot confole themfelves for your abfence; I fancy they will be forc'd to make their own picture in a pretty babe, before you come home : 'twill be a noble fubject for a family piece. Come then, and having peopled Ireland with a world of beautiful fhadows, come to us, and fee with that eye

(which

(which like the eye of the world, creates beauties by looking on them) fee, I fay, how England has alter'd the airs of all its heads in your abfence: and with what fneaking city attitudes our moft celebrated perfonages appear, in the mere mortal works of our painters.

Mr. Fortefcue is much yours; Gay commemorates you; and laftly (to climb by juft fteps and degrees) my Lord Burlington defires you may be put in mind of him. His gardens flourifh, his ftructures rife, his pictures arrive, and (what is far more valuable than all) his own good qualities daily extend themfelves to all about him : of whom I the meaneft (next to fome Italian fiddlers and Englifh Bricklayers) am a living inftance. Adieu.

LETTER III.

To the fame.

Nov. 14, 1716,

IF I had not done my utmoft to lead my life fo pleafantly as to forget all misfortunes, I fhould tell you I reckoned your abfence no fmall one; but I hope you have alfo had many good and pleafant reafons to forget your friends on this fide the world. If a wifh could tranfport me to you and your prefent companions, I could do the fame. Dr. Swift, I believe, is a very good landlord, and a chearful hoft at his own table : I fuppofe he has perfectly learnt himfelf, what he has taught fo many others, *rupta non infanire lagena:* elfe he would not make a proper hoft for your humble fervant, who (you know) tho' he drinks a glafs as feldom as any man, contrives to break one as often. But 'tis a confolation to me, that I can do this, and many other enormities, under my own roof.

But that you and I are upon equal terms in all friendly lazinefs, and have taken an inviolable oath to each other, always to do what we will; I fhould reproach you for fo long a filence. The beft amends you can make for fay-

ing

ing nothing to me is by faying all the good you can of me, which is, that I heartily love and efteem the Dean and Dr. Parnelle.

Gay is yours and theirs. His fpirit is awakened very much in the cafe of the Dean, which has broke forth in a courageous couplet or two upon Sir Richard Blackmore : He has printed it with his name to it, and bravely affigns no other reafon, than that the faid Sir Richard has abufed Dr. Swift. I have alfo fuffered in tho like caufe, and fhall fuffer more : unlefs Parnelle fends me his Zoilus and Book-worm (which the Bifhop of Clögher, I hear, greatly extols) it will be fhortly, *concurrere Bellum atque Virum* —I love you all, as much as I defpife moft wits in this dull country. Ireland has turned the tables upon England; and if I have no poetical friend in my own nation, I'll be as proud as Scipio, and fay (fince I am reduced to fkin and bone) *Ingrata patria, ne offa quidem habeas.*

LETTER IV.

To the fame.

Nov. 29, 1716.

THAT you have not heard from me of late, afcribe not to the ufual lazinefs of your correfpondent, but to a ramble to Oxford, where your name is mentioned with honour, even in a land flowing with Tories. I had the good fortune there to be often in the converfation of Dr. Clarke : He entertain'd me with feveral drawings, and particularly with the original defigns of Inigo Jones's Whitehall. I there faw and reverenced fome of your firft pieces; which future painters are to look upon as we Poets do on the Culex of Virgil and Batrocom. of Homer.

Having nam'd this latter piece, give me leave to afk what is become of Dr. Parnelle and his frogs * ? *Oblitufque meorum, oblivifcendus et illis,* might be Horace's wifh, but

_____

* He tranflated the Batrochom. of Homer, which is printed amongft his Poems.

will never be mine while I have such *meorums* as Dr. Parnelle and Dr. Swift. I hope the Spring will reftore you
to us, and with you all the beauties and colours of nature.
Not but I congratulate you on the pleafure you muft take
in being admir'd in your own country, which fo feldom
happens to prophets and poets : but in this you have the
advantage of Poets ; you are mafter of an art that muft
profper and grow rich, as long as people love, or are
proud of themfelves, or their own perfons. However,
you have ftay'd long enough, methinks, to have painted
all the numberlefs hiftories of old Ogygia. If you have
begun to be hiftorical, I recommend to your hand the
ftory which every pious Irifhman ought to begin with,
that of St. Patrick; to the end you may be obliged (as
Dr. P. was, when he tranflated the Batrachomuomachia)
to come into England, to copy the Frogs, and fuch other
vermin as were never feen in that land fince the time of
that Confeffor.

I long to fee you a hiftory painter. You have already
done enough for the private, do fomething for the public; and be not confined, like the reft, to draw only fuch
filly ftories as our own faces tell of us. The Ancients too
expect you fhould do them right; thofe ftatues from
which you learned your beautiful and noble ideas, demand
it as a piece of gratitude from you, to make them truly
known to all nations, in the account you intend to write
of their characters. I hope you think more warmly than
ever of that defign.

As to your enquiry about your houfe, when I come
within the walls, they put me in mind of thofe of Car-
thage, where your friend, like the wandering Trojan,

animum Pictura pafcit inani.

For the fpacious manfion, like a Turkifh Caravanferah,
entertains the vagabonds with only bare lodging. I rule
the family very ill, keep bad hours, and lend out your
pictures about the town. See what it is to have a poet
in your houfe ! Frank indeed does all he can in fuch a

circumftance; for, confidering he has a wild beaft in it, he conftantly keeps the door chain'd : every time it is open'd, the links rattle, the rufty hinges roar. The houfe feems fo fenfible that you are its fupport; that it is ready to drop in your abfence; but I ftill truft myfelf under its roof, as depending that providence will preferve fo many Raphael's, Titian's, and Guido's, as are lodged in your Cabinet. Surely the fins of one poet can hardly be fo heavy, as to bring an old houfe over the heads of fo many painters. In a word, your houfe is falling; but what of that? I am only a lodger *.

LETTER V.

The Hon: Mr. CRAGGS to Mr. POPE.

Paris, Sept. 2, 1716.

LAST poft brought me the favour of your letter of the 10th Aug: O. S. It would be taking too much upon me to decide, that it was a witty one; I never pretend to more judgment than to know what pleafes me; and can affure you, it was a very agreeable one. The proof I can give you of my fincerity in this opinion is, that I hope and defire you would not ftop at this, but continue more of them.

I am in a place where pleafure is continually flowing: The Princes fet the example, and the fubjects follow at a diftance. The Ladies are of all parties †, by which means the converfation of the men is very much foftened and fafhioned from thofe blunt difputes on politics, and rough jefts, we are fo guilty of; while the freedom of the women takes away all formality and conftraint. I muft own, at the fame time; thefe beauties are a little too artificial for my tafte : you have feen a French picture the original is more painted, and fuch a cruft of powder and effence in their hair, that you can fee no difference between black and red. By difufing ftays and indulging themfelves at table; they run out of all fhape ; but as to

* Alluding to the ftory of the Irifhman.
† i. e. In all companies.

that;

that, they may give a good reafon, they prefer conveniency to parade, and are, by this means, as ready, as they
are generally willing, to be charitable. \

I am furpriz'd to find I have wrote fo much fcandal;
I fancy I am either fetting up for a wit, or imagine I
muſt write in this ſtyle to a wit; I hope you'll prove a
good-natur'd one, and not only let me hear from you
fometimes, but forgive the fmall encouragement you
meet with. I won't trouble myfelf to finiſh finely; a
true compliment is better than a good one, and I can
affure you without any, that I am very fincerely,

Sir, Yours, &c.

LETTER VI.

To Mr. FENTON

SIR,   May 5.

I Had not omitted anfwering yours of the 18th of laſt
 month, but out of a defire to give you fome certain
and fatisfactory account, which way, and at what time,
you might take your journey. I am now commiffioned
to tell you, that Mr. Craggs will expect you on the rifing
of the parliament, which will be as foon as he can receive
you in the manner he would receive a man de belles Lettres, that is, in tranquillity and full leifure. I dare fay
your way of life (which, in my taſte, will be the beſt in
the world, and with one of the beſt men in the world)
muſt prove highly to your contentment. And I muſt
add, it will be ſtill the more a joy to me, as I ſhall
reap a particular advantage from the good I ſhall have
done in bringing you together, by feeing it in my own
neighbourhood. Mr. Craggs has taken a houfe clofe by
mine, whither he propofes to come in three weeks: in
the mean time I heartily invite you to live with me;
where a frugal and philofophical diet, for a time, may
give you a higher relifh of that elegant way of life you
will enter into after. I defire to know by the firſt poſt,
how foon I may hope for you.

K 2   I am

. I am a little fcandalized at your complaint that your time lies heavy on your hands, when the Mufes have put fo many good materials into your head to employ them. As to your queftion, What I am doing? I anfwer, Juft what I have been doing fome years, my duty; fecondly, relieving myfelf with neceffary amufements, or exercifes, which fhall ferve me inftead of phyfic as long as they can; thirdly, reading till I am tired; and laftly, writing when I have no other thing in the world to do, or no friend to entertain in company.

My mother is, I thank God, the eafier, if not the bet-ter, for my cares; and I am the happier in that regard, as well as in the confcioufnefs of doing my beft. My next felicity is in retaining the good opinion of honeft men, who think me not quite undeferving of it; and in finding no injuries from others hurt me, as long as I know my-felf. I will add the fincerity with which I act towards in-genious and undefigning men, and which makes me always (even by a natural bond) their friend; therefore believe me very affectionately   Your, &c.

LETTER VII.

Rev. Dean BERKLEY*, to Mr. POPE.

Naples, Oct. 22, N. S. 1717.

I Have long had it in my thoughts to trouble you with a letter, but was difcouraged for want of fomething that I could think worth fending fifteen hundred miles. Italy is fuch an exhaufted fubject, that I dare fay you'd eafily forgive my faying nothing of it; and the imagina-tion of a Poet is a thing fo nice and delicate, that it is no eafy matter to find out images capable of giving plea-fure to one of the few, who (in any age) have come up to that character. I am neverthelefs lately returned from an ifland, where I paffed three or four months; which,

* Afterwards Bifhop of Cleyne in Ireland, author of the Dialogues of Hy-las and Philonous, the Minute Philofopher, &c.

were it fet out in its true colours, might, methinks, amufe you agreeably enough for a minute or two. The ifland Inarime is an epitome of the whole earth, containing, within the compafs of eighteen miles, a wonderful variety of hills, vales, ragged rocks, fruitful plains, and barren mountains, all thrown together in a moft romantic confufion. The air is, in the hotteft feafon, conftantly refrefhed by cool breezes from the fea. The vales produce excellent wheat and Indian corn, but are moftly covered with vineyards, intermix'd with fruit-trees. Befides the common kinds, as cherries, apricots, peaches, &c. they produce oranges, limes, almonds, pomegranates, figs, water-melons, and many other fruits unknown to our climates, which lie every where open to the paffenger. The hills are the greater part covered to the top with vines, fome with chefnut groves, and others with thickets of myrtle and lentifcus. The fields in the northern fide are divided by hedge-rows of myrtle. Several fountains and rivulets add to the beauty of this landfcape, which is likewife fet off by the variety of fome barren fpots, and naked rocks. But that which crowns the fcene is a large mountain, rifing out of the middle of the ifland (once a terrible Volcano, by the ancients called Mons Epomeus) ; its lower parts are adorned with vines, and other fruits ; the middle affords pafture to flocks of goats and fheep ; and the top is a fandy pointed rock, from which you have the fineft profpect in the world, furveying at one view, befides feveral pleafant iflands lying at your feet, a tract of Italy about three hundred miles in length, from the promontory of Antium to the Cape of Palinurus : the greater part of which hath been fung by Homer and Virgil, as making a confiderable part of the travels and adventures of their two Heroes. The iflands Caprea, Prochyta, and Parthenope, together with Cajeta, Cumæ, Monte Mifeno, the habitations of Circe, the Syrens, and the Læftrigones, the bay of Naples, the promontory of Minerva, and the whole Campagnia felice, make but a part of this noble landfcape ; which would demand an

imagi-

imagination as warm, and numbers as flowing, as your own, to defcribe it. The inhabitants of this delicious ifle, as they are without riches and honours, fo are they without the vices and follies that attend them; and were they but as much ftrangers to revenge, as they are to avarice and ambition, they might in fact anfwer the poetical notions of the golden age. But they have got, as an alloy to their happinefs, an ill habit of murdering one another on flight offences. We had an inftance of this the fecond night after our arrival, a youth of eighteen being fhot dead by our door; and yet by the fole fecret of minding our own bufinefs, we found a means of living fecurely among thofe dangerous people. Would you know how we pafs the time at Naples? Our chief entertainment is the devotion of our neighbours: befides the gaiety of their churches (where folks go to fee what they call *una bella Devotione*, i. e. a fort of religious Opera) they make fireworks almoft every week, out of devotion; the ftreets are often hung with arras, out of devotion; and (what is ftill more ftrange) the ladies invite gentlemen to their houfes, and treat them with mufic and fweetmeats, out of devotion; in a word, were it not for this devotion of its inhabitants, Naples would have little elfe to recommend it, befide the air and fituation. Learning is in no very thriving ftate here, as indeed no where elfe in Italy; however, among many pretenders, fome men of tafte are to be met with. A friend of mine told me, not long fince, that being to vifit Salvini at Florence, he found him reading your Homer: he liked the notes extremely, and could find no other fault with the verfion, but that he thought it approached too near a paraphrafe; which fhews him not to be fufficiently acquainted with our language. I wifh you health to go on with that noble work; and when you have that, I need not wifh you fuccefs. You will do me the juftice to believe, that whatever relates to your welfare is fincerely wifhed by

Your, &c,

LETTERS

LETTER VIII.

Mr. POPE to *⁎*.

Dec. 12, 1718.

THE old project of a Window in the bosom, to render the Soul of man visible, is what every honest friend has manifold reason to wish for; yet even that would not do in our case, while you are so far separated from me, and so long. I begin to fear you'll die in Ireland, and that Denunciation will be fulfilled upon you, *Hibernus es, et in Hiberniam reverteris.* I should be apt to think you in Sancho's case; some Duke has made you Governor of an island, or wet place, and you are administring laws to the wild Irish. But I must own, when you talk of Building and Planting, you touch my string; and I am as apt to pardon you, as the fellow that thought himself Jupiter would have pardon'd the other madman who call'd himself his brother Neptune. Alas, Sir, do you know whom you talk to? one that has been a Poet, was degraded to a Translator, and at last, thro' mere dulness, is turned an Architect. You know Martial's censure, *Præconem facito vel Architectum.* However, I have one way left, to plan, to elevate, and to surprize (as Bays says); the next news you may expect to hear, is, that I am in debt.

The history of my transplantation and settlement, which you desire, would require a volume, were I to enumerate the many projects, difficulties, vicissitudes, and various fates attending that important part of my life : much more, should I describe the many Draughts, Elevations, Profiles, Perspectives, &c. of every Palace and Garden propos'd, intended, and happily raised, by the strength of that faculty wherein all great Geniuses excel, Imagination. At last, the gods and fate have fix'd me on the borders of the Thames, in the districts of Richmond and Twickenham : it is here I have passed an entire

entire year of my life, without any fix'd abode in London, or more than cafting a tranfitory glance (for a day
or two at moft in a month) on the pomps of the Town.
It is here I hope to receive you, Sir, returned from eter-
nizing the Ireland of this age. For you my ftruꞗures
rife; for you my colonades extend their wings; for you
my groves afpire, and rofes bloom; and, to fay truth, I
hope pofterity (which, no doubt, will be made acquainted
with all thefe things) will look upon it as one of the principal motives of my Architeꞗure, that it was a manfion
prepar'd to receive you, againft your own fhould fall to
duft, which is deftin'd to be the tomb of poor Frank and
Betty, and the immortal monument of the fidelity of two
fuch Servants, who have excell'd in conftancy the very
Rats of your family.

What more can I tell you of myfelf? fo much, and
yet all put together fo little, that I fcarce care or know
how to do it. But the very reafons that are againft putting it upon paper, are as ftrong for telling it you in perfon; and I am uneafy to be fo long denied the fatisfaꞗion
of it.

At prefent I confider you bound in by the Irifh Sea,
like the ghofts in Virgil,

Trifti palus inamabilis unda
Alligat, et novies Styx circumfufa coërcet!

and I can't exprefs how I long to renew our old intercourfe and converfation, our morning conferences in bed
in the fame room, our evening walks in the park, our
amufing voyages on the water, our philofophical fuppers,
our leꞗures, our differtations, our gravities, our reveries, our fooleries, our what not?—This awakens the
memory of fome of thofe who have made a part in all
thefe. Poor Parnelle, Garth, Rowe! You juftly re-
prove me for not fpeaking of the death of the laft: Parnelle was too much in my mind, to whofe memory I am
ereꞗing the beft Monument I can. What he gave me to
publifh, was but a fmall part of what he left behind him;
but it was the beft, and I will not make it worfe by enlarging

larging it. I'd fain know if he be buried at Chefter, or Dublin; and what care has been, or is, to be taken for his Monument, &c.   Yet I have not neglected my devoirs to Mr. Rowe; I am writing this very day his epitaph for Weftminfter-Abbey.—After thefe, the beft-natur'd of men, Sir Samuel Garth, has left me in the trueft concern for his lofs.   His death was very heroical, and yet unaffected enough to have made a faint or a philofopher famous.   But ill tongues, and worfe hearts, have branded even his laft moments, as wrongfully as they did his life, with irreligion.   You muft have heard many tales on this fubject; but if ever there was a good Chriftian, without knowing himfelf to be fo, it was Dr. Garth.

Your, &c.

LETTER IX.

To Mr. ****.

Sept. 17.

THE gaiety of your letter proves you not fo ftudious of Wealth as many of your profeffion are, fince you can derive matter of mirth from want of bufinefs.   You are none of thofe Lawyers who deferve the motto of the devil, *Circuit quærens quem devoret*.   But your *Circuit* will at leaft procure you one of the greateft of temporal bleffings, Health.   What an advantageous circumftance is it, for one that loves rambling fo well, to be a grave and reputable rambler; while (like your fellow Circuiteer, the Sun) you travel the round of the earth, and behold all the iniquities under the heavens!   You are much a fuperior genius to me in rambling: you, like a pigeon (to which I would fooner compare a Lawyer than to a Hawk) can fly fome hundred leagues at a pitch; I, like a poor fquirrel, am continually in motion indeed, but it is about a cage of three feet: my little excurfions are but like thofe of a fhop-keeper, who walks every day a mile or two before his own door, but minds his bufinefs all the while.   Your letter of the caufe lately before you,

L   I could

I could not but communicate to fome ladies of your acquaintance. I am of opinion, if you continued a correfpondence of the fame fort during a whole Circuit, it could not fail to pleafe the fex, better than half the novels they read; there would be in them what they love above all things, a moft happy union of Truth and Scandal. I affure you the Bath affords nothing equal to it: it is on the contrary full of *grave and fad* men, Mr. Baron S. Lord Chief Juftice A. Judge P. and Counfellor B. who has a large pimple on the tip of his nofe, but thinks it inconfiftent with his gravity to wear a patch, notwithftanding the precedent of an eminent Judge. I am, dear Sir,

Your, &c.

LETTER X.

To the Earl of BURLINGTON.

MY LORD,

IF your Mare could fpeak, fhe would give an account of what extraordinary company fhe had on the road; which fince fhe cannot do, I will.

It was the enterprizing Mr. Lintot, the redoubtable rival of Mr. Tonfon, who, mounted on a ftone-horfe (no difagreeable companion to your Lordfhip's mare) overtook me in Windfor-foreft. He faid, he heard I defign'd for Oxford, the feat of the Mufes, and would, as my bookfeller, by all means accompany me thither.

I afk'd him where he got his horfe? He anfwer'd, he got it of his Publifher: " For that rogue, my Printer
" (faid he) difappointed me: I hoped to put him in
" good humour by a treat at the tavern, of a brown fri-
" caffee of rabbits, which coft two fhillings, with two
" quarts of wine, befides my converfation. I thought
" myfelf cockfure of his horfe, which he readily promis'd
" me, but faid that Mr. Tonfon had juft fuch another
" defign of going to Cambridge, expecting there the
" copy of a new kind of Horace from Dr. ——; and if
" Mr.

" Mr. Tonfon went, he was pre-engaged to attend him,
" being to have the printing of the faid copy.

" So in fhort, I borrow'd this ftone-horfe of my Pub-
" lifher, which he had of Mr. Oldmixon for a debt; he
" lent me too the pretty boy you fee after me : he was
" a fmutty dog yefterday, and coft me near two hours
" to wafh the ink off his face ; but the Devil is a fair-
" condition'd Devil, and very forward in his Catechife :
" if you have any more bags, he fhall carry them."

I thought Mr. Lintot's civility not to be neglected, fo
gave the boy a fmall bag, containing three fhirts, and an
Elzevir Virgil; and mounting in an inftant, proceeded
on the road, with my man before, my courteous ftationer
befide, and the aforefaid devil behind. ·

Mr. Lintot began in this manner: " Now, damn them!
" what if they fhould put it into the news-paper, how
" you and I went together to Oxford? what would I
" care ? If I fhould go down into Suffex, they would fay
" I was gone to the Speaker. But what of that ! If my
" fon were but big enough to go on with the bufinefs,
" by G—d I would keep as good company as old Jacob."

Hereupon I enquir'd of his fon. " The lad (fays he)
" has fine parts, but is fomewhat fickly, much as you
" are—I fpare for nothing in his education at Weftmin-
" fter. Pray don't you think Weftminfter to be the beft
" fchool in England? moft of the late Miniftry came
" out of it, fo did many of this Miniftry; I hope the
" boy will make his fortune."

Don't you defign to let him pafs a year at Oxford?
" To what purpofe ? (faid he) the Univerfities do but
" make Pedants, and I intend to breed him a man of
" bufinefs."

As Mr. Lintot was talking, I obferv'd he fat uneafy on
his faddle, for which I expreffed fome folicitude: Nothing, fays he, I can bear it well enough : but fince we
have the day before us, methinks it would be very pleafant for you to reft a-while under the woods. When we
were alighted, " See here, what a mighty pretty Horace

L 2   " I

" I have in my pocket! what if you amus'd yourfelf in
" turning an ode, till we mount again? Lord! if you
" pleas'd, what a clever Mifcellany might you make at
" leifure hours." Perhaps I may, faid I, if we ride on;
. the motion is an aid to my fancy, a round trot very much
awakens my fpirits: then jog on a pace, and I'll think as
hard as I can.

Silence enfued for a full hour; after which Mr. Lintot
lugg'd the reins, ftop'd fhort, and broke out, " Well,
" Sir, how far have you gone?" I anfwer'd, Seven
miles. " Z—ds, Sir, faid Lintot, I thought you had
" done feven ftanza's. Oldfworth, in a ramble round
" Wimbledon hill, would tranflate a whole ode in half
" this time. I'll fay that for Oldfworth (tho' I loft by
" his Timothy's) he tranflates an ode of Horace the
" quickeft of any man in England. I remember Dr.
" King would write verfes in a tavern three hours after
" he could not fpeak: and there's Sir Richard, in that
" rumbling old chariot of his, between Fleet-ditch and
" St. Giles's-pound, fhall make you half a Jobb."

Pray, Mr. Lintot (faid I) now you talk of Tranflators, what is your method of managing them? " Sir
" (reply'd he) thofe are the faddeft pack of rogues in the
" world: in a hungry fit, they'll fwear they underftand
" all the languages in the univerfe: I have known one
" of them take down a Greek book upon my counter,
" and cry, Ah, this is Hebrew, I muft read it from the
" latter end. By G—d, I can never be fure in thefe
" fellows; for I neither underftand Greek, Latin,
" French, nor Italian, myfelf. But this is my way; I
" agree with them for ten fhillings per fheet, with a
" provifo, that I will have their doings correfted by
" whom I pleafe; fo by one or other they are led at laft
" to the true fenfe of an author; my judgment giving
" the negative to all my tranflators." But how are you
fecure thofe correftors may not impofe upon you? " Why
" I get any civil gentleman (efpecially any Scotchman)
" that comes into my fhop, to read the original to me

                                        " in

" in Englifh; by this I know whether my firft tranflator
". be deficient, and whether my corrector merits his mo-
" ney or not ?

" I'll tell you what happen'd to me laft month : I bar-
" gain'd with S** for a new verfion of Lucretius to pub-
" lifh againft Tonfon's; agreeing to pay the author fo
" many fhillings at his producing fo many lines. He
" made a great progrefs in a very fhort time, and I gave
" it to the corrector to compare with the Latin; but he
" went directly to Creech's tranflation, and found it the
" fame word for word, all but the firft page. Now,
" what d'ye think I did ? I arrefted the tranflator for a
" cheat; nay, and I ftopt the corrector's pay too, upon
" this proof that he had made ufe of Creech inftead of
" the original."

Pray tell me next how you deal with the Critics ?
" Sir (faid he) nothing more eafy. I can filence the
" moft formidable of them : the rich ones, for a fheet a-
" piece of the blotted manufcript, which cofts me no-
" thing; they'll go about with it to their acquaintance,
" and pretend they had it from the author, who fubmit-
" ted to their correction : this has given fome of them
" fuch an air, that in time they come to be confulted
" with, and dedicated to as the top Critics of the town.
" —As for the poor critics, I'll give you one inftance of
" my management, by which you may guefs at the reft.
" A lean man, that look'd like a very good fcholar, came
" to me t'other day ; he turn'd over your Homer, fhook
" his head, fhrugg'd up his fhoulders, and pifh'd at eve-
" ry line of it: One would wonder (fays he) at the
" ftrange prefumption of fome men; Homer is no fuch
" eafy tafk, that every ftripling, every verfifier—He
" was going on, when my wife call'd to dinner: Sir,
" faid I, will you pleafe to eat a piece of beef with me ?
" Mr. Lintot, faid he, I am forry you fhould be at the
" expence of this great book; I am really concern'd on
" your account—Sir, I am much oblig'd to you : if you
" can dine upon a piece of beef, together with a flice of
" pudding

" pudding—Mr. Lintot, I do not fay but Mr. Pope, if
" he would condefcend to advife with men of learning—
" Sir, the pudding is upon the table, if you pleafe to go
" in—My critic complies, he comes to a tafte of your
" poetry, and tells me in the fame breath, that the book
" is commendable, and the pudding excellent.

" Now, Sir (concluded Mr. Lintot) in return to the
" franknefs I have fhewn, pray tell me, Is it the opinion
" of your friends at court, that my Lord Lanfdown will
" be brought to the bar, or not ?" I told him, I heard
he would not, and I hop'd it, my Lord being one I had
particular obligations to.´   " That may be (reply'd Mr.
" Lintot) but by G—d, if he is not, I fhall lofe the
" printing of a very good Trial."

Thefe, my Lord, are a few traits by which you may
difcern the genius of Mr. Lintot, which I have chofen
for the fubject of a letter.   I dropt him as foon as I got
to Oxford, and paid a vifit to my Lord Carleton at Mid-
dleton.

The converfations I enjoy here, are not to be prejudiced by my pen, and the pleafures from them only to
be equall'd when I meet your Lordfhip.   I hope in a few
days to caft myfelf from your horfe at your feet.

I am, &c.

LETTER XI.

To the Duke of BUCKINGHAM.

[In anfwer to a Letter in which he inclofed the Defcription of Buckingham-
houfe, written by him to the D. of Sh.]

PLINY was one of thofe few authors who had a warm
houfe over his head; nay, two houfes, as appears by
two of his epiftles. I believe, if any of his contemporary
authors durft have inform'd the public where they lodged,
we fhould have found the garrets of Rome as well inha-
bited as thofe of Fleet-ftreet; but 'tis dangerous to let
creditors into fuch a fecret, therefore we may prefume

4   that

that then, as well as now-a-days, no-body knew where they lived but their bookfellers.

It feems, that when Virgil came to Rome, he had no lodging at all : he firft introduc'd himfelf to Auguftus by an epigram, beginning *Noĉte pluit tota*—an obfervation which probably he had not made, unlefs he had lain all night in the ftreet.

Where Juvenal lived we cannot affirm ; but in one of his fatires he complains of the exceflive price of lodgings; neither do I believe he would have talk'd fo feelingly of Codrus's bed, if there had been room for a bedfellow in it.

I believe, with all the oftentation of Pliny, he would have been glad to have changed both his houfes for your Grace's one ; which is a country-houfe in the fummer, and a town-houfe in the winter, and muft be owned to be the propereft habitation for a wife man, who fees all the world change every feafon without ever changing himfelf.

I have been reading the defcription of Pliny's houfe, with an eye to yours ; but finding they will bear no comparifon, will try if it can be match'd by the large country-feat I inhabit at prefent, and fee what figure it may make by the help of a florid defcription.

You muft expeĉt nothing regular in my defcription, any more than in the houfe ; the whole vaft edifice is fo disjointed, and the feveral parts of it fo detach'd one from the other, and yet fo joining again, one cannot tell how, that, in one of my poetical fits, I imagined it had been a village in Amphion's time, where the cottages having taken a country-dance together, had been all out, and ftood ftone-ftill with amazement ever fince.

You muft excufe me, if I fay nothing of the Front; indeed I don't know which it is. A ftranger would be grievoufly difappointed, who endeavour'd to get into the houfe the right way. One would reafonably expeĉt, after the entry through the porch, to be let into the hall : alas, nothing lefs ! you find yourfelf in the houfe of

office,

office. From the parlour you think to ſtep into the drawing-room; but upon opening the iron-nail'd door, ⋅ you are convinc'd by a flight of birds about your ears, and a cloud of duſt in your eyes, that it is the Pigeon-houſe. If you come into the chapel, you find its altars, like thoſe of the ancients, continually ſmoaking, but it is with the ſteams of the adjoining kitchen.

The great hall within is high and ſpacious, flank'd on one ſide with a very long table, a true image of ancient hoſpitality : the walls are all over ornamented with mon-ſtrous horns of animals, about twenty broken pikes, ten or a dozen blunderbuſſes, and a ruſty match-lock muſquet or two, which we were inform'd had ſerv'd in the civil wars. Here is one vaſt arch'd window beautifully dark-en'd with divers ſcutcheons of painted glaſs; one ſhining pane in particular bears date 1286, which alone preſerves the memory of a Knight, whoſe iron armour is long ſince periſh'd with ruſt, and whoſe alabaſter noſe is moulder'd from his monument. The face of dame Eleanor in an-other piece, owes more to that ſingle pane, than to all the glaſſes ſhe ever conſulted in her life. After this, who can ſay that glaſs is frail, when it is not half ſo frail as human beauty, or glory! and yet I can't but ſigh to think that the moſt authentic record of ſo ancient a fami-ly ſhould lie at the mercy of every infant who flings a ſtone. In former days there have din'd in this hall gar-ter'd Knights, and courtly Dames, attended by uſhers, ſewers, and ſeneſchals; and yet it was but laſt night, that an owl flew hither and miſtook it for a barn.

This hall lets you (up and down) over a very high threſhold into the great parlour. Its contents are a broken-belly'd virginal, a couple of cripled velvet chairs, with two or three milldew'd pictures of mouldy anceſtors, who look as diſmally as if they came freſh from hell with all their brimſtone about them; theſe are carefully ſet at the farther corner, for the windows being every where broken, make it ſo convenient a place to dry poppies and muſtard-ſeed, that the room is appropriated to that uſe.

Next

Next this parlour, as I faid before, lies the pigeon-houfe, by the fide of which runs an entry, which lets you on one hand and t'other into a bed-chamber, a but-tery, and a fmall hole call'd the chaplain's ftudy; then follow a brew-houfe, a little green and gilt parlour, and the great ftairs, under which is the dairy ; a little farther on the right, the fervants hall, and by the fide of it, up fix fteps, the old lady's clofet for her private devotions; which has a lattice into the hall, intended (as we imagine) that at the fame time as fhe pray'd, fhe might have an eye on the men and maids. There are upon the ground-floor, in all, twenty-fix apartments, among which I muft not forget a chamber which has in it a large antiquity of timber, that feems to have been either a bedftead, oi a cyder-prefs.

The kitchen is built in form of the Rotunda, being one vaft vault to the top of the houfe ;· where one aper-ture ferves to let out the fmoke, and let in the light. By the blacknefs of the walls, the circular fires, vaft caul-drons, yawning mouths of ovens and furnaces, you would. think it either the forge of Vulcan, the cave of Poly-pheme, or the temple of Moloch. The horror of this place has made fuch an impreffion on the country people, that they believe the Witches keep their Sabbath here, and that once a year the Devil treats them with infernal venifon, a roafted tyger ftuff'd with ten penny nails.

Above ftairs we have a number of rooms : you never pafs out of one into another but by the afcent or defcent of two or three ftairs.   Our beft room is very long and low, of the exaft proportion of a band-box.   In moft of thefe rooms there are hangings of the fineft work in the world, that is to fay, thofe which Arachne fpins from her own bowels.   Were it not for this only furniture, the whole would be a miferable fcene of naked walls, flaw'd cielings, broken windows, and rufty locks.   The roof is fo decay'd, that, after a favourable fhower, we may ex-pet a crop of mufhrooms between the chinks of our floors.   All the doors are as little and low as thofe to the cabbins of packet-boats. Thefe rooms have for many years had no other inhabitants than certain rats, whofe very age renders them worthy of this feat; for the very rats of this venerable houfe are grey : fince thefe have not yet quitted it, we hope at leaft that this ancient man-fion may not fall during the fmall remnant thefe poor animals have to live, who are now too infirm to remove to another. There is yet a fmall fubfiftence left them in the few remaining books of the library.

We had never feen half what I had defcribed, but for a ftarch'd, grey-headed Steward, who is as much an an-tiquity as any in this place, and looks like an old family picture walk'd out of its frame. He entertain'd us, as we pafs'd from room to room, with feveral relations of the family ; but his obfervations were particularly curious when we came to the cellar : he inform'd us where ftood .the triple rows of butts of fack, and where were ranged the bottles of tent, for toafts in a morning : he pointed to the ftands that fupported the iron-hoop'd hogfheads of ftrong beer ; then ftepping to a corner, he lugg'd out the tatter'd fragments of an unframed picture : " This (fays " he, with tears) was poor Sir Thomas ! once mafter of " all this drink. He had two fons, poor young mafters ! " who never arrived to the age of this beer ; they both " fell ill in this very room, and never went out on their " own legs." He could not pafs by a heap of broken bottles, without taking up a piece, to fhow us the Arms of the family upon it. He then led us up the Tower by dark winding ftone fteps, which landed us into feveral little rooms, one above another. One of thefe was nail'd up, and our guide whifper'd to us as a fecret, the occa-fion of it : it feems the courfe of this noble blood was a little interrupted, about two centuries ago, by a freak of the lady Frances, who was here taken in the fact with a neighbouring Prior, ever fince which the room has been nailed up, and branded with the name of the Adultery-Chamber. The ghoft of lady Frances is fuppofed to walk there ; and fome prying maids of the family report,

that

that they have feen a lady in a fardingale through the key-hole; but this matter is hufht up, and the fervants are forbid to talk of it.

I muft needs have tired you by this long defcription: but what engaged me in it was, a generous principle to preferve the memory of that, which itfelf muft foon fall into duft, nay, perhaps part of it, before this letter reaches your hands.

Indeed we owe this old houfe the fame kind of gratitude that we do to an old friend, who harbours us in his declining condition, nay even in his laft extremities. How fit is this retreat for uninterrupted ftudy, where no one that paffes by can dream there is an inhabitant; and even thofe who would dine with us, dare not ftay under our roof! Any one that fees it, will own, I could not have chofen a more likely place to converfe with the dead in. I had been mad indeed, if I had left your Grace for any one but Homer. But when I return to the living, I fhall have the fenfe to endeavour to converfe with the beft of them; and fhall therefore, as foon as poffible, tell you in perfon how much I am, &c.

LETTER XII.

The D. of BUCKINGHAM to Mr. POPE.

YOU defire my opinion as to the late difpute in France concerning Homer: and I think it excufable (at an age, alas! of not much pleafure) to amufe myfelf a little in taking notice of a controverfy, than which nothing is at prefent more remarkable (even in a nation who value themfelves fo much upon the Belles Lettres) both on account of the illuftrious fubject of it, and of the two perfons engaged in the quarrel.

The one is extraordinary in all the Lyric kind of Poetry, even in the opinion of his very adverfary. The other, a Lady (and of more value for being fo) not only of great Learning, but with a Genius admirably turn'd to that fort of it which moft becomes her Sex, for foft-

nefs,

nefs, genteelnefs, and promoting of virtue; and fuch as (one would think) is not fo liable as other parts of fcholarfhip, to rough difputes, or violent animofity.

Yet it has fo happen'd, that no writers, even about Divinity itfelf, have been more outrageous or uncharitable, than thefe two polite authors; by fuffering their judgments to be a little warped (if I may ufe that expreffion) by the heat of their eager inclinations, to attack or defend fo great an Author under debate. I wifh, for the fake of the public, which is now fo well entertained by their quarrel, it may not end at laft in their agreeing to blame a third man who is not fo prefumptuous as to cenfure both, if they fhould chance to hear it.

To begin with matter of fact. M. D'Acier has well judg'd, that the beft of all Poets certainly deferved a better tranflation, at leaft into French profe, becaufe to fee it done in verfe was defpair'd of: I believe, indeed, from a defect in that language, incapable of mounting to any degree of excellence fuitable to fo very great an undertaking.

She has not only perform'd this tafk as well as profe can do it (which is indeed but as the wrong fide of tapeftry is able to reprefent the right *) fhe has added to it alfo many learned and ufeful annotations; with all which, fhe moft obligingly delighted not only her own fex, but moft of ours, ignorant of the Greek, and confequently her adverfary himfelf, who frankly acknowledges that ignorance.

'Tis no wonder therefore, if, in doing this, fhe is grown fo enamour'd of that unfpeakably-charming Author, as to have a kind of horror at the leaft mention of a man bold enough to blame him.

Now as to M. de la Motte, he being already defervedly famous for all forts of Lyric poetry, was fo far introduced by her into thofe beauties of the Epic kind (tho' but in that way of tranflation) as not to refift the pleafure and hope of reputation, by attempting that in verfe, which

---

* A thought of Cervantes.

3   had

had been applauded fo much for the difficulty of doing it even in profe; knowing how this, well executed, muft extremely tranfcend the other.

But as great Poets are a little apt to think they have an ancient right of being excus'd for vanity on all occafions, he was not content to out-do M. D'Acier, but endea-vour'd to out-do Homer himfelf, and all that ever in any age or nation went before him in the fame enterprize; by leaving out, altering, or adding whatever he thought beft.

Againft this prefumptuous attempt, Homer has been in all times fo well defended, as not to need my fmall affiftance; yet I muft needs fay, his excellencies are fuch, that for their fakes he deferves a much gentler touch for his feeming errors. Thefe, if M. de la Motte had tran-flated as well as the reft, with an apology for having re-tained them only out of mere veneration; his judgment, in my opinion, would have appear'd much greater than by the beft of his alterations, though I admit them to be written very finely. I join with M. de la Motte in won-dering at fome odd things in Homer, but 'tis chiefly be-caufe of his fublime ones, I was about to fay his divine ones, which almoft furprize me at finding him any where in the fallible condition of human nature.

And now we are wondering, I am in a difficulty to guefs what can be the reafon of thefe exceptions againft Homer, from one who has himfelf tranflated him, con-trary to the general cuftom of tranflators. Is there not a little of that in it? I mean to be fingular, in getting above the title of a Tranflator, tho' fufficiently honour-able in this cafe. For fuch an ambition no body has lefs occafion, than one who is fo fine a Poet in other kinds; and who muft have too much wit to believe, any altera-tion of another can entitle him to the denomination of an *Epic Poet* himfelf: tho' no man in this age feems more capable of being a good one, if the French tongue would bear it. Yet in his tranflation he has done too well, to leave any doubt (with all his faults) that her's can be ever parallel'd with it.

Befides,

Befides, he could not be ignorant, that finding faults is the moft eafy and vulgar part of a critic; whereas nothing fhews fo much fkill and tafte both, as the being thoroughly fenfible of the fublimeft excellencies.

What can we fay in excufe of all this? *Humanum eft errare:* fince as good a Poet as, I believe, the French language is capable of, and as fharp a Critic as any nation can produce, has, by too much cenfuring Homer, fubjected a tranflation to cenfure, that would have otherwife' ftood the teft of the fevereft adverfary.

But fince he would needs chufe that wrong way of criticifm, I wonder he mifs'd a ftone fo eafy to be thrown againft Homer, not for his filling the Iliad with fo much' flaughter (for that is to be excufed, fince a War is not capable of being defcribed without it) but with fo many various particulars of wounds and horror, as fhew the writer (I am afraid) fo delighted that way himfelf, as not the leaft to doubt his reader being fo alfo. Like Spanioletta, whofe difmal pictures are the more difagreeable for being always fo movingly painted. Even Hector's laft parting from his fon and Andromache hardly makes us amends for his body's being dragg'd thrice round the town. M. de la Motte, in his ftrongeft objections about that difmal combat, has fufficient caufe to blame his inraged adverfary; who here gives an inftance, that it is impoffible to be vio · lent without committing fome miftake; her paffion for Homer blinding her too much to perceive the very groffeft of his failings: by which warning I am become a little more capable of impartiality, though in a difpute about that very Poet for whom I have the greateft veneration.

M. D'Acier might have confider'd a little, that whatever were the motives of M. de la Motte to fo bold a proceeding, it could not darken that fame which I am fure fhe thinks fhines fecurely, even after the vain attempts of Plato himfelf againft it: caus'd only perhaps by a like reafon with that of Madam D'Acier's anger againft M. de la Motte, namely, the finding that in profe his genius (great as it was) could not be capable

of

of the fublime heights of poetry, which therefore he baniſhed out of his commonwealth.

Nor were theſe objeƈtions to Homer any more leſſen-
ing of her merit in tranſlating him as well as that way is
capable of, viz. fully, plainly, and elegantly, than the
moſt admirable verſes can be any diſparagement to as excellent proſe.

The beſt excuſe for all this violence is, its being in a
cauſe which gives a kind of reputation even to ſuffering,
notwithſtanding ever ſo ill a management of it.

The worſt of defending even Homer in ſuch a paſſionate
manner, is its being more a proof of her weakneſs, than
of his being liable to none. For what is it can excuſe
Homer any more than Heƈtor, for flying at the firſt ſight
of Achilles? whoſe terrible aſpeƈt ſure needed not ſuch
an inexcuſable fright to ſet it off; and methinks all that
account of Minerva's reſtoring his dart to Achilles, comes
a little too late, for excuſing Heƈtor's ſo terrible apprehenſion at the very firſt.

LETTER XIII.

To the Duke of BUCKINGHAM.

Sept. 1, 1718.

I Am much honour'd by your Grace's compliance with
my requeſt, in giving me your opinion of the French
diſpute concerning Homer. And I ſhall keep my word,
in fairly telling wherein I diſagree from you. It is but
in two or three very ſmall points, not ſo much of the diſpute, as of the parties concern'd in it. I cannot think
quite ſo highly of the Lady's learning, tho' I reſpeƈt it
very much. It is great complaiſance in that polite nation, to allow her to be a Critic of equal rank with her
huſband. To inſtance no further, his remarks on Horace ſhew more good Senſe, Penetration, and a better
Taſte of his author, and thoſe upon Ariſtotle's Art of
Poetry

Poetry more Skill and Science, than any of her's on any author whatever *. In truth, they are much more flight, dwell more in generals, and are befides, for the moft part, lefs her own; of which her Remarks upon Homer are an example, where Euftathius is tranfcribed ten times for once that he is quoted. Nor is there at all more depth of learning in thofe upon Terence, Plautus, or (where they were moft wanted) upon Ariftophanes, only the Greek fcholia upon the latter are fome of the beft extant.

Your Grace will believe me, that I did not fcarch to find defects in a Lady; my employment upon the Iliad forced me to fee them; yet I have had fo much of the French complaifance as to conceal her thefts; for where-ever I have found her notes to be wholly another's (which is the cafe in fome hundreds) I have barely quoted the true Proprietor, without obferving upon it. If Madam D'Acier has ever feen my obfervations, fhe will be fen-fible of this conduct; but what effect it may have upon a Lady, I will not anfwer for.

In the next place, as to M. de la Motte, I think your Grace hardly does him right, in fuppofing he could have no idea of the beauties of Homer's Epic Poetry, but what he learn'd from Madam D'Acier's Profe-tranflation. There had been a very elegant Profe-tranflation before, that of Monfieur de la Valterie; fo elegant, that the ftyle of it was evidently the original and model of the famous Telemaque. Your Grace very juftly animadverts againft the too great difpofition of finding faults in the one, and of confeffing none in the other. But doubtlefs, as to Violence, the Lady has infinitely the better of the Gentleman. Nothing can be more polite, difpaffionate, or fenfible, than M. de la Motte's manner of managing the difpute : and fo much as I fee your Grace admires the beauty of his verfe (in which you have the fuffrage too of the Archbifhop of Cambray) I will venture to fay, his profe is full as good. I think therefore when you fay, no difputants even in Divinity could be more outrageous

* This is a juft Character of that excellent Critic's writings.

and

and uncharitable than thefe two authors, you are a little too hard upon M. de la Motte. Not but that (with your Grace) I doubt as little of the zeal of Commentators as of the zeal of Divines, and am as ready to believe of the paffions and pride of mankind in general, that (did but the fame interefts go along with them) they would carry the learned world to as violent extremes, animofities, and even perfecutions, about variety of opinions in Criticifm, as ever they did about Religion : and that, in defect of Scripture to quarrel upon, we fhould have French, Italian, and Dutch Commentators ready to burn one another about Homer, Virgil, Terence, and Horace.

I do not wonder your Grace is fhock'd at the flight of Hector upon the firft appearance of Achilles, in the twenty-fecond Iliad. However (to fhew myfelf a true Commentator, if not a true Critic) I will endeavour to excufe, if not to defend it, in my Notes on that book. And to fave myfelf what trouble I can, inftead of doing it in this letter, I will draw up the fubftance of what I have to fay for it in a feparate paper, which I'll fhew your Grace when next we meet. I will only defire you to allow me, that Hector was in an abfolute certainty of death, and deprefs'd over and above with the confcience of being in an ill caufe. If your heart be fo great, as not to grant the firft of thefe will fink the fpirit of a Hero, you'll at leaft be fo good as to allow the fecond may. But, I can tell your Grace, no lefs a Hero than my Lord Peterborow, when a perfon complimented him for never being afraid, made this anfwer; " Sir, fhew me a dan-" ger that I think an imminent and real one, and I pro-" mife you I'll be as much afraid as any of you."

I am your Grace's, &c.

LETTER XIV.

From Dr. Arbuthnot.

London, Sept. 7, 1714.

I Am extremely obliged to you for taking notice of a poor old diftreffed courtier, commonly the moft defpifcable thing in the world. This blow has fo rous'd *Scriblerus*, that he has recover'd his fenfes, and thinks and talks like other men. From being frolickfome and gay, he is turn'd grave and morofe. His lucubrations lie neglected among old news-papers, cafes, petitions, and abundance of unanfwerable letters. I wifh to God they had been among the papers of a noble Lord, fealed up. Then might Scriblerus have pafs'd for the Pretender; and it would have been a moft excellent and laborious work for the Flying Poft, or fome fuch author, to have allegoriz'd all his adventures into a plot, and found out myfteries fomewhat like the Key to the Lock. Martin's office is now the fecond door on the left hand in Doverfireet, where he will be glad to fee Dr. Parnelie, Mr. Pope, and his old friends, to whom he can ftill afford a half pint of claret. It is with fome pleafure that he contemplates the world ftill bufy, and all mankind at work, for him. I have feen a letter from Dean Swift; he keeps up his noble fpirit, and tho' like a man knock'd down, you may behold him ftill with a ftern countenance, and aiming a blow at his adverfaries. I will add no more, being in hafte, only, that I will never forgive you if you don't ufe my aforefaid houfe in Dover-ftreet with the fame freedom as you did that in St. James's; for as our friendfhip was not begun upon the relation of a courtier, fo I hope it will not end with it. I will always be proud to be reckon'd amongft the number of your friends and humble fervants.

LET,

I Am glad your Travels delighted you; improve you, I am fure they could not; you are not fo much a youth as that, tho' you run about with a King of fixteen, and (what makes him ftill more a child) a King of Frenchmen. My own time has been more melancholy, fpent in an attendance upon death, which has feized one of our family : my mother is fomething better, though at her advanced age every day is a climacteric. There was joined to this an indifpofition of my own, which I ought to look upon as a flight one, compared with my mother's, becaufe my life is not of half the confequence to any body that her's is to me. All thefe incidents have hinder'd my more fpeedy reply to your obliging letter.

The article you enquire of, is of as little concern to me, as you defire it fhould ; namely, the railing papers about the Odyffey. If the book has merit, it will extinguifh all fuch nafty fcandal; as the Sun puts an end to ftinks, merely by coming out.

I wifh I had nothing to trouble me more ; an honeft mind is not in the power of any difhoneft one. To break its peace, there muft be fome guilt or confcioufnefs, which is inconfiftent with its own principles : not but malice and injuftice have their day, like fome poor fhort-lived vermin that die in fhooting their own ftings. Falfhood is Folly (fays Homer) and liars and calumniators at laft hurt none but themfelves, even in this world; in the next, 'tis charity to fay, God have mercy on them ! they were the devil's vicegerents upon earth, who is the father of lies, and, I fear, has a right to difpofe of his children.

I've had an occafion to make thefe reflections of late more juftly than from any thing that concerns my writings, for it is one that concerns my morals, and (which

I ought

I ought to be as tender of as my own) the good character of another very innocent perfon, who, I'm fure, fhares your friendfhip no lefs than I do. No creature has better natural difpofitions, or would act more rightly or reafonably in every duty, did fhe act by herfelf, or from herfelf; but you know it is the misfortune of that family to be governed like a fhip, I mean the Head guided by the Tail, and that by every wind that blows in it.

LETTER XVI.

Mr. POPE to the Earl of OXFORD.

MY LORD,   Oct. 21, 1721.

YOUR Lordfhip may be furprized at the liberty I take in writing to you; tho' you will allow me always to remember, that you once permitted me that honour, in conjunction with fome others who better deferved it. I hope you will not wonder I am ftill defirous to have you think me your grateful and faithful fervant; but, I own, I have an ambition yet farther, to have others think me fo, which is the occafion I give your Lordfhip the trouble of this. Poor Parnelle, before he died, left me the charge of publifhing thefe few remains of his: I have a ftrong defire to make them, their author, and their publifher, more confiderable, by addrefling and dedicating them all to you. There is a pleafure in bearing teftimony to truth, and a vanity perhaps, which at leaft is as excufable as any vanity can be. I beg you, my Lord, to allow me to gratify it, in prefixing this paper of honeft verfes to the book. I fend the book itfelf, which, I dare fay, you'll receive more fatisfaction in perufing, than you can from any thing written upon the fubject of yourfelf: therefore I am a good deal in doubt, whether you will care for fuch an addition to it. All I fhall fay for it is, that 'tis the only dedication I ever writ, and fhall be the only one, whether you accept of it or not; for I will not bow the knee to a lefs man than my Lord Oxford, and I expect to fee no greater in my time.

After

After all, if your Lordſhip will tell my Lord Harley that I muſt not do this, you may depend upon a ſuppreſ-ſion of theſe verſes (the only copy whereof I ſend you) but you never ſhall ſuppreſs that great, ſincere, and en-tire reſpeƈt, with which I am always,

My Lord,

Your, etc.

LETTER XVII.

The Earl of OXFORD to Mr. POPE.

SIR,   Brampton-Caſtle, Nov. 6, 1721.

I Received your packet, which could not but give me great pleaſure, to ſee you preſerve an old friend in your memory; for it muſt needs be, very agreeable to be remember'd by thoſe we highly value. But then how much ſhame did it cauſe me, when I read your very fine verſes incloſ'd? my mind reproach'd me how far ſhort I came of what your great friendſhip and delicate pen would partially deſcribe me. You aſk my conſent to publiſh it: to what ſtraits doth this reduce me? I look back indeed to thoſe evenings I have uſefully and pleaſantly ſpent, with Mr. Pope, Mr. Parnelle, Dean Swift, the Doƈtor, &c. I ſhould be glad the world knew you admitted me to your friendſhip; and ſince your affeƈtion is too hard for your judgment, I am contented to let the world know how well Mr. Pope can write upon a barren ſubjeƈt. I return you an exaƈt copy of the verſes, that I may keep the Original, as a teſtimony of the only error you have been guilty of. I hope very ſpeedily to embrace you in London, and to aſſure you of the particular eſteem and friendſhip wherewith I am

Your, &c.

OXFORD.

L E T T E R S

TO AND FROM

EDWARD BLOUNT, Efq;

From the Year 1714 to 1725.

LETTER I.

Mr. POPE to EDWARD BLOUNT, Efq;

August 27, 1714.

WHatever ftudies on the one hand, or amufements on the other, it fhall be my fortune to fall into, I fhall be equally incapable of forgetting you in any of them. The tafk I undertook, though of weight enough in itfelf, has had a voluntary increafe by the inlarging my defign of the *Notes*; and the neceffity of confulting a number of books has carried me to Oxford : but I fear, thro' my Lord Harcourt's and Dr. Clark's means, I fhall be more converfant with the pleafures and company of the place, than with the books and manufcripts of it.

I find ftill more reafon to complain of the negligence of the Geographers in their maps of old Greece, fince I looked upon two or three more noted names in the public libraries here. But with all the care I am capable of, I have fome caufe to fear the Engraver will prejudice me in a few fituations. I have been forced to write to him in fo high a ftyle, that, were my epiftle intercepted, it would raife no fmall admiration in an ordinary man. There is fcarce an order in it of lefs importance, than to

remove

remove fuch and fuch mountains, alter the courfe of fuch and fuch rivers, place a large city on fuch a coaft, and raife another in another country. I have fet bounds to the fea, and faid to the land, Thus far fhalt thou advance, and no farther *. In the mean time, I who talk and command at this rate, am in danger of lofing my horfe, and ftand in fome fear of a country juftice †. To difarm me, indeed, may be but prudential, confidering what armies I have at prefent on foot, and in my fervice; an hundred thoufand Grecians are no contemptible body; for all that I can tell, they may be as formidable as four thoufand priefts; and they feem proper forces to fend againft thofe in Barcelona. That fiege deferves as fine a poem as the Iliad, and the machining part of poetry would be the jufter in it, as they fay the inhabitants expect angels from heaven to their affiftance. May I venture to fay, who am a Papift, and fay to you who are a Papift, that nothing is more aftonifhing to me, than that people fo greatly warm'd with a fenfe of liberty, fhould be capable of harbouring fuch weak fuperftition, and that fo much bravery and fo much folly can inhabit the fame breafts?

I could not but take a trip to London on the death of the Queen, mov'd by the common curiofity of mankind, who leave their own bufinefs to be looking upon that of other men's. I thank God, that, as for myfelf, I am below all the accidents of ftate-changes by my circumftances, and above them by my philofophy. Common charity of man to man, and univerfal good-will to all, are the points I have moft at heart; and I am fure, thofe are not to be broken for the fake of any governors, or government. I am willing to hope the beft; and what I more wifh than my own or any particular man's advancement, is, that this turn may put an end entirely to the divifions of Whig and Tory; that the parties may love each other as well as I love them both, or at leaft hurt

* This relates to the map of ancient Greece, laid down by our Author in his obfervations on the fecond Iliad.

† Some of the laws were, at this time, put in force againft the Papifts.

each other as little as I would either : and that our own
people may live as quietly as we fhall certainly let theirs ;
that is to fay, that want of power itfelf in us may not be
a furer prevention of harm, than want of will in them.
I am fure, if all Whigs and all Tories had the fpirit of one
Roman Catholic that I know, it would be well for all
Roman Catholics ; and if all Roman Catholics had always
had that fpirit, it had been well for all others ; and we
had never been charged with fo wicked a fpirit as that of
perfecution.

I agree with you in my fentiments of the ftate of our
nation fince this change : I find myfelf juft in the fame
fituation of mind you defcribe as your own, heartily
wifhing the good, that is, the quiet of my country, and
hoping a total end of all the unhappy divifions of mankind by party-fpirit, which at beft is but the madnefs of
many for the gain of a few.

I am, &c.

LETTER II.

From Mr. BLOUNT.

IT is with a great deal of pleafure I fee your letter, dear
Sir, written in a ftyle that fhews you full of health,
and in the midft of diverfions : I think thofe two things
neceffary to a man who has fuch undertakings in hand as
yours.   All lovers of Homer are indebted to you for taking fo much pains about the fituation of his Hero's kingdoms ; it will not only be of great ufe with regard to his
works, but to all that read any of the Greek hiftorians ;
who generally are ill underftood thro' the difference of
the maps as to the places they treat of, which makes one
think one author contradicts another.   You are going to
fet us right ; and 'tis an advantage every body will gladly
fee you engrofs the glory of.

You can draw rules to be free and eafy, from formal
pedants ; and teach men to be fhort and pertinent, from
tedious commentators.   However, I congratulate your
happy

happy deliverance from fuch authors, as you (with all your humanity) cannot wifh alive again to converfe with. Critics will quarrel with you, if you dare to pleafe without their leave; and Zealots will fhrug up their fhoulders at a man, that pretends to go to Heaven out of their form, drefs, and diet. I would no more make a judgment of an author's genius from a damning critic, than I would of a man's religion from an unfaving zealot.

I could take great delight in affording you the new glory of making a Barccloniad (if I may venture to coin fuch a word :) I fancy you would find a jufter parallel than it feems at firft fight; for the Trojans too had a great mixture of folly with their bravery; and I am out of countenance for them when I read the wife refult of their council, where, after a warm debate between Antenor and Paris about reftoring Helen, Priam fagely determines that they fhall go to fupper. And as for the Greeks, what can equal their fuperftition in facrificing an innocent lady?

Tantum Religio potuit, &c.

I have a good opinion of my politics, fince they agree with a man who always thinks fo juftly as you. I wifh it were in our power to perfuade all the nation into as calm and fteady a difpofition of mind.

We have receiv'd the late melancholy news, with the ufual ceremony, of condoling in one breath for the lofs of a gracious Queen, and in another rejoicing for an illuftrious King. My views carry me no farther, than to wifh the peace and welfare of my country; and my morals and politics teach me to leave all that to be adjufted· by our reprefentatives above, and to divine providence. It is much at one to you and me, who fit at the helm, provided they will permit us to fail quietly in the great fhip. Ambition is a vice that is timely mortify'd in us poor papifts; we ought in recompence to cultivate as many virtues in ourfelves as we can, that we may be truly great. Among my ambitions, that of being a fincere friend is one of the chief: yet I will confefs that I have

a fecret pleafure to have fome of my defcendants know,
that their Anceftor was great with Mr. Pope.

I am, &c.

LETTER III.

From Mr. B L O U N T.

Nov. 11, 1715.

IT is an agreement of long date between you and me,
that you fhould do with my letters juft as you pleafed,
and anfwer them at your leifure; and that is as foon as I
fhall think you ought. I have fo true a tafte of the fub-
ftantial part of your friendfhip, that I wave all ceremonials; and am fure to make you as many vifits as I can,
and leave you to return them whenever you pleafe, affuring you they fhall at all times be heartily welcome to me.

The many alarms we have from your parts, have no
effect upon the genius that reigns in our country, which
is happily turn'd to preferve peace and quiet among us.
What a difmal fcene has there been opened in the North,
what ruin have thofe unfortunate rafh gentlemen drawn
upon themfelves and their miferable followers, and per-
chance upon many others too, who upon no account
would be their followers? However, it may look unge-
nerous to reproach people in diftrefs. I don't remember
you and I ever ufed to trouble ourfelves about politics,
but when any matter happened to fall into our difcourfe,
we us'd to condemn all undertakings that tended towards
the difturbing the peace and quiet of our country, as
contrary to the notions we had of morality and religion,
which oblige us on no pretence whatfoever to violate the
laws of charity. How many lives have there been loft in
hot blood, and how many more are there like to be taken
off in cold? If the broils of the nation affect you, come
down to me; and though we are farmers, you know Eu-
meus made his friends welcome. You fhall here worfhip
the Echo at your eafe; indeed we are forced to do fo,
becaufe we can't hear the firft report, and therefore are

obliged

obliged to liften to the fecond; which, for fecurity fake,
I do not always believe neither.

'Tis a great many years fince I fell in love with the
character of Pomponius Atticus : I long'd to imitate him
a little, and have contriv'd hitherto to be, like him, engaged in no party, but to be a faithful friend to fome in
both : I find myfelf very well in this way hitherto, and
live in a certain peace of mind by it, which, I am perfuaded, brings a man more content than all the perqui-
fites of wild ambition. I with pleafure join with you in
wifhing, nay, I am not afhamed to fay, in praying for
the welfare, temporal and eternal, of all mankind. How
much more affectionately then fhall I do fo for you, fince
I am, in a moft particular manner, and with all fincerity,

Yours, &c.

LETTER IV.

Jan. 24, 1715-16.

I Know of nothing that will be fo interefting to you at
prefent, as fome circumftances of the laft act of that
eminent comic poet, and our friend, Wycherley. He
had often told me, as I doubt not he did all his acquaintance, that he would marry as foon as his life was defpair'd of : accordingly, a few days before his death, he
underwent the ceremony, and join'd together thofe two
facraments which, wife men fay, fhould be the laft we receive ; for if you obferve, Matrimony is placed after Extreme unction in our Catechifin, as a kind of hint of the
order of time in which they are to be taken. The old man
then lay down, fatisfy'd in the confcience of having by
this one act paid his juft debts, obliged a woman, who (he
was told) had merit, and fhewn an heroic refentment of
the ill ufage of his next heir. Some hundred pounds which
he had with the Lady, difcharged thofe debts ; a jointure
of four hundred a year made her a recompence ; and the
nephew he left to comfort himfelf, as well as he could,
with the miferable remains of a mortgaged eftate. I faw

our

our friend twice after this was done, lefs peevifh in his
ficknefs than he ufed to be in his health; neither much
afraid of dying, nor (which in him had been more likely)
much afhamed of marrying. The evening before he ex-
pired, he called his young wife to the bed-fide, and earneftly entreated her not to deny him one requeft, the laft
he fhould make. Upon her affurances of confenting to
it, he told her, " My dear, it is only this, that you
" will never marry an old man again." I cannot help-
remarking, that ficknefs, which often deftroys both wit
and wifdom, yet feldom has power to remove that talent
which we call humour: Mr. Wycherley fhew'd his, even
in this laft compliment; tho' I think his requeft a little
hard, for why fhould he bar her from doubling her jointure on the fame eafy terms?

So trivial as thefe circumftances are, I fhould not be
difpleas'd myfelf to know fuch trifles, when they concern
or charaäerife any eminent perfon. The wifeft and wit-
tieft of men are feldom wifer or wittier than others in
thefe fober moments: at leaft, our friend ended much in
the charaäer he had lived in; and Horace's rule for a
play, may as well be apply'd to him as a play-wright,

> Servetur ad imum
> Qualis ab inceptu procefferit, et fibi conftet.

I am, &c.

L E T T E R V.

Feb. 10, 1715-16.

I AM juft return'd from the country, whither Mr.
Rowe accompanied me, and pafs'd a week in the Foreft. I need not tell you how much a man of his turn
entertain'd me; but I muft acquaint you, there is a vivacity and gaiety of difpofition almoft peculiar to him,
which make it impoffible to part from him without that
uneafinefs which generally fucceeds all our pleafures. I
have been juft taking a folitary walk by moon-fhine, full
of

of reflections on the tranfitory nature of all human delights; and giving my thoughts a loofe in the contemplation of thofe fatisfactions which probably we may hereafter tafte in the company of feparate fpirits, when we fhall range the walks above, and perhaps gaze on this world at as vaft a diftance as we now do on thofe worlds. The pleafures we are to enjoy in that converfation, muft undoubtedly be of a nobler kind, and (not unlikely) may proceed from the difcoveries each fhall communicate to another, of God and of Nature; for the happinefs of minds can furely be nothing but knowledge.

The higheft gratification we receive here from company is mirth, which at the beft is but a fluttering, unquiet motion, that beats about the breaft for a few moments, and after leaves it void and empty. Keeping good company, even the beft, is but a lefs fhameful art of lofing time. What we here call fcience and ftudy, are little better: the greater number of arts to which we apply ourfelves, are mere groping in the dark; and even the fearch of our moft important concerns in a future being, is but a needlefs, anxious, and uncertain hafte to be knowing, fooner than we can, what without all this folicitude we fhall know a little later. We are but curious impertinents in the cafe of futurity. 'Tis not our bufinefs to be guefling what the ftate of fouls fhall be, but to be doing what may make our own ftate happy; we cannot be knowing, but we can be virtuous.

If this be my notion of a great part of that high fcience, Divinity, you will be fo civil as to imagine I lay no mighty ftrefs upon the reft. Even of my darling poetry I really make no other ufe, than horfes of the bells that gingle about their ears (tho' now and then they tofs their heads as if they were proud of them) only to jog on a little more merrily.

Your obfervations on the narrow conceptions of mankind in the point of friendfhip, confirm me in what I was fo fortunate as at my firft knowledge of you to hope, and fince fo amply to experience. Let me take fo much

decent

decent pride and dignity upon me, as to tell you, that, but for opinions like thefe which I difcover'd in your mind, I had never made the trial I have done; which has fucceeded fo much to mine, and, I believe, not lefs to your fatisfaction : for, if I know you right, your plea-fure is greater in obliging me, than I can feel on my part, till it falls in my power to oblige you.

Your remark, that the variety of opinions in politics or religion is often rather a gratification, than an objec-tion, to people who have fenfe enough to confider the beautiful order of nature in her variations; makes me think you have not conftrued Joannes Secundus wrong, in the verfe which precedes that which you quote : *Bene nota fides*, as I take it, does no way fignify the Roman Catholic religion, tho' Secundus was of it. I think it was a generous thought, and one that flow'd from an exalted mind, That it was not improbable but that God might be delighted with the various methods of worfhipping him, which divided the whole world. I am pretty fure you and I fhould no more make good Inquifitors to the modern tyrants in faith, than we could have been qualified for Lictors to Procruftes, when he converted refractory members with the rack. In a word, I can only repeat to you what I think I have formerly faid; that I as little fear God will damn a man who has Charity, as I hope that any prieft can fave him without it.

I am, &c.

LETTER VI.

March 20, 1715-16.

I Find that a real concern is not only a hindrance to fpeaking, but to writing too : the more time we give ourfelves to think over one's own or a friend's unhappi-nefs, the more unable we grow to exprefs the grief that proceeds from it. It is as natural to delay a letter at fuch a feafon as this, as to retard a melancholy vifit to a per-fon one cannot relieve. One is afhamed, in that circumstance,

ftance, to pretend to entertain people with trifling, infignificant affectations of forrow on the one hand, or unfeafonable and forced gaieties on the other. 'Tis a kind of profanation of things facred, to treat fo folemn a matter as a generous voluntary fuffering, with compliments, or heroic gallantries. Such a mind as your's has no need of being fpirited up into honour; or like a weak woman, praifed into an opinion of its own virtue. 'Tis enough to do and fuffer what we ought; and men fhould know, that the noble power of fuffering bravely is as far above that of enterprizing greatly, as an unblemifh'd confcience and inflexible refolution are above an accidental flow of fpirits, or a fudden tide of blood. If the whole religious bufinefs of mankind be included in refignation to our Maker, and charity to our fellow-creatures, there are now fome people who give us as good an opportunity of practifing the one, as themfelves have given an inftance of the violation of the other. Whoever is really brave, has always this comfort when he is opprefs'd, that he knows himfelf to be fuperior to thofe who injure him: for the greateft power on earth can no fooner do him that injury, but the brave man can make himfelf greater by forgiving it.

If it were generous to feek for alleviating confolations in a calamity of fo much glory, one might fay, that to be ruin'd thus in the grofs, with a whole people, is but like perifhing in the general conflagration, where nothing we can value is left behind us.

Methinks the moft heroic thing we are left capable of doing, is to endeavour to lighten each other's load, and (opprefs'd as we are) to fuccour fuch as are yet more opprefs'd. If there are too many who cannot be affifted but by what we cannot give, our money; there are yet others who may be relieved by our counfel, by our countenance, and even by our chearfulnefs. The misfortunes of private families, the mifunderftandings of people whom diftreffes make fufpicious, the coldneffes of relations whom change of religion may difunite, or the neceffities

of

of half-ruined eftates render unkind to each other; thefe
at leaft may be foftened, in fome degree, by a general
well-managed humanity among ourfelves; if all thofe
who have your principles of belief, had alfo your fenfe
and conduct. But indeed moft of them have given
lamentable proofs of the contrary; and 'tis to be apprehended, that they who want fenfe, are only religious
thro' weaknefs, and good-natur'd thro' fhame. Thefe
are narrow-minded creatures that never deal in effentials,
their faith never looks beyond ceremonials, nor their
charity beyond relations. As poor as I am, I would
gladly relieve any diftreffed, confcientious French refu-
gee at this inftant: what muft my concern then be, when
I perceive fo many anxieties now tearing thofe hearts,
which I have defired a place in, and clouds of melancholy
rifing on thofe faces, which I have long look'd upon with
affection? I begin already to feel both what fome apprehend, and what others are yet too ftupid to apprehend.
I grieve with the old, for fo many additional inconveniences and chagrins, more than their fmall remain of
life feemed deftined to undergo; and with the young,
for fo many of thofe gaieties and pleafures (the portion
of youth) which they will by this means be deprived of.
This brings into my mind one or other of thofe I love
beft, and among them the widow and fatherlefs, late of
—. As I am certain no people living had an earlier and
truer fenfe of others misfortunes, or a more generous refignation as to what might be their own, fo I earneftly
wifh that whatever part they muft bear, may be render'd
as fupportable to them, as it is in the power of any friend
to make it.

But I know you have prevented me in this thought, as
you always will in any thing that is good or generous: I
find by a letter of your lady's (which I have feen) that
their eafe and tranquillity is part of your care. I believe
there's fome fatality in it, that you fhould always, from
time to time, be doing thofe particular things that make
me enamour'd of you.

I write

I write this from Windfor-Foreft, of which I am come to take my laft look. We here bid our neighbours adieu, much as thofe who go to be hang'd do their fellow prifoners, who are condemned to follow them a few weeks after. I parted from honeft Mr. D* with tendernefs: and from old Sir William Trumbull as from a venerable prophet, foretelling with lifted hands the miferies to come, from which he is juft going to be remov'd himfelf.

Perhaps now I have learnt fo far as

> Nos dulcia linquimus arva,

my next leffon may be

> Nos Patriam fugimus.

Let that, and all elfe be as heaven pleafes! I have provided juft enough to keep me a man of honour. I believe you and I fhall never be afhamed of each other. I know I wifh my country well, and, if it undoes me, it fhall not make me wifh it otherwife.

LETTER VII.

From Mr. BLOUNT.

March 24, 1715-16.

YOUR letters give me a gleam of fatisfaction, in the midft of a very dark and cloudy fituation of thoughts, which it would be more than human to be exempt from at this time, when our homes muft either be left, or be made too narrow for us to turn in. Poetically fpeaking, I fhould lament the lofs Windfor-foreft and you fuftain of each other, but that, methinks, one can't fay you are parted, becaufe you will live by and in one another, while verfe is verfe. This confideration hardens me in my opinion rather to congratulate you, fince you have the pleafure of the profpect whenever you take it from your fhelf, and at the fame time the folid cafh you fold it for, of which Virgil in his exile knew nothing in thofe days, and which will make every place eafy to you. I, for my part, am not fo happy; my *parva rura* are faften'd to me, fo that I can't exchange them, as you have, for more portable means of fubfiftance; and yet I hope to gather enough to make the *Patriam fugimus* fupportable to me: 'tis what I am refolved on with my *Penate*. If therefore you afk me, to whom you fhall complain? I will exhort you to leave lazinefs and the elms of St. James's Park, and choofe to join the other two propofals in one, fafety and friendfhip (the leaft of which is a good motive for moft things, as the other is for almoft every thing) and go with me where war will not reach us, nor paultry conftables fummon us to veftries.

The future epiftle you flatter me with will find me ftill here, and I think I may be here a month longer. Whenever I go from hence, one of the few reafons to make meregret my home will be, that I fhall not have the pleafure of faying to you,

Hic tamen hanc mecum poteris requiefcere noɓtem,

which would have rendered this place more agreeable, than ever it elfe could be to me; for I proteft, it is with the utmoft fincerity that I affure you I am entirely,

Dear Sir,

Your, &c.

LETTER VIII.

June 22, 1716.

IF a regard both to public and private affairs may plead a lawful excufe in behalf of a negligent corrofpondent, I have really a very good title to it. I cannot fay whether 'tis a felicity or unhappinefs, that I am obliged at this time to give my whole application to Homer; when without that employment, my thoughts muft turn upon what is lefs agreeable, the violence, madnefs, and refentment of modern War-makers *, which are likely to prove (to fome people at leaft) more fatal, than the fame qualities in Achilles did to his unfortunate countrymen.

* This was written in the year of the affair of Prefton.

Tho

Tho' the change of my scene of life, from Windsor-forest to the side of the Thames, be one of the grand Æra's of my days, and may be called a notable period in so inconsiderable a history, yet you can scarce imagine any hero passing from one stage of life to another, with so much tranquility, so easy a transition, and so laudable a behaviour. I am become so truly a citizen of the world (according to Plato's expression) that I look with equal indifference on what I have left, and on what I have gained. The times and amusements past are not more like a dream to me, than those which are present: I lie in a refreshing kind of inaction, and have one comfort at least from obscurity, that the darkness helps me to sleep the better. I now and then reflect upon the enjoyment of my friends, whom, I fancy, I remember much as separate spirits do us, at tender intervals, neither interrupting their own employments, nor altogether careless of ours, but in general constantly wishing us well, and hoping to have us one day in their company.

To grow indifferent to the world is to grow philosophical, or religious (which soever of those turns we chance to take) and indeed the world is such a thing, as one that thinks pretty much, must either laugh at, or be angry with: but if we laugh at it, they say we are proud; and if we are angry with it, they say we are ill natur'd. So the most politic way is to seem always better pleas'd than one can be, greater admirers, greater lovers, and in short greater fools than we really are: so shall we live comfortably with our families, quietly with our neighbours, favoured by our masters, and happy with our mistresses. I have filled my paper, and so adieu.

LETTER IX.

Sept. 8, 1717.

I Think your leaving England was like a good man's leaving the world, with the blessed conscience of

having

having acted well in it; and I hope you have received your reward, in being happy where you are. I believe, in the religious country you inhabit, you'll be better pleafed to find I confider you in this light, than if I compared you to thofe Greeks and Romans, whofe conftancy in fuffering pain, and whofe refolution in purfuit of a generous end, you would rather immitate than boaft of.

But I had a melancholy hint the other day, as if you were yet a martyr to the fatigue your virtue made you undergo on this fide the water. I beg if your health be reftored to you, not to deny me the joy of knowing it. Your endeavours of fervice and good advice to the poor papifts, put me in mind of Noah's preaching forty years to thofe folks that were to be drowned at laft. At the worft I heartily wifh your ark may find an Arrarat, and the wife and family (the hopes of the good patriarch) land fafely after the deluge, upon the fhore of Totnefs.

If I durft mix prophane with facred hiftory, I would chear you with the old tale of Brutus, the wandering Trojan, who found on that very coaft the happy end of his peregrinations and adventures.

I have very lately read Jeffery of Monmouth (to whom your Cornwall is not a little beholden) in the tranflation of a clergyman in my neighbourhood. The poor man is highly concerned to vindicate Jeffry's veracity as an hiftorian: and told me he was perfectly aftonifhed, we of the Roman communion could doubt of the legends of his Giants, while we believe thofe of our faints. I am forced to make a fair compofition with him: and, by crediting fome of the wonders of Corinæus and Gogmagog, have brought him fo far already, that he fpeaks refpectfully of St. Chriftopher's carrying Chrift, and the refufcitation of St. Nicholas Tolentine's chicken. Thus we proceed apace in converting each other from all manner of infidelity.

Ajax and Hector are no more to be compared to Corinæus and Arthur, than the Guelphs and Ghibellines are to the Mohocks of ever dreadful memory. This amazing
writer

writer has made me lay afide Homer for a week, and
when I take him up again, I fhall be very well prepared
to tranflate, with belief and reverence, the fpeech of A-
chilles's horfe.

You'll excufe all this trifling or any thing elfe which
prevents a fheet full of compliment: and believe there is
nothing more true (even more true than any thing in Jeffry is falfe) than that I have a conftant affection for you,
and am, &c.

P. S. I know you will take part in rejoicing for the
victory of Prince Eugene over the Turks, in the zeal
you bear to the Chriftian intereft, tho' your Coufin of
Oxford (with whom I dined yefterday) fays, there is no
other difference in the Chriftians beating the Turks, or
the Turks beating the Chriftians, than whether the Emperor fhall firft declare war againft Spain, or Spain declare it againft the Emperor.

LETTER X.

Nov. 27, 1717.

THE queftion you propofed to me is what at prefent I
am the moft unfit man in the world to anfwer, by
my lofs of one of the beft of fathers.

He had lived in fuch a courfe of temperance as was
enough to make the longeft life agreeable to him, and in
fuch a courfe of piety as fufficed to make the moft fudden
death fo alfo. Sudden indeed it was: however, I heartily
beg of God to give me fuch a one, provided I can lead
fuch a life. I leave him to the mercy of God, and to the
piety of a religion that extends beyond the grave : *Si qua
eft ea cura*, &c.

He has left me to the ticklifh management of fo narrow
a fortune, that any one falfe ftep would be fatal. My
mother is in that difpirited ftate of refignation, which is
the effect of long life, and the lofs of what is dear to us.
We are really each of us in want of a friend, of fuch an
humane turn as yourfelf, to make almoft any thing defirable

firable to us. I feel your abfence more than ever, at the fame time I can lefs exprefs my regards to you than ever: and fhall make this, which is the moft fincere letter I ever writ to you, the fhorteft and fainteft perhaps of any you have ever received. 'Tis enough if you reflect, that barely to remember any perfon when one's mind is taken up with a fenfible forrow, is a great degree of friendfhip. I can fay no more but that I love you, and all that are yours; and that I wifh it may be very long before any of yours fhall feel for you what I now feel for my father.
Adieu.

LETTER XI.

Rentcomb in Gloucefterfhire, Oct. 3, 1721.

YOUR kind letter has overtaken me here, for I have been in and about this country ever fince your departure. I am well pleafed to date this from a place fo well known to Mrs. Blount, where I write as if I were dictated to by her anceftors, whofe faces are all upon me. I fear none fo much as Sir Chriftopher Guife, who being in his fhirt, feems as ready to combat me, as her own Sir John was to demolifh Duke Lancaftere. I dare fay your lady will recollect his figure. I look'd upon the manfion, walls, and terraces: the plantations, and flopes, which nature has made to command a variety of vallies and rifing woods; with a veneration mix'd with a pleafure, that reprefented her to me in thofe puerile amufements, which engaged her fo many years ago in this place. I fancied I faw her fober over a fampler, or gay over a jointed baby. I dare fay fhe did one thing more, even in thofe early times; "remember'd her creator in the days of her youth."

You defcribe fo well your hermitical ftate of life, that none of the ancient anchorites could go beyond you, for a cave in a rock, with a fine fpring, or any of the accommodations that befit a folitary. Only I don't remember to have read, that any of thofe venerable and holy perfonages took with them a lady, and begat fons and
daugh-

daughters. You muſt modeſtly be content to be accounted a patriarch. But were you a little younger, I ſhould rather rank you with Sir Amadis, and his fellows. If piety be ſo romantic, I ſhall turn hermit in good earneſt; for I ſee, one may go ſo far as to be poetical, and hope to ſave one's ſoul at the ſame time. I really wiſh myſelf ſomething more, that is, a prophet; for I wiſh I were, as Habakkuk, to be taken by the hair of his head, and viſit Daniel in his den. You are very obliging in ſaying, I have now a whole family upon my hands to whom to diſcharge the part of a friend; I aſſure you, I like them all ſo well, that I will never quit my hereditary right to them; you have made me yours, and conſequently them mine. I ſtill ſee them walking on my green at Twickenham, and gratefully remember, not only their green gowns, but the inſtruꝛtions they gave me how to ſlide down and trip up the ſteepeſt ſlopes of my mount.

Pray think of me ſometimes, as I ſhall often of you: and know me for what I am, that is,

Your, &c.

LETTER XII.

Oꝛt. 21, 1721.

YOUR very kind and obliging manner of enquiring after me among the firſt concerns of life, at your reſuſcitation, ſhould have been ſooner anſwer'd and acknowledged. I ſincerely rejoice at your recovery from an illneſs which gave me leſs pain than it did you, only from my ignorance of it. I ſhould have elſe been ſeriouſly and deeply afflicted, in the thought of your danger by a fever. I think it a fine and a natural thought, which I lately read in a letter of Montaign's publiſh'd by P. Coſte, giving an account of the laſt words of an intimate friend of his: " Adieu my friend! the pain I feel will " ſoon be over; but I grieve for that you are to feel, " which is to laſt you for life."

I join with your family in giving God thanks for lending us a worthy man ſomewhat longer. The comforts

you

you receive from their attendance, put me in mind of what old Fletcher of Saltoune faid one day to me: " Alas I have nothing to do but to die; I am a poor in- " dividual; no creature to wifh or to fear, for my life or " death: 'Tis the only reafon I have to repent being a " fingle man; now I grow old I am like a tree without a " prop, and without young trees to grow round me, for " company and defence."

I hope the gout will foon go after the fever, and all evil things remove far from you. But pray tell me, when will you move towards us? If you had an interval to get hither, I care not what fixes you afterwards, ex- cept the gout. Pray come, and never ftir from us again. Do away your dirty acres, caft them to dirty people, fuch as in the fcripture-phrafe poffefs the land. Shake off your earth like the noble animal in Milton,

> The tawny lyon, pawing to get free
> His hinder parts, he fprings as broke from bonds,
> And rampant fhakes his brinded main: the ounce,
> The lizard, and the tyger, as the mole
> Rifing, the crumbled earth above them threw
> In hillocks!

But, I believe, Milton never thought thefe fine verfes of his fhould be apply'd to a man felling a parcel of dirty acres; tho' in the main, I think, it may have fome re- femblance. For, God knows! this little fpace of ground nourifhes, buries, and confines us, as that of Eden did thofe creatures, till we can fhake it loofe, at leaft in our affections and defires.

Believe, dear Sir, I truly love and value you: let Mrs. Blount know that fhe is in the lift of my *Memento Domi- ne, famulorum famularumque's,* &c. My poor mother is far from well, declining; and I am watching over her, as we watch an expiring taper, that even when it looks brighteft, waftes fafteft. I am (as you will fee from the whole air of this letter) not in the gayeft nor eafieft hu- mour, but always with fincerity,

Your, &c.

3

LET-

LETTER XIII.

June 27, 1723.

YOU may truly do me the juſtice to think no man is more your ſincere well-wiſher than myſelf, or more the ſincere well wiſher of your whole family ; with all which, I cannot deny but I have a mixture of envy to you all, for loving one another ſo well ; and for enjoy-ing the ſweets of that life, which can only be taſted by people of good-will.

They from all ſhades the darkneſs can exclude,
And from a deſert baniſh ſolitude.

Torbay is a paradiſe, and a ſtorm is but an amuſement to ſuch people.   If you drink tea upon a promontory that over-hangs the ſea, it is preferable to an aſſembly : and the whiſtling of the wind better muſic to contented and loving minds, than the opera to the ſpleenful, ambitious, diſeas'd, diſtaſted, and diſtracted ſouls which this world af-fords ; nay, this world affords no other.   Happy they, who are baniſh'd from us ! but happier they, who can baniſh themſelves ; or more properly baniſh the world from them !

Alas ! I live at Twickenham !

I take that period to be very ſublime, and to include more than a hundred ſentences that might be writ to ex-preſs diſtraction, hurry, multiplication of nothings, and all the fatiguing perpetual buſineſs of having no buſineſs to do.   You'll wonder I reckon tranſlating the Odyſſey as nothing.   But whenever I think ſeriouſly (and of late I have met with ſo many occaſions of thinking ſeriouſly, that I begin never to think otherwiſe) I cannot but think theſe things very idle ; as idle, as if a beaſt of burden ſhould go on jingling his bells, without bearing any thing valuable about him, or ever ſerving his maſter.

Life's vain Amuſements, amidſt which we dwell ;
Not weigh'd, or underſtood, by the grim God of Hell !

ſaid a heathen poet ; as he. is tranſlated by a chriſtian Biſhop, who has, firſt by his exhortations, and ſince by his example, taught me to think as becomes a reasonable creature—but he is gone !

I remember I promis'd to write to you, as soon as I should hear you were got home. You must look on this as the firſt day I've been myſelf, and paſs over the mad interval un-imputed to me. How punctual a correſpondent I ſhall henceforward be able, or not able to be, God knows: but he knows, I ſhall ever be a punctual and grateful friend, and all the good wiſhes of ſuch an one will ever attend you.

LETTER XIV.

Twick'nam, June 2, 1725.

YOU ſhew yourſelf a juſt man and a friend in thoſe gueſſes and ſuppoſitions you make at the poſſible reaſons of my ſilence ; every one of which is a true one. As to forgetfulneſs of you, or yours, I aſſure you, the promiſcuous converſations of the town ſerve only to put me in mind of better, and more quiet, to be had in a corner of the world (undiſturb'd, innocent, ſerene, and ſenſible) with ſuch as you. Let no acceſs of any diſtruſt make you think of me differently in a cloudy day from what you do in the moſt ſun-ſhiny weather. Let the young ladies be aſſured I make nothing new in my gardens, without wiſhing to ſee the print of their fairy ſteps in every part of them. I have put the laſt hand to my works of this kind, in happily finiſhing the ſubterraneous way and grotto : I there found a ſpring of the cleareſt water, which falls in a perpetual rill, that echoes thro' the cavern day and night. From the river Thames, you ſee thro' my arch up a walk of the wilderneſs, to a kind of open temple, wholly compos'd of ſhells in the ruſtic manner ; and from that diſtance under the temple you look down thro' a ſloping arcade of trees, and ſee the ſails on the river paſſing ſuddenly and vaniſhing, as thro' a perſpective glaſs. When you ſhut the doors of this grotto, it becomes on the inſtant, from a luminous room, a *Camera*

2   *obſcura* ;

obscura; on the walls of which, all objects of the river,
hills, woods, and boats, are forming a moving picture in
their visible radiations : and when you have a mind to
light it up, it affords you a very different scene; it is
finished with shells interspersed with pieces of looking-
glafs in angular forms; and in the cieling is a star of the
fame material, at which, when a lamp (of an orbicular
figure of thin alabafter) is hung in the middle, a thoufand
pointed rays glitter, and are reflected over the place.
There are connected to this grotto, by a narrower paffage,
two porches, one towards the river of fmooth ftones full
of light, and open ; the other toward the garden fhadow'd
with trees, rough with fhells, flints, and iron ore. The
bottom is pav'd with fimple pebble, as is alfo the adjoining walk up the wildernefs to the temple, in the natural
tafte, agreeing not ill with the little dripping murmur,
and the aquatic idea of the whole place. It wants nothing
to complete it but a good ftatue with an infcription, like
that beautiful antique one which you know I am fo fond
of,

> Hujus Nympha loci, facri cuftodia fontis,
>   Dormio, dum blandæ fentio murmur aquæ.
> Parce meum, quifquis tangis cava marmora, fomnum
>   Rumpere ; fi bibas, five lavere, tace.
>
> Nymph of the grot, thefe facred fprings I keep,
> And to the murmur of thefe waters fleep ;
> Ah fpare my flumbers, gently tread the cave !
> And drink in filence, or in filence lave !

You'll think I have been very poetical in this defcription, but it is pretty near the truth. I wifh you were
here to bear teftimony how little it owes to Art, either
the place itfelf, or the image I give of it.

I am, &c.

LETTER XV.

Sept. 13, 1725.

I Should be afham'd to own the receipt of a very kind
letter from you, two whole months from the date of

this ;

this; if I were not more afhamed to tell a lye, or to make an excufe, which is worfe than a lye (for being built upon fome probable circumftance, it makes ufe of a degree of truth to falfify with, and is a lye guarded.) Your letter has been in my pocket in conftant wearing, till that, and the pocket, and the fuit, are worn out; by which means I have read it forty times, and I find by fo doing, that I have not enough confidered and re-fle&ed upon many others you have obliged me with; for true friendfhip, as they fay of good writing, will bear reviewing a thoufand times, and ftill difcover new beau-ties.

I have had a fever, a fhort one, but a violent: I am now well; fo it fhall take up no more of this paper.

I begin now to expe& you in town to make the winter to come more tolerable to us both. The fummer is a kind of heaven, when we wander in a paradifaical fcene among groves and gardens; but at this feafon, we are, like our poor firft parents, turn'd out of that agreeable, though folitary life, and forced to look about for more people to help to bear our labours, to get into warmer houfes, and live together in cities.

I hope you are long fince perfe&ly reftor'd, and rifen from your gout, happy in the delights of a contented fa-mily, fmiling at ftorms, laughing at greatnefs, merry over a Chriftmas fire, and exercifing all the fun&ions of an old Patriarch in charity and hofpitality. I will not tell Mrs. B* what I think fhe is doing; for I conclude it is her opinion, that he only ought to know it for whom it is done; and fhe will allow herfelf to be far enough advanced above a fine lady, not to defire to fhine before men.

Your daughters perhaps may have fome other thoughts, which even their mother muft excufe them for, becaufe fhe is a mother. I will not however fuppofe thofe thoughts get the better of their devotions, but rather excite them and affift the warmth of them; while their prayer may be, that they may raife up and breed as irreproachable a

young

young family as their parents have done. In a word, I fancy you all well, eafy, and happy, juft as I wifh you; and next to that, I wifh you all with me.

Next to God, is a good man: next in dignity, and next in value. *Minuifti eum paullo minus ab angelis.* If therefore I wifh well to the good and the deferving, and defire they only fhould be my companions and correfpondents, I muft very foon and very much think of you. I want your company, and your example. Pray make hafte to town, fo as not again to leave us: difcharge the load of earth that lies on you, like one of the mountains under which the poets fay, the giants (the men of the earth) are whelmed: leave earth, to the fons of the earth, your converfation is in heaven; which, that it may be accomplifh'd in us all, is the prayer of him who maketh this fhort fermon; value (to you) three-pence. Adieu.

Mr. Blount died in London the following year, 1736.

LETTER

L E T T E R S

TO AND FROM

The Hon. R O B E R T D I G B Y.

From the Year 1714 to 1727.

L E T T E R I.

To the Hon. R O B E R T D I G B Y.

June 2, 1717.

I Had pleas'd myfelf fooner in writing to you, but that
I have been your fucceffor in a fit of ficknefs, and am
not yet fo much recovered, but that I have thoughts of
ufing your * phyficians. They are as grave perfons as
any of the faculty, and (like the ancients) carry their
own medicaments about with them. But indeed the moderns are fuch lovers of raillery, that nothing is grave
enough to efcape them. Let them laugh, but people
will ftill have their opinions: as they think our Doctors
affes to them, we'll think them affes to our Doctors.

I am glad you are fo much in a better ftate of health,
as to allow me to jeft about it. My concern, when I
heard of your danger, was fo very ferious, that I almoft
take it ill that Dr. Evans fhould tell you of it, or you
mention it. I tell you fairly, if you and a few more
fuch people were to leave the world, I would not give
fix-pence to ftay in it.

* Affes.

I am

I am not fo much concerned as to the point whether you are to live fat or lean : moft men of wit or honefty are ufually decreed to live very lean, fo I am inclined to the opinion that 'tis decreed you fhall; however, be comforted, and reflect, that you'll make the better Bufto for it.

'Tis fomething particular in you, not to be fatisfied with fending me your own books, but to make your acquaintance continue the frolic. Mr. Wharton forced me to take Gorboduc, which has fince done me great credit with feveral people, as it has done Dryden and Oldham fome difkindnefs, in fhewing there is as much difference between their Gorboduc and this, as between Queen Anne and King George. It is truly a fcandal, that men fhould write with contempt of a piece which they never once faw, as thofe two poets did, who were ignorant even of the fex, as well as fenfe, of Gorboduc.

Adieu! I am going to forget you: this minute you took up all my mind; the next I fhall think of nothing but the reconciliation with Agamemnon, and the recovery of Brifeis. I fhall be Achilles's humble fervant thefe two months (with the good leave of all my friends.) I have no ambition fo ftrong at prefent, as that noble one of Sir Salathiel Lovel, recorder of London, to furnifh out a decent and plentiful execution, of Greeks and Trojans. It is not to be exprefs'd how heartily I wifh the death of all Homer's heroes, one after another. The Lord preferve me in the day of battle, which is juft approaching! join in your prayers for me, and know me to be always

Your, &c.

LETTER II.

London, March 31, 1718.

TO convince you how little pain I give myfelf in correfponding with men of good-nature and good underftanding, you fee I omit to anfwer your letters till a
time,

time, when another man would be afhamed to own he
had received them.   If therefore you are ever moved on
my account by that fpirit, which I take to be as familiar
to you as a quotidian ague, I mean the fpirit of goodnefs,
pray never ftint it, in any fear of obliging me to a civility beyond my natural inclination. I dare truft you, Sir,
not only with my folly when I write, but with my negligence when I do not; and expect equally your pardon
for either.

If I knew how to entertain you thro' the reft of this
paper, it fhould be fpotted and diverfified with conceits
all over; you fhould be put out of breath with laughter
at each fente. :e, and paufe at each period, to look back
over how much wit you have paffed.   But I have found
by experience, that people now-a-days regard writing as
little as they do preaching: the moft we can hope is to
be heard juft with decency and patience, once a week, by
folks in the country. Here in town we hum over a piece
of fine writing, and we whiftle at a fermon.   The ftage
is the only place we feem alive at; there indeed we ftare,
and roar, and clap hands for K. George and the government.   As for all other virtues but this loyalty, they are
an obfolete train, fo ill drefs'd, that men, women, and
children, hifs them out of all good company.

Humility knocks fo fneakingly at the door, that every
footman outraps it, and makes it give way to the free
entrance of pride, prodigality, and vain-glory.

My Lady Scudamore, from having rufticated in your
company too long, really behaves herfelf fcandaloufly
among us : fhe pretends to open her eyes for the fake of
feeing the fun, and to fleep becaufe it is night; drinks
tea at nine in the morning, and is thought to have faid
her prayers before; talks, without any manner of fhame,
of good books, and has not feen Cibber's play of the Non-
juror.   I rejoiced the other day to fee a libel on her toi-
lette, which gives me fome hope that you have, at leaft,
a tafte of fcandal left you, in defect of all other vices.

Upon the whole matter, I heartily wifh you well; but
as I cannot entirely defire the ruin of all the joys of this
.   city,

city, fo all that remains is to wifh you would keep your happinefs to yourfelves, that the happieft here may not die with envy at a blifs which they cannot attain to.

I am, &c.

LETTER III.

From Mr. D I G B Y.

Colefhill, April 17, 1718.

I Have read your letter over and over with delight. By your defcription of the town, I imagine it to lie under fome great enchantment, and am very much concerned for you and all my friends in it. I am the more afraid, imagining, fince you do not fly thofe horrible monfters, rapine, diffimulation, and luxury, that a magic circle is drawn about you, and you cannot efcape. We are here in the country in quite another world, furrounded with bleffings and pleafures, without any occafion of exerting our irafcible facultics; indeed we cannot boaft of good-breeding and the art of life, but yet we don't live un-pleafantly in primitive fimplicity and good humour. The fafhions of the town affect us but juft like a raree-fhow; we have a curiofity to peep at them, and nothing more. What you call pride, prodigality, and vain-glory, we cannot find in pomp and fplendor at this diftance; it appears to us a fine glittering fcene, which, if we don't envy you, we think you happier than we are, in your enjoying it. Whatever you may think to perfuade us of the humility of Virtue, and her appearing in rags amongft you, we can never believe : our uninform'd minds reprefent her fo noble to us, that we neceffarily annex fplendor to her : and we could as foon imagine the order of things inverted, and that there is no man in the moon, as believe the contrary. I can't forbear telling you we indeed read the fpoils of Rapine as boys do the Englifh Rogue, and hug ourfelves full as much over it; yet our rofes are not without thorns. Pray give me the pleafure of hearing (when you are at leifure) how foon I may expect to fee the next volume of Homer. I am, &c.

YOU'LL think me very full of myfelf, when, after long filence (which however, to fay truth, has rather been employed to contemplate of you, than to forget you) I begin to talk of my own works. I find it is in the finifhing a book, as in concluding a feffion of parliament, one always thinks it will be very foon, and finds it very late. There are many unlook'd-for incidents to retard the clearing any public account, and fo I fee it is in mine. I have plagued myfelf, like great minifters, with undertaking too much for one man; and with a defire of doing more than was expected from me, have done lefs than I ought.

For having defign'd four very laborious and uncommon forts of Indexes to Homer, I'm forced, for want of time, to publifh two only; the defign of which you will own to be pretty, tho' far from being fully executed. I've alfo been obliged to leave unfinifh'd in my defk the heads of two Effays; one on the Theology and Morality of Homer, and another on the Oratory of Homer and Virgil. So they muft wait for future editions, or perifh: and (one way or other, no great matter which) *dabit Deus his quoque finem.* I think of you every day, I affure you, even without fuch good memorials of you as your fifters, with whom I fometimes talk of you, and find it one of the moft agreeable of all fubjects to them. My Lord Digby muft be perpetually remember'd by all who ever knew him, or knew his children. There needs no more than an acquaintance with your family, to make all elder fons wifh they had fathers to their lives end.

I can't touch upon the fubject of filial love, without putting you in mind of an old woman, who has a fincere, hearty, old-fafhion'd refpect for you, and conftantly blames her fon for not having writ to you oftener to tell you fo.

I very much wifh (but what fignifies my wifhing? my

2   lady

lady Scudamore wifhes, your fifters wifh) that you were
with us, to compare the beautiful contraft this feafon affords us, of the town and the country. No ideas you
could form in the winter can make you imagine what
Twickenham is (and what your friend Mr. Johnfon of
Twickenham is) in this warmer feafon. Our river glit-
ters beneath an unclouded fun, at the fame time that its
banks retain the verdure of fhowers: our gardens are of-
fering their firft nofegays; our trees, like new acquaintance brought happily together, are ftretching their arms
to meet each other, and growing nearer and nearer every
hour; the birds are paying their thankfgiving fongs for
the new habitations I have made them; my building rifes
high enough to attract the eye and curiofity of the paffenger from the river, where, upon beholding a mixture of
beauty and ruin, he enquires what houfe is falling, or what
church is rifing? So little tafte have our common Tritons
of Vitruvius; whatever delight the poetical gods of the
river may take, in reflecting on their ftreams, by Tufcan
Porticos, or Ionic Pilafters.

But (to defcend from all this pomp of ftyle) the beft
account of what I am building, is, that it will afford me
a few pleafant rooms for fuch a friend as yourfelf, or a
cool fituation for an hour or two for Lady Scudamore,
when fhe will do me the honour (at this public houfe on
the road) to drink her own cyder.

The moment I am writing this, I am furprized with the
account of the death of a friend of mine, which makes
all I have here been talking of, a mere jeft! Building,
gardens, writings, pleafures, works, of whatever ftuff
man can raife! none of them (God knows) capable of
advantaging a creature that is mortal, or of fatisfying a
foul that is immortal! Dear Sir,

I am, &c.

LETTER V.

From Mr. Digby.

May 21, 1720.

Your letter, which I had two pofts ago, was very medicinal to me; and 1 heartily thank you for the relief it gave me. I was fick of the thoughts of my not having, in all this time, given you any teftimony of the affeΧtion I owe you, and which I as conftantly indeed feel as I think of you. This indeed was a troublefome ill to me, till, after reading your letter, I found it was a moft idle weak imagination to think I could fo offend you. Of all the impreffions you have made upon me, I never receiv'd any with greater joy than this of your abundant good-nature, which bids me be affured of fome fhare of your affeΧions.

I had many other pleafures from your letter; that your mother remembers me, is a very fincere joy to me; I cannot but reflecⁿt how alike you are; from the time you do any one a favour, you think yourfelves obliged as thoſe that have received one. This is indeed an old-fafhioned refpecⁿt, hardly to be found out of your houfe. I have great hopes, however, to fee many old-fafhioned virtues revive, fince you have made our age in love with Homer; I heartily wifh you, who are as good a citizen as a poet, the joy of feeing a reformation from your works. I am in doubt whether I fhould congratulate your having finifhed Homer, while the two effays you mention are not completed; but if you expecⁿt no great trouble from finifhing thefe, 1 heartily rejoice with you.

I have fome faint notion of the beauties of Twickenham from what I here fee round me. The verdure of fhowers is poured upon every tree and field about us; the gardens unfold variety of colours to the eye every morning, the hedges breath is beyond all perfume, and the fong of birds we hear as well as you. But tho' I hear and

fee

fee all this, yet I think they would delight me more if you was here. I found the want of thefe at Twickenham, while I was there with you, by which I guefs what an increafe of charms it muft now have. How kind is it in you to wifh me there, and how unfortunate are my cir-cumftances that allow me not to vifit you? If I fee you, I muft leave my father alone, and this uneafy thought would difappoint all my propofed pleafures; the fame cir-cumftance will prevent my profpect of many happy hours with you in Lord Bathurft's wood, and, I fear, of feeing you till winter, unlefs Lady Scudamore comes to Sher-burne, in which cafe I fhall prefs you to fee Dorfetfhire, as you propofed. May you have a long enjoyment of your new favourite Portico. Your, &c.

LETTER VI.

From Mr. DIGBY.

Sherburne, July 9, 1720.

THE London language and converfation is, I find, quite changed fince I left it, tho' it is not above three or four months ago. No violent change in the na-tural world ever aftonifhed a Philofopher fo much as this does me. I hope this will calm all Party rage, and in-troduce more humanity than has of late obtained in con-verfation. All fcandal will fure be laid afide, for there can be no fuch difeafe any more as Spleen in this new golden age. I am pleafed with the thoughts of fee-ing nothing but a general good humour when I come up to town; I rejoice in the univerfal riches I hear of, in the thought of their having this effect. They tell me you was foon content; and that you cared not for fuch an in-creafe as others wifhed you. By this account I judge you the richeft man in the South-fea, and congratulate you accordingly. I can wifh you only an increafe of health, for of riches and fame you have enough.

Your, &c.

LET-

LETTER VII.

July 20, 1720.

YOUR kind defire to know the ftate of my health had not been unfatisfied fo long, had not that ill ftate been the impediment. Nor fhould I have feem'd an un-concern'd party in the joys of your family, which I heard of from lady Scudamore, whofe fhort Efchantillon of a letter (of a quarter of a page) I value as the fhort glympfe of a vifion afforded to fome devout hermit; for it includes (as thofe revelations do) a promife of a better life in the Elyfian groves of Cirencefter, whither, I could fay almoft in the ftyle of a fermon, the Lord bring us all, &c. Thither may we tend, by various ways, to one blifsful bower : thither may health, peace, and good hu-mour wait upon us as affociates : thither may whole car-goes of nectar (liquor of life and longevity !) by mortals call'd fpaw-water, be conveyed; and there (as Milton has it) may we, like the deities,

On flow'rs repos'd, and with frefh garlands crown'd,
Quaff immortality and joy.

When I fpeak of garlands, I fhould not forget the green veftments and fcarfs which your fifters promis'd to make for this purpofe : I expect you too in green, with a hunt-ing horn by your fide, and a green hat, the model of which you may take from Ofborne's defcription of King James the firft.

What words, what numbers, what oratory, or what poetry, can fuffice, to exprefs how infinitely I efteem, value, love, and defire you all, above all the great ones of this part of the world; above all the Jews, jobbers, bubblers, fubfcribers, projectors, directors, governors, treafurers, &c. &c. &c. in fæcula fæculorum.

Turn your eyes and attention from this miferable mer-cenary period ; and turn yourfelf, in a juft contempt of thefe fons of Mammon, to the contemplation of books, gardens, and marriage; in which I now leave you, and return (wretch that I am !) to water-gruel and Palladio.

I am, &c.

LET-

LETTER VIII.

From Mr. DIGBY.

Sherburne, July 30.

I Congratulate you, dear Sir, on the return of the Golden age; for fure this muft be fuch, in which money is fhower'd down in fuch abundance upon us. I hope this overflowing will produce great and good fruits, and bring back the figurative moral golden-age to us. I have fome omens to induce me to believe it may; for when the Mufes delight to be near a Court, when I find you frequently with a Firft minifter, I can't but expect, from fuch an intimacy, an encouragement and revival of the polite arts. I know, you defire to bring them into honour, above the golden Image which is fet up and worfhipped; and, if you cannot effect it, adieu to all fuch hopes. You feem to intimate in yours, another face of things from this inundation of wealth, as if beauty, wit, and valour, would no more engage our paffions in the pleafurable purfuit of them, tho' affifted by this increafe : if fo, and if monfters only as various as thofe of Nile arife from this abundance, who that has any fpleen about him will not hafte to town to laugh ? What will become of the play-houfe? who will go thither, while there is fuch entertainment in the ftreets ? I hope we fhall neither want good Satire nor Comedy ; if we do, the age may well be thought barren of geniufes, for none has ever produced better fubjects.   Your, &c.

LETTER IX.

From Mr. DIGBY.

Colefhill, Nov. 12, 1720.

I Find in my heart that I have a taint of the corrupt age we live in. I want the public Spirit fo much admired in old Rome, of facrificing every thing that is dear

to

to us to the commonwealth. I even feel a more intimate
concern for my friends who have fuffered in the S. Sea,
than for the public, which is faid to be undone by it.
But I hope the reafon is, that I do not fee fo evidently
the ruin of the public to be a confequence of it, as I do
the lofs of my friends. I fear there are few befides yourfelf that will be perfuaded by old Hefiod, that *half is
more than the whole.* I know not whether I do not rejoice
in your Sufferings ; fince they have fhewn me your
mind is principled with fuch a fentiment, I affure you I
expect from it a performance greater ftill than Homer.
I have an extreme joy from your communicating to me
this affection of your mind;

Quid voveat dulci Nutricula majus alumno?

Believe me, dear Sir, no equipage could fhew you to my
eye in fo much fplendor. I would not indulge this fit of
philofophy fo far as to be tedious to you, elfe I could pro-
fecute it with pleafure.

I long to fee you, your Mother, and your Villa ; till
then I will fay nothing of Lord Bathurft's wood, which I
faw in my return hither. Soon after Chriftmas I defign
for London, where I fhall mifs Lady Scudamore very
much, who intends to ftay in the country all winter. I
am angry with her, as I am like to fuffer by this refolution, and would fain blame her, but cannot find a caufe.
The man is curfed that has a longer letter than this to
write with as bad a pen ; yet I can ufe it with pleafure, to
fend my fervices to your good mother, and to write myfelf

Your, &c.

LETTER X.

Sept. 1, 1722.

D Octor Arbuthnot is going to Bath, and will ftay there
a fortnight or more: perhaps you would be comforted to have a fight of him, whether you need him or not.
I think him as good a Doctor as any man for one that is ill,
and a better Doctor for one that is well. He would do admirably

mirably for Mrs. Mary Digby: fhe needed only to follow his hints, to be in eternal bufinefs and amufement of
mind, and even as active as fhe could defire. But indeed
I fear fhe would out-walk him; for (as Dean Swift obferv'd to me the very firft time I faw the Doctor) "He is
" a man that can do every thing but walk." His brother,
who is lately come into England, goes alfo to the Bath;
and is a more extraordinary man than he, worth your
going thither on purpofe to know him. The fpirit of
philanthropy, fo long dead to our world, is reviv'd in
him: he is a philofopher all of fire; fo warmly, nay, fo
wildly in the right, that he forces all others about him
to be fo too, and draws them into his own Vortex. He
is a ftar that looks as if it were all fire, but is all benig-
nity, all gentle and beneficial influence. If there be
other men in the world that would ferve a friend, yet he
is the only one, I believe, that could make even an enemy ferve a friend.

As all human life is chequer'd and mixed with acquifitions and loffes (tho' the latter are more certain and ir-
remediable, than the former lafting or fatisfactory) fo at
the time I have gain'd the acquaintance of one worthy
man, I have loft another, a very eafy, humane, and gen-
tlemanly neighbour, Mr. Stonor. 'Tis certain, the lofs
of one of this character puts us naturally upon fetting a
greater value on the few that are left, tho' the degree of
our efteem may be different. Nothing, fays Seneca, is
fo melancholy a circumftance in human life, or fo foon
reconciles us to the thought of our own death, as the reflection and profpect of one friend after another dropping
round us! Who would ftand alone, the fole remaining ruin,
the laft tottering column of all the fabric of friendfhip,;
once fo large, feemingly fo ftrong, and yet fo fuddenly
funk and buried? I am, &c.

LETTER XI.

I Have belief enough in the goodnefs of your whole family, to think you will all be pleas'd that I am arriv'd
in fafety at Twickenham; tho' it is a fort of earneft that

you will be troubled again with me, at Sherburne, or Colefhill; for however I may like one of your places, it may be in that as in liking one of your family; when one fees the reft, one likes them all. Pray make my fervices acceptable to them: I wifh them all the happinefs they may want, and the continuance of all the happinefs they have; and I take the latter to comprize a great deal more than the former. I muft feparate Lady Scudamore from you, as, I fear, fhe will do herfelf before this letter reaches you: fo I wifh her a good journey, and I hope one day to try if fhe lives as well as you do: tho' I much queftion if fhe can live as quietly: I fufpect the bells will be ringing at her arrival, and on her own and Mifs Scudamore's birth-days, and that all the clergy in the country come to pay refpects; both the clergy and their bells expecting from her and from the young lady, further bufinefs and further employment. Befides all this, there dwells on the one fide of her the Lord Coningfby, and on the other Mr. W*. Yet I fhall, when the days and the year is come about, adventure upon all this for her fake.

I beg my Lord Digby to think me a better man than to content myfelf with thanking him in the common way. I am, in as fincere a fenfe of the word, his fervant, as you are his fon, or he your father.

I muft in my turn infift upon hearing how my laft fellow-travellers got home from Clarendon, and defire Mr. Philips to remember me in his Cyder, and to tell Mr. W*. that I am dead and buried.

I wifh the young ladies, whom I almoft robb'd of their good name, a better name in return, (even that very name to each of them, which they fhall like beft, for the fake of the man that bears it.)   Your, &c.

LETTER XII.

1722.

YOUR making a fort of apology for your not writing, is a very genteel reproof to me. I know I was to blame, but I know I did not intend to be fo, and (what

2   is

is the happieft knowledge in the world) I know you will forgive me : for fure nothing is more fatisfactory than to be certain of fuch a friend as will overlook one's failings, fince every fuch inftance is a conviction of his kindnefs.

If I am all my life to dwell in intentions, and never to rife to actions, I have but too much need of that gentle difpofition which I experience in you. But I hope better things of myfelf, and fully purpofe to make you a vifit this fummer at Sherburne. I'm told you are all upon removal very fpeedily, and that Mrs. Mary Digby talks, in a letter to Lady Scudamore, of feeing my Lord Bathurft's wood in her way. How much I wifh to be her guide thro' that enchanted foreft, is not to be expreft: I look upon myfelf as the magician appropriated to the place, without whom no mortal can penetrate into the receffes of thofe facred fhades. I could pafs whole days, in only defcribing to her the future, and as yet vifionary beauties, that are to rife in thofe fcenes: the palace that is to be built, the pavillions that are to glitter, the colonades that are to adorn them : nay more the meeting of the Thames and the Severn, which (when the noble ownerhas finer dreams than ordinary) are to be led into each other's embraces thro' fecret caverns of ' not above twelve or fifteen miles, till they rife and celebrate their marriage in the midft of an immenfe ampitheatre, which is to be the admiration of pofterity, a hundred years hence. But till the deftin'd time fhall arrive that is to manifeft thefe wonders, Mrs. Digby muft content herfelf with feeing what is at prefent no more than the fineft wood in England.

The objects that attract this part of the world, are of a quite different nature. Women of quality are all turn'd followers of the camp in Hyde-park this year, whither all the town refort to magnificent entertainments given by the officers, &c. The Scythian Ladies that dwelt in the waggons of war, were not more clofely attached to the luggage. The matrons, like thofe of Sparta, attend their fons to the field, to be witneffes of their glorious deeds ; and the maidens with all their charms difplay'd,

provoke

provoke the fpirit of the foldiers: Tea and Coffee fupply
the place of Lacedemonian black broth.   This camp feems
crown'd with perpetual victory, for every fun that rifes
in the thunder of cannon, fets in the mufic of violins.
Nothing is yet wanting but the conftant prefence of the
Princefs to reprefent the *Mater exercitus.*

   At Twickenham the world goes otherwife.   There are
certain old people who take up all my time, and will
hardly allow me to keep any other company.   They were
introduced here by a man of their own fort, who has
made me perfectly rude to all contemporaries, and
won't fo much as fuffer me to look upon them.   The
perfon I complain of is the Bifhop of Rochefter.   Yet
he allows me (from fomething he has heard of your character, and that of your family, as if you were of the old
fect of moralifts) to write three or four fides of paper to
you, and to tell you (what thefe fort of people never tell
but with truth and religious fincerety) that I am, and ever
will be,   Your, &c.

LETTER XIII.

THE fame reafon that hinder'd your writing, hinder'd
mine, the pleafing expectation to fee you in town.
Indeed fince the willing confinement I have lain under
here with my mother (whom it is natural and reafonable
I fhould rejoice with, as well as grieve) I could the better
bear your abfence from London, for I could hardly have
feen you there; and it would not have been quite reafonable to have drawn you to a fick room hither from
the firft embraces of your friends.   My mother is now
(I thank God) wonderfully recovered, tho' not fo much
as yet to venture out of her chamber, but enough to enjoy a few particular friends, when they have the good nature
to look upon her.   I may recommend to you the room we
fit in, upon one (and that a favourite) account, that it
is the very warmeft in the houfe; we and our fires will
equally fmile upon your face.   There is a Perfian pro-
                                                        verb

verb that fays (I think very prettily) " The converfa-
" tion of a friend brightens the eyes." This I take to
be a fplendour ftill more agreeable than the fires you fo
delightfully defcribe.

That you may long enjoy your own fire-fide in the me-
taphorical fenfe, that is, all thofe of your family who
make it pleafing to fit and fpend whole wintry months
together, (a far more rational delight, and better felt by
an honeft heart, than all the glaring entertainments, numerous lights, and falfe fplendours, of an affembly of
empty heads, aching hearts, and falfe faces.) This is my
fincere wifh to you and yours.

You fay you propofe much pleafure in feeing fome few
faces about town of my acquaintance. I guefs you mean
Mrs. Howard's and Mrs. Blount's. And I affure you,
you ought to take as much pleafure in their hearts, if
they are what they fometimes exprefs with regard to you.

Believe me, dear Sir, to you all, a very faithful fervant.

LETTER XIV.

From Mr. DIGBY.

Sherburne, Aug. 14, 1725.

I Can't return from fo agreeable an entertainment as
yours in the country, without acknowledging it. I
thank you heartily for the new agreeable idea of life you
there gave me; it will remain long with me, for it is very
ftrongly impreffed upon my imagination. I repeat the
memory of it often, and fhall value that faculty of the
mind now more than ever, for the power it gives me of
being entertained in your villa, when abfent from it.
As you are poffeffed of all the pleafures of the country,
and, as I think, of a right mind, what can I wifh you
but health to enjoy them? This I fo heartily do, that I
fhould be even glad to hear your good mother might loofe
all her prefent pleafures in her unwearied care of you, by
your better health convincing them it is unneceffary.

I am

I am troubled, and shall be so, till I hear you have receiv'd this litter : for you gave me the greatest pleasure
imaginable in yours, and I am impatient to acknowledge
it. If I any ways deserve that friendly warmth and affection, with which you write, it is, that I have a heart
full of love and esteem for you: so truly, that I should
loose the greatest pleasure of my life if I lost your good
opinion. It rejoices me very much to be reckoned by
you in the class of honest men ; for tho' I am not troubled
over much about the opinion most may have of me, yet,
I own, it would grieve me not to be thought well of, by
you and some few others. I will not doubt my own
strength, yet I have this further security to maintain my
integrity, that I cannnot part with that, without forfeit-
ing your esteem with it.

Perpetual disorder and ill health have for some years
so disguised me, that I sometimes fear I do not to my
best friends enough appear what I really am. Sickness
is a great oppressor : it does great injury to a zealous
heart, stifling its warmth, and not suffering it to break out
in action. But, I hope, I shall not make this complaint
much longer. I have other hopes that please me too,
tho' not so well grounded; these are, that you may yet
make a journey westward with Lord Bathurst ; but of
the probability of this I do not venture to reason, because I would not part with the pleasure of that belief.
It grieves me to think how far I am removed from you,
and from that excellent Lord, whom I love ! Indeed I remember him, as one that has made sickness easy to me,
by bearing with my infirmities in the same manner that
you have always done. I often too consider him in other
lights that make him valuable to me. With him, I know
not by what connection, you never fail to come into my
mind, as if you were inseparable. I have, as you guess,
many philosophical reveries in the shades of Sir Walter
Raleigh, of which you are a great part. You generally
enter there with me, and like a good genius, applaud and
strengthen all my sentiments that have honour in them.

This

This good office which you have often done me unknow..
ingly, I muſt acknowledge now, that my own breaſt may
not reproach me with ingratitude, and diſquiet me when
I would muſe again in that ſolemn ſcene. I have not room.
now left to aſk you many queſtions I intended about the
Odyſſey. I beg I may know how far you have carried
Ulyſſes on his journey, and how you have been entertained with him on the way? I deſire I may hear of your
health, of Mrs. Pope's, and of every thing elſe that belongs to you.

How thrive your garden plants? how look the trees?
how ſpring the Brocoli and the Fenochio? hard names to
ſpell! how did the poppies bloom? and how is the great
room approv'd? what parties have you had of pleaſure?
what in the grotto? what upon the Thames? I would
know how all your hours paſs, all you ſay, and all you
do; of which I ſhould queſtion you yet farther, but my
paper is full and ſpares you. My brother Ned is wholly
yours, and ſo my father deſires to be, and every ſoul here
whoſe name is Digby. My ſiſter will be yours in particular. What can I add more? I am, &c.

LETTER XV.

October 10.

I Was upon the point of taking a much greater journey
than to Bermudas, even to that *undiſcover'd country, from
whoſe bourn no traveller returns!*

A fever carried me on the high gallop towards it for ſix
or ſeven days—But here you have me now, and that is
all I ſhall ſay of it: ſince which time an impertinent
lameneſs kept me at home twice as long; as if fate ſhould
ſay (after the other dangerous illneſs) " You ſhall nei-
" ther go into the other world, nor any where you like
" in this." Elſe who knows but I had been at Hom-lacy?

I conſpire in your ſentiments, emulate your pleaſures,
wiſh for your company. You are all of one heart and
one ſoul, as was ſaid of the primitive Chriſtians: 'tis like
the

the kingdom of the juft upon earth ; not a wicked wretch
to interrupt you, but a fet of try'd, experienc'd friends
and fellow comforters, who have feen evil men and evil
days ; and have, by a fuperior rectitude of heart fet yourfelves above them, and reap your reward. Why will
you ever, of your own accord, end fuch a millenary year
in London ? tranfmigrate (if I may fo call it) into other
creatues, in that fcene of folly militant, when you may
reign for ever at Hom-lacy in fenfe and reafon triumphant? I appeal to a third lady in your family, whom I take
to be the moft innocent, and the leaft warp'd by idle
fafhion and cuftom of you all ; I appeal to her, if you
are not every foul of you better people, better companions, and happier where you are ? I defire her opinion
under her hand in your next letter, I mean Mifs Scudamore's *. I am confident if fhe would or durft fpeak her
fenfe, and employ that reafoning which God has given
her, to infufe more thoughtfulnefs into you all ; thofe arguments could not fail to put you to the blufh, and keep
you out of town, like people fenfible of your own felicities. I am not without hopes, if fhe can detain a parli-
ament-man and a lady of quality from the world one
winter, that I may come upon you with fuch irrefiftable
arguments another year as may carry you all with me to
Bermudas †, the feat of all earthly happinefs, and the new
Jerufalem of the righteous.

Don't talk of the decay of the year, the feafon is
good where the people are fo : 'tis the beft time of the
year for a painter; there is more variety of colours in the
leaves, the profpects begin to open, thro' the thinner woods,
over the valleys ; and thro' the high canopies of trees to
the higher arch of heaven : the dews of the morning im-
pearl every thorn, and fcatter diamonds on the verdant
mantle of the earth ; the frofts are frefh and wholefome :
what would you have ? the Moon fhines too, tho' not
for lovers thefe cold nights, but for aftronomers.

* Afterwards Duchefs of Beaufort, at this time very young.
† About this time the Rev. Dean Berkley conceived his project of erecting
a fettlement in Bermudas for the Propagation of the Chriftian faith, and in-
troduction of Sciences into America.

Have

Have ye not reflecting Telefcopes ‡, whereby ye may innocently magnify her fpots and blemifhes? Content yourfelves with them, and do not come to a place where your own eyes become reflecting Telefcopes, and where thofe of all others are equally fuch upon their neighbours. Stay you at leaft (for what I have faid before relates on-ly to the ladies: don't imagine I'll write about any eyes but theirs) ftay, I fay, from that idle, bufy-looking San-hedrin, where wifdom and no wifdom is the eternal debate, not (as it lately was in Ireland) an accidental one.

If, after all, you will difpife good advice, and refolve to come to London, here you will find me, doing juft the things I fhould not, living where I fhould not, and as worldly, as idle, in a word as much an Anti-Bermudanift as any body.   Dear Sir, make the ladies know I am their fervant, you know I am   Yours, &c.

<hr>

LETTER XVI.

Aug. 12.

I Have been above a month ftrolling about in Buck-inghamfhire and Oxfordfhire, from garden to garden, but ftill returning to Lord Cobham's with frefh fatisfac-tion. I fhould be forry to fee my Lady Scudamore's, till it has had the full advantage of Lord B*'s improve-ments; and then I will expect fomething like the waters of Rifkins, and the woods of Oakley together, which (without flattery) would be at leaft as good as any thing in our world: For as to the hanging gardens of Babylon, the Paradife of Cyrus, and the Sharawaggi's of China, I have little or no ideas of them, but, I dare fay, Lord B* has becaufe they were certainly both very great, and very wild. I hope Mrs. Mary Digby is quite tired of his Lordfhip's*Extravagante Bergerie:* and that fhe is juft now fiting, or rather reclining on a bank, fatigued with over-much dancing and finging at his unwearied requeft and inftigation. I know your love of eafe fo well, that you might be in danger of being too quiet to enjoy quiet, and

‡ Thefe inftruments were juft then brought to perfection.

too philofophical to be a philofopher; were it not for the ferment Lord B. will put you into. One of his Lordfhip's maxims is, that a total abftinence from intemperance or bufinefs, is no more philofophy, than a total confopiation of the fenfes is repofe : one muft feel enough of its contrary to have a relifh of either. But, after all, let your temper work, and be as fedate and contemplative as you will, I'll engage you fhall be fit for any of us, when you come to town in the winter. Folly will laugh you into all the cuftoms of the company here; nothing will be able to prevent your converfion to her, but indifpofition, which, I hope, will be far from you. I am telling the worft that can come of you; for as to vice, you are fafe; but folly is many an honeft man's, nay, every good humour'd man's lot: nay, it is the feafoning of life; and fools (in one fenfe) are the falt of the earth : a little is excellent, tho' indeed a whole mouthful is juftly call'd the Devil.

So much for your diverfions next winter, and for mine. I envy you much more at prefent, than I fhall then ; for if there be on earth an image of paradife, it is in fuch perfect Union and Society as you all poffefs. I would have my innocent envies and wifhes of your ftate known to you all; which is far better than making you compliments, for it is inward approbation and efteem. My Lord Digby has in me a fincere fervant, or would have, were there any occafion in me to manifeft it.

LETTER XVII.

Decemb. 28, 1724.

IT is now the feafon to wifh you a good end of one year, and a happy beginning of another : but both thefe you know how to make yourfelf, by only continuing fuch a life as you have been long accuftomud to lead. As for good works, they are things I dare not name, either to thofe that do them, or to thofe that do them not: the firft are too modeft, and the latter too felfifh, to bear the mention of what are become of either too old fafhion'd, or too private, to conftitute any part of the vanity or reputation of the prefent age. However, it were to be wifh'd people would now and then look upon good works as they do upon old wardrobes, merely in cafe any of them fhould by chance come into fafhion again : as ancient fardingales revive in modern hoop'd peticoats, (which may be properly compared to charities, as they cover a multitude of fins.)
. They tell me that at Colefhill certain antiquated charities,

ties, and obfolete devotions are yet fubfifting : that a thing called Chriftian chearfulnefs (not incompatible with Chrift-mas pyes and plum-broth) whereof frequent is the mention in old fermons and almanacks, is really kept alive and in practice ; that feeding the hungry, and giving alms to the poor, do yet make a part of good houfe-keeping, in a la-titude not more remote from London than fourfcore miles : and laftly, that prayers and roaft beef annually make fome people as happy as a whore and a bottle. · But here in town, I affure you, men, women, and children have done with with thefe things. Charity not only begins, but ends at home. Inftead of the four cardinal virtues, now reign four courtly ones : we have cunning for prudence, rapine for juftice, time ferving for fortitude, and luxury for temperance. Whatever you may fancy where you live in a ftate of ignorance, and fee hothing but quiet, religion, and good-humour, the cafe is juft as I tell you where peo-ple underftand the world, and know how to live with credit and glory.

I wifh that heaven would open the eyes of men, and make them fenfible which of thefe is right; whether, upon a due conviction, we are to quit faction, and gaming, and high feeding, and all manner of luxury, and to take to your country way ? or you to leave prayers, and almf-giving, and reading, and exercife, and come into our meafures ? I wifh, (I fay) that this matter were as clear to all men as it is to   Your affectionate, &c.

L E T T E R XVIII.

DEAR SIR,   April 21, 1726.

I Have a great inclination to write to you, tho' I cannot by writing any more than 1 could by words, exprefs what part I bear in your fufferings. Nature and efteem in you are join'd to aggravate your affliction: the latter I have in a degree equal even to yours, and a tye of friendfhip approaches near to the tendernefs of nature : yet, God knows, no man living is lefs fit to comfort you, as no man is more deeply fenfible than myfelf of the greatnefs of the lofs. That very virtue which fecures his prefent ftate from all the forrows incident to ours, does but aggrandife our fenfation of its being remov'd from our fight, from our affection, and from our imitation; for the friendfhip and fociety of good men does not only make us happier, but it makes us better. Their death does but complete

T 2   their

their felicity before our own, who probably are not yet arrived to that degree of perfection which merits an immediate reward. That your dear brother, and my dear friend was fo, I take his very removal to be a proof; Providence would certainly lend virtuous men to a world that fo much wants them, as long as in its juftice to them it could fpare them to us. May my foul be with thofe who have meant well, and have acted well to that meaning! and, I doubt not, if this prayer be granted, I fhall be with him. Let us preferve his memory in the way he would beft like, by recollecting what his behaviour would have been, in every incident of our lives to come, and doing in each juft as we think he would have done; fo we fhall have him always before our eyes, and in our minds, and (what is more) in our lives and manners, I hope when we fhall meet him next, we fhall be more of a piece with him, and confequently not to be evermore feparated from him. I will add but one word that relates to what remains of yourfelf and me, fince fo valued a part of us is gone; it is to beg you to accept, as yours by inheritance, of the vacancy he has left in a heart, which (while he could fill it with fuch hopes, wifhes and affections for him as fuited a mortal creature) was truly and warmly his ; and fhall (I affure you in the fincerity of forrow for my own lofs) be faithfully at your fervice while I continue to love his memory, that is, while I continue to be myfelf.

Mr. Digby died in the year 1726, and is buried in the church of Sherburne in Dorfetfhire, with an Epitaph written by the Author.

L E T T E R S

TO AND FROM

Dr. A T T E R B U R Y,

Biſhop of ROCHESTER,

From the Year 1716 to 1723.

L E T T E R I.

The Biſhop of ROCHESTER to Mr. POPE.

Decemb. 1716.

I Return your * Preface, which I have read twice with
pleaſure. The modeſty and good ſenſe there is in it,
muſt pleaſe every one that reads it : and ſince there is nothing that can offend, I ſee not why you ſhould balance
a moment about printing it—always provided, that there
is nothing ſaid there which you may have occaſion to un-
ſay hereafter; of which you yourſelf are the beſt and the
only judge. This is my ſincere opinion, which I give,
becauſe you aſk it : and which I would not give, tho'
aſked, but to a man I value as much as I do you; being
ſenſible how improper it is, on many accounts, for me to
interpoſe in things of this nature ; which I never underſtood well, and now underſtand ſomewhat leſs than ever I
did. But I can deny you nothing; eſpecially ſince you
have had the goodneſs often, and patiently, to hear what
I have ſaid againſt rhyme, and in behalf of blank verſe;
with little diſcretion, perhaps, but, I am ſure, without
the leaſt prejudice; being myſelf equally incapable of
writing well in either of thoſe ways, and leaning therefore
to neither ſide of the queſtion, but as the appearance of
reaſon inclines me. Forgive me this error, if it be one;
an error of above thirty years ſtanding, and which therefore I ſhall be very loth to part with. In other matters
which relate to polite writing, I ſhall ſeldom differ from

* The general preface to Mr. Pope's Poems, firſt printed 1717, the year
after the date of this letter.

you

you; or, if I do, fhall, I hope, have the prudence to
conceal my opinion. I am as much as I ought to be, that
is, as much as any man can be,   Your, &c.

L E T T E R II.

The Bifhop of ROCHESTER to Mr. POPE.

Feb. 18, 1717.

I Hoped to find you laft night at Lord Bathurft's, and
came but a few minutes after you had left him. I
brought *Gorboduc* * with me; and Dr. Arbuthnot telling
me he fhould fee you, I depofited the book in his hands:
out of which, I think, my Lord Bathurft got it before we
parted, and from him therefore you are to claim it. If
Gorboduc fhould ftill mifs his way to you, others are to
anfwer for it; I have delivered up my truft. I am not
forry your † Alcander is burnt; had I known your intentions, I would have interceded for the firft page, and put
it, with your leave, among my curiofities. In truth, it
is the only inftance of that kind I ever met with, from a
perfon good for any thing elfe, nay, for every thing elfe
to which he is pleas'd to turn himfelf.

Depend upon it, I fhall fee you with great pleafure at
Bromley; and there is no requeft you can make to me,
that I fhall not moft readily comply with. I wifh you
health and happinefs of all forts, and would be glad to be
inftrumental in any degree towards helping you to the
leaft fhare of either. I am always, every where, moft
affectionately and faithfully   Your, &c.

L E T T E R III.

The Bifhop of ROCHESTER to Mr. POPE.

Bromley, Nov 8, 1717.

I Have nothing to fay to you on that melancholy fubject,
with an account of which the printed papers have furnifhed me, but what you have already faid to yourfelf.

When you have paid the debt of tendernefs you owe
to the memory of a father, I doubt not but you will turn
your thoughts towards improving that accident to your
own eafe and happinefs. You have it now in your power
to purfue that method of thinking and living which you

* A Tragedy, written in the Reign of Edward the fixth (and much the
beft performance of that Age) by Sackville, afterwards Earl of Dorfet, and
Lord Treafurer to Queen Elizabeth. It was then very fcarce, but lately reprinted by R. Dodfley in Pall-mall.
† An Heroic Poem writ at 15 years old.

                                                    like

like beſt. `Give me leave, if I am not a little too early in my applications of this kind, to congratulate you upon it; and to aſſure you that there is no man living who wiſhes you better, or would be more pleas'd to contribute any ways to your ſatisfaction or ſervice.

I return you your Milton, which, upon collation, I find to be reviſed, and augmented, in ſeveral places, as the title page of my third edition pretends it to be. When I ſee you next, I will ſhew you the ſeveral paſſages alter'd, and added by the author, beſide what you mentioned to me.

I proteſt to you, this laſt peruſal of him has given me ſuch new degrees, I will not ſay of pleaſure, but of admiration and aſtoniſhment, that I look upon the ſublimity of Homer, and the majeſty of Virgil, with ſomewhat leſs reverence than I uſed to do. I challenge you, with all your partiality, to ſhew me, in the firſt of theſe, any thing equal to the Allegory of Sin and Death, either as to the greatneſs and juſtneſs of the invention, or the height and beauty of the colouring. What I look'd upon as a rant of Barrow's, I now begin to think a ſerious truth, and could almoſt venture to ſet my hand to it,

> Hæc quicunque legit, tantum ceciniſſe putabit
> Mæoniden Ranas, Virgilium Culices.

But more of this when we meet. When I left the town, the D. of Buckingham continued ſo ill, that he receiv'd no meſſages; oblige me ſo far as to let me know how he does; at the ſame time I ſhall know how you do, and that will be a double ſatisfaction to   Your, &c.

LETTER IV.
The Anſwer.

MY LORD,   Nov. 20, 1717.

I Am truly obliged by your kind condolence on my Father's death, and the deſire you expreſs that I ſhould improve this incident to my advantage. I know your Lordſhip's friendſhip to me is ſo extenſive, that you include in that wiſh both my ſpiritual and my temporal advantage; and it is what I owe to that friendſhip, to open my mind unreſervedly to you on this head. It is true, I have loſt a parent for whom no gains I could make would be any equivalent. But that was not my only tye: I thank God another ſtill remains (and long may it remain) of the ſame tender nature: *Genitrix eſt mihi*—and excuſe me if I ſay with Euryalus,

> nequeam lacrymas perferre parentis,

A rigid divine may call it a carnal tye; but fure it is a virtuous one: at leaft I am more certain that it is a duty of nature to preferve a good parent's life and happinefs, than I am of any fpeculative point whatever.

> Ignaram hujus quodcunque pericli
> Hanc ego, nunc, linquam?

For fhe, my Lord, would think this feparation more grievous than any other; and I, for my part, know as little as poor Euryalus did, of the fuccefs of fuch an adventure (for an Adventure it is, and no fmall one, in fpite of the moft pofitive divinity.) Whether the change would be to my fpiritual advantage, God only knows: this I know, that I mean as well in the religion I now profefs, as I can poffibly ever do in another. Can a man who thinks fo, juftify a change, even if he thought both equally good? To fuch an one, the part of *Joining* with any one body of Chriftians might perhaps be eafy, but I think it would not be fo, to *Renounce* the other.

Your Lordfhip has formerly advis'd me to read the beft controverfies between the Churches. Shall I tell you a fecret? I did fo at fourteen years old (for I loved reading, and my father had no other books) there was a collection of all that had been written on both fides in the reign of King James the fecond: I warm'd my head with them, and the confequence was, that I found myfelf a Papift and a Proteftant by turns, according to the laft book I read *. I am afraid moft Seekers are in the fame cafe; and when they ftop, they are not fo properly converted, as outwitted. You fee how little glory you would gain by my converfion. And after all, I verily believe your Lordfhip and I are both of the fame religion, if we were thoroughly underftood by one another, and that all honeft and reafonable chriftians would be fo, if they did but talk enough together every day, and had nothing to do together but to ferve God, and live in peace with their neighbour.

As to the *temporal* fide of the queftion, I can have no difpute with you; it is certain, all the beneficial circumftances of life, and all the fhining ones, lie on the part you would invite me to. But if I could bring myfelf to fancy, what I think you do but fancy, that I have any talents for active life, I want health for it; and befides, it is a real truth, I have lefs Inclination (if poffible) than

---

* This is an excellent defcription of every Reader labouring in religious controverfy, without poffeffing the *principles* on which a right judgment of the points in queftion is to be regulated.

Ability.

Ability. Contemplative life is not only my fcene, but it
is my habit too. I begun my life where moft people end
theirs, with a dif relifh of all that the world calls ambition : I don't know why 'tis called fo, for to me it always
feem'd to be rather *ftooping* than *climbing.* I'll tell you my
politic and religious fentiments in a few words. In my
politics, I think no further than how to preferve the peace
of my life, in any government under which I live ; nor
in my religion, than to preferve the peace of my confcience, in any church with which I communicate. I
hope all churches and all governments are fo far of God,
as they are rightly underftood, and rightly adminiftred :
and where they are, or may be wrong, I leave it to God
alone to mend or reform them ; which, whenever he does,
it muft be by greater inftruments than I am. I am not a
Papift, for I renounce the temporal invafions of the papal
power, and deteft their arrogated authority over Princes
and States. I am a Catholic in the ftricteft fenfe of the
word. If I was born under an abfolute prince, I would
be a quiet fubject ; but I thank God I was not. I have a
due fenfe of the excellence of the Britifh conftitution. In
a word, the things I have always wifhed to fee are not a
Roman Catholic, or a French Catholic, or a Spanifh Catholic, but a true Catholic : and not a King of Whigs, or
a King of Tories, but a King of England ; which God of
his mercy grant his prefent Majefty may be, and all future
Majefties. You fee, my Lord, I end like a preacher : this
is *Sermo ad Clerum*, not *ad Populum.* Believe me, with infinite obligation and fincere thanks, ever   Your, &c.

LETTER V.

Sept. 23, 1720.

I Hope you have fome time ago receiv'd the Sulphur, and
the two volumes of Mr. Gay, as inftances (how fmall
ones foever) that I wifh you both health and diverfion.
What I now fend for your perufal, I fhall fay nothing of ;
not to foreftal, by a fingle word, what you promis'd to fay
upon that fubject. Your Lordfhip may criticife from Virgil to thefe Tales ; as Solomon wrote of every thing from
the cedar to the hyffop. I have fome caufe, fince I laft
waited on you at Bromley, to look upon you as a prophet
in that retreat, from whom oracles are to be had, were
mankind wife enough to go thither to confult you : the
fate of the South-fea fcheme has, much fooner than I expected, verify'd what you told me. Moft people thought
the time would come, but no man prepared for it ; no man
confider'd it would come *like a Thief in the Night*, exactly

as it happens in the cafe of our death. Methinks God has punifhed the avaritious, as he often punifhes finners, in their own way, in the very fin itfelf: the thirft of gain was their crime; that thirft continued, became their punifhment and ruin. As for the few who have the good fortune to remain with half of what they imagined they had (among whom is your humble fervant) I would have them fenfib'e of their felicity, and convingd of the truth of old Hefiod's maxim, wno, after half his eftate was fwallowed by the *Directors* of thofe days, refolved, that *half* to be *more than the whole.*

Does not the fate of thefe people put you in mind of two paffages; one in Job, the other from the Pfalmift?

Men fhall groan out of the CITY, *and hifs them out of their* PLACE.

They have dreamed out their dream; and awakening, have found nothing in their hands.

Indeed the univerfal poverty, which is the confequence of univerfal avarice, and which will fall hardeft upon the guiltlefs and induftrious part of mankind, is truly lamentable. The univerfal deluge of the S. Sea, contrary to the old deluge, has drowned all, except a few *Unrighteous* men: but it is fome comfort to me that I am not one of them, even tho' I were to furvive and rule the world by it. I am much pleas'd with a thought of Dr. Arbuthnot's; he fays the government and South Sea company have only lock'd up the money of the people, upon conviction of their Lunacy (as is ufual in the cafe of Lunatics) and intend to reftore them as much as may be fit for fuch people, as faft as they fhall fee them return to their fenfes.

The latter part of your letter does me fo much honour, and fhews me fo much kindnefs, that I muft both be proud and pleas'd, in a great degree; but I affure you, my Lord, muc more the laft than the firft. For I certainly know, and fee, from my own heart, which truly refpects you, that there may be a ground for your partiality, one way; but I find not the leaft fymptoms in my head, of any foundation for the other. In a word, the beft reafon I know for my being pleas'd, is, that you continue your favour towards me; the beft I know for being proud, would be that you might cure me of it; for I have found you to be fuch a phyfician, as does not only *repair* but *improve.* I am, with the finccreft efteem, and moft grateful acknowledgment, Your, &c.

L E T-

LETTER VI.

From the Bishop of ROCHESTER.

THE Arabian Tales, and Mr. Gay's books, I receiv'd not till Monday night, together with your letter; for which I thank you. I have had a fit of the gout upon me ever since I returned hither from Westminster on Saturday night last: it has found its way into my hands as well as legs, so that I have been utterly incapable of writing. This is the first letter that I have ventured upon; which will be written, I fear, *vacillantibus literis,* as Tully says, Tyro's letters were, after his recovery from an illness. What I said to you in mine about the Monument, was in-tended only to quicken, not to alarm you. It is not worth your while to know what I meant by it; but when I see you, you shall. I hope you may be at the Deanry to-wards the end of October, by which time, I think of set-tling there for the winter. What do you think of some such short inscription as this in Latin, which may, in a few words, say all that is to be said of Dryden, and yet nothing more than he deserves?

JOHANNI DRYDENO,

CVI POESIS ANGLICANA

VIM SVAM AC VENERES DEBET;

ET SIQVA IN POSTERVM AVGEBITVR LAVDE,

EST ADHVC DEBITVRA:

HONORIS ERGO P. etc.

To shew you that I am as much in earnest in the affair as you yourself, something I will send you too of this kind in English. If your design holds of fixing Dryden's name only below, and his Busto above—may not lines like these be grav'd just under the name?

This Sheffield rais'd, to Dryden's ashes just,
Here fix'd his Name, and there his laurel'd Bust.
What else the Muse in Marble might express,
Is known already; Praise would make him less.

Or thus—

More needs not; where acknowledg'd Merits reign,
Praise is impertinent; and Censure vain.

This you'll take as a proof of my zeal at least, tho' it be none of my talent in Poetry. When you have read it over, I'll forgive you if you should not once in your life-time again think of it.

U 2

And now, Sir, for your *Arabian Tales*. Ill as I have been, almost ever since they came to hand, I have read as much of them, as ever I shall read while I live. Indeed they do not please my taste : they are writ with so romantic an air, and, allowing for the difference of Eastern manners, are yet, upon any suppofition that can be made, of so wild and abfurd a contrivance (at least to my northern underftanding) that I have not only no pleasure, but no patience, in perufing them. They are to me like the odd paintings on Indian fcreens, which at first glance may furprize and please a little ; but when you fix your eye intently upon them, they appear so extravagant, difproportioned, and monftrous, that they give a judicious eye pain, and make him feek for relief from some other object.

They may furnish the mind with some new images ; but I think the purchafe is made at too great an expence : for to read thofe two volumes through, liking them as little as I do, would be a terrible penance ; and to read them with pleafure, would be dangerous on the other fide, becaufe of the infection. I will never believe that you have any keen relifh of them, till I find you write worfe than you do, which, I dare fay, I never shall. Who that *Petit de la Croife* is, the pretended author of them, I cannot tell : but obferving how full they are in the defcriptions of drefs, furniture, &c. I cannot help thinking them the product of some Woman's imagination ; and believe me, I would do any thing but break with you, rather than be bound to read them over with attention.

I am forry that I was so true a prophet in refpect of the S. Sea ; forry, I mean, as far as your lofs is concern'd : for in the general I ever was, and still am of opinion, that had that project taken root and flourifh'd, it would by degrees have overturn'd our conftitution. Three or four hundred millions was fuch a weight, that which-foever way it had leaned, muft have borne down all before it— But of the dead we muft fpeak gently ; and therefore, as Mr. Dryden fays fomewhere, *Peace be to its Manes !*

Let me add one reflection, to make you eafy in your ill luck. Had you got all that you have loft beyond what you ventur'd, confider that your fuperfluous gains would have fprung from the ruin of feveral families that now want neceffaries ; a thought, under which a good and good-natured man that grew rich by fuch means, could not, I perfuade myself, be perfectly eafy. Adieu, and believe me ever,

Your, &c.

LET-

LETTER VII.

From the Bifhop of ROCHESTER.

March 26, 1721.

YOU are not yourfelf gladder you are well, than I am; efpecially fince I can pleafe myfelf with the thought, that when you had loft your health elfewhere, you reco-vered it here. May thefe lodgings never treat you worfe, nor you at any time have lefs reafon to be fond of them! I thank you for the fight of your * Verfes; and with the freedom of an honeft, tho' perhaps injudicious friend, muft tell you, that tho' I could like fome of them, if they were any body's elfe but yours; yet as they are yours, and to be own'd as fuch, I can fcarce like any of them. Not but that the four firft lines are good, efpecially the fecond couplet; and might, if followed by four others as good, give reputation to a writer of a lefs eftablifhed fame; but from you I expeƈt fomething of a more perfeƈt kind, and which the oftener it is read, the more it will be ad-mired. When you barely exceed other writers, you fall much beneath yourfelf: 'tis your misfortune now to write without a rival, and to be tempted by that means to be more carelefs, than you would otherwife be in your com-pofures.

Thus much I could not forbear faying, tho' I have a motion of confequence in the Houfe of Lords to-day, and muft prepare for it. I am even with you for your ill pa-per; for I write upon worfe, having no other at hand. I wifh you the continuance of your health moft heartily; and am ever   Your, &c.

I have fent Dr. Arbuthnot the † Latin MS. which I could not find when you left me; and I am fo angry at the writer for his defign, and his manner of executing it, that I could hardly forbear fending him a line of Virgil along with it. The chief Reafoner of that philofophic farce is a *Gallo Ligur*, as he is call'd—what that means in Englifh or French, I can't fay—but all he fays, is in fo loofe and flippery and trickifh a way of reafoning, that I could not forbear applying the paffage of Virgil to him,

* Epitaph on Mr. Harcourt.

† Written by Huetius, bifhop of Avranches. He was a mean reafoner; as may be feen by a vaft collection of fanciful and extravagant conjeƈures, which he call'd a *demonftration*; mixed up with much reading, which his friends called learning, and delivered (by the allowance of all) in good Latin. This not being received for what he would give it, he compofed a treatife *of the weak-nefs of the human underftanding*: a poor fyftem of fcepticifm; indeed little other than an abftract from *Sextus Empiricus*.

Vane

Vane Ligur, fruſtraque animis elate ſuperbis !
Nequicquam patrias tentaſti lubricus artes—

To be ſerious, I hate to ſee a book gravely written, and
in all the forms of argumentation, which proves nothing,
and which ſays nothing; and endeavours only to put us
into a way of diſtruſting our own faculties, and doubting
whether the marks of truth and falſhood can in any caſe
be diſtinguiſhed from each other. Could that bleſſed point
be made out (as it is a contradiction in terms to ſay it can)
we ſhould then be in the moſt uncomfortable and wretched
ſtate in the world ; and I would in that caſe be glad to exchange my Reaſon, with a dog for his Inſtinct, to-morrow.

LETTER VIII.

L. Chancellor HARCOURT to Mr. POPE.

Decemb. 6, 1722.

I Cannot but ſuſpect myſelf of being very unreaſonable
in begging you once more to review the incloſ'd.
Your friendſhip draws this trouble on you. I may freely
own to you, that my tenderneſs makes me exceeding hard
to be ſatisfied with any thing which can be ſaid on ſuch an
unhappy ſubject. I cauſ'd the Latin Epitaph to be as often alter'd before I could approve of it.

When once your Epitaph is ſet up, there can be no alteration of it; it will remain a perpetual monument of
your friendſhip, and, I aſſure myſelf, you will ſo ſettle it,
that it ſhall be worthy of you. I doubt whether the word,
deny'd, in the third line, will juſtly admit of that conſtruction, which it ought to bear (viz.) renounced, deſerted,
&c. *deny'd* is capable, in my opinion, of having an ill
ſenſe put upon it, as too great uneaſineſs, or more good-
nature, than a wiſe man ought to have. I very well remember you told me, you could ſcarce mend thoſe two
lines, and therefore I can ſcarce expect your forgiveneſs
for my deſiring you to reconſider them.

Harcourt ſtands dumb, and Pope is forc'd to ſpeak.
I can't perfectly, at leaſt without further diſcourſing you,
reconcile myſelf to the firſt part of that line ; and the word,
forc'd (which was my own, and, I perſuade myſelf, for
that reaſon only ſubmitted to by you) ſeems to carry too
doubtful a conſtruction for an Epitaph, which, as I apprehend, ought as eaſily to be underſtood as read. I ſhall
acknowledge it as a very particular favour, if at your beſt
leiſure you will peruſe the incloſed, and vary it, if you
think it capable of being amended, and let me ſee you any
morning next week. I am, &c.

3   LETTER

LETTER IX.

The Bifhop of ROCHESTER to Mr. POPE.

Sept. 27, 1721.

I Am now confined to my bed-chamber, and to the matted room, wherein I am writing, feldom venturing to be carried down even into the parlour to dinner, unlefs when company to whom I cannot excufe myfelf, comes, which I am not ill-pleas'd to find is now very feldom. This is my cafe in the funny part of the year: what muft I expect, when

inverfum contriftat Aquarius annum?

" If thefe things be done in the green tree, what fhall " be done in the dry?" Excufe me for employing a fentence of Scripture on this occafion; I apply it very ferioufly. One thing relieves me a little, under the ill profpect I have of fpending my time at the Deanry this winter, that I fhall have the opportunity of feeing you oftener; tho', I am afraid, you will have little pleafure in feeing me there. So much for my ill ftate of health, which I had not touch'd on, had not your friendly letter been fo full of it. One civil thing that you fay in it, made me think you had been reading Mr. Waller; and poffefs'd of that image at the end of his copy, à la malade, had you not beftow'd it on one who has no right to the leaft part of the character. If you have not read the verfes lately, I am fure you remember them becaufe you forget nothing.

> With fuch a grace you entertain,
> And look with fuch contempt on pain, &c.

I mention them not on the account of that couplet, but one that follows; which ends with the very fame rhymes and words (appear and clear) that the couplet but one after that does—and therefore in my Waller there is a various reading of the firft of thefe couplets; for there it runs thus:

> So lightnings in a ftormy air
> Scorch more, than when the fky is fair.

You will fay that I am not very much in pain, nor very bufy, when I can relifh thefe amufements; and you will fay true: for at prefent I am in both thefe refpects very eafy. I had not ftrength enough to attend Mr. Prior to his grave, elfe I would have done it, to have fhew'd his friends that I had forgot and forgiven what he wrote on me. He is buried, as he defired, at the feet of Spencer; and I will take care to make good, in every refpect, what

I faid

I said to him when living; particularly as to the Triplet he wrote for his own Epitaph; which, while we were in good terms, I promis'd him should never appear on his tomb while I was Dean of Weftminfter.

I am pleafed to find you have fo much pleafure, and (which is the foundation of it) fo much health at Lord Bathurft's: may both continue till I fee you! may my Lord have as much fatisfaction in building the houfe in the wood, and ufing it when built, as you have in defigning it! I cannot fend a wifh after him that means him more happinefs, and yet, I am fure, I wifh him as much as he wifhes himfelf. I am, &c.

LETTER X.

From the fame.

Bromley, Oct. 15, 1721.

NOtwithstanding I write this on Sunday even, to acknowledge the receipt of yours this morning, yet I forefee it will not reach you till Wednefday morning. And before fet of fun that day I hope to reach my winterquarters at the Deanry. I hope, did I fay? I recall that word, for it implies defire; and, God knows, that is far from being the cafe: for I never part with this place but with regret, tho' I generally keep here what Mr. Cowley calls the worft of company in the world, my own; and fee either none befide, or what is worfe than none, fome of the *Arrii*, or *Sebofi* of my neighbourhood: Characters, which Tully paints fo well in one of his Epiftles, and complains of the too civil, but impertinent interruption they gave him in his retirement. Since I have named thofe gentlemen, and the book is not far from me, I will turn to the place, and by pointing it out to you, give you the pleafure of perufing the epiftle, which is a very agreeable one, if my memory does not fail me.

I am furpriz'd to find that my Lord Bathurft and you are parted fo foon; he has been fick, I know, of fome late tranfactions; but fhould that ficknefs continue ftill in fome meafure, I prophefy, it will be quite off by the beginning of November: a letter or two from his London friends, and a furfeit of folitude, will foon make him change his refolution and his quarters. I vow to you, I could live here with pleafure all the winter, and be contented with hearing no more news than the London Journal, or fome fuch trifling paper, affords me, did not the duty of my place require, abfolutely require my attendance at Weftminfter, where I hope the Prophet will now and then remember

member he has a bed and a candleftick. In fhort, I long to
fee you, and hope you will come if not a day, yet at leaft
an hour fooner to town than you intended, in order to afford me that fatisfaction. I am now, I thank God! as
well as ever I was in my life, except that I can walk fcarce
at all without crutches: And I would willingly compound
the matter with the gout to be no better, could I hope to
be no worfe; but that is a vain thought, I expect a new
attack long before Chriftmas. Let me fee you therefore
while I am in a condition to relifh you, before the days
(and the nights) come, when I fhall (and muft) fay
have no pleafure in them.

I will bring your fmall volume of paftorals along with
me, that you may not be difcouraged from lending me
books, when you find me fo punctual in returning them.
Shakefpeare fhall bear it company, and be put into your
hands as clear and as fair as it came out of them, tho' you,
I think, have been dabbling here and there with the text:
I have had more reverence for the writer and the printer,
and left every thing ftanding juft as I found it. However,
I thank you for the pleafure you have given me in putting
me upon reading him once more before I die.

I believe I fhall fcarce repeat that pleafure any more,
having other work to do, and other things to think of, but
none that will interfere with the offices of friendfhip, in
the exchange of which with you, Sir, I hope to live and
die   Your, &c.

P. S. Addifon's works came to my hands yefterday. I
cannot but think it a very odd fet of incidents, that the
book fhould be dedicated by a * dead man to † a dead man;
and even that the new ‡ patron to whom Tickell chofe to infcribe his verfes, fhould be dead alfo before they were publifhed. Had I been in the Editor's place I fhould have
been a little apprehenfive for myfelf, under a thought that
every one who had any hand in that work was to die before
the publication of it. You fee, when I am converfing
with you, I know not how to give over, till the very bottom of the paper admonifhes me once more to bid you adieu!

LETTER XI.

My Lord,   Feb. 8, 1721-2.

IT is fo long fince I have had the pleafure of an hour with
your Lordfhip, that I fhould begin to think myfelf no longer *amicus omnium horarum*, but for finding myfelf fo in my

* Mr. Addifon.   † Mr. Crapgs.   ‡ Lord Warwick.

conftant thoughts of you.   In thofe I was with you many
hours this very day, and had you (where I wifh and hope
one day to fee you really) in my garden at Twitnam.
When I went laft to town, and was on wing to the Deanry,
I heard your Lordfhip was gone the day before to Bromley,
and there you continued till after my return hither.   I fincerely wifh you whatever you wifh yourfelf, and all you
wifh your friends or family.   All I mean by this word or
two, is juft to tell you fo, till in perfon I find you as I defire, that is, find you well: eafy, refign'd, and happy you
will make yourfelf, and (I believe) every body that converfes with you; if I may judge of your power over other
men's minds and affections, by that which you will ever
have over thofe of   Your, &c.

- - - - - - - - - - - - - - -

LETTER XII.

From the Bifhop of ROCHESTER.

Feb. 26, 1721-2.

PERMIT me, dear Sir, to break into your retirement,
and to defire of you a complete copy of thofe verfes on
Mr. Addifon * ; fend me alfo your laft refolution, which
fhall punctually be obferved in relation to my giving out
any copy of it; for I am again folicited by another Lord,
to whom I have given the fame anfwer as formerly.   No
fmall piece of your writing has been ever fought after fo
much : it has pleas'd every man without exception, to whom
it has been read.   Since you now therefore know where
your real ftrength lies, I hope you will not fuffer that talent to lye unemploy'd.   For my part, I fhould be fo glad
to fee you finifh fomething of that kind, that I could be
content to be a little fneer'd at in a line or fo, for the fake of
the pleafure I fhould have in reading the reft.   I have
talk'd my fenfe of this matter to you once or twice, and
now I put it under my hand, that you may fee it is my deliberate opinion.   What weight that may have with you I
cannot fay: but it pleafes me to have an opportunity of
fhewing you how well I wifh you, and how true a friend
I am to your fame, which I defire may grow every day,
and in every kind of writing, to which you fhall pleafe to
turn your pen.   Not but that I have fome little intereft in
the propofal, as I fhall be known to have been acquainted
with a man that was capable of excelling in fuch different

_____

* An imperfect Copy was got out, very much to the Author's furprize, who
never would give any.

manners,

manners, and did fuch honour to his country and language; and yet was not difpleas'd fometimes to read what was written by his humble fervant.

LETTER XIII.

March 14, 1721-2.

I Was difappointed (much more than thofe who common-ly ufe that phrafe on fuch occafions) in miffing you at the Deanry, where I lay folitary two nights. Indeed I truly partake in any degree of concern that affects you, and I wifh every thing may fucceed as you defire in your own family, and in that which, I think, you no lefs account your own, and is no lefs your family, the whole world: for I take you to be one of the true friends of it, and to your power its protector. Tho' the noife and daily buftle for the public be now over, I dare fay a good man is ftill tendring its welfare; as the fun in the winter, when feeming to retire from the world, is preparing benedictions and warmth for a better feafon. No man wifhes your Lord-fhip more quiet, more tranquility, than I, who know you fhould underftand the value of it; but I don't wifh you a jot lefs concern'd or lefs active than you are, in all fincere and therefore warm defires of public good.

I beg the kindnefs (and 'tis for that chiefly I trouble you with this letter) to favour me with notice as foon as you return to London, that I may come and make you a proper vifit of a day or two: for hitherto I have not been your vi-fitor, but your lodger, and I accufe myfelf of it. I have now no earthly thing to oblige my being in town (a point of no fmall fatisfaction to me) but the beft reafon, the feeing a friend. As long, my Lord, as you will let me call you fo (and I dare fay you will, till I forfeit, what, I think, I never fhall, my veracity and integrity) I fhall efteem myfelf fortunate, in fpite of the South fea, Poe-try, Popery, and Poverty.

I can't tell you how forry I am, you fhould be troubled a-new by any fort of people. I heartily wifh, *Quod fuper-eft, ut tibi vivas*—that you may teach me how to do the fame: who, without any real impediment to acting and living rightly, do act and live as foolifhly as if I were a Great man.   I am, &c.

X 2   LET-

LETTER XIV.
From the Bishop of ROCHESTER.

March 16, 1721-2.

AS a visitant, a lodger, a friend (or under what other denomination soever) you are always welcome to me; and will be more so, I hope, every day that we live: for, to tell you the truth, I like you as I like myself, best when we have both of us least business. It has been my fate to be engaged in it much and often, by the stations in which I was placed: but, God, that knows my heart, knows I never lov'd it: and am still less in love with it than ever, as I find less temptation to act with any hope of success. If I am good for any thing, 'tis *in angulo cum libello*; and yet a good part of my time has been spent, and perhaps must be spent, far otherwise. For I will never, while I have health, be wanting to my duty in my post, or in any respect, how little soever I may like my employment, and how hopeless soever I may be in the discharge of it.

In the mean time the judicious world is pleas'd to think that I delight in work which I am obliged to undergo, and aim at things which I from my heart despise; let them think as they will, so I might be at liberty to act as I will, and spend my time in such a manner as is most agreeable to me. I cannot say I do so now, for I am here without any books, and if I had them could not use them to my satisfaction, while my mind is taken up in a more melancholy * manner; and how long, or how little a while it may be so taken up, God only knows, and to his will I implicitly resign myself in every thing.   I am, &c.

LETTER XV.

MY LORD,   March 19, 1721-2.

I AM extremely sensible of the repeated favour of your kind letters, and your thoughts of me in absence, even among thoughts of much nearer concern to yourself on the one hand, and of much more importance to the world on the other, which cannot but engage you at this juncture. I am very certain of your good-will, and of the warmth which is in you inseparable from it.

Your remembrance of Twitenham is a fresh instance of that partiality. I hope the advance of the fine season will set you upon your legs, enough to enable you to get into my garden, where I will carry you up a Mount, in a point of view to shew you the glory of my little kingdom. If you approve it, I shall be in danger to boast, like Nebu-

* In his Lady's last sickness.

chadnezzar,

chadnezzar, of the things I have made, and to be turn'd to
converfe, not with the beafts of the field, but with the
birds of the grove, which I fhall take to be no great pun-
nifhment.   For indeed I heartily defpife the ways of the
world, and moft of the great ones of it.

Oh keep me innocent, make others great !

And you may judge how comfortably I am ftrengthen'd
in this opinion, when fuch as your Lordfhip bear teftimony
to its vanity and emptinefs.   *Omnis, inane eft*, with the picture of one ringing on the globe with his finger, is the beft
thing I have the luck to remember in that great Poet
Quarles (not that I forget the Devil at bowls; which I
know to be your Lordfhips favourite cut, as well as favourite diverfion.)

The fituation here is pleafant, and the view rural enough,
to humour the moft retired, and agree with the moft contemplative.   Good air, folitary groves, and fparing diet,
fufficient to make you fancy yourfelf (what you are in temperance, tho' elevated into a greater figure by your ftation)
one of the Fathers of the Defart.   Here you may think
(to ufe an author's words, whom you fo juftly prefer to all his
followers that you'll recieve them kindly, tho'_taken from
his worft work * ;)

That in Eliah's banquet you partake,
Or fit a gueft with Daniel, at his Pulfe.

I am fincerely free with you, as you defire I fhould, and
approve of your not having your coach here, for if you
would fee Lord C* or any body elfe, I have another chariot, befides that little one you laugh'd at when you compared me to Homer in a nut-fhell.   But if you would be
entirely private, no body fhall know any thing of the matter.   Believe me (my Lord) no man is with more perfect
acquiefcence, nay with more willing acquiefcence (not even
any of your own Sons of the Church)   Your obedient, &c,

LETTER XVI.

From the Bifhop of ROCHESTER.

April 6, 1722.

UNDER all the leifure in the world, I have no leifure,
no ftomach to write to you : the gradual approaches
of death are before my eyes.   I am convinced that it muft
be fo; and yet make a fhift to flatter myfelf fometimes with
the thought, that it may poffibly be otherwife.   And that
very thought, tho' it is directly contrary to my reafon,

* The *Paradife Regain'd*. I fuppofe this was in compliment to the Bifhop.
It could never be his own opinion.

does

does for a few moments make me eafy—however not eafy
enough in good earneft to think of any thing but the melancholy objeft that employs them. Therefore wonder not
that I do not anfwer your kind letter : I fhall anfwer it too
foon, I fear, by accepting your friendly invitation. When
I do fo, no conveniencies will be wanting : for I'll fee no
body but you and your mother, and the fervants. Vifits
to ftatefmen always were to me (and are now more than
ever) infipid things; let the men that expeft, that wifh
to thrive by them, pay them that homage : I am free.
When I want them, they fhall hear of me at their doors :
and when they want me, I fhall be fure to hear of them at
mine. But probably they will defpife me fo much, and I
fhall court them fo little, that we fhall both of us keep our
diftance.

When I come to you, 'tis in order to be with you only ;
a prefident of the council, or a ftar and garter will make
no more impreffion upon my mind, at fuch a time, than
the hearing of a bagpipe, or the fight of a puppet-fhew.
I have faid to greatnefs fome time ago—*Tuas tibi res habeto,
Egomet curabo meas.* The time is not far off when we fhall
all be upon the level : and I am refolv'd, for my part, to
anticipate that time, and be upon the level with them now ;
for he is fo, that neither feeks nor wants them. Let them
have more virtue and lefs pride, and then I'll court them as
much as any body : but till they refolve to diftinguifh
themfelves fome way elfe than by their outward trappings,
I am determined (and, I think, I have a right) to be as
proud as they are : tho' I truft in God, my pride is neither
of fo odious a nature as theirs, nor of fo mifchievous a confequence.

I know not how I have fallen into this train of thinking
—When I fat down to write I intended only to excufe myfelf for not writing, and to tell you that the time drew
nearer and nearer, when I muft diflodge ; I am preparing
for it; for I am at this moment building a vault in the
Abbey for me and mine. 'Twas to be in the Abbey, becaufe of my relation to the place; but 'tis at the weft door
of it : as far from Kings and Cæfars as the fpace would
admit of.

I know not but I may ftep to town to-morrow, to fee
how the work goes forward ; but, if I do, I fhall return
hither in the evening. I would not have given you the
trouble of this letter but that they tell me it will coft you
nothing, and that our privilege of Franking (one of the
moft valuable we have left) is again allow'd us.

Your, &c.

LET-

LETTER XVII.

From the Bishop of ROCHESTER.

Bromley, May 25, 1722.

I Had much ado to get hither laſt night, the water being ſo rough that the ferrymen were unwilling to venture.   The firſt thing I ſaw this morning after my eyes
were open, was your letter, for the freedom and kindneſs
of which I thank you.   Let all compliments be laid aſide
between us for the future; and depend upon me as your
faithful friend in all things within my power, as one that
truly values you, and wiſhes you all manner of happineſs.
I thank you and Mrs. Pope for my kind reception, which
has left a pleaſing impreſſion upon me that will not ſoon be
effaced.

Lord * has preſs'd me terribly to ſee him at *, and told
me in a manner betwixt kindneſs and reſentment, that it is
but a few miles beyond Twitenham.

I have but a little time left, and a great deal to do in it;
and muſt expect that ill health will render a good ſhare of
it uſeleſs: and therefore what is likely to be left at the
foot of the account, ought by me to be cheriſh'd, and not
thrown away in compliments.   You know the motto of
my ſun dial, *Vivite, ait, fugio.*   I will, as far as I am able,
follow its advice, and cut off all unneceſſary avocations
and amuſements.   There are thoſe that intend to employ
me this winter in a way I do not like: If they perſiſt in
their intentions, I muſt apply myſelf to the work they cut
out for me, as well as I can.   But withal, that ſhall not
hinder me from employing myſelf alſo in a way which they
do not like.   The givers of trouble one way ſhall have
their ſhare of it another; that at laſt they may be induced
to let me be quiet, and live to myſelf, with the few (the very few) friends I like; for that is the point, the ſingle
point I now aim at; tho' I know the generality of the
world who are unacquainted with my intentions and views,
think the very reverſe of this character belongs to me.   I
don't know how I have rambled into this account of myſelf;
when I ſat down to write, I had no thought of making that
any part of my letter.

You might have been ſure without my telling you, that
my right hand is at eaſe; elſe I ſhould not have overflow'd
at this rate.   And yet I have not done, for there is a kind
intimation in the end of yours, which I underſtood, becauſe it ſeems to tend towards employing me in ſomething
that is agreeable to you.   Pray explain yourſelf, and believe

lieve that you have not an acquaintance in the world that would be more in earneft on fuch an occafion than I, for I love you, as well as efteem you.

All the while I have been writing, Pain, and a fine Thrufh have been feverally endeavouring to call off my attention; but both in vain, nor fhould I yet part with you, but that the turning over a new leaf frights me a little, and makes me refolve to break thro' a new temptation, before it has taken too faft hold on me. I am, &c.

LETTER XVIII.

From the fame.

June 15, 1722.

YOU have generally written firft, after our parting; I will now be before-hand with you in my enquiries, how you got home, and how you do, and whether you met with Lord *, and deliver'd my civil reproach to him in the manner I defired? I fuppofe you did not, becaufe I have heard nothing either from you, or from him on that head; as I fuppofe, I might have done, if you had found him.

I am fick of thefe men of quality; and the more fo, the oft'ner I have any bufinefs to tranfact with them: They look upon it as one of their diftinguifhing privileges, not to be punctual in any bufinefs, of how great importance foever: nor to fet other people at eafe, with the lofs of the leaft part of their own. This conduct of his vexes me; but to what purpofe? or how can I alter it?

I long to fee the original MS. of Milton: but don't know how to come at it, without your repeated affiftance.

I hope you won't utterly forget what pafs'd in the coach about Sampfon Agoniftes. I fhall not prefs you as to time, but fome time or other, I wifh you would review and polifh that piece. If upon a new perufal of it (which I defire you to make) you think as I do, that it is written in the very fpirit of the Ancients; it deferves your care, and is capable of being improv'd, with little trouble, into a perfect model and ftandard of Tragic poetry—always allowing for its being a ftory taken out of the Bible; which is an objection that at this time of day, I know, is not to be got over

I am, &c.

LET-

LETTER XIX.

July 27.

I Have been as conſtantly at Twitenham as your Lord-ſhip has at Bromley, ever ſince you ſaw Lord Bathurſt. At the time of the Duke of Marlborough's funeral, I in-tend to lie at the Deanry, and moralize one evening with you on the vanity of human glory.

The Duchefs's * letter concerns me nearly, and you know it, who know all my thoughts without diſguiſe : I muſt keep clear of Flattery ; I will : and as this is an ho-neſt reſolution, I dare hope, your Lordſhip will not be ſo unconcern'd for my keeping it, as not to aſſiſt me in ſo do-ing. I beg therefore you would repreſent thus much at leaſt to her Grace, that as to the fear ſhe ſeems touch'd with [That the Duke's memory ſhould have no advantage but what he muſt give himſelf, without being beholden to any one friend] your Lordſhip may certainly, and agree-ably to your character, both of rigid honour and chriſtian plainneſs, tell her, that no man can have any other ad-vantage : and that all offerings of friends in ſuch a caſe paſs for nothing. But be ſo good as to confirm what I've re-preſented to her, that an inſcription in the antient way, plain, pompous, yet modeſt, will be the moſt uncommon, and therefore the moſt diſtinguiſhing manner of doing it. And ſo, I hope, ſhe will be ſatisfied, the Duke's honour be preſerv'd, and my integrity alſo : which is too ſacred a thing to be forfeited, in conſideration of any little (or what people of quality may call great) honour or diſtinction whatever, which thoſe of their rank can beſtow on one of mine ; and which indeed they are apt to over-rate, but never ſo much, as when they imagine us under any obli-gation to ſay one untrue word in their favour.

I can only thank you my Lord, for the kind tranſition you make from common buſineſs, to that which is the only real buſineſs of every reaſonable creature. Indeed I think more of it than you imagine, tho' not ſo much as I ought. I am pleas'd with thoſe Latin verſes extremely, which are ſo very good that I thought them yours, 'till you call'd them an Horatian Cento, and then I recollected the *disjecti membra poetæ.* I won't pretend I am ſo totally in thoſe ſen-timents which you compliment me with, as I yet hope to

* The Duchefs of Buckingham.

be: You tell me I have them, as the civileft method to'
put me in mind how much it fits me to have them. I ought,
firft, to prepare my mind by 'a better knowledge even of
good prophane writers, efpecially the Moralifts, &c. before I can be worthy of tafting that fupreme of books, and
fublime of all writings.   In which, as in all the interme-
diate ones, you may (if your friendfhip and' charity toward me continue fo far) be the beft guide to

Your, &c.

LETTER XX.

From the Bifhop of ROCHESTER.

July 30, 1722.

I Have written to the Duchefs * juft as you defir'd, and
referred her to our meeting in town for a further account
of it. I have done it the rather becaufe your opinion in
the cafe is fincerely mine : and if it had not been fo, you
yourfelf fhould not have induced me to give it.   Whether,
and how far fhe will acquiefce in it, I cannot fay : efpecially in a cafe where fhe thinks the Duke's honour concern'd,
but fhould fhe feem to perfift a little at prefent, her good
fenfe (which I depend upon) will afterwards fatisfy her
that we are in the right.

I go to-morrow to the Deanry, and I believe, I fhall ftay
there, till I have faid Duft to duft, and fhut up that † laft
fcene of pompous vanity.

'Tis a great while for me to ftay there at this time of the
year; and I know I fhall often fay to myfelf, while I am
expecting the funeral,

> O Rus, quando ego te aufpiciam! quandoque licebit
> Ducere folicitæ jucunda oblivia vitæ ?

In this cafe I fhall fancy I hear the ghoft of the dead,
thus intreating me,

> At tu facratæ ne parce malignus arenæ
>   Offibus et capiti inhumato
> Particulam dare————
> Quanquam feftinas, non eft mora longa ; licebit,
>   Injecto ter pulvere, curras.

---

* Duchefs of Buckingham.
† This was the Funeral of the Duke of Marlborough, at which the Bifhop
officiated as Dean of Weftminfter, in Aug. 1722.

There

There is an anfwer for me fomewhere in *Hamlet* to this requeft, which you remember, tho' I don't.   *Poor Ghoft!*
thou fhalt be fatisfied!—or fomething like it.   However that
be, take care you do not fail in your appointment, that the
company of the living may make me fome amends for my
attendance on the dead.

I know you will be glad to hear that I am well : I fhould
always could I always be here—

Sed me
Imperiofa trahit Proferpina : vive, valeque.

You are the firft man I fent to this morning, and the laft
man I defire to converfe with this evening, tho' at twenty,
miles diftance from you.

Te, veniente die, Te, decedente, requiro.

LETTER XXI.

From the Bifhop of ROCHESTER.

DEAR SIR,   The Tower, April, 10, 1723.

I Thank you for all the inftances of your friendfhip, both
before, and fince my misfortunes.   A little time will
complete them, and feparate you and me for ever.   But in
what part of the world foever I am, I will live mindful of
of your fincere kindnefs to me ; and will pleafe myfelf with
the thought, that I ftill live in your efteem and affe&ion,
as much as ever I did; and that no accidents of life, no
diftance of time, or place, will alter you in that refpe&.
It never can me ; who have lov'd and valued you, ever fince
I knew you, and fhall not fail to do it when I am not allowed to tell you fo ; as the cafe will foon be.   Give my
faithful fervices to Dr. Arbuthnot, and thanks for what
he fent me, which was much to the purpofe, if any thing
can be faid to be to the purpofe, in a cafe that is already
determined.   Let him know my Defence will be fuch, that
neither my friends need blufh for me, nor will my enemies have great occafion of triumph, tho' fure of the vi&ory.
I fhall want his advice before I go abroad, in many things.
But I queftion whether I fhall be permitted to fee him, or
any body, but fuch as are abfolutely neceffary towards
the difpatch of my private affairs.   If fo, God blefs you
both ; and may no part of the ill fortune that attends me,
ever purfue either of you! I know not but I may call upon
you at my hearing, to fay fomewhat about my way of
fpending my time at the Deanry, which did not feem cal-

culat

culated towards managing plots and confpiracies. But of
that I fhall confider—You and I have fpent many hours together upon much pleafanter fubjeats ; and, that I may
preferve the old cuftom, I fhall not part with you now till
I have clos'd this letter, with three lines of Milton, which
you will, I know, readily and not without fome degree of
concern apply to your ever affeationate, &c.

Some nat'ral Tears he dropt, but wip'd them foon:
The World was all before him, where to chufe
His place of reft, and *Providence* his Guide.

LETTER XXII.

The Anfwer.

April 20, 1723.

IT is not poffible to exprefs what I think, and what I feel;
only this, that I have thought and felt for nothing but
you, for fome time paft: and fhall think of nothing fo
long for the time to come. The greateft comfort I had
was an intention (which I would have made practicable)
to have attended you in your journey, to which I had
brought that perfon to confent, who only could have hindered me, by a tye which, though it may be more tender,
I do not think more ftrong, than that of friendfhip. But
I fear there will be no way left me to tell you this great
truth, that I remember you, that I love you, that I am
grateful to you, that I entirely efteem and value you : no
way but that one, which needs no open warrant to author-
ize it, or fecret conveyance to fecure it; which no bills can
preclude, and no Kings prevent; a way that can reach to
any part of the world where you may be, where the very
whifper, or even the wifh of a friend muft not be heard, or
even fufpeated : by this way, I dare tell my efteem and af-
feation of you, to your enemies in the gates, and you, and
they, and their fons, may hear of it.
You prove yourfelf, my Lord, to know me for the
friend I am ; in judging that the manner of your Defence,
and your Reputation by it, is a point of the higheft concern to me : and affuring me, it fhall be fuch, that none
of your friends fhall blufh for you. Let me further prompt
you to do yourfelf the beft and moft lafting juftice: the inftruments of your Fame to pofterity will be in your own
hands. May it not be, that providence has appointed you to
fome great and ufeful work, and calls you to it this fevere

5   way ?

way? You may more eminently and more effectually ferve the Public even now, than in the ftations you have fo honourably fill'd. Think of Tully, Bacon, and Clarendon * : is it not the latter, the difgraced part of their lives, which you moft envy, and which you would choofe to have liv'd? I am tenderly fenfible of the wifh you exprefs, that no part of your misfortune may purfue me. But, God knows, I am every day lefs and lefs fond of my native country (fo torn as it is by Party-rage) and begin to confider a friend in exile as a friend in death ; one gone before, where I am not unwilling or unprepared to follow after ; and where (however various or uncertain the roads and voyages of another world may be) I cannot but entertain a pleafing hope that we may meet again.

I faithfully affure you, that in the mean time there is no one, living or dead, of whom I fhall think oftener or better than of you. I fhall look upon you as in a ftate between both, in which you will have from me all the paffions and warm wifhes that can attend the living, and all the refpect and tender fenfe of lofs, that we feel for the dead. And I fhall ever depend upon your conftant friendfhip, kind memory, and good offices, tho' I were never to fee or hear the effects of them : like the truft we have in benevolent fpirits, who tho' we never fee or hear them, we think, are conftantly ferving us, and praying for us.

Whenever I am wifhing to write to you, I fhall conclude you are intentionally doing fo to me. And every time that I think of you, I will believe you are thinking of me. I never fhall fuffer to be forgotten (nay to be but faintly remember'd) the honour, the pleafure, the pride I muft ever have, in reflecting how frequently you have delighted me, how kindly you have diftinguifh'd me, how cordially you have advis'd me ! In converfation, in ftudy, I fhall always want you, and wifh for you : In my moft lively, and in my moft thoughtful hours, I fhall equally bear about me, the impreffions of you : And perhaps it will not be in This life only, that I fhall have caufe to remember and acknowledge the friendfhip of the Bifhop of Rochefter.

I am, &c.

---

* Clarendon indeed wrote his beft works in his banifhment ; but the beft of Bacon's were written before his difgrace, and the beft of Tully's after his return from exile.

LETTER

LETTER XXIII.

To the fame.

May, 1723.

ONCE more I write to you, as I promis'd, and this once,
I fear, will be the laft! the Curtain will foon be
drawn between my friend and me, and nothing left but to
wifh you a long good-night. May you enjoy a ftate of
repofe in this life, not unlike that fleep of the foul which
fome have believ'd is to fucceed it, where we lye utterly
forgetful of that world from which we are gone, and ripen-
ing for that to which we are to go. If you retain any memory of the paft, let it only image to you what has pleas'd
you beft; fometimes prefent a dream of an abfent friend,
or bring you back an agreeable converfation. But upon
the whole, I hope you will think lefs of the time paft than
of the future; as the former has been lefs kind to you than
the latter infallibly will be. Do not envy the world your
ftudies; they will tend to the benefit of men againft whom
you can have no complaint, I mean of all Pofterity; and, perhaps, at your time of life, nothing elfe is worth your care.
What is every year of a wife man's life but a cenfure or
critic on the paft? Thofe whofe date is the fhorteft, live
long enough to laugh at one half of it: the boy defpifes
the infant, the man the boy, the philofopher both, and
the Chriftian all. You may now begin to think your man-
hood was too much a puerility; and you'll never fuffer
your age to be but a fecond infancy. The toys and bau-
bles of your childhood are hardly now more below you, than
thofe toys of our riper and of our declining years, the drums
and rattles of ambition, and the dirt and bubbles of avarice.
At this time, when you are cut off from a little fociety,
and made a citizen of the world at large, you fhould bend
your talents not to ferve a party, or a few, but all mankind. Your Genius fhould mount above that mift in which
its participation and neighbourhood with earth long involv'd
it; to fhine abroad and to heaven, ought to be the bufinefs
and the glory of your prefent fituation. Remember it was at
fuch a time, that the greateft lights of antiquity dazzled
and blazed the moft, in the retreat, in their exile, or in
their death: but why do I talk of dazzling or blazing? it
was then that they did good, that they gave light, and that
they became guides to mankind.

Thofe aims alone are worthy of fpirits truly great, and
fuch I therefore hope will be yours. Refentment indeed
may

may remain, perhaps cannot be quite extinguished, in the nobleft minds; but revenge never will harbour there: higher principles than thofe of the firft, and better principles than thofe of the latter, will infallibly influence men, whofe thoughts and whofe hearts are enlarged, and caufe them to prefer the whole to any part of mankind, efpecially to fo fmall a part as one's fingle felf.

Believe me, my Lord, I look upon you as a fpirit entered into another life *, as one juft upon the edge of Immortality; where the paffions and affections muft be much more exalted, and where you ought to defpife all little views, and all mean retrofpects. Nothing is worth your looking back; and therefore look forward, and make (as you can) the world look after you. But take care that it be not with pity, but with efteem and admiration.

I am with the greateft fincerity, and paffion for your fame as well as happinefs,   Your, &c.

LETTER XXIV.

From the Bifhop of ROCHESTER.

Paris, Nov. 23, 1731.

YOU will wonder to fee me in print; but how could I avoid it? The dead and the living, my friends and my foes, at home and abroad, call'd upon me to fay fomething; and the reputation of an † Hiftory which I and all the world value, muft have fuffered, had I continued filent. I have printed it here, in hopes that fomebody may venture to reprint it in England, notwithftanding thofe two frightening words at the clofe of it ‡. Whether that happens or not, it is fit you fhould have a fight of it, who, I know, will read it with fome degree of fatisfaction, as it is mine, tho' it fhould have (as it really has) nothing elfe to recommend it. Such as it is, *Extremum hoc munus morientis habeto*; for that may well be the cafe, confidering that within a few months I am entering into my feventieth

---

* The Bifhop of Rochefter went into exile the month following, and continued in it till his death, which happen'd at Paris on the fifteenth day of February, in the year 1732.

† Earl of Clarendon's.

‡ The Bifhop's Name, fet to his Vindication of Bifhop Smalridge, Dr. Aldrich, and himfelf, from the fcandalous Reflections of Oldmixon, relating to the Publication of Lord Clarendon's Hiftory. Paris, 1731, 4to, fince reprinted in England.

year:

year: after which, even the healthy and the happy cannot much depend upon life, and will not if they are wife, much defire it. Whenever I go, you will loofe a friend who loves and values you extremely, if in my circum-ftances I can be faid to be loft to any one, when dead, more than I am already whilft living. I expected to have heard from you by Mr. Morrice, and wonder a little that I did not; but he owns himfelf in a fault, for not giving you due notice of his motions. It was not amifs that you forebore writing, on a head wherein I promis'd more than I was able to perform. Difgrac'd men fancy fometimes, that they preferve an influence, where when they endea-vour to exert it, they foon fee their miftake. I did fo, my good friend, and acknowledge it under my hand. You founded the coaft and found out my error, it feems, be-fore I was aware of it; but enough on this fubject.

What are they doing in England to the honour of letters; and particularly what are you doing? *Ipfe quid audes? Quæ circumvolitas agilis Thyma?* Do you purfue the moral plan you marked out, and feemed fixteen months ago fo intent upon? Am I to fee it perfected ere I die, and are you to enjoy the reputation of it while you live? or do you rather chufe to leave the marks of your friendfhip, like the legacies of a will, to be read and enjoyed only by thofe who furvive you? Were I as near you as I have been, I fhould hope to peep into the manufcript before it was finifhed. But alas! there is, and will ever probably be a great deal of land and fea between us. How many books have come out of late in your parts, which you think I fhould be glad to perufe? Name them: the catalogue, I believe, will not coft you much trouble. They muft be good one's indeed to chal-lenge any part of my time, now I have fo little of it left. I, who fquandered whole days heretofore, now hufband hours when the glafs begins to run low, and care not to mifpend them on trifles. At the end of the Lottery of Life, our laft minutes, like tickets left in the wheel, rife in their valuation: they are not of fo much worth perhaps in them-felves as thofe which preceded, but we are apt to prize them more, and with reafon. I do fo, my dear friend, and yet think the moft precious minutes of my life are well employed, in reading what you write. But this is a fatisfaction I cannot much hope for, and therefore muft be-take myfelf to others lefs entertaining. Adieu! dear Sir, and forgive me engaging with one, whom you, I think, have reckoned among the heroes of the Dunciad. It was ne-ceffary for me either to accept of his dirty challenge, or to have fuffered in the efteem of the world by declining it.

My

My refpects to your Mother; I fend one of thefe papers
for Dean Swift, if you have an opportunity, and think
it worth while to convey it.   My Country at this diftance
feems to me a ftrange fight; I know not how it appears
to you, who are in the midft of the fcene, and yourfelf a
part of it; I wifh you would tell me.   You may write
iafely to Mr. Morice, by the honeft hand that conveys
this, and will return into thefe parts before Chriftmas;
fketch out a rough draught of it, that I may be able to judge
whether a return to it be really eligible, or whether I
fhould not, like the Chemift in the bottle, upon hearing
Don Quevedo's account of Spain, defire to be corked up
again.

After all, I do and muft love my Country, with all its
faults and blemifhes; even that part of the conftitution
which wounded me unjuftly, and itfelf through my fide,
fhall ever be dear to me.   My laft wifh fhall be like that
of father Paul, *Efto perpetua!* and when I die at a diftance
from it, it will be in the fame manner as Virgil defcribes
the expiring Peloponnefian,

> Sternitur,
>   et dulces moriens reminifcitur Argos.

Do I ftill live in the memory of my friends, as they certainly do in mine? I have read a good many of your paper
fquabbles about me, and am glad to fee fuch free concef-
fions on that head, tho' made with no view of doing me
a pleafure, but merely of loading another.

I am, &c.

LETTER XXV.

From the Bifhop of ROCHESTER.

On the death of his Daughter.

Montpelier, Nov. 20, 1729.

I Am not yet Mafter enough of myfelf, after the late
wound I have receiv'd, to open my very heart to you,
and am not content with lefs than that, whenever I converfe with you.   My thoughts are at prefent vainly, but
pleafingly employed, on what I have loft, and can never
recover.   I know well I ought, for that reafon, to call
them off to other fubjects, but hitherto I have not been able
to do it.   By giving them the rein a little, and fuffering

VOL. IV.   Z   them

them to fpend their force, I hope in fome time to check
and fubdue them. *Multis fortunæ vulneribus perculfus, huic
uni me imparem fenfi, et pene fuccubui.* This is weaknefs not
witilom, I own; and on that account fitter to be trufted to
the bofom of a friend, where I may fafely lodge all my infirmities. As foon as my mind is in fome meafure corrected and calm'd, I will endeavour to follow your advice, and
turn it to fomething of ufe and moment; if I have ftill life
enough left to do any thing that is worth reading and preferving. In the mean time I fhall be pleas'd to hear that
you proceed in what you intend, without any fuch melancholy interruption as I have met with. Your mind is as
yet unbroken by age and ill accidents, your knowledge
and judgment are at the height: ufe them in writing
fomewhat that may teach the prefent and future times, and
if not gain equally the applaufe of both, may yet raife the envy
of the one, and fecure the admiration of the other. Employ not your precious moments, and great talents, on little men and little things; but choofe a fubject every way
worthy of you, and handle it as you can, in a manner
which nobody elfe can equal or imitate. As for me, my
abilities, if I ever had any, are not what they were: and
yet I will endeavour to recollect and employ them.

gelidus tardante fenecta
Sanguis hebet, frigentque effœto in corpore vires.

However, I fhould be ingrateful to this place, if I did not
own that I have gained upon the gout in the fouth of
France, much more than I did at Paris, tho' even there I
fenfibly improved. I believe my cure had been perfected
but the earneft defire of meeting one I dearly loved, called
me abruptly to Montpelier; where after continuing two
months, under the cruel torture of a fad and fruitlefs expectation, I was forced at laft to take a long journey to Tou-
loufe; and even there I had mifs'd the perfon I fought, had
fhe not, with great fpirit and courage, ventured all night
up the Garonne to fee me, which fhe above all things defired to do before fhe died. By that means fhe was brought
where I was, between feven and eight in the morning, and
liv'd twenty hour's afterwards, which time was not loft on
either fide, but pafs'd in fuch a manner as gave great fatisfaction to both, and fuch as, on her part, every way became her circumftances and character. For fhe had her
fenfes to the very laft gafp, and exerted them to give me,
in thofe few hours, greater marks of Duty and Love than
fhe had done in all her life-time, tho' fhe had never been
want-

wanting in either. The laft words fhe faid to me were
the kindeft of all; a' reflection on the goodnefs of God,
which had allowed us in this manner to meet once more,
before we parted for ever. Not many minutes after that,
fhe laid herfelf on her pillow, in a fleeping pofture,

placidaque ibi demum morte quievit.

udge you, Sir, what I felt, and ftill feel on this occafion,
and fpare me the trouble of defcribing it. At my age, under my infirmities, among utter ftrangers, how fhall I find
out proper reliefs and fupports? I can have none, but thofe
with which reafon and religion furnifh me, and thofe I lay
hold on, and grafp as faft as I can. I hope that He, who
laid the burthen upon me (for wife and good purpofes no
doubt) will enable me to bear it in like manner as I have
borne others, with fome degree of fortitude and firmnefs.

You fee how ready I am to relapfe into an argument
which I had quitted once before in this letter. I fhall
probably again commit the fame fault, if I continue to
write ; and therefore I ftop fhort here, and with all fincerity, affection, and efteem, bid you adieu! till we meet
either in this world, if God pleafes, or elfe in another.

I am, &c.

Z 2

L E T T E R S

M̱r.   G A Y,

From 1712 to 1732.

L E T T E R I.

Binfield, Nov. 13, 1712.

YOU writ me a very kind Letter fome months ago, and told me you were then upon the point of taking a journey into Devonfhire. That hindered my anfwering you, and I have fince feveral times inquired of you, without any fatisfaction; for fo I call the knowledge of your welfare, or of any thing that concerns you. I paft two months in Suffex, and fince my return, have been again very ill. I writ to Lintot in hopes of hearing of you, but had no anfwer to that point. Our friend Mr. Cromwell too has been filent all this year; I believe he has been difpleafed at fome or other of my freedoms *, which I very innocently take, and moft with thofe I think moft my friends. But this I know nothing of; perhaps he may have opened to you: and if I know you right, you are of a temper to cement friendfhips, and not to divide them. I really much love Mr. Cromwell, and have a true affection for yourfelf, which if I had any intereft in the world, or power with thofe who have, I fhould not be long without manifefting to you. I defire you will not, either out of modefty, or a vicious diftruft of another's value for you (thofe two

---

* We fee by the Letters to Mr. Cromwell, that Mr. Pope was wont to rally him on his turn for trifling and pedantic criticifm. So he loft his two early friends Cromwell and Wycherly, by his zeal to correct the bad poetry of the one, and the bad tafte of the other.

eternal

eternal foes to merit) imagine that your letters and converfation are not always welcome to me. There is no man
more entirely fond of good-nature or ingenuity than myfelf,
and I have feen too much of thofe qualities in you to be
any thing lefs than

Your, &c.

LETTER II.

Dec. 24, 1712.

IT has been my good fortune within this month paft, to
hear more things that have pleafed me than (I think)
almoft in all my time befide. But nothing upon my word
has been fo home-felt a fatisfaction as the news you tell me
of yourfelf : and you are not in the leaft miftaken, when you
congratulate me upon your own good fuccefs : for I have more
people out of whom to be happy, than any ill-natured man
can boaft of. I may with honefty affirm to you, that, notwithftanding the many inconveniences and difadvantages
they commonly talk of in the *Res angufti domi*, I have never found any other, than the inability of giving people of
merit the only certain proof of our value for them, in doing them fome real fervice. For after all, if we could but
think a little, felf love might make us philofophers, and
convince us *quantuli indiget Natura!* Ourfelves are eafily
provided for ; 'tis nothing but the circumftantials, and the
apparatus or equipage of human life, that coft fo much
the furnifhing. Only what a luxurious man wants for horfes,
and footmen, a good-natured man wants for his friends, or
the indigent.

I fhall fee you this winter with much greater pleafure
than I could the laft ; and, I hope, as much of your time,
as your attendance on the Duchefs * will allow you to fpare
to any friend, will not be thought loft upon one who is as
much fo as any man. I muft alfo put you in mind, tho'
you are now fecretary to this Lady, that you are likewife
fecretary to nine other ladies, and are to write fometimes
for them too. He who is forced to live wholly upon thofe
Ladies favours, is indeed in as precarious a condition as
any He who does what Chaucer fays for fuftenance ; but they
are very agreeable companions, like other Ladies, when a
man only paffes a night or fo with them at his leifure, and
away, I am

Your, &c.

* Duchefs of Monmouth, to whom he was juft then made Secretary.

LETTER

LETTER III.

Aug. 23, 1713.

JUST as I received yours, I was fet down to write to you with fome fhame that I had fo long deferred it. But I can hardly repent my neglect, when it gives me the knowledge how little you infift upon ceremony, and how much a greater fhare in your memory I have, than I deferve. I have been near a week in London, where I am like to remain, till I become, by Mr. Jervas's help, *Elegans formarum fpectator.* I begin to difcover beauties that were till now imperceptible to me. Every corner of an eye, or turn of a nofe or ear, the fmalleft degree of light or fhade on a cheek, or in a dimple, have charms to diftract me. I no longer look upon Lord Plaufible as ridiculous, for admiring a Lady's fine tip of an ear and pretty elbow (as the *Plain Dealer* has it) but am in fome danger even from the ugly and difagreeable, fince they may have their retired beauties, in one trait or other about them. You may guefs in how uncafy a ftate I am, when every day the performances of others appear more beautiful and excellent, and my own more defpicable. I have thrown away three Dr. Swifts, each of which was once my vanity, two Lady Bridgwaters, a Duchefs of Montague, befides half a dozen Earls, and one Knight of the garter. I have crucified Chrift over again in effigy, and made a Madona as old as her mother St. Anne. Nay, what is yet more miraculous, I have rivall'd St. Luke himfelf in painting, and as, 'tis faid, an angel came and finifhed his piece, fo you would fwear, a devil put the laft hand to mine, 'tis fo begrimed and fmutted. However, I comfort myfelf with a Chriftian reflection, that I have not broken the commandment, for my pictures are not the likenefs of any thing that is in heaven above, or in earth below, or in the water under the earth. Neither will any body adore or worfhip them, except the Indians fhould have a fight of them, who, they tell us, worfhip certain idols purely for their uglinefs.

I am very much recreated and refrefhed with the news of the advancement of the *Fan* *, which, I doubt not, will delight the eye and fenfe of the Fair, as long as that agreeable machine fhall play in the hands of pofterity. I am glad your fan is mounted fo foon, but I would have you

---

* A Poem of Mr. Gay's, fo intitled.

varnifh

varnifh and glaze it at your leifure, and polifh the fticks as much as you can. You may then caufe it to be borne in the hands of both fexes, no lefs in Britain than it is in China; where it is ordinary for a Mandarine to fan himfelf cool after a debate, and a Statefman to hide his face with it when he tells a grave lye.

I am, &c.

LETTER IV.

DEAR MR. GAY,   Sept. 23, 1714.

WELCOME to your native foil ! * welcome to your friends ! thrice welcome to me ! whether returned in glory, bleft with court intereft, the love and familiarity of the great, and filled with agreeable hopes ; or melancholy with dejeftion, contemplative of the changes of fortune, and doubtful for the future : Whether returned a triumphant Whig, or a defponding Tory, equally all hail ! equally beloved and welcome to me ! If happy, I am to partake in your elevation : if unhappy you have ftill a warm corner in my heart, and a retreat at Binfield in the worft of times at your fervice. If you are a Tory, or thought fo by any man, I know it can proceed from nothing but your gratitude to a few people who endeavoured to ferve you, and whofe politics were never your concern. If you are a Whig, as I rather hope, and as I think, your principles and mine (as brother poets) had ever a bias to the fide of liberty, I know you will be an honeft man and an inoffenfive one. Upon the whole, I know you are incapable of being fo much of either party as to be good for nothing. Therefore once more, whatever you are, or in whatever ftate you are, all hail !

One or two of your old friends complain'd they had heard nothing from you fince the Queen's death ; I told them no man living lov'd Mr. Gay better than I, yet I had not once written to him in all his voyage. This I thought a convincing proof, how truly one may be a friend to another without telling him fo every month. But they had reafons to themfelves to allege in your excufe ; as men who really value one another, will never want fuch as make their friends and themfelves eafy. The late univerfal concern

* In the beginning of this year Mr. Gay went over to Hanover with the Earl of Clarendon, who was fent thither by Queen Anne. On her death they returned to England : and it was on this occafion that Mr. Pope met him with this friendly welcome.

in public affairs, threw us all into a hurry of spirits: even
I, who am more a philosopher than to expect any thing
from any Reign, was borne away with the current, and
full of the expectation of the Succeffor. During your
journey I knew not whither to aim a letter after you; that
was a fort of shooting flying: add to this, the demand Homer had upon me, to write fifty verses a day, befides
learned notes, all which are at a conclufion for this year.
Rejoice with me, O my Friend, that my labour is over;
come and make merry with me in much feafting : We will
feed among the lilies (by the lilies I mean the Ladies.)
Are not the Rofalindas of Britain as charming as the
Bloufalindas of the Hague? or have the two great Paftoral poets of our nation renounced love at the fame time ?
for Philips, immortal Philips, hath deferted, yea, and in a
ruftic manner, kicked his Rofalinda. Dr. Parnell and I
have been infeparable ever fince you went. We are now
at the Bath, where (if you are not, as I heartily hope,
better engaged) your coming would be the greateft pleafure to us in the world. Talk not of expences : Homer
fhall fupport his children. I beg a line from you directed
to the Poft-houfe in Bath. Poor Parnell is in an ill ftate
of health.

Pardon me if I add a word of advice in the poetical way.
Write fomething on the King, or Prince, or Princefs.
On whatfoever foot you may be with the court, this can
do no harm.—I fhall never know where to end, and am
confounded in the many things I have to fay to you,
though they all amount but to this, that I am entirely as
ever,   Your, &c.

LETTER V.

London, Nov. 8, 1717.

I Am extremely glad to find by a Letter of yours to Mr.
Fortefcue, that you have received one from me; and
I beg you to keep, as the greateft of curiofities, that let-
ter of mine which you received, and I never writ.

But the truth is, that we were made here to expect you in
a fhort time, that I was upon the ramble moft part of the
Summer, and have concluded the feafon in grief, for the
death of my poor father.

I fhall not enter into a detail of my concerns and troubles, for two reafons; becaufe I am really afflicted and
need no airs of grief, and becaufe they are not the concerns

cerns and troubles of any but myfelf. But I think you (without too great a compliment) enough my friend, to be pleafed to know he died eafily, without a groan, or the ficknefs of two minutes; in a word, as filently and peacefully as he lived.

Sic mihi contingat vivere, ficque mori!

I am not in the humour to fay gay things, nor in the affeftation of avoiding them. I can't pretend to entertain either Mr. Pultney or you, as you have done both my Lord Burlington and me, by your letter to Mr. Lowndes*. I am only forry you have no greater quarrel to Mr. Lowndes, and wifh you paid fome hundreds a year to the land-tax. That gentleman is lately become an inoffen-five perfon to me too: fo that we may join heartily in our addreffes to him, and (like true patriots) rejoice in all that good done to the nation and government, to which we contribute nothing ourfelves.

I fhould not forget to acknowledge your letter fent from Aix; you told me then that writing was not good with the waters, and, I find fince, you are of my opinion, that 'tis as bad without the waters. But, I fancy, it is not writ-ing but thinking, that is fo bad with the waters; and then you might write without any manner of prejudice, if you writ like our brother poets of thefe days.

The Duchefs, Lord Warwick, Lord Stanhope, Mrs. Bellenden, Mrs. Lepell, and I can't tell who elfe, had your letters: Dr. Arbuthnot and I expeft to be treated like friends. I would fend my fervices to Mr. Pultney, but that he is out of favour at court; and make fome com-pliment to Mrs. Pulteney, if fhe were not a Whig. My Lord Burlington tells me fhe has as much out-fhined all the French ladies, as fhe did the Englifh before: I am forry for it, becaufe it will be detrimental to our holy re-ligion, if heretical women fhould eclipfe thofe Nuns and orthodox Beauties, in whofe eyes alone lie all the hopes we can have, of gaining fuch fine gentlemen as you to our church.   Yours, &c.

I wifh you joy of the birth of the young prince, becaufe he is the only prince we have from whom you have had no expeftations and no difappointments.

---

* A Poem intituled, *To my ingenious and worthy friend W. Lowndes, Efq; Au-thor of that celebrated treatife in Folio, call'd the* LAND-TAX BILL

LETTER VI.

From Mr. GAY to Mr. F———.

Stanton-Harcourt Aug, 9, 1718.

THE only news that you can expect to have from me
here, is news from heaven, for I am quite out of the
world, and there is scarce any thing can reach me except
the noise of thunder, which undoubtebly you have heard
too. We have read in old authors of high towers levell'd
by it to the ground, while the humble valleys have escap'd:
the only thing that is proof against it is the laurel, which,
however, I take to be no great security to the brains of
modern authors. But to let you see that the contrary to
this often happens, I must acquaint you, that the highest
and most extravagant heap of towers in the universe, which
is in this neighbourhood, stand still undefaced, while a
cock of barley in our next field has been confumed to
ashes. Would to God that this heap of barley had been
all that had perished! for unhappily beneath this little
shelter sat two much more constant Lovers than ever were
found in romance under the shade of a beech-tree. John
Hewet was a well-set man of about five and twenty, Sarah
Drew might be rather called comely than beautiful, and
was about the same age. They had pass'd through the various labours of the year together, with the greatest satisfaction; if she milk'd, 'twas his morning and evening care
to bring the cows to her hand; it was but last fair that he
bought her a present of green silk for her straw hat, and the
posie on her silver ring was of his chusing. Their love
was the talk of the whole neighbourhood; for scandal never
affirmed that they had any other views than the lawful
possession of each other in marriage. It was that very
morning that he had obtain'd the consent of her parents,
and it was but till the next week that they were to wait to
be happy. Perhaps in the intervals of their work they
were now talking of the wedding cloaths, and John was
suiting several forts of poppies and field flowers to her
complexion, to chuse her a knot for the wedding-day.
While they were thus busied (it was on the last of July between two and three in the afternoon) the clouds grew
black, and such a storm of lightning and thunder enfued,
that all the labourers made the best of their way to what
shelter the trees and hedges afforded. Sarah was frighted,
and fell down in a swoon, on a heap of barley. John, who
never separated from her, sat down by her side, having
raked

raked together two or three heaps, the better to fecure her
from the ftorm. Immediately there was heard fo loud a crack,
as if heaven had fplit afunder; every one was now folicitous for the fafety of his neighbour, and call'd to one another throughout the field; No anfwer being returned to
thofe who called to our Lovers, they ftept to the place
where they lay, they perceived the barley all in a fmoke,
and then fpied this faithful pair: John with one arm
about Sarah's neck, and the other held over her as to
ikreen her from the lightning. They were ftruck dead,
and ftiffen'd in this tender pofture. Sarah's left eye-brow
was fing'd, and there appeared a black fpot on her breaft:
her lover was all over black, but not the leaft figns of life
were found in either. Attended by their melancholy companions, they were convey'd to the town, and the next day
were interr'd in Stanton-Harcourt Church-yard. My
Lord Harcourt, at Mr. Pope's and my requeft, has caufed
a ftone to be placed over them, upon condition that we
furnifh'd the Epitaph, which is as follows;

> When Eaftern lovers feed the fun'ral fire,
> On the fame pile the faithful pair expire:
> Here pitying Heav'n that virtue mutual found,
> And blafted both, that it might neither wound.
> Hearts fo fincere th' Almighty faw well pleas'd,
> Sent his own lightning, and the victims feiz'd.

But my Lord is apprehenfive the country people will not
underftand this, and Mr. Pope fays he'll make one with
fomething of Scripture in it, and with as little of poety as
Hopkins and Sternhold *.

Your, &c.

* The Epitaph was this,

> Near this place lie the bodies of
> JOHN HEWET and MARY DREW,
> an induftrious young Man
> and Virtuous Maid of this Parifh;
> Who, being at Harveft Work
> (with feveral others)
> were in one inftant killed by Lightning
> the laft day of July 1718.
> Think not by rig'rous Judgment feiz'd,
> A Pair fo faithful could expire;
> Victims fo pure Heav'n faw well pleas'd,
> And fnatch'd them in celeftial fire.

> Live well, and fear no fudden fate;
> When God calls Virtue to the grave,
> Alike 'tis Juftice foon or late,
> Mercy alike to kill or fave.

> Virtue unmov'd can hear the call,
> And face the flafh that melts the ball,

LETTER VII.

DEAR GAY. Sept. 11, 1722.

I Thank you for remembering me ; I would do my beft to forget myfelf, but that, I find, your idea is fo clofely connected to me, that I muft forget both together, or neither. I am forry I could not have a glympfe either of you, or of the Sun (your father) before you went for Bath : But now it pleafes me to fee him, and hear of you. Pray put Mr. Congreve in mind that he has one on this fide of the world who loves him ; and that there are more men and women in the univerfe than Mr. Gay and my Lady Duchefs. There are ladies in and about Richmond, that pretend to value him and yourfelf ; and one of them at leaft may be thought to do it without affectation, namely Mrs. Howard.

Pray confult with Dr. Arbuthnot and Dr. Cheyne, to what exact pitch your belly may be fuffer'd to fwell, not to outgrow theirs, who are, yet, your betters. Tell Dr. Arbuthnot that even pigeon-pies and hogs puddings are thought dangerous by our governors ; for thofe that have been fent to the Bifhop of Rochefter are open'd and prophanely pry'd into at the Tower : 'Tis the firft time dead pigeons have been fufpected of carrying intelligence. To be ferious, you and Mr Congreve and the Doctor will be fenfible of my concern and furprize at his commitment, whofe welfare is as much my concern as any friend's I have. I think myfelf a moft unfortunate wretch : I no fooner love, and, upon knowledge fix my efteem to any man, but he either dies like Mr. Craggs, or is fent to imprifonment, like the Bifhop. God fend him as well as I wifh him, manifeft him to be as innocent as I believe him, and make all his enemies know him as well as I do, that they may think of him as well !

If you apprehend this period to be of any danger in being addrefled to you, tell Mr. Congreve or the Doctor, it is writ to them. I am Your, &c.

LETTER VIII.

July 13, 1722.

I Was very much pleafed, not to fay obliged, by your kind letter, which fufficiently warm'd my heart to have anfwered it fooner, had I not been deceived (a way one often
ten

ten is deceived) by hearkening to women ; who told me that both Lady Burlington and yourself were immediately to return from Tunbridge, and that my Lord was gone to bring you back.   The world furnishes us with too many examples of what you complain of in yours, and I affure you, none of them touch and grieve me fo much as what relates to you.   I think your fentiments upon it are the very fame I fhould entertain : I wifh thofe we call great men had the fame notions, but they are really the moft little creatures in the world ; and the moft interefted, in all but one point ; which is, that they want judgment * to know their greateft intereft, to encourage and chufe honeft men for their friends.

I have not once feen the perfon you complain of, whom I have of late thought to be, as the Apoftle admonifheth, one flesh with his wife.   ,,

Pray make my fincere compliments to Lord Burlington, whom I have long known to have a ftronger bent of mind to be all that is good and honourable, than almoft any one of his rank.

I have not forgot yours to Lord Bolingbroke, tho' I hope to have fpeedily a fuller opportunity, he returning for Flanders and France next month.

Mrs. Howard has writ you fomething or other in a letter, which, fhe fays, fhe repents.   She has as much good-nature as if fhe had never feen any ill-nature, and had been bred among lambs and turtle-doves, inftead of Princes and court-ladies.

By the end of this week, Mr. Fortefcue will pafs a few days with me : we fhall remember you in our potations, and wifh you a fisher with us, on my grafs-plat.   In the mean time we wifh you fuccefs as a fisher of women at the Wells, a rejoicer of the comfortlefs and widow, and a play-fellow of the maiden.   I am   Your, &c.

LETTER IX.

Sept. 11, 1722.

I Think it obliging in you to defire an account of my health.   The truth is, I have never been in a worfe ftate in my life, and find whatever I have try'd as a remedy fo ineffectual, that I gave myfelf intirely over.   I wifh your health may be fet perfectly right by the waters ; and be affured, I not only wifh that, and every thing elfe for

* Inftead of—*that they want judgment*, propriety of ex. reffion, requires he fhould have faid——*there where they want judgment*.

you,

you, as common friends wish, but with a zeal not usual among those we call so. I am always glad to hear of, and from you; always glad to see you, what ever accidents or amusements have interven'd to make me do either less than usual. I not only frequently think of you, but constantly do my best to make others do it, by mentioning you to all your acquaintance. I desire you to do the same for me to those you are now with: do me what you think justice in regard to those who are my friends, and if there are any, whom I have unwillingly deserved so little of as to be my enemies, I don't desire you to forfeit their opinion, or your own judgment in any case. Let time convince those who know me not, that I am an inoffensive person; tho' (to say truth) I don't care how little I am indebted to Time, for the world is hardly worth living in, at least to one that is never to have health a week together. I have been made to expect Dr. Arbuthnot in town this fortnight, or else I had written to him. If he, by never writing to me, seems to forget me, I consider I do the same seemingly to him, and yet I don't believe he has a more sincere friend in the world than I am: therefore I will think him mine. I am his, Mr. Congreve's, and   Your, &c.

LETTER X.

I Faithfully assure you, in the midst of that melancholy with which I have been so long encompassed, in an hourly expectation almost of my Mother's death; there was no circumstance that rendered it more insupportable to me, than that I could not leave her to see you. Your own present escape from so imminent danger, I pray God may prove less precarious than my poor Mother's can be; whose life at best can be but a short Reprieve or a longer dying. But I fear, even that is more than God will please to grant me, for, these two days past, her most dangerous symptoms are returned upon her; and unless there be a sudden change, I must, in a few days, if not in a few hours, be deprived of her. In the afflicting prospect before me, I know nothing that can so much alleviate it as the view now given me (Heaven grant it may increase!) of your recovery. In the sincerity of my heart, I am excessively concern'd not to be able to pay you, dear Gay, any part of the debt, I very gratefully remember I owe you on a like sad occasion, when you was here comforting me in her last great illness. May your health augment as fast as I fear hers must decline: I believe that would be very fast—may the life that

is added to you be paft in good fortune and tranquillity, rather of your own giving to yourfelf, than from any expectations or truft in others. May you and I live together
without wifhing more felicity or acquifitions than Friendfhip can give and receive without obligations to Greatnefs.
God keep you, and three or four more of thofe I have
known as long, that I may have fomething worth the fur-
viving my Mother.   Adieu, dear Gay, and believe me
(while you live and while I live)   Your, &c.
    As I told you in my laft letter, I repeat it in this: Do
not think of writing to me. The Doctor, Mrs. Howard,
and Mrs. Blount give me daily accounts of you.

LETTER XI.

Sunday Night,

I Truly rejoiced to fee your hand-writing, though I feared
  the trouble it might give you. I wifh I had not known
that you are ftill fo exceffively weak. Every day for a
week paft I had hopes of being able in a day or two more
to fee you. But my Mother advances not at all, gains
no ftrength, and feems but upon the whole to wait for the
next cold day to throw her into a Diarrhœa, that muft, if
it return, carry her off. This being daily to be feared,
makes me not dare to go a day from her, left that fhould
prove to be her laft. God fend you a fpeedy recovery, and
fuch a total one as, at your time of life, may be expected.
You need not call the few words I writ to you either kind
or good; that was, and is, nothing. But whatever I have
in my nature of kindnefs, I really have for you, and whatever good I could do, I would, among the very firft, be
glad to do to you. In your circumftance the old Roman
farewell is proper, *Vive memor noftri.*   Your, &c.
    I fend you a very kind letter of Mr. Digby, between
whom and me two letters have pafs'd concerning you.

LETTER XII.

NO words can tell you the great concern I feel for you;
  I affure you it was not, and is not leffened, by the
immediate apprehenfion I have now every day lain under
of loofing my mother. Be affured no duty lefs than that
fhould have kept me one day from attending your condition: I would come and take a room by you at Hampftead, to be with you daily, were fhe not ftill in danger of
death. I have conftantly had particular accounts of you
from the Doctor, which have not ceafed to alarm me yet.
God

God preferve your life, and reftore your health. I really
beg it for my own fake, for I feel I love you more than I
thought in health, tho' I always loved you a great deal.
If I am fo unfortunate as to bury my poor mother, and yet
have the good fortune to have my prayers heard for you,
I hope we may live moft of our remaining days together.
If, as I believe, the air of a better clime as the Southern
part of France, may be thought ufeful for your recovery,
thither would I go with you infallibly; and it is very probable we might get the Dean with us, who is in that abandoned ftate already in which I fhall fhortly be, as to other
cares and duties. Dear Gay, be as chearful as your fufferings will permit: God is a better friend than a Court; even
any honeft man is a better. I promife you my entire friendfhip in all events, heartily praying for your recovery.

Your, &c.

Do not write, if you are ever fo able: the Doctor tells
me all.

LETTER XIII.

I Am glad to hear of the progrefs of your recovery, and
the oftener I hear it, the better, when it becomes eafy
to you to give it me. I fo well remember the confolation
you were to me in my Mother's former illnefs, that it doubles my concern at this time not to be able to be with you,
or you able to be with me. Had I loft her, I would have
been no where elfe but with you during your confinement.
I have now paft five weeks without once going from home,
and without any company but for three or four of the days.
Friends rarely ftretch their kindnefs fo far as ten miles.
My Lord Bolingbroke and Mr. Bethel have not forgotten
to vifit me: the reft (except Mrs. Blount once) were contented to fend meffages. I never paffed fo melancholy a
time, and now Mr. Congreve's death touches me nearly.
It was twenty years and more that I have known him:
Every year carries away fomething dear with it, till we
outlive all tendernefſes, and become wretched individual ̄
again as we begun. Adieu! This is my birth-day, and
this is my reflection upon it.

> With added days if life give nothing new,
> But, like a fieve, let ev'ry pleafure thro';
> Some Joy ftill loft, as each vain year runs o'er,
> And all we gain, fome fad Reflection more!
> Is this a birth-day?—'Tis alas too clear,
> 'Tis but the fun'ral of the former year.

Your, &c.

LETTER XIV.
To the Honourable Mrs. ———

June 20.

WE cannot omit taking this occasion to congratulate you upon the increase of your family, for your Cow is this morning very happily delivered of the better fort, I mean a female calf; she is as like her mother as she can stare. All Knights Errants Palfreys were distinguished by lofty names; we see no reason why a Pastoral Lady's sheep and calves should want names of the softer sound; we have therefore given her the name of Cæsar's wife, Calfurnia: imagining, that as Romulus and Remus were suckled by a wolf, this Roman lady was suckled by a cow, from whence she took that name. In order to celebrate this birth-day, we had a cold dinner at Marble-hill *. Mrs. Susan offered us wine upon the occasion, and upon such an occasion we could not refuse it. Our entertainment consisted of flesh and fish, and the lettuce of a Greek Island called Cos. We have some thoughts of dining there to-morrow, to celebrate the day after the birth-day, and on Friday to celebrate the day after that, where we intend to entertain Dean Swift; because we think your hall the most delightful room in the world except that where you are. If it was not for you, we would forswear all courts; and really it is the most mortifying thing in nature, that we can neither get into the court to live with you, nor you get into the country to live with us; so we will take up with what we can get that belongs to you, and make ourselves as happy as we can in your house.

I hope we shall be brought into no worse company, when you all come to Richmond: for whatever our friend Gay may wish as to getting into Court, I disclaim it, and desire to see nothing of the court but yourself, being wholly and solely   Your, etc.

LETTER XV.
July 21.

YOU have the same share in my memory that good things generally have; I always know (whenever I reflect) that you should be in my mind; only I reflect too seldom.

* Mrs. Howard's House. -

However, you ought to allow me the indulgence I allow all my friends (and if I did not, they would take it) in confideration that they have other avocations, which may prevent the proofs of their remembring me, though they preferve for me all the friendfhip and good-will which I deferve from them. In like manner I expect from you, that my paft life of twenty years may be fet againft the omiffion of (perhaps) one month: and if you complain of this to any other, 'tis you are in the fpleen, and not I in the wrong. If you think this letter fplenetic, confider I have juft received the news of the death of a friend, whom I efteemed almoft as many years as you; poor Fenton. He died at Eafthamftead, of indolence and inactivity; let it not be your fate, but ufe exercife. I hope the Duchefs * will take care of you in this refpect, and either make you gallop after her, or teize you enough at home to ferve inftead of exercife abroad. Mrs. Howard is fo concerned about you, and fo angry at me for not writing to you, and at Mrs. Blount for not doing the fame, that I am piqu'd with jealoufy and envy at you, and hate you as much as if you had a great place at court; which you will confefs a proper caufe of envy and hatred, in any Poet militant or unpenfioned. But to fet matters even, I own I love you; and own, I am, as I ever was, and juft as I ever fhall be, Your, etc.

LETTER XVI.

Dear Sir, Oct. 6, 1727.

I Have many years ago magnify'd, in my own mind, and repeated to you, a ninth Beatitude, added to the eight in the Scripture; " Bleffed is he who expects nothing, for " he fhall never be difappointed." I could find in my heart to congratulate you on this happy difmiffion from all Court-dependance; I dare fay I fhall find you the better and the honefter man for it, many years hence: very probably the healthfuller, and the chearfuller into the bargain. You are happily rid of many curfed ceremonies, as well as of many ill and vicious habits, of which few or no men efcape the infection, who are hackney'd and tramelled in the ways of a court. Princes indeed, and Peers (the lackies of Princes) and Ladies (the fools of |Peers) will fmile on you the lefs; but men of worth and real

* Of Queenfberry.

friends

friends will look on you the better. There is a thing, the only thing which Kings and Queens cannot give you (for they have it not to give) Liberty, and which is worth all they have; which, as yet, I thank God, Englishmen need not ask from their hands. You will enjoy that, and your own integrity, and the satisfactory consciousness of having *not* merited such graces from courts as are bestowed only on the mean, servile, flattering, interested, and undeserving. The only steps to the favour of the Great are such complacencies, such compliances, such distant decorums, as delude them in their vanities, or engage them in their passions. He is their greatest favourite, who is the falsest: and when a man, by such vile gradations, arrives at the height of grandeur and power, he is then at best but in a circumstance to be hated, and in a condition to be hanged, for serving their ends: so many a Minister has found it !

I believe you did not want advice, in the letter you sent by my Lord Grantham; I presume you writ it not, without: and you could not have better, if I guess right at the person who agreed to your doing it, in respect to any decency you ought to observe: for I take that person to be a perfect judge of decencies and forms. I am not without fears even on that person's account: I think it a bad omen: but what have I to do with Court-omens?—Dear Gay, adieu. I can only add a plain uncourtly speech: While you are no body's servant, you may be any one's friend; and as such I embrace you, in all conditions of life. While I have a shilling, you shall have six-pence, nay eight-pence, if I can contrive to live upon a groat. I am faithfully   Your, etc.

LETTER XVII.

From Mr. GAY to Mr. POPE.

Aug. 2, 1728.

'TWAS two or three weeks ago that I writ you a letter; I might indeed have done it sooner; I thought of you every post-day upon that account, and every other day upon some account or other. I must beg you to give Mrs. B. my sincere thanks for her kind way of thinking of me, which I have heard of more than once from our friend at court, who seem'd in the letter she writ to be in high health

and fpirits. Confidering the multiplicity of pleafures and
delights that one is over-run with in thofe places, I wonder how any body hath health and fpirits enough to fupport them : I am heartily glad fhe has, and whenever I hear
fo, I find it contributes to mine. You fee I am not free
from dependance, tho' I have lefs attendance than I had
formerly : for a great deal of my own welfare ftill depends
upon hers. Is the widow's houfe to be difpos'd of yet ? I
have not given up my pretenfions to the Dean ; if it was
to be parted with, I wifh one of us had it ; I hope you wifh
fo too, and that Mrs. Blount and Mrs. Howard wifh the
fame, and for the very fame reafon that I wifh it. All I
could hear of you of late hath been by advertifements in
news-papers, by which one would think the race of Curls
was multiplied ; and, by the indignation fuch fellows fhow
againft you, that you have more merit than any body alive
could have. Homer himfelf hath not been worfe us'd by
the French. I am to tell you that the Duchefs makes you
her compliments, and is always inclin'd to like any thing
you do ; that Mr. Congreve admires, with me, your fortitude : and loves, net envies, your performance, for we
are not Dunces.   Adieu.

LETTER XVIII.

April 18, 1730.

IF my friendfhip were as effectual as it is fincere, you
would be one of thofe people who would be vaftly ad-
vantaged and enrich'd by it. I ever honour'd thofe Popes
who were moft famous for Nepotifm ; 'tis a fign that the
old fellows loved Somebody, which is not ufual in fuch
advanced years. And I now honour Sir Robert Walpole
for his extenfive bounty and goodnefs to his private friends
and relations. But it vexes me to the heart when I reflect,
that my friendfhip is fo much lefs effectual than theirs ;
nay fo utterly ufelefs that it cannot give you any thing,
not even a dinner at this diftance, nor help the General
whom I greatly love, to catch one fifh. My only confolation is to think you happier than myfelf, and to begin to
envy you, which is next to hating you (an excellent remedy for love.) How comes it that Providence has been
fo unkind to me (who am a greater object of compaffion
than any fat man alive) that I am forced to drink wine,
while you riot in water, prepared with oranges by the hand
of

of the Duchefs of Queenfberry? that I am condemned to
live by a highway fide, like an old Patriarch, receiving
all guefts, where my portico (as Virgil has it)

Mane falutantum totis vomit aedibus undam,

while you are wrapt in the Idalian Groves, fprinkled with
rofe-water, and live in burrage, balm, and burnet up to
the chin, with the Duchefs of Queenfberry; that I am
doom'd to the drudgery of dining at court with the ladies
in waiting at Windfor, while you are happily banifh'd
with the Duchefs of Queenfberry? So partial is Fortune
in her difpenfations! for I deferved ten times more to be
banifh'd than you, and I know fome Ladies who merit it
better than even her Grace. After this I muft not name
any, who dare do fo much for you as to fend you their
fervices. But one there is, who exhorts me often to write
to you, I fuppofe, to prevent or excufe her not doing it
herfelf; fhe feems (for that is all I'll fay for a courtier)
to wifh you mighty well. Another, who is no courtier,
frequently mentions you, and does certainly wifh you
well.—I fancy, after all, they both do fo.

I writ to Mr. Fortefcue, and told him the pains you
took to fee him. The Dean is well; I have had many accounts of him from Irifh evidence, but only two letters
thefe four months, in both which you are mentioned kindly: he is in the north of Ireland, doing I know not what,
with I know not whom. Mr. Cleland always fpeaks of
you: he is at Tunbridge, wondering at the fuperior car-
nivoracity of our friend: he plays now with the old Duchefs, nay dines with her, after fhe has won all his money.
Other news I know not, but that Counfellor Bickford has
hurt himfelf, and has the ftrongeft walking-ftaff I ever
faw. He intends fpeedily to make you a vifit with it at
Amefbury. I am my Lord Duke's, my Lady Duchefs's,
Mr. Dormer's, General Dormer's, and   Your, etc.

LETTER XIX.

Sept. 11, 1730.

I May with great truth return your fpeech, that I think
of you daily; oftner indeed than is confiftent with the
character of a reafonable man, who is rather to make himfelf eafy with the things and men that are about him than
uneafy

uneafy for thofe which he wants.   And you, whofe abfence is in a manner perpetual to me, ought rather to be
remembered as a good man gone, than breathed after as
one living.   You are taken from us here, to be laid up in
a more bleffed ftate with fpirits of a higher kind : fuch I
reckon his Grace and her Grace, fince their banifhment
from an earthly court to a heavenly one, in each other
and their friends; for, I conclude, none but true friends,
will confort or affociate with them afterwards.   I can't
but look upon myfelf (fo unworthy as a man of Twitnam
feems, to be rank'd with fuch rectify'd and fublimated
beings as you) as a feparated fpirit too from Courts and
courtly fopperies.   But, I own, not altogether fo divefted of terrene matter, nor altogether fo fpiritualized, as
to be worthy admiffion to your depths of retirement and
contentment.   I am tugg'd back to the world and its regards too often ; and no wonder, when my retreat is but
ten miles from the capital.   I am within ear-fhot of reports, within the vortex of lies and cenfures.   I hear fometimes of the lampooners of beauty, the calumniators of
virtue, the jokers at reafon and religion.   I prefume thefe
are creatures and things as unknown to you, as we of this
dirty orb are to the inhabitants of the planet Jupiter; except a few fervent prayers reach you on the wings of the
poft, from two or three of your zealous votaries at this
diftance : as one Mrs. H. who lifts up her heart now and
then to you, from the midft of the Colluvies and fink of
human greatnefs at W—r ; one Mrs. B. that fancies you
may remember her while you liv'd in your mortal and too
tranfitory ftate at Peterfham ; one Lord B. who admir'd
the Duchefs before fhe grew a Goddefs ; and a few others.

To defcend now to tell you what are our wants, our
complaints, and our miferies here ; I muft ferioufly fay,
the lofs of any one good woman is too great to be borne
eafily : and poor Mrs. Rollinfon, tho' a private woman,
was fuch.   Her hufband is gone into Oxfordfhire very melancholy, and thence to the Bath, to live on, for fuch is
our fate, and duty.   Adieu.   Write to me as often as you
will, and (to encourage you) I will write as feldom as if
you did not.   Believe me

Your, etc,

LETTER

LETTER XX.

DEAR SIR,   Octob. 1, 1730.

I Am fomething like the fun at this feafon, withdrawing
from the world, but meaning it mighty well, and re-
folving to fhine whenever I can again.   But I fear the
clouds of a long winter will overcome me to fuch a degree,
that any body will take a farthing candle for a better guide,
and more ferviceable companion. My friends may remember my brighter days, but will think (like the Irifhman)
that the moon is a better thing when once I am gone.
I don't fay this with any allufion to my poetical capacity as
a fon of Apollo, but in my companionable one (if you'll
fuffer me to ufe a phrafe of the Earl of Clarendon's), for
I fhall fee or be feen of few of you this winter.   I am
grown too faint to do any good, or to give any pleafure.
I not only, as Dryden finely fays, feel my notes decay as
a poet, but feel my fpirits flag as a companion, and fhall
return again to where I firft began, my books.   I have
been putting my library in order, and enlarging the chim-
ney in it, with equal intention to warm my mind and body
(if I can) to fome life.   A friend (a woman-friend, God
help me!) with whom I have fpent three or four hours a
day thefe fifteen years, advifed me to pafs more time in my
ftudies : I reflected, fhe muft have found fome reafon for
this admonition, and concluded fhe would complete all
her kindneffes to me by returning me to the employment
I am fitteft for; converfation with the dead, the old, and
the worm-eaten.

Judge therefore if I might not treat you as a beatify'd
fpirit, comparing your life with my ftupid ftate.   For as
to my living at Windfor with the ladies, etc. it is all a
dream; I was there but two nights, and all the day
out of that company. I fhall certainly make as little court
to others as they do to me ; and that will be none at all.
My fair-weather friends of the fummer are going away for
London, and I fhall fee them and the butterflies together,
if I live till next year ; which I would not defire to do, if
it were only for their fakes. But we that are writers, ought
to love pofterity, that pofterity may love us ; and I would
willingly live to fee the children of the prefent race, merely
in hope they may be a little wifer than their Parents.

                                        I am, etc.

LETTER

LETTER XXI.

IT is true that I write to you very feldom, and have no pretence of writing which fatisfies me, becaufe I have nothing to fay that can give you much pleafure : only merely that I am in being, which in truth is of little confequence to one from whofe converfation I am cut off by fuch accidents or engagements as feparate us. I continue, and ever fhall, to wifh you all good and happinefs : I wifh that fome lucky event might fet you in a ftate of eafe and independency all at once ; and that I might live to fee you as happy as this filly world and fortune can make any one. Are we never to live together more, as once we did ? I find my life ebbing apace, and my affeⓚions ftrengthening as my age increafes ; not that I am worfe, but better, in my health than laft winter ; but my mind finds no amendment nor improvement, nor fupport to lean upon, from thofe about me : and fo I find myfelf leaving the world, as faft as it leaves me. Companions I have enough, friends few, and thofe too warm in the concerns of the world, for me to bear pace with ; or elfe fo divided from me, that they are but like the dead whofe remembrance I hold in honour. Nature, temper, and habit from my youth made me have but one ftrong defire ; all other ambitions, my perfon, education, conftitution, religion, etc. confpired to remove far from me. That defire was to fix and preferve a few lafting dependable friendfhips : and the accidents which have difappointed me in it, have put a period to all my aims. So I am funk into an idlenefs, which makes me neither care nor labour to be noticed by the reft of mankind ; I purpofe no rewards to myfelf, and why fhould I take any fort of pains ? here I fit and fleep, and probably here I fhall fleep till I fleep for ever, like the old man of Verona. I hear of what paffes in the bufy world with fo little attention, that I forget it the next day : and as to the learned world there is nothing paffes in it. I have no more to add, but that I am with the fame truth as ever,

Your, etc.

LETTER XXII.

Oꝗ. 23, 1730.

YOUR letter is a very kind one, but I can't fay fo pleafing to me as many of yours have been, thro' the account you give of the dejeⓚion of your fpirits. I wifh the

too

too conſtant uſe of water does not contribute to it; I find
Dr. Arbuthnot and another very knowing phyſician of that
opinion. I alſo wiſh you were not ſo totally immerſed in
the country; I hope your return to town will be a prevalent remedy againſt the evil of too much recollection. I
wiſh it partly for my own ſake. We have lived little together of late, and we wantto be phyſicians for one another.
It is a remedy that agreed very well with us both for many
years, and I fancy our conſtitutions would mend upon the
old medicine of *Studiorum ſimilitudo*, etc. I believe we both
of us want whetting; there are ſeveral here who will do
you that good office, merely for the love of wit, which
ſeems to be bidding the town a long and laſt adieu. I can
tell you of not one thing worth reading, or ſeeing; the whole
age ſeems reſolved to juſtify the Dunciad, and it may ſtand
for a public Epitaph or monumental Inſcription like that
at Thermopylae, on a *whole people periſh'd!* There may indeed be a Wooden image or two of Poetry ſet up, to preſerve the memory that there once were bards in Britain;
and (like the Giants at Guildhall) ſhew the bulk and bad
taſte of our anceſtors: At preſent the poor Laureat * and
Stephen Duck ſerve for this purpoſe; a drunken ſot of a
Parſon holds forth the emblem of *Inſpiration*, and an honeſt
induſtrious *Threſher* not unaptly repreſents *Pains* and *Labour*. I hope this Phænomenon of Wiltſhire has appeared
at Ameſbury, or the Ducheſs will be thought inſenſible
to all bright qualities and exalted geniuſes, in court and
country alike. But he is a harmleſs man, and therefore I
am glad.

This is all the news talk'd of at court, but it will pleaſe
you better to hear that Mrs. Howard talks of you, though
not in the ſame breath with the Threſher, as they do of
me. By the way, have you ſeen or convers'd with Mr.
Chubb, who is a wonderful Phænomenon of Wiltſhire?
I have read thro' his whole volume † with admiration of
the writer; tho' not always with approbation of the doctrine. I have paſt juſt three days in London in four months,
two at Windſor, half a one at Richmond, and have not
taken one excurſion into any other country. Judge now

* Euſden.
† This was his quarto Volume, written before he had given any ſigns of
thoſe extravagances, which have ſince rendered him ſo famous. As the Court
ſet up Mr. *Duck* for the rival of Mr. Pope, the City at the ſame time conſidered *Chubb*, as one who would eclipſe Locke. The modeſty of the court Poet
kept him ſober in a very intoxicating ſituation, while the vanity of this new-
fangled Philoſopher aſſiſted his ſage admirers in turning his head.

whether I can live in my library. Adieu. Live mindfu
of one of your firſt friends, who will be ſo till the laſt.
Mrs. Blount deſerves your remembrance, for ſhe never
forgets you, and wants nothing of being a friend *.

I beg the Duke's and her Grace's acceptance of my ſervices; the contentment you exprefs in their company
pleafes me, tho' it be the bar to my own, in dividing you
from us. I am ever very truly

Your, etc.

L E T T E R XXIII.

Oƈt. 2, 1732.

SIR Clem. Cotterel tells me you will ſhortly come to
town. We begin to want comfort in a few friends
about us, while the winds whiftle, and the waters roar.
The ſun gives us a parting look, but 'tis a cold one ; we
are ready to change thoſe diſtant favours of a lofty beauty,
for a grofs material fire that warms and comforts more. I
wiſh you could be here till your family come to town ;
you'll live more innocently, and kill fewer harmlefs creatures, nay none, except by your proper deputy, the but-
cher. It is fit for confcience fake, that you ſhould come
to town, and that the Duchefs ſhould ſtay in the country,
where no innocents of another ſpecies may ſuffer by her. I
hope ſhe never goes to church : the Duke ſhould lock you
both up, and lefs harm would be done. I adviſe you to
make man your game, hunt and beat about here for cox-
combs, and trufs up Rogues in Satire : I fancy they'll turn
to a good account, if you can produce them freſh, or make
them keep : and their relations will come, and buy their
bodies of you.

The death of Wilks leaves Cibber without a collegue,
abfolute and perpetual diƈtator of the ſtage, tho' indeed
while he lived he was but as Bibulus to Cæſar. However,
ambition finds ſomething to be gratify'd with in a mere
name ; or elſe, God have mercy upon poor ambition !
Here is a dead vacation at prefent, no politics at court,
no trade in town, nothing ſtirring but poetry. Every
man, and every boy, is writing verſes on the Royal Hermitage : I hear the Queen is at a lofs which to prefer ; but

---

* Alluding to thofe lines in the Epift. *on the characters of Women.*
  " With ev'ry pleafing, every prudent part,
  " Say what can *Cloe* want ?—She wants a heart."

for

for my own part, I like none fo well as Mr. Poyntz's in
Latin. You would oblige my Lady Suffolk if you tried
your Mufe on this occafion. I am fure I would do as much
for the Duchefs of Queenfberry, if fhe defired it. Several of your friends affure me it is expected from you : one
fhould not bear in mind, all one's life, any little indignity
one receives from a Court; and therefore I am in hopes,
neither her Grace will hinder you, nor you decline it.

The volume of Mifcellanies is juft publifh'd, which
concludes all our fooleries of that kind. All your friends
remember you, and, I affure you, no one more than

Your, etc.

LETTER XXIV.

From Mr. GAY to Mr. POPE.

Oct. 7, 1732.

I Am at laft returned from my Somerfetfhire expedition,
but fince my return I cannot fo much boaft of my health
as before I went, for I am frequently out of order with
my colical complaints, fo as to make me uneafy and difpirited, tho' not to any violent degree. The reception
we met with, and the little excurfions we made were every
way agreeable. I think the country abounds with beautiful profpects. Sir William Wyndham is at prefent amufing himfelf with fome real improvements, and a great
many vifionary caftles. We were often entertained with
fea-views and fea-fifh, and were at fome places in the neighbourhood, among which I was mightily pleafed with Dun-
ftar-Caftle near Minehead. It ftands upon a great eminence, and hath a profpect of that town, with an extenfive view of the Briftol Channel, in which are feen two
fmall iflands call'd the Steep Holmes and Flat Holmes,
and on t'other fide we could plainly diftinguifh the divifions of fields on the Welch coaft. All this journey I perform'd on horfeback, and am very much difappointed that
at prefent I feel myfelf fo little the better for it. I have
indeed followed riding and exercife for three months fuc-
ceffively, and really think I was as well without it; fo
that I begin to fear the illnefs I have fo long and fo often
complain'd of, is inherent in my conftitution, and that I
have nothing for it but patience *.

* Mr. Gay died the November following at the Duke of Queenfberry's
houfe in London, aged 45 years.

As to your advice about writing Panegyric, 'tis what I have not frequently done. I have indeed done it sometimes against my judgment and inclinations, and I heartily repent of it. And at prefent, as I have no defire of reward, and fee no juft reafon of praife, I think I had better let it alone. There are flatterers good enough to be found, and I would not interfere in any Gentleman's profeffion. I have feen no verfes on thefe fublime occafions ; fo that I have no emulation : Let the patrons enjoy the authors, and the authors their patrons, for i know myfelf unworthy.

I am, etc.

LETTER XXV.

Mr. CLELAND to Mr. GAY *.

Decemb. 16, 1731.

I Am aftonifh'd at the complaints occafioned by a late Epiftle to the Earl of Burlington; and fhould be afflicted were there the leaft juft ground for them. Had the writer attacked Vice, at a time when it is not only tolerated but triumphant, and fo far from being conceal'd as a Defect, that it is proclaimed with oftentation as a Merit ; I fhould have been apprehenfive of the confequence : Had he fatirized Gamefters of a hundred thoufand pounds fortune, acquir'd by fuch methods as are in daily practice, and almoft univerfally encouraged ; had he over warmly defended the Religion of his country againft fuch books as come from every prefs, are publicly vended in every fhop, and greedily bought by almoft every rank of men : or had he called our excellent weekly writers by the fame names which they openly beftow on the greateft men in the Miniftry, and out of the Miniftry, for which they are all unpunifhed, and moft rewarded : in any of thefe cafes, indeed, I might have judged him too prefumptuous, and perhaps have trembled for his rafhnefs.

I could not but hope better for this fmall and modeft Epiftle. which attacks no one Vice whatfoever ; which deals only in Folly, and not Folly in general, but a fingle fpecies of it ; that only branch, for the oppofite excellency of which, the Noble Lord to whom it is written muft neceffarily be celebrated. I fancied it might efcape cenfure,

---

* This was written by th. fame hand that wrote the *Letter to the Publifher*, prefixed to the Dunciad.

efpecially

efpecially feeing how tenderly thefe follies are treated, and really lefs accufed than apologized for.

Yet hence the Poor are cloath'd, the Hungry fed,
Health to himfelf, and to his Infants Bread
The Lab'rer bears.

Is this fuch a crime, that to impute it to a man muft be a grievous offence ? 'Tis an innocent Folly, and much more beneficent than the want of it; for ill Tafte employs more hands, and diffufes expence more than a good one. Is it a moral defect ? No, it is but a natural one; a want of tafte. It is what the beft good man living may be liable to. The worthieft Peer may live exemplarily in an ill-favour'd houfe, and the beft reputed citizen be pleafed with a vile garden. I thought (I fay) the author had the common liberty to obferve a defect, and to compliment a friend for a quality that diftinguifhes him : which I know not how any quality fhould do, if we were not to remark that it was wanting in others.

But, they fay, the fatire is perfonal. I thought it could not be fo, becaufe all it's reflections are on things. His reflections are not on the man, but his houfe, garden, etc. Nay, he refpects (as one may fay) the Perfons of the Gladiator, the Nile, and the Triton; he is only forry to fee them (as he might be to fee any of his friends) ridiculous by being in the wrong place, and in bad company. Some fancy, that to fay, a thing is Perfonal, is the fame as to fay, it is unjuft, not confidering, that nothing can be juft that is not perfonal. I am afraid that " all writings and difcourfes as touch no man, will mend no man." The good-natured, indeed, are apt to be alarmed at any thing like fatire; and the guilty readily concur with the weak, for a plain reafon, becaufe the vicious look upon folly as their frontier:

Jam proximus ardet
Ucalegon.

No wonder thofe who know ridicule belongs to them, find an inward confolation in removing it from themfelves as far as they can; and it is never fo far, as when they can get it fixed in their beft characters. No wonder thofe who are Food for Satirifts fhould rail at them as creatures of prey; every beaft born for our ufe would be ready to call a man fo.

I know no remedy, unlefs people in our age would as
little

little frequent the theatres, as they begin to do the churches;
unlefs comedy were forfaken, fatire filent, and every man
left to do what feems good in his own eyes, as if there
were no King, no Prieft, no Poet, in Ifrael.

But I find myfelf obliged to touch a point, on which I
muft be more ferious; it well deferves I fhould: I mean
the malicious application of the character of Timon, which,
I will boldly fay, they would impute to the perfon moft
different in the world from a Man-hater, to the perfon
whofe tafte and encouragement of wit have often been
fhewn in the righteft place. The author of that epiftle muft
certainly think fo, if he has the fame opinion of his own
merit as authors generally have; for he has been diftin-
guifhed by this very perfon.

Why, in God's name, muft a Portrait, apparently
collected from twenty different men, be applied to one
only? Has it his eye? no, it is very unlike. Has it his
nofe or mouth? no, they are totally differing. What then,
I befeech you? Why, it has the mole on his chin. Very
well; but muft the picture therefore be his, and has no
other man that blemifh?

Could there be a more melancholy inftance how much
the tafte of the public is vitiated, and turns the moft falu-
tary and feafonable phyfick into poifon, than if amidft the
blaze of a thoufand bright qualities in a great man, they
fhould only remark there is a fhadow about him; as what
eminence is without? I am confident the author was incapable of imputing any fuch to one, whofe whole life (to
ufe his own expreffion in print of h m) is a *continued feries
of good* and *generous actions.*

I know no man who would be more concerned, if he
gave the leaft pain of offence to any innocent perfon; and
none who would be lefs concerned, if the fatire were challenged by any one at whom he would really aim at. If
ever that happens, I dare engage, he will own it, with all
the freedom of one whofe cenfures are juft, and who fets
his name to them.

LETTER XXVI.

To the Earl of BURLINGTON.

My LORD,   March 7, 1731.

THE clamour rais'd about my Epiſtle to you, could not give me ſo much pain, as I receiv'd pleaſure in ſeeing the general zeal of the world in the cauſe of a Great man who is beneficent, and the particular warmth of your Lordſhip in that of a private man who is innocent.

It was not the Poem that deſerv'd this from you; for as I had the honour to be your Friend, I could not treat you quite like a Poet ; but ſure the writer deſerved more candour, even from thoſe who knew him not, than to promote a report which, in regard to that noble perſon, was impertinent, in regard to me, villainous. Yet I had no great cauſe to wonder, that a character belonging to twenty ſhould be applied to one ; ſince, by that means nineteen would eſcape the ridicule.

I was too well content with my knowledge of that noble perſon's opinion in this affair, to trouble the public about it. But ſince Malice and Miſtake are ſo long a dying, I have taken the opportunity of a third edition to declare his belief, not only of my innocence, but of their malignity ; of the former of which my own heart is as conſcious, as, I fear, ſome of theirs muſt be of the latter. His humanity feels a concern for the injury done to me, while his greatneſs of mind can bear with indifference the inſult offered to himſelf *.

However, my Lord, I own that critics of this ſort can intimidate me, nay half incline me to write no more : That would be making the Town a compliment which, I think, it deſerves ; and which ſome, I am ſure, would take very kindly. This way of Satire is dangerous, as long as ſlander rais'd by fools of the loweſt rank, can find any countenance from thoſe of a higher. Even from the conduct ſhewn on this occaſion, I have learnt there are ſome who would rather be wicked than ridiculous ; and therefore it may be ſafer to attack Vices than Follies. I will therefore leave my betters in the quiet poſſeſſion of their Idols, their Groves and their High-places ; and change my ſubject from their pride to their meanneſs,

* Alludes to the Letter the Duke of Ch* wrote to Mr. Pope on this occaſion.

from

from their vanities to their miferies ; and as the only certain way to avoid mifconftructions, to leffen offence, and
not to multiply ill-natured applications, I may probably,
in my next, make ufe of real names inftead of fictitious
ones.   I am,
My Lord,
Your moft affectionate, etc.

L E T T E R   XXVII *.

Cirencefter.

IT is a true faying that misfortunes alone prove one's
friendfhips: they fhow us not only that of other people
for us, but our own for them.   We hardly know ourfelves
any otherwife.   I feel my being forced to this Bath-jour-
ney as a misfortune ; and to follow my own weltare pre-
ferably to thofe I love, is indeed a new thing to me : my
health has not ufually got the better of my tenderneffes
and affections.   I fet out with a heavy heart, wifhing I
had done this thing the laft feafon ; for every day I defer
it, the more I am in danger of that accident, which I dread
the moft, my Mother's death (efpecially fhould it happen
while I am away.)   And another Reflection pains me,
that I have never, fince I knew you, been fo long feparated
from you, as I now muft be.   Methinks we live to be
more and more ftrangers, and every year teaches you to
live without me : This abfence may, I fear, make my return lefs welcome and lefs wanted to you, than once it feem'd,
even after but a fortnight.   Time ought not in reafon to
diminifh friendfhip, when it confirms the truth of it by
experience.

The journey has a good deal diforder'd me, notwithftanding my refting-place at Lord Bathurft's.   My Lord is
too much for me, he walks, and is in fpirits all day long :
I rejoice to fee him fo.   It is a right diftinction, that I
am happier in feeing my friends fo many degrees above
me, be it in fortune, health, or pleafures, than I can be in
fharing either with them : for in thefe fort of enjoyments
I cannot keep pace with them, any more than I can walk
with a ftronger man.   I wonder to find I am a companion
for none but old men, and forget that I am not a young fellow myfelf.   The worft is that reading and writing, which I
have ftill the greateft relifh for, are growing painful to my

* To Mrs. B.

eyes.

eyes. But if I can preferve the good opinion of one or two friends, to fuch a degree as to have their indulgence to my weaknefies, I will not complain of life : And if I could live to fee you confult your eafe and quiet, by be-coming independent on thofe who will never help you to either, I doubt not of finding the latter part of my life pleafanter than the former, or prefent. My uneafineffes of body I can bear ; my chief uneafinefs of mind is in your regard. You have a temper that would make you *eafy* and *beloved.* (which is all the happinefs one needs to wifh in this world) and content with moderate things. All your point is not to lofe that temper by facrificing yourfelf to others, out of a miftaken tendernefs, which hurts you, and pro-fits not them. And this you muft do foon, or it will be too late : Habit will make it as hard for you to live inde-pendent, as for L——— to live out of a Court.

You muft excufe me for obferving what I think any de-fect in you ; you grow too indolent, and give things up too eafily : which would be otherwife, when you found and felt yourfelf your own : Spirits would come in, as ill-ufage went out. While you live under a kind of perpe-tual dejection and oppreffion, nothing at all belongs to you, not your own *Humour*, nor your own *Senfe.*

You can't conceive how much you would find refolution rife, and chearfulnefs grow upon you, if you'd once try to live independent for two or three months. I never think tenderly of you but this comes acrofs me, and therefore excufe my repeating it, for whenever I do not, I diffem-ble half that I think of you : Adieu, pray write, and be particular about your health.

LETTER XXVIII *.

YOUR letter dated at nine o'clock on Tuefday (night as I fuppofe) has funk me quite. Yefterday I hoped ; and yefterday I fent you a line or two for our poor Friend Gay, inclos'd in a few words to you ; about twelve or one o'clock you fhould have had it. I am troubled about that, tho' the prefent caufe of our trouble be fo much greater †. Indeed I want a friend, to help me to bear it better. We want each other. I bear a hearty fhare with Mrs. Howard,

* To the fame.
† Mr. Gay's death, which happen'd in Nov. 1732, at the Duke of Queenf-berry's houfe in London, aged 46.

who has loft a man of a moft honeft heart; fo honeft an one, that I wifh her Mafter had none lefs honeft about him. The world after all is a little pitiful thing; not performing any one promife it makes us, for the future, and every day taking away and annulling the joys of the paft. Let us comfort one another, and, if poffible, ftudy to add as much more friendfhip to each other, as death has deprived us of in him. I promife you more and more of mine, which will be the way to deferve more and more of yours.

I purpofely avoid faying more. The fubject is beyond writing upon, beyond cure or eafe by reafon or reflection, beyond all but one thought, that is the will of God.

So will the death of my mother be! which now I trem-ble at, now refign to, now bring clofe to me, now fet far-ther off: Every day alters, turns me about, and confufes my whole frame of mind. Her dangerous diftemper is a-gain return'd, her fever coming onward again, tho' lefs in pain; for which laft however I thank God.

I am unfeignedly tired of the world, and receive no-thing to be called a pleafure in it, equivalent to counter-vail either the death of one I have fo long lived with, or of one I have fo long lived for. I have nothing left but to turn my thoughts to one comfort; the laft we ufually think of, tho' the only one we fhould in wifdom depend upon, in fuch a difappointing place as this. I fit in her room, and fhe is always prefent before me, but when I fleep. I wonder I am fo well: I have fhed many tears, but now I weep at nothing. I would above all things fee you, and think it would comfort you to fee me fo equal-temper'd and fo quiet. But pray dine here; you may, and fhe know nothing of it, for fhe dozes much, and we tell her of no earthly thing, left it run in her mind, which often trifles have done. If Mr. Bethell had time, I wifh he were your companion hither. Be as much as you can with each other: Be affur'd I love you both, and be far-ther affur'd, that friendfhip will increafe as I live on.

LETTER XXIX.

To Hugh Bethell, Efq.

July 12, 1723.

I Affure you unfeignedly any memorial of your good-
nature and friendlinefs is moft welcome to me, who
know thofe tenders of affection from you are not like the
common traffic of compliments and profeffions, which
moft people only give that they may receive; and is at
beft a commerce of Vanity, if not of Falfehood. I am
happy in not immediately wanting the fort of good offices
you offer: but if I did want them, I fhould not think myfelf unhappy in receiving them at your hands: this really
is fome compliment, for I would rather moft men did me
a fmall injury, than a kindnefs. I know your humanity,
and allow me to fay, I love and value you for it: 'Tis a
much better ground of love and value, than all the qualities
I fee the world fo fond of: They generally admire in the
wrong place, and generally moft admire the things they
don't comprehend, or the things they can never be the
better for. Very few can receive pleafure or advantage
from wit which they feldom tafte, or learning which they
feldom underftand: much lefs from the quality, high birth,
or fhining circumftances of thofe to whom they profefs
efteem, and who will always remember how much they
are their Inferiors. But humanity and fociable virtues are
what every creature wants every day, and ftill wants more
the longer he lives, and moft the very moment he dies. It
is ill travelling either in a ditch or on a terras; we fhould
walk in the common way, where others are continually
paffing on the fame level, to make the journey of life fupportable by bearing one another company in the fame
circumftances.—Let me know how I may convey over the
Odyffeys for your amufement in your journey, that you
may compare your own travels with thofe of Ulyffes; I
am fure yours are undertaken upon a more difinterefted,
and therefore a more heroic motive. Far be the omen
from you, of returning as he did, alone, without faving
a friend.

There is lately printed a book * wherein all human virtue
is reduced to one teft, that of Truth, and branch'd out

---

* Mr. Wollafton's excellent book of *the Religion of Nature delineated.* The
Queen was fond of it, and that made the reading, and the talking of it fafhi-
o:able.

in

in every inftance of our duty to God and man. If you
have not feen it, you muft, and I will fend it together
with the Odyffey. The very women read it, and pretend
to be charmed with that beauty which they generally think
the leaft of. They make as much ado about *truth*, fince
this book appear'd, as they did about *health* when Dr.
Cheyne's came out: and will doubtlefs be as conftant in
the purfuit of one, as of the other. Adieu.

L E T T E R. XXX.

To the fame.

Aug. 9, 1726.

I Never am unmindful of thofe I think fo well of as yourfelf; their number is not fo great as to confound one's
memory. Nor ought you to decline writing to me, upon
an imagination, that I am much employed by other people.
For though my houfe is like the houfe of a Patriarch of
old, ftanding by the highway-fide and receiving all travellers, neverthelefs I feldom go to bed without the reflection, that one's chief bufinefs is to be really at home:
and I agree with you in your opinion of company, amufements, and all the filly things which mankind would fain
make pleafures of, when in truth they are labour and
forrow.

I condole with you on the death of your Relation, the
E. of C. as on the fate of a mortal man: Efteem I never
had for him, but concern and humanity I had: the latter
was due to the infirmity of his laft period, tho' the former
was not due to the triumphant and vain part of his courfe.
He certainly knew himfelf beft at laft, and knew beft the
little value of others, whofe neglect of him, whom they fo
grofsly follow'd and flatter'd in the former fcene of his
life, fhew'd him as worthlefs as they could imagine him to
be, were he all that his worft enemies believ'd of him:
For my own part, I am forry for his death, and wifh he
had lived long enough to fee fo much of the faithleffnefs of
the world, as to have been above the mad ambition of go-
verning fuch wretches as he muft have found it to be compos'd of.

Tho' you could have no great value for this Great man,
yet acquaintance itfelf, the cuftom of feeing the face, or
entering under the roof, of one that walks along with us
in the common way of the world, is enough to create a

wifh

wiſh at leaſt for his being above ground, and a degree of uneaſineſs at his removal. 'Tis the loſs of an object familiar to us : I ſhould hardly care to have an old poſt pull'd up, that I remember'd ever ſince I was a child. And add to this the reflection (in the caſe of ſuch as were not the beſt of their Species) what their condition in another life may be, it is yet a more important motive for our concern and compaſſion. To ſay the truth, either in the caſe of death or life, almoſt every body and every thing is a cauſe or object for humanity, even proſperity itſelf, and health itſelf ; ſo many weak pitiful incidentals attend on them.

I am ſorry any relation of yours is ill, whoever it be, for you don't name the perſon. But I conclude it is one of thoſe to whoſe houſes, you tell me, you are going, for I know no invitation with you is ſo ſtrong as when any one is in diſtreſs, or in want of your aſſiſtance : The ſtrongeſt proof in the world of this, was your attendance on the late Earl.

I have been very melancholy for the loſs of Mr. Blount. Whoever has any portion of good-nature will ſuffer on theſe occaſions ; but a good mind rewards its own ſufferings. I hope to trouble you as little as poſſible, if it be my fate to go before you. I am of old Ennius's mind, *Nemo me decoret lachrymis* — I am but a *Lodger* here : this is not an abiding city, I am only to ſtay out my leaſe : for what has Perpetuity and mortal man to do with each other ? But I could be glad you would take up with an Inn at Twittenham, as long as I am Hoſt of it : if not, I would take up freely with any Inn of yours.—Adieu, dear Sir : Let us while away this life : and (if we can) meet in another.

LETTER XXXI.

To the ſame.

June 24, 1727.

YOU are too humane and conſiderate (things few people can be charged with.) Do not ſay you will not expect letters from me ; upon my word I can no more forbear writing ſometimes to you, than thinking of you. I know the world too well, not to value you who are an example of acting, living, and thinking, above it, and contrary to it.

I thank God for my Mother's unexpected recovery,
tho'

tho' my hope can rife no higher than from reprieve to reprieve, the fmall addition of a few days to the many fhe
has already feen.   Yet fo fhort and tranfitory as this light
is, it is all I have to warm or fhine upon me ; and when
it is out, there is nothing elfe that will live for me, or con-
fume itfelf in my fervice.   But I would have you think
this is not the chief motive of my concern about her : Gratitude is a cheap virtue, one may pay it very punctually, for
it cofts us nothing, but our memory of the good done.
And I owe her more good, than ever I can pay, or
fhe at this age receive, if I could.   I do not think the
tranquillity of the mind ought to be difturbed for many
things in this world : but thofe offices that are neceffary
duties either to our friends or ourfelves, will hardly prove
any breach of it ; and as much as they take away from our
indolence and eafe of body, will contribute to our peace
and quiet of mind by the content they give.   They often
afford the higheft pleafure ; and thofe who do not feel that,
will hardly ever find another to match it, let them love
themfelves ever fo dearly.   At the fame time it muft be
own'd, one meets with cruel difappointments in feeing fo
often the beft endeavours ineffectual to make others happy,
and very often, (what is moft cruel of all) thro' their own
means *.   But ftill I affirm, thofe very difappointments
of a virtuous man are greater pleafures than the utmoft
gratifications and fucceffes of a mere felf-lover.

    The great and fudden event which has juft now happen-
ed §, puts the whole world (I mean this whole world) into
a new ftate : The only ufe I have, fhall, or wifh to make
of it, is to obferve the difparity of men from themfelves in
a week's time ; the defultory leaping and catching of new
motions, new modes, new meafures : and that ftrange fpirit and life, with which men broken and difappointed refume their hopes, their folicitations, their ambitions ! It
would be worth your while as a Philofopher, to be bufy
in thefe obfervations, and to come hither to fee the fury
and buftle of the Bees this hot feafon, without coming fo
near as to be ftung by them.

                                                Your, etc.

* See Letter xxvii, from Cirencefter.
§ The death of K. George the Firft, which happened the 11th of June,
1717.

' L E T T E R

LETTER XXXII.

To the fame

June 17, 1728.

AFter the publifhing of my Boyifh Letters to Mr. Crom-well, you will not wonder if I fhould forfwear wri-ting a letter again while I live ; fince I do not correfpond with a friend upon the terms of any other free fubject of this kingdom. But to you I can never be filent or refer-ved ; and, I am fure, my opinion of your heart is fuch, - that I could open mine to you in no manner which I could fear the whole world fhould know. I could publifh my own heart too, I will venture to fay, for any mifchief or malice there is in it : but a little too much folly or weaknefs might, (I fear) appear, to make fuch a fpectacle either in-ftructive or agreeable to others.

I am reduced to beg of all my acquaintance to fecure me from the like ufage for the future, by returning me any letters of mine which they may have preferved ; that I may not be hurt, after my death, by that which was the hap-pinefs of my life, their partiality and affection to me.

I have nothing of myfelf to tell you, only that I have had but indifferent health. I have not made a vifit to Lon-don : Curiofity and the love of Diffipation die apace in me. I am not glad nor forry for it, but I am very forry for thofe who have nothing elfe to live on.

I have read much, but writ no more. I have fmall hopes of doing good, no vanity in writing, and little ambition to pleafe a world not very candid or deferving. If I can preferve the good opinion of a few friends, it is all I can expect, confidering how little good I can do even to them to merit it. Few people have your candour, or are fo will-ing to think well of another from whom they receive no benefit, and gratify no vanity. But of all the foft fen-fations, the greateft pleafure is to give and receive mutual Truft. It is by Belief and firm Hope, that men are made happy in this life, as well as in the other. My confidence in your good opinion, and dependance upon that of one or two more, is the chief cordial drop I tafte, amidft the Infipid, the Difagreeable, the Cloying, or the Dead-fweet, which are the common draughts of life. Some pleafures are too pert, as well as others too flat, to be relifh'd long : and vivacity in fome cafes is worfe than dulnefs. There-fore indeed for many years I have not chofen my compa-nions for any of the qualities in fafhion, but almoft entirely for that which is moft out-of-fafhion, fincerity. Before

I am

I am aware of it, I am making your panegyric, and perhaps my own too, for next to poſſeſſing the beſt of qualities is the eſteeming and diſtinguiſhing thoſe who poſſeſs it. I truly love and value you, and ſo I ſtop ſhort.

LETTER XXXIII.

To the Earl of PETERBOROW.

My LORD,   Aug. 24, 1728.

I Preſume you may before this time be returned, from the contemplation of many Beauties, animal and vegetable, in Gardens; and poſſibly ſome rational, in Ladies; to the better enjoyment of your own at Bevis-Mount. I hope, and believe, all you have ſeen will only contribute to it. I am not ſo fond of making compliments to Ladies as I was twenty years ago, or I would ſay there are ſome very reaſonable, and one in particular there. I think you happy, my Lord, in being at leaſt half the year almoſt as much your own maſter as I am mine the whole year: and with all the diſadvantageous incumbrances of quality, parts, and honour, as mere a gardener, loiterer, and labourer, as he who never had Titles, or from whom they are taken. I have an eye in the laſt of theſe glorious appellations to the ſtyle of a Lord degraded or attainted: methinks they give him a better title than they deprive him of, in calling him Labourer: *Agricultura*, ſays Tully, *proxima Sapientiae*, which is more than can be ſaid by moſt modern Nobility, of Grace or Right Honourable, which are often *proxima Stultitiae*. The Great Turk, you know, is often a Gardener, or of a meaner trade: and are there not (my Lord) ſome circumſtances in which you would reſemble the Great Turk? The two Paradiſes are not ill connected, of Gardens and Gallantry; and ſome there are (not to name my Lord B.) who pretend they are both to be had, even in this life, without turning Muſſelmen.

We have as little politics here within a few miles of the Court (nay perhaps at the Court) as you at Southampton; and our Miniſters, I dare ſay, have leſs to do. Our weekly hiſtories are only full of the feaſts given to the Queen and Royal Family by their ſervants, and the long and laborious walks her Majeſty takes every morning. Yet if the graver Hiſtorians hereafter ſhall be ſilent of this

year's

year's events, the amorous and anecdotical may make posterity some amends, by being furnished with the gallantries of the Great at home; and 'tis some comfort, that if
the Men of the next age do not read of us, the Women may.

From the time you have been absent, I've not been to
wait on a certain great man, thro' modesty, thro' idleness,
and thro' respect. But for my comfort I fancy, that any
great man will as soon forget one that does him no harm,
as he can one that has done him any good. Believe me,
my Lord, yours.

LETTER XXXIV.

From the Earl of PETERBOROW.

I Must confess that in going to Lord Cobham's, I was
not led by curiosity. I went thither to see what I had
seen, and what I was sure to like.

I had the idea of those gardens so fix'd in my imagination by many descriptions, that nothing surprized me;
Immensity and Van Brugh appear in the whole, and in
every part. Your joining in your letter animal and vegetable beauty, makes me use this expression: I confess the
stately Sacharissa at Stow, but am content with my little
Amoret.

I thought you indeed more knowing upon the subject,
and wonder at your mistake; why will you imagine women
insensible to Praise, much less to yours? I have seen them
more than once turn from their Lover to their Flatterer.
I am sure the Farmeress at Bevis in her highest mortifica-
tions, in the middle of her Lent *, would feel emotions of
vanity, if she knew you gave her the character of a reasonable woman.

You have been guilty again of another mistake, which
hinder'd me shewing your letter to a friend: when you join
two ladies in the same compliment, tho' you gave to both
the beauty of Venus, and the wit of Minerva, you would
please neither.

If you had put me into the Dunciad, I could not have
been more disposed to criticise your letter. What, Sir,
do you bring it in as a reproach, or as a thing uncommon
to a Court, to be without politics? With politics indeed
the Richlieu's and such folks have brought about great
things in former days; but what are they, Sir, who,
without policy, in our times, can make ten Treaties in a
year, and secure everlasting Peace?

* The Countess of Peterborow, a Roman-catholic.

I can no longer difagree with you, tho' in jeft. Oh how heartily I join with you in your contempt for Excellency and Grace, and in your efteem of that moft noble title, Loi-erer. If I were a man of many plums, and a good heathen, I would dedicate a Temple to Lazinefs.: No man fure could blame my choice of fuch a Deity, who confiders that when I have been fool enough to take pains, I always met with fome wife man able to undo my labours.

Your, etc.

LETTER XXXV.

YOU were in a very polemic humour when you did me the honour to anfwer my laft. I always underftood, like a true controvertift, that to anfwer is only to cavil and quarrel : however, I forgive you ; you did it (as all Po-lemics do) to fhew your parts. Elfe was it not very vex-atious, to deny me to commend two women at a time ? It is true, my Lord, you know women as well as men : but fince you certainly love them better, why are you fo uncha-ritable in your opinion of them ? Surely one Lady may al-low another to have the thing fhe herfelf leaft values, Reafon, when Beauty is unconteſted. Venus herfelf could allow Minerva to be Goddefs of Wit, when Paris gave her the apple (as the fool herfelf thought) on a better account. I do fay, that Lady P* is a reafonable woman ; and I think, fhe will not take it amifs, if I fhould infift upon efteeming her, inftead of Toafting her, like a filly thing I could name, who is the Venus of thefe days. I fee you had forgot my letter, or would not let her know how much I thought of her in this reafonable way : but I have been kinder to you, and have fhewn your letter to one who will take it candidly.

But for God's fake, what have you faid about Politi-cians ? you made me a great compliment in the truft you repofed in my prudence, or what mifchief might not I have done you with fome that affect that denomination ? Your Lordfhip might as fafely have fpoken of Heroes. What a blufter would the God of the winds have made, had one that we know puff'd againft Æolus, or (like Xerxes) whipp'd the feas ? They had dialogued it in the language of the Rehearfal,

I'll give him flaſh for flaſh—
I'll give him daſh for daſh—

But

But all now is fafe ; the Poets are preparing fongs of joy, and Halcyon-days are the word.

I hope, my Lord, it will not be long before your dutiful affection brings you to town. I fear it will a little raife your envy to find all the Mufes employed in celebrating a Royal work *, which your own partiality will think inferior to Bevis-Mount. But if you have any inclination to be even with them, you need but put three or four Wits into any hole in your Garden, and they will out-rhyme all Eaton and Weftminfter. I think, Swift, Gay, and I could undertake it, if you don't think our Heads too expenfive : but the fame hand that did the others, will do them as cheap. If all elfe fhould fail, you are fure at leaft of the head. hand, and heart of your fervant.

Why fhould you fear any difagreeable news to reach us at Mount Bevis ? Do as I do even within ten miles of London, let no news whatever come near you. As to public affairs we never knew a deader feafon : 'tis all filent, deep tranquillity. Indeed, they fay, 'tis fometimes fo juft before an Earthquake. But whatever happens, cannot we obferve the wife neutrality of the Dutch, and let all about us fall by the ears ? Or if you, my Lord, fhould be prick'd on by any old fafhion'd notions of Honour and Romance, and think it neceffary for the General of the Marines to be in action, when our Fleets are in motion ; meet them at Spithead, and take me along with you. I decline no danger where the glory of Great Britain is concern'd ; and will contribute to empty the largeft bowl of punch that fhall be rigg'd on fuch an occafion. Adieu, my Lord, and may as many Years attend you, as may be happy and honourable !

LETTER XXXVI.

From the Earl of PETERBOROW.

YOU muft receive my letters with a juft impartiality, and give grains of allowance for a gloomy or rainy day ; I fink grievoufly with the weather-glafs, and am quite fpiritlefs when opprefs'd with the thoughts of a Birthday or a Return.

Dutiful affection was bringing me to town, but undutiful lazinefs, and being much out of order, keep me in the

* The Hermitage.

country ;

country; however, if alive, I muſt make my appearance
at the Birth-day. Where you ſhewed one letter you may
ſhew the other; ſhe that never was wanting in any good
office in her power, will make a proper excuſe, where a
ſin of Omiſſion, I fear, is not reckoned as a venial ſin.

I conſent you ſhall call me polemic, or aſſociate me to
any ſect or Corporation, provided you do not join me to
the Charitable Rogues, or to the Pacific Politicians of
the preſent age. I have read over * Barkley in vain, and
find, after a ſtroke given on the left, I cannot offer the
right cheek for another blow: all I can bring myſelf to,
is to bear mortification from the fair ſex with patience.

You ſeem to think it vexatious that I ſhall allow you but
one woman at a time, either to praiſe, or love. If I difpute with you upon this point, I doubt every jury will
give a verdict againſt me. So, Sir, with a Mahometan
indulgence, I allow you pluralities, the favourite privilege of our church.

I find you do not mend upon correction; again I tell you,
you muſt not think of women in a reaſonable way: you
know we always make Goddeſſes of thoſe we adore upon
earth; and do not all the good men tell us, we muſt lay
aſide Reaſon in what relates to the Deity?

'Tis well the Poets are preparing ſongs of joy: 'tis well
to lay in antidotes of ſoft rhyme, againſt the rough proſe
they may chance to meet with at Weſtminſter. I ſhould
have been glad of any thing of Swift's: pray when you
write to him next, tell him I expect him with impatience,
in a place as odd, and as much out of the way as himſelf.

Yours.

LETTER XXXVII.

From the ſame.

WHenever you apply as a good Papiſt to your female
Mediatrix, you are ſure of ſucceſs; but there is not
a full aſſurance of your entire ſubmiſſion to Mother-
church, and that abates a little of your authority. However, if you will accept of country-letters, ſhe will cor-
reſpond from the hay-cock, and I will write to you upon
the ſide of my wheelbarrow: ſurely ſuch letters might
eſcape examination.

---

* Barkley's Apology for the Quakers.

Your

Your idea of the Golden Age is, that every fhepherd might pipe where he pleafed. As I have lived longer, I am more moderate in my wifhes, and would be content with the liberty of not piping where I am not pleafed.

Oh how I wifh, to myfelf and my friends, a freedom which Fate feldom allows, and which we often refufe ourfelves! why is our Shepherdefs * in voluntary flavery? why muft our Dean fubmit to the Colour of his coat, and live abfent from us? and why are you confined to what you cannot relieve?

I feldom venture to give accounts of my journeys beforehand, becaufe I take refolutions of going to London, and keep them no better than quarrelling lovers do theirs. But the devil will drive me thither about the middle of next month, and I will call upon you, to be fprinkled with holy water, before I enter the place of Corruption. Your, etc.

LETTER XXXVIII.

From the fame.

I Am under the greateft impatience to fee Dr. Swift at Bevis-Mount, and muft fignify my mind to him by another hand, it not being permitted me to hold correfpondence with the faid Dean, for no letter of mine can come to his hands.

And whereas it is apparent, in this Proteftant land, moft efpecially under the care of divine providence, that nothing can fucceed or come to a happy iffue but by Bribery; therefore let me know what he expects to comply with my defires, and it fhall be remitted unto him.

For tho' I would nor corrupt any man for the whole world, yet a benevolence may be given without any offence to confcience; every one muft confefs, that gratification and corruption are two diftinct terms; nay at worft many good men hold, that for a good end, fome very naughty meafures may be made ufe of.

But, Sir, I muft give you fome good news in relation to myfelf, becaufe, I know, you wifh me well; I am cur'd of fome difeafes in my old age, which tormented me very much in my youth.

I was poffeffed with violent and uneafy paffions, fuch as

* Mrs. H.

a peevifh

a peevifh concern for Truth, and a faucy love for my Country.

When a Chriftian Prieft preached againft the Spirit of the Gofpel, when an Englifh Judge determined againft Magna Charta, when the Minifter acted againft Common Senfe, I ufed to fret.

Now, Sir, let what will happen, I keep myfelf in temper: As I have no flattering hopes, fo I banifh all ufelefs fears; but as to the things of this world, I find myfelf in a condition beyond expectation; it being evident from a late Parliamentary inquiry, that I have as much ready money, as much in the funds, and as great a perfonal eftate, as Sir Robert S-tt-n.

If the Tranflator of Homer find fault with this unheroic difpofition, or (what I more fear) if the Draper of Ireland acufe the Englifhman of want of fpirit: I filence you both with one line out of your own Horace, *Quid te exempta juvat fpinis e pluribus una?* For I take the whole to be fo corrupted, that a cure in any part would be of little avail.

Your, etc.

LETTER XXXIX.

Dr. Swift to the Earl of Peterborow.

MY LORD,

I Never knew or heard of any perfon fo volatile and fo fix'd as your Lordfhip: You, while your imagination is carrying you thro' every corner of the world, where you have or have not been, can at the fame time remember to do offices of favour and kindnefs to the meaneft of your friends; and in all the fcenes you have paffed, have not been able to attain that one quality peculiar to a great man, of forgetting every thing but injuries. Of this I am a living witnefs againft you; for being the moft infignificant of all your old humble fervants, you were fo cruel as never to give me time to afk a favour, but prevented me, in doing whatever you thought I defired, or could be for my credit or advantage.

I have often admired at the capricioufnefs of Fortune in regard to your Lordfhip. She hath forced Courts to act againft their oldeft and moft conftant maxims; to make you a General becaufe you had courage and conduct; an Ambaffador, becaufe you had wifdom and knowledge in the interefts of Europe; and an Admiral on account of your

fkill

ſkill in maritime affairs : whereas, according to the uſual method of Court-proceedings, I ſhould have been at the head of the Army, and you of the Church, or rather a Curate under the Dean of St. Patrick's.

The Archbiſhop of Dublin laments that he did not ſee your Lordſhip till he was juſt upon the point of leaving the Bath : I pray God you may have found ſucceſs in that journey, elſe I ſhall continue to think there is a fatality in all your Lordſhip's undertakings, which only terminate in your own honour, and the good of the public, without the leaſt advantage to your health or fortune.

I remember Lord Oxford's Miniſtry us'd to tell me, that not knowing where to write to you, they were forced to write at you. It is ſo with me, for you are in one thing an Evangelic man, that you know not where to lay your head, and, I think, you have no houſe. Pray, my Lord, write to me, that I may have the pleaſure, in this ſcoundrel country, of going about, and ſhewing my depending Par-ſons a letter from the Earl of Peterborow.

I am, etc.

LETTER XL.

To * * * * †.

Sept. 13.

I Believe you are by this time immers'd in your vaſt Wood ; and one may addreſs to you as to a very abſtract-ed perſon, like Alexander Selkirk, or the * Self-taught Philoſopher. I ſhould be very curious to know what ſort of contemplations employ you. I remember the latter of thoſe I mentioned, gave himſelf up to a devout exerciſe of making his head giddy with various circumrotations, to imitate the motions of the celeſtial bodies. I don't think it at all impoſſible that Mr. L * may be far advanced in that exerciſe, by frequent turns towards the ſeveral aſpects of the heavens, to which you may have been pleaſed to direct him in ſearch of proſpects and new avenues. He will be tract-able in time as birds are tamed by being whirl'd about ; and doubtleſs come not to deſpiſe the meaneſt ſhrubs or coppice-wood, though natually he ſeems more inclined to admire God, in his greater works, the tall timber : for as Virgil has it, *Non omnes arbuſta juvant, humileſque myricae.*

† Lord Bathurſt.
* The title of an Arabic Treatiſe of the Life of Hai Ebn Yocktan.

I wiſh

I wifh myfelf with you both, whether you are in peace or at war, in violent argumentation or fmooth confent, over Gazettes in the morning, or over Plans in the evening. In that laft article, I am of opinion your Lordfhip has a lofs of me ; for generally after the debate of a whole day, we acquicfced at night in the beft conclufion of which human Reafon fcems capable in all great matters, to fall faft afleep ! And fo we ended, unlefs immediate Revelation (which ever muft overcome human reafon) fuggefted fome new lights to us, by a vifion in bed. But laying afide Theory, I am told, you are going directly to Practice. Alas, what a Fall will that be ? A new Building is like a new Church ; when once it is fet up, you muft mantain it in all the forms, and with all the inconveniences ; then ceafe the pleafant luminous days of infpiration, and there is an end of miracles at once !

That this Letter may be all of a piece, I'll fill the reft with an account of a confultation lately held in my neigh- bourhood about defigning a princely garden. Several Critics were of feveral opinions: One declared he would not have too much Art in it ; for my notion (faid he) of gardening is, that it is only fweeping nature * : Another told them that Gravel walks were not of a good tafte, for all the fineft abroad were of loofe fand : A third advis'd pe- remptorily there fhould not be one Lyme-tree in the whole plantation : A fourth made the fame exclufive claufe ex- tend to Horfe-chefnuts, which he affirmed not to be Trees, but Weeds : Dutch Elms were condemned by a fifth ; and thus about half the trees were profcribed, contrary to the Paradife of God's own planting, which is exprefs- ' ly faid to be planted with *all trees*. There were fome who could not bear Ever-greens, and call'd them Never- greens ; fome, who were angry at them only when cut into fhapes, and gave the modern Gardeners the name of Ever-green Taylors ; fome, who had no diflike to Cones and Cubes, but would have them cut in Foreft-trees ; and fome who were in a paffion againft any thing in fhape, even againft clipt hedges, which they call green walls. Thefe (my Lord) are our Men of Tafte, who pretend to prove it by tafting little or nothing. Sure fuch a Tafte is like fuch a ftomach, not a good one but a weak one. We have the fame fort of Critics in poetry : one is fond of nothing but Heroics, another cannot relifh Tragedies, another hates Paftorals, all little wits delight in Epigrams.

* An Expreffion of Sir T. H.

Will

Will you give me leave to add, there are the fame in Divinity; where many leading Critics are for rooting up more than they plant, and would leave the Lord's Vineyard either very thinly furnifhed, or very oddly trimm'd.

I have lately been with my Lord * *, who is a zealous, yet a charitable Planter, and has fo bad a Tafte, as to like all that is good. He hath a difpofition to wait on you in his way to the Bath, and if he can go and return to London in eight or ten days, I am not without a hope of feeing your Lordfhip with the delight I always fee you. Every where I think of you, and every where I wifh for you.   I am, etc.

LETTER XLI.

To Mr. C———.

Sept. 2, 1732.

I Affure you I am glad of your letter, and have long wanted nothing but the permiffion you now give me, to be plain and unreferved upon this head. I wrote to you concerning it long fince ; but a friend of yours and mine was of opinion, it was taking too much upon me, and more than I could be entitled to by the mere merit of long acquaintance, and good will. I have not a thing in my heart relating to any friend, which I would not, in my own nature, declare to all mankind. The truth is what you guefs ; I could not efteem your conduct, to an object of mifery fo near you as Mrs. ———, and I have often hinted it to yourfelf : The Truth is, I cannot yet efteem it for any reafon I am able to fee. But this I promife, I acquit you as far as your own mind acquits you. I have now no further caufe of complaint, for the unhappy Lady gives me now no further pain : fhe is no longer an object either of yours or my compaffion ; the hardfhips done her, are lodg'd in the hands of God, nor has any man more to do in them, except the perfons concern'd in occafioning them.

As for the interruption of our Correfpondence, I am forry you feem to put the Teft of my friendfhip upon that, becaufe it is what I am difqualified from toward my other acquaintance, with whom I cannot hold any frequent commerce. I'll name you the obftacles which I can't furmount : want of health, want of time, want of good eyes : and one yet ftronger than them all, I write not upon the terms of other

men. For however glad I might be, of expreſſing my
reſpeᏐ, opening my mind, or venting my concerns, to
my private friends; I hardly dare while there are Curls
in the World. If you pleaſe to reflecᏐ either on the impertinence of weak admirers, the malice of low enemies,
the avarice of mercenary bookſellers, or the ſilly curioſity
of people in general; you'll confeſs I have ſmall reaſon to
indulge correſpondences: in which too I want materials,
as I live altogether out of town, and have abſtraᏐed my
mind (I hope) to better things than common news. I wiſh
my friends would ſend me back thoſe forfeitures of my diſcretion, commit to my juſtice what I truſted only to their
indulgence, and return me at the year's end, thoſe trifling
letters, which can be to them but a day's amuſement, but
to me may prove a diſcredit as laſting and extenſive, as
the aforeſaid weak admirers, mean enemies, mercenary
ſcriblers, or curious ſimpletons, can make it.

I come now to a particular you complain of, my not
anſwering your queſtion about ſome Party-papers, and
their authors. This indeed I could not tell you, becauſe
I never was, or will be privy to ſuch papers: And if by
accident, thro' my acquaintance with any of the writers,
I had known a thing they conceal'd; I ſhould certainly
never be the reporter of it.

For my waiting on you at your country-houſe, I have
often wiſh'd it; it was my compliance to a ſuperior duty
that hinder'd me, and one which you are too good a Chriſtian to wiſh I ſhould have broken, having never ventur'd
to leave my mother (at her great age) for more than a week,
which is too little for ſuch a journey.

Upon the whole, I muſt acquit myſelf of any aᏐ or
thought, in prejudice to the regard I owe you, as ſo long
and obliging an acquaintance and correſpondent. I am
ſure I have all the good wiſhes for yourſelf and your family, that become a friend: There is no accident that can
happen to your advantage, and no aᏐion that can redound
to your credit, which I ſhould not be ready to extol, or
to rejoice in. And therefore I beg you to be aſſured, I am
in diſpoſition and will, tho' not ſo much as I would be in
teſtimonies or writing,

                                        Yours, etc.

LETTER

LETTER XLII.

To Mr. RICHARDSON.

Jan. 13, 1732.

I Have at laſt got my mother ſo well, as to allow myſelf to be abſent from her for three days. As Sunday is one of them, I do not know whether I may propoſe to you to employ it in the manner you mentioned to me once. Sir Godfrey call'd employing the pencil the prayer of a painter, and affirmed it to be his proper way of ſerving God, by the talent he gave him. I am ſure, in this inſtance, it is ſerving your friend; and, you know, we are allowed to do that (nay even to help a neighbour's ox or aſs) on the Sabbath: which tho' it may ſeem a general precept, yet in one ſenſe particulary applies to you, who have help'd many a human ox, and many a human aſs to the likeneſs of man, not to ſay God.

Believe me, dear Sir, with all good wiſhes for yourſelf and your family (the happineſs of which tyes I know by experience, and have learn'd to value from the late danger of loſing the beſt of mine)

Your, etc.

LETTER XLIII.

To the ſame.

Twickenham, June 10, 1733.

AS I know, you and I mutually deſire to ſee one another, I hoped that this day our wiſhes would have met, and brought you hither. And this for the very reaſon which poſſibly might hinder your coming, that my poor Mother is dead *. I thank God her death was eaſy, as her life was innocent; and as it coſt her not a groan, or even a ſigh, there is yet upon her countenence ſuch an expreſſion of Tranquillity, nay, almoſt of Pleaſure, that it is even amiable to behold it. It would afford the fineſt Image of a Saint expir'd, that ever Painting drew; and it would be the greateſt obligation which even that obliging Art could ever beſtow on a friend, if you could come and ſketch it for me. I am ſure, if there be no very prevalent obſtacle,

* Mrs, Pope died the 7th of June, 1733, aged 93.

you

you will leave any common bufinefs to do this: and I
hope to fee you this evening as late as you will, or to-morrow morning as early, before this winter-flower is faded.
I will defer her interment till to-morrow night. I know
you love me, or I could not have written this—I could
not (at this time) have written at all—Adieu! May you
die as happily!   Your, etc.

LETTER XLIV.

To the fame.

IT is hardly poffible to tell you the joy your pencil gave
me, in giving me another friend, fo much the fame!
and which (alas for mortality!) will out-laft the other.
Pofterity will, thro' your means, fee the man whom it
will for ages honour *, vindicate, and applaud, when envy
is no more, and when (as I have already faid in the Effay
to which you are fo partial)

The fons fhall blufh their fathers were his fees.

That Effay has many faults, but the poem you fent me
has but one, and that I can eafily forgive. Yet I would
not have it printed for the world, and yet I would not
have it kept unprinted neither—but all in good time.
I'm glad you publifh your Milton. B—ly will be angry
at you, and at me too fhortly for what I could not help, a
Satyrical Poem on Verbal Criticifm by Mr. Mallet, which
he has infcribed to me, but the Poem itfelf is good (another caufe of anger to any Critic.) As for myfelf, I refolve to go on in my quiet, calm, moral courfe, taking
no fort of notice of man's anger, or woman's fcandal, with
Virtue in my eyes, and Truth upon my tongue. Adieu.

LETTER XLV,

To Mr. BETHEL,

Aug. 9, 1733.

YOU might well think me negligent or forgetful of you,
if true friendfhip and fincere efteem were to be mea-
fured by common forms and compliments. The truth is,

* Lord Bolingbroke.

I could

I could not write then, without faying fomething of my
own condition, and of my lofs of fo old and fo deferving a
parent, which really would have troubled you ; or I muſt
have kept a filence upon that head, which would not have
fuited that freedom and fincere opening of the heart which
is due to you from me. I am now pretty well ; but my
home is uneafy to me ftill, and I am therefore wandering
about all this fummer. I was but four days at Twickenham
fince the occafion that made it fo melancholy. I have been
a fortnight in Effex, and am now at Dawley (whofe maſter is your fervant) and going to Cirencefter to Lord Bathurſt. I ſhall alfo fee Southampton with Lord Peterborow. The Court and Twit'nam I ſhall forfake together. I
wiſh I did not leave our friend †, who deferves more quiet,
and more health and happinefs, than can be found in fuch
a family. The reſt of my acquaintance are tolerably
happy in their various ways of life, whether court, country, or town ; and Mr. Cleland is as well in the Park, as
if he were in Paradife. I heartily hope, Yorkſhire is the
fame to you ; and that no evil, moral or phyfical, may
come near you.

I have now but too much melancholy leifure, and no
other care but to finiſh my Effay on Man: there will be
in it one line that may offend you (I fear) and yet I will
not alter or omit it, unlefs you come to town and prevent me before I print it, which will be in a fortnight
in all probability. In plain truth, I will not deny myfelf
the greateſt pleafure I am capable of receiving, becaufe another may have the modefty not to ſhare it. It is all a poor
poet can do, to bear teftimony to the virtue he cannot reach :
befides, that, in this age, I fee too few good Examples not
to lay hold on any I can find. You fee what an intereſted
man I am. Adieu.

LETTER XLVI.

To ———— †.

Sept. 7, 1733.

YOU cannot think how melancholy this place makes
me ; every part of this wood puts into my mind poor
Mr. Gay, with whom I paſt once a great deal of pleafant
time in it, and another friend who is near dead, and quite
loſt to us, Dr. Swift. I really can find no enjoyment in

† Mrs. B.

the

the place; the fame fort of uneafinefs as I find at Twit'-nam, whenever I pafs near my Mother's room.

I've not yet writ to Mrs. *. I think I fhould, but have nothing to fay that will anfwer the character they confider me in, as a Wit; befides, my eyes grow very bad (whatever is the caufe of it) I'll put them out for nobody but a friend; and, I proteft, it brings tears into them almoft to write to you, when I think of your ftate and mine. I long to write to Swift, but cannot. The greateft pain I know, is to fay things fo very fhort of one's meaning, when the heart is full.

I feel the going out of life faft enough, to have little appetite left to make compliments, at beft ufelefs, and for the moft part unfelt fpeeches. 'Tis but in a very narrow circle that Friendfhip walks in this world, and I care not to trade out of it more than I needs muft; knowing well, it is but to two or three (if quite fo many) that any man's welfare or memory can be of confequence: The reft, I believe, I may forget, and be pretty certain they are already even, if not before-hand with me.

Life, after the firft warm heats are over, is all downhill: and one almoft wifhes the journey's end, provided we were fure but to lie down eafy, whenever the Night fhall overtake us.

I dream'd all laft night of —. She has dwelt (a little more than perhaps is right) upon my fpirits: I faw a very deferving gentleman in my travels, who has formerly, I have heard, had much the fame misfortune: and (with all his good breeding and fenfe) ftill bears a cloud and melancholy caft, that never can quite clear up, in all his behaviour and converfation. I know another, who, I believe, could promife, and eafily keep his word, never to laugh in his life. But one muft do one's beft, not to be ufed by the world as that poor lady was by her fifter; and not feem too good, for fear of being thought affected, or whimfical.

It is a real truth, that to the laft of my moments, the thought of you and the beft of my wifhes for you, will attend you, told or untold: I could wifh you had once the conftancy and refolution to act for yourfelf, whether before or after I leave you (the only way I ever fhall leave you) you muft determine; but reflect that the firft would make me, as well as yourfelf, happier; the latter could make you only fo. Adieu.

LETTER

LETTER XLVII.

From Dr. ARBUTHNOT.

Hampſtead, July, 17, 1734.

I Little doubt of your kind concern for me, nor of that of the Lady you mention. I have nothing to repay my friends with at preſent, but prayers and good wiſhes. I have the ſatisfaction to find that I am as officiouſly ſerv'd by my friends, as he that has thouſands to leave in legacies; beſides the aſſurance of their ſincerity. God Almighty has made my bodily diſtreſs as eaſy as a thing of that nature can be. I have found ſome relief, at leaſt ſome times, from the air of this place. My nights are bad, but many poor creatures have worſe.

As for you, my good friend, I think, ſince our firſt acquaintance, there have not been any of thoſe little ſuſpicions or jea'ouſies that often affect the ſincereſt friendſhips; I am ſure not on my ſide. I muſt be ſo ſincere as to own, that though I could not help valuing you for thoſe Talents which the world prizes, yet they were not the foundation of my friendſhips; they were quite of another ſort; nor ſhall I at preſent offend you by enumerating them: And I make it my Laſt Requeſt, that you will continue that Noble Diſdain and Abhorrence of Vice, which you ſeem naturally endued with; but ſtill with a due regard to your own ſafety; and ſtudy more to reform than chaſtiſe, tho' the one cannot be effected without the other.

Lord Bathurſt I have always honour'd, for every good quality that a perſon of his rank ought to have: Pray, give my reſpects and kindeſt wiſhes to the family. My venifon ſtomach is gone, but I have thoſe about me, and often with me, who will be very glad of his preſent. If it is left at my houſe, it will be tranſmitted ſafe to me.

A recovery in my caſe, and at my age, is impoſſible; the kindeſt wiſh of my friends is Euthanaſia. Living or dying, I ſhall always be   Yours, etc.

LETTER XLVIII.

To Dr. ARBUTHNOT.

July 26, 1734.

I Thank you for your letter, which has all thoſe genuine marks of a good mind by which I have ever diſtinguiſh'd yours,

yours, and for which I have so long loved you. Our friendship has been conflant; becaule it was grounded on good principles, and therefore not only uninterrupted by any Diftruft, but by any Vanity, much lefs any Intereft.

What you recommend to me with the folemnity of a Laft Requeft, fhall have its due weight with me. That difdain and indignation againft Vice, is (I thank God) the only difdain and indignation I have: It is fincere, and it will be a lafting one. But fure it is as impoffible to have a juft abhorrence of Vice, without hating the Vicious, as to bear a true love for Virtue, without loving the Good. To reform and not to chaftife, I am afraid, is impoffible ; and that the beft Precepts, as well as the beft Laws, would prove of fmall ufe, if there were no Examples to enforce them. To attack Vices in the abftract, without touching Perfons, may be fafe fighting indeed, but it is fighting with Shadows. General propofitions are obfcure, mifty, and uncertain, compar'd with plain, full, and home examples : Precepts only apply to our Reafon, which in moft men is but weak : Examples are pictures, and ftrike the Senfes, nay raife the Paffions, and call in thofe (the ftrongeft and moft general of all motives) to the aid of reformation. Every vicious man makes the cafe his own ; and that is the only way by which fuch men can be affected, much lefs deterr'd. So that to chaftife is to re- form. The only fign by which I found my writings ever did any good, or had any weight, has been that they raifed the anger of bad men. And my greateft comfort, and encouragement to proceed, has been to fee, that thofe who have no fhame, and no fear of any thing elfe, have ap- pear'd touch'd by my Satires.

As to your kind concern for my Safety, I can guefs what occafions it at this time. Some Characters * I have drawn are fuch, that if there be any who deferve them, 'tis evidently a fervice to mankind to point thofe men out ; yet fuch as, if all the world gave them, none, I think, will own they take to themfelves. But if they fhould, thofe of whom all the world think in fuch a manner, muft be men I cannot fear. Such in particular as have the meannefs to do mifchiefs in the dark, have feldom the courage to juftify them in the face of day ; the talents that make a Cheat or Whifperer, are not the fame that qualify a man for an Infulter ; and as to private villainy, it is not

* The Character of Sporus in the Epiftle to Dr. Arbuthnot.

fo

fo fafe to join in an Affaffination, as in a Libel *. I will confult my fafety fo far as I think becomes a prudent man : but not fo far as to omit any thing which I think becomes an honeft one. As to perfonal attacks beyond the law, every man is liable to them : as for danger within the law, I am not guilty enough to fear any. For the good opinion of all the world, I know, it is not to be had : for that of worthy men, I hope, I fhall not forfeit it : for that of the Great, or thofe in power, I may wifh I had it ; but if thro' mifreprefentations (too common about perfons in that ftation) I have it not, I fhall be forry, but not miferable in the want of it.

It is certain, much freer Satirifts than I, have enjoy'd the encouragement and protection of the Princes under whom they lived. Auguftus and Mæcenas made Horace their companion, though he had been in arms on the fide of Brutus.; and allow me to remark, it was out of the fuffering Party too, that they favour'd and diftinguifh'd Virgil. You will not fufpect me of comparing myfelf with Virgil and Horace, nor even with another Court-favourite, Boileau †. I have always been too modeft to imagine my Panegyrics were Incenfe worthy of a Court ; and that, I hope, will be thought the true reafon why I have never offer'd any. I would only have obferv'd, that it was under the greateft Princes and beft Minifters, that moral Satirifts were moft encouraged ; and that then Poets exercifed the fame jurifdiction over the Follies, as Hiftorians did over the Vices of men. It may alfo be worth confidering, whether Auguftus himfelf makes the greater figure in the writings of the former, or of the latter ? and whether Nero and Domitian do not appear as ridiculous for their falfe Tafte and Affectation in Perfius and Juvenal, as odious for their bad Government in Tacitus and Suetonius ? In the firft of thefe reigns it was, that Horace was protected and carefs'd ; and in the latter that Lucan was put to death, and Juvenal banifh'd.

I would not have faid fo much, but to fhew you my whole heart on this fubject ; and to convince you, I am deliberately bent to perform that Requeft which you make your laft to me, and to perform it with Temper, Juftice, and Refolution. As your Approbation (being the Teftimony of a found head and an honeft heart) does greatly confirm me herein, I wifh you may live to fee the effect it may hereafter have upon me, in fomething more deferving

* See the following Letter to a Noble Lord.
† See Letter VII. to Mr. Warburton.
VOL. IV. G g of

of that approbation.   But if it be the Will of God, (which
I know, will also be yours) that we muft feparate, I hope
it will be better for You than it can be for me.   You are
fitter to live, or to die, than any man I know.   Adieu,
my dear friend! and may God preferve your life eafy, or
make your death happy *.

* This excellent perfon died Feb. 27, 1734-5.

[We find by Letter xix. to Dr. Atterbury, that the Duchefs of Buckinghamfhire would have had Mr. Pope to draw her hufband's Character. But though
he refufed this office, yet in his Epiftle *on the Characters of Women*, thefe lines,

> *To heirs unknown defcends th' unguarded ftore,*
> *Or wanders, heav'n-directed, to the poor,*

are fuppofed to mark her out in fuch a manner as not to be miftaken for another ; and having faid of himfelf, that *be held a lie in profe and verfe to be the
fame*: All this together gave a handle to his enemies, fince his death, to publifh the following Paper (intitled *The Character of Katharine*, etc.) as written
by him. To which (in vindication of the deceafed Poet) we have fubjoined a
Letter to a friend, that will let the reader fully into the hiftory of the *writing*
and *publication* of this extraordinary CHARACTER.]

The CHARACTER of KATHARINE, late Duchefs of Buckinghamfhire and Normanby.

By the late Mr. POPE.

SHE was the daughter of James the Second, and of the
Countefs of Dorchefter, who inherited the Integrity
and Virtue of her father with happier fortune. She was
married firft to James Earl of Anglefey ; and fecondly, to
John Sheffield Duke of Buckinghamfhire and Normanby ;
with the former fhe exercifed the virtues of *Patience* and
Suffering, as long as there was any hopes of doing good by
either ; with the latter all other *conjugal virtues*. The man
of fineft fenfe and fharpeft difcernment, fhe had the happinefs to pleafe ; and in that, found her only pleafure.
When he died, it feemed as if his fpirit was only breathed
into her, to fulfil what he had begun, to perform what he
had concerted, and to preferve and watch over what he had
left, *his only fon* ; in the care of whofe health, the forming
of whofe mind, and the improvement of whofe fortune,
fhe acted with the conduct and fenfe of the Father, foften'd,
but not overcome, with the tendernefs of the Mother.
Her Underftanding was fuch as muft have made a figure,
had it been in a man; but the modefty of her fex threw a veil
over its luftre, which neverthelefs fupprefs'd only the expreffion, not the exertion of it ; for her fenfe was not fuperior to her Refolution, which, when once fhe was in the
right, preferv'd her from making it only a tranfition to the
wrong, the frequent weaknefs even of the beft women.
She often followed wife counfel, but fometimes went before it, always with fuccefs. She was poffeffed of a fpirit
which affifted her to get the better of thofe accidents which
admitted of any redrefs, and enabled her to fupport out-
wardly, with decency and dignity, thofe which admitted

of

of none ; yet melted inwardly, through almoſt her whole
life, at a ſucceſſion of melancholy and affecting objects,
the loſs of all her Children, the misfortunes of *Relations
and Friends, public and private*, and the death of thoſe who
were deareſt to her. Her heart was as compaſſionate as it
was great : her Affections warm even to ſolicitude : her
Friendſhip not violent or jealous, but rational and perſe-
vering : her Gratitude equal and conſtant to the living ;
to the dead boundleſs and heroical. What perſon ſoever
ſhe found worthy of her eſteem, ſhe would not give up for
any power on earth ; and the greateſt on earth whom ſhe
could not eſteem, obtain'd from her no farther tribute than
Decency. Her Good-will was wholly directed by merit,
not by accident ; not meaſured by the regard they profeſs'd
for her own deſert, but by her idea of theirs : And as there
was no merit which ſhe was not able to imitate, there was
none which ſhe could envy : therefore her Converſation
was as free from detraction as her Opinions from prejudice
or prepoſſeſſion. As her Thoughts were her own, ſo were
her Words ; and ſhe was as ſincere in uttering her judgment, as impartial in forming it. She was a ſafe Companion, many were ſerv'd, none ever ſuffer'd by her acquaintance : inoffenſive, when unprovoked ; when provoked, not ſtupid : but the moment her enemy ceaſed to
be hurtful, ſhe could ceaſe to act as an enemy. She was
therefore not a bitter but conſiſtent enemy : (tho' indeed,
when forced to be ſo, the more a finiſh'd one for having been
long a making.) And her proceeding with ill people was
more in a calm and ſteady courſe, like Juſtice, than in
quick and paſſionate onſets, like Revenge. As for thoſe
of whom ſhe only thought ill, ſhe conſidered them not ſo
much as once to wiſh them ill ; of ſuch, her Contempt was
great enough to put a ſtop to all other paſſions that could
hurt them. Her Love and Averſion, her Gratitude and
Reſentment, her Eſteem and Neglect, were equally open
and ſtrong, and alterable only from the alteration of the
perſons who created them. Her Mind was too noble to
be inſincere, and her Heart too honeſt to ſtand in need of
it ; ſo that ſhe never found cauſe to repent her conduct
either to a friend or an enemy. There remains only to
ſpeak of her Perſon, which was moſt amiably majeſtic ;
the niceſt eye could find no fault in the lineaments of her
Face or proportion of her Body ; it was ſuch, as pleas'd
wherever ſhe had a deſire it ſhould ; yet ſhe never envied
that of any other, which might better pleaſe in general :
In the ſame manner, as being content that her merits were

eſteemed

efteemed where fhe defired they fhould, fhe never depre-
ciated thofe of any other that were efteemed or preferred
elfewhere. For fhe aimed not at a general love or a general efteem where fhe was not known ; it was enough to be
pofiefs'd of both wherever fhe was. Having lived to the
age of Sixty-two years ; not courting Regard, but receiving it from all who knew her; not loving Bufinefs, but
difcharging it fully wherefoever duty or friendfhip engaged
her in it ; not following Greatnefs, but not declining to
pay refpeft, as far as was due from independency and
difintereft ; having honourably abfolv'd all the parts of life,
fhe forfook this World, where fhe had left no aft of duty
or virtue undone, for that where alone fuch afts are rewarded, on the 13th Day of March 1742-3 *.

Mr. Pope to James Moyser of Beverly, Efq.

Dear Sir,   Bath, July 11, 1743.

I Am always glad to hear of you, and where I can, I
always inquire of you. But why have you omitted to
tell me one word of your own health ? The account of our
Friend's † is truly melancholy, added to the circumftance
of his being detained (I fear, without much hope) in a
foreign country, from the comfort of feeing (what a good
man moft defires and beft deferves to fee to the Jaft hour)
his Friends about him. The public news ‡ indeed gives
every Englifhman a reafonable joy, and I truly feel it with
you, as a national joy, not a party one ; nay as a general
joy, to all nations where bloodfhed and mifery muft have
been introduced, had the ambition and perfidy of ——
prevail'd.

I come now to anfwer your friend's queftion. The
whole of what he has heard of my writing the Charafter
of the old § Duke of Buckingham is untrue. I do not remember ever to have feen it in MS. nor have I ever feen
the pedigree he mentions, otherwife than after the Duchefs had printed it with the Will, and fent one to me, as,
I fuppofe, fhe did to all her acquaintance. I do not wonder it fhould be reported I writ that Charafter, after a
ftory which I will tell you in your ear, and to yourfelf

* " The above Charafter was written by Mr. Pope fome years before her
" Grace's Death." So the printed Edition.
† Mr. Bethel.
‡ The Viftory at Dettingen.
§ He fays the old Duke, becaufe he wrote a very fine Epitaph for the Son.

only

only. There was another *Character written of her Grace* by herself (with what help, I know not) but she shewed it me in her blots, and preffed me, by all the adjurations of Friendship, to give her my sincere opinion of it. I acted honeftly and did fo. She feemed to take it patiently, and upon many exceptions which I made, engaged me to take the whole, and to felect out of it juft as much as I judged might ftand, and return her the Copy. I did fo. Immediately fhe picked a quarrel with me, and we never faw each other in five or fix years. In the mean time fhe fhewed this *Character* (as much as was extracted of it in my hand-writing) as a Compofition of my own in her praife. And very probably it is *now in the hands of Lord Harvey.* Dear Sir, I fincerely wifh you, and your whole family (whofe welfare is fo clofely connected) the beft health and trueft happinefs; and am (as is alfo the Mafter of this place)

Your, etc.

A LETTER to a NOBLE LORD.

On occasion of some Libels written and propagated at
Court, in the year 1732-3.

MY LORD,   NOV. 30, 1733.

YOUR Lordship's* Epistle has been publish'd some days,
but I had not the pleasure and pain of seeing it till
yesterday : Pain, to think your Lordship should attack me
at all ; Pleasure, to find that you can attack me so weakly.
As I want not the humility, to think myself in every way
but *one* your inferior, it seems but reasonable that I
should take the only method either of self-defence or re-
taliation, that is left me, against a person of your quality
and power. And as by your choice of this weapon, your
pen, you generously (and modestly too, no doubt) meant
to put yourself upon a level with me ; I will as soon believe
that your Lordship would give a wound to a man unarm'd,
as that you would deny me the use of it in my own
defence.

I presume you will allow me to take the same liberty,
in my answer to so *candid, polite*, and *ingenious* a Nobleman,
which your Lordship took in yours, to so *grave, religious*,
and *respectable* a Clergyman † : As you answered his *Latin*
in *English*, permit me to answer your *Verse* in *Prose*. And
tho' your Lordship's reason for not writing in *Latin*, might
be stronger than mine for not writing in *Verse*, yet I may
plead *Two good* ones, for this conduct : the one that I want
the Talent of spinning *a thousand lines in a* Day ‡ (which, I
think, is as much *Time* as this subject deserves) and the
other, that I take your Lordship's *Verse* to be as much *Prose*
as this letter. But no doubt it was your choice, in writing
to a friend, to renounce all the Pomp of Poetry, and give
us this excellent model of the familiar.

When I consider the *great difference* betwixt the rank your
Lordship holds in the *World*, and the rank which your *writings* are like to hold in the *learned world*, I presume that
distinction of style is but necessary, which you will see ob-

* Entitled, *An Epistle to a Doctor of Divinity from a Nobleman at Hampton-
Court*, *Aug.* 28, 1733, and printed the November following for J. Roberts.
Fol.
† Dr. S.

‡ *And Pope with justice of such lines may say,
His Lordship spins a thousand in a day*. Epist. p. 6.

serv'd

serv'd thro' this letter. When I speak of *you*, my Lord, it will be with all the deference due to the inequality which Fortune has made between you and myself: but when I speak of your *writings*, my Lord, I muſt, I can do nothing but trifle.

I ſhould be oblig'd indeed to leſſen this *Reſpect*, if all the Nobility (and eſpecially the elder brothers) are but ſo many hereditary fools *, if the privilege of Lords be to want brains †, if noblemen can hardly write or read ‖, if all their buſineſs is but to dreſs and vote §, and all their employment in court to tell lies, flatter in public, ſlander in private, falſe to each other, and follow nothing but ſelf-intereſt ┼. Bleſs me, my Lord, what an account is this you give of them? and what would have been ſaid of me, had I immolated, in this manner, the whole body of the Nobility, at the ſtall of a well-fed Prebendary?

Were it the mere *Exceſs* of your Lordſhip's *Wit*, that carried you thus triumphantly over all the bounds of decency, I might conſider your Lordſhip on your *Pegaſus*, as a ſprightly hunter on a mettled horſe; and while you were trampling down all our works, patiently ſuffer the injury, in pure admiration of the *Noble Sport*. But ſhould the caſe be quite otherwiſe, ſhould your Lordſhip be only like a *Boy that is run away with*; and run away with by a *very Fool*; really common charity, as well as reſpect for a noble family, would oblige me to ſtop your career, and to *help you down* from *this Pegaſus*.

Surely the little praiſe of a *Writer* ſhould be a thing below your ambition: You, who were no ſooner born, but in the lap of the Graces; no ſooner at ſchool, but in the arms of the Muſes; no ſooner in the World, but you practiſ'd all the ſkill of it; no ſooner in the Court, but you poſſeſs'd all the art of it! Unrival'd as you are, in making

* *That to good blood by old preſcriptive rules*
  Gives right ſucceſſively to be Fools.

† *Nor wonder that my Brain no more affords,*
  But recollect the privilege of Lords.

¶ *And when you ſee me fairly write my name;*
  For England's ſake wiſh all could do the ſame.

§ *Whilſt all our buſineſs is to dreſs and vote.* ibid.

┼ *Courts are only larger families,*
  The growth of each, few truths, and many lies:
  *   I private ſatyrize, in public flatter.*
  Few to each other, all is one point true;
  Whiſt at one I point, nor need explain. Adieu. p. ult.

a figure

a figure, and in making a speech, methinks, my Lord, you may well give up the poor talent of turning a Diftich. And why this fondnefs for Poetry ? Profe admits of the two excellencies you moft admire, Diction and Fiction: It admits of the talents you chiefly poffefs, a moft fertile invention, and moft florid expreffion; it is with profe, nay the plaineft profe, that you beft could teach our nobility to vote, which, you juftly obferve, is half at leaft of their bufinefs * : And, give me leave to prophefy, it is to your talent in profe, and not in verfe, to your fpeaking, not your writing, to your art at court, not your art of poetry, that your Lordfhip muft owe your future figure in the world.

My Lord, whatever you imagine, this is the advice of a Friend, and one who remembers he formerly had the honour of fome profeffion of Friendfhip from you : Whatever was his *real fhare* in it, whether fmall or great, yet as your Lordfhip could never have had the leaft *Lofs* by continuing it, or the leaft *Intereft* by withdrawing it; the misfortune of lofing it, I fear, muft have been owing to his own *deficiency* or *neglect*. But as to any *actual fault* which deferved to forfeit it in fuch a degree, he protefts he is to this day guiltlefs and ignorant. It could at moft be but a fault of *omiffion*; but indeed by omiffions, men of your Lordfhip's uncommon merit may fometimes think themfelves fo injur'd, as to be capable of an inclination to injure another; who, tho' very much below their quality, may be above the injury.

I never heard of the leaft difpleafure you had conceived againft me, till I was told that an imitation I had made of † *Horace* had offended fome perfons, and among them your Lordfhip. I could not have apprehended that a few *general ftrokes* about a *Lord fcribling carelefly*, a *Pimp* or a *Spy* at Court, a *Sharper* in a gilded chariot, etc. that thefe, I fay, fhould be ever applied as they have been, by *any malice* but that which is the greateft in the world, *the Malice of ill people to themfelves.*

Your Lordfhip fo well knows (and the whole Court and town thro' your means fo well know) how far the refentment was carried upon that imagination, not only in the *Nature* of the *Libel* ‡ you propagated againft me, but in the extraordinary *manner, pace*, and *prefence* in which it was

---

* *All their bufinefs is to drefs and vote.*
† The firft Satire of the fecond Book, printed in 1732.
‡ *Verfes to the Imitator of Horace*, afterwards printed by J. Roberts, 1732, Fol.

propagated *; that I shall only say, it seem'd to me to exceed the bounds of justice, common sense, and decency.

I wonder yet more, how a *Lady*, of great wit, beauty,
and fame for her poetry, (between whom and your Lord-
ship there is a *natural*, a *just*, and a *well grounded esteem:*) could
be prevailed upon to take a part in that proceeding. Your
resentments against me indeed might be equal, as my offence to you both was the same ; for neither had I the
least misunderstanding with that Lady, till after I was the
Author of my own misfortune in discontinuing her acquaintance. I may venture to own a truth, which cannot be
unpleasing to either of you ; I assure you my reason for so
doing, was merely that you had both *too much wit* for
me † ; and that I could not do, with *mine*, many things
which you could with *yours*. The injury done you in withdrawing myself could be but small, if the value you had
for me was no greater than you have been pleas'd since
to profess. But surely, my Lord, one may say, neither
the Revenge, nor the Language you held, bore any *proportion* to the pretended offence : The appellations of ‡ *Foe*
to *human kind*, an *Enemy* like the *Devil* to all that have *Being* ;
ungrateful, *unjust*, deserving to be *whipt, blanketed, kicked*,
nay *kill'd* ; a *Monster*, an *Assassin*, whose conversation every
man ought to *shun*, and against whom *all doors* should be
shut ; I beseech you, my Lord, had you the least right to
give, or to encourage or justify any other in giving
such language as this to me ? Could I be treated in terms
more strong or more atrocious, if, during my acquaintance
with you, I had been a *Betrayer*, a *Backbiter*, a *Whisperer*,
an *Eves-dropper*, or an *Informer* ? Did I in all that time
ever throw a *false Dye*, or palm a *foul Card* upon you ? Did
I ever *borrow*, *steal*, or accept, either *Money, Wit*, or *Advice* from you ? Had I ever the honour to join with either of
you in one *Ballad, Satire, Pamphlet*, or *Epigram*, on any
person *living or dead ?* Did I ever do you so great an injury
as to put off *my own Verses* for *yours*, especially on *those Persons* whom they might *most offend ?* I am confident you cannot answer in the affirmative ; and I can truly affirm, that,
ever since I lost the happiness of your conversation, I have

---

* *It was for this reason that this Letter, as soon as it was printed, was
communicated to the Q*

† *Once, and but once, his heedless youth was bit,*
  And lik'd that dang'rous thing, a female Wit.
See the Letter to Dr. Arbuthnot amongst the Variations.

‡ *See the aforesaid Verses to the Imitator of Horace.*

not publiſhed or written, one ſyllable of, or to either of you; never hitch'd your *names* in a *Verſe*, or trifled with your *good names* in *company*. Can I be honeſtly charged with any other crime but an *Omiſſion* (for the word *Neglect*, which I us'd before, ſlip'd my pen unguardedly) to continue my admiration of you all my life, and ſtill to contemplate, face to face, your many excellencies and perfections? I am perſuaded you can reproach me truly with no great *Faults*, except my *natural ones*, which I am as ready to own, as to do all juſtice to the contrary *Beauties* in you. It is true, my Lord, I am ſhort, not well ſhap'd, generally ill-dreſs'd, if not ſometimes dirty : Your Lordſhip and Ladyſhip are ſtill in bloom ; your Figures ſuch, as rival the *Apollo* of *Belvedere*, and the *Venus* of *Medicis* ; and your faces ſo finiſh'd, that neither ſickneſs or paſſion can deprive them of *Colour* ; I will allow your own in particular to be the fineſt that ever *Man* was bleſt with : preſerve it, my Lord, and reflect, that to be a Critic, would coſt it too many *frowns*, and to be a Stateſman, too many *wrinkles!* I further confeſs, I am now ſomewhat old ; but ſo your Lordſhip and this excellent Lady, with all your beauty, will (I hope) one day be. I know your Genius and hers ſo perfectly *tally*, that you cannot but join in admiring each other, and by conſequence in the contempt of all ſuch as myſelf. You have both, in my regard, been like—(Your Lordſhip, I know, loves a *Simile*, and it will be one ſuitable to your *Quality*) you have been like *Two Princes*, and I like a *poor Animal* ſacrificed between them to cement a laſting League : I hope I have not bled in vain; but that ſuch an amity may endure for ever! For tho' it be what common *underſtandings* would hardly conceive, Two *Wits* however may be perſuaded, that it is in Friendſhip as in Enmity, The more *danger*, the more *honour*.

Give me the liberty, my Lord, to tell you, why I never replied to thoſe *Verſes* on the *Imitator* of *Horace?* They regarded nothing but my *Figure*, which I ſet no value upon; and my *Morals*, which, I knew, needed no defence : Any honeſt man has the pleaſure to be conſcious, that it is out of the power of the *Wittieſt*, nay the *Greateſt Perſon* in the Kingdom, to leſſen him *that way*, but at the expence of his own *Truth*, *Honour*, or *Juſtice*.

But tho' I declined to explain myſelf juſt at the time when I was ſillily threaten'd, I ſhall now give your Lordſhip a frank account of the offence you imagined to be meant to you. *Fanny* (my Lord) is the plain Engliſh of

runnixs,

Fannius, a real perfon, who was a foolifh Critic, and an enemy of *Horace :* perhaps a Noble one, for fo (if your Latin be gone in earneft *) I muft acquaint you, the word *Beatus* may be conftrued.

> *Beatus Fannius! ultro.*
> *Delatis cap:is et* imagine.

This *Fannius* was, it feems, extremely fond both of his *Poetry* and his *Perfon,* which appears by the pictures and *Statues* he caufed to be made of himfelf, and by his great diligence to propagate *bad Verfes* at *Court,* and get them admitted into the library of *Auguftus.* He was moreover of a delicate or *effeminate complexion,* and conftant at the Affemblies and Operas of thofe days, where he took it into his head to *flander poor Horace.*

> *Ineptus*
> Fannius, *Hermogenis* laedat *conviva Tigelli.*

till it provoked him at laft juft to *name* him, give him a *lafh,* and fend him whimpering to the *Ladies.*

> Difcipularum *inter jubeo plorare cathedras.*

So much for *Fanny,* my Lord. The word *ftins* (as Dr. *Freind,* or even Dr. *Sherwin* could affure you) was the literal tranflation of *deduci* ; a metaphor taken from a *Silk-worm,* my Lord, to fignify any *flight, filken,* or (as your Lordfhip and the Ladies call it) † *flimzy* piece of work. I prefume your Lordfhip has enough of this, to convince you there was nothing *perfonal* but to *that Fannius,* who (with all his fine accomplifhments) had never been heard of, but for *that Horace* he injur'd.

In regard to the right honourable Lady, your Lordfhip's friend, I was far from defigning a perfon of her condition by a name fo derogatory to her, as that of *Sappho* ; a name proftituted to every infamous Creature that ever wrote Verfe or Novels. I proteft I never *apply'd* that name to her in any verfe of mine, *public* or private ; and (I firmly believe) not in any *Letter* or *Converfation.* Whoever could invent a Falfehood to fupport an accufation, I pity ; and whoever can believe fuch a Character to be theirs, I pity

---

* *all I learn'd from Dr.* Freind *at fchool,*
Has quite deferted this poor John Tret head,
And left plain native Englifh in its ftead. Epift. **p. 2.**

† *Weak texture of his flimzy brain,* p. 6.

ftill

ftill more. God forbid the Court or Town fhould have the complaifance to *join* in that opinion! Certainly I meant it only of fuch modern *Sapphos*, as imitate much more the *Lewdnefs* than the *Genius* of the ancient one; and upon whom their wretched brethren frequently beftow both the *Name* and the *Qualification* there mentioned *.

There was another reafon why I was filent as to that paper—I took it for a *Lady's* (on the printer's word in the title-page) and thought it too prefuming, as well as indecent, to contend with one of that *Sex* in *altercation:* For I never was fo mean a creature as to commit my Anger againft a *Lady* to *paper*, tho' but in a *private Letter.* But foon after, her denial of it was brought to me by a Noble perfon of *real Honour and Truth.* Your Lordfhip indeed faid you had it from a Lady, and the Lady faid it was your Lordfhip's; fome thought the beautiful by-blow had *Two Fathers*, or (if one of them will hardly be allow'd a man) *Two Mothers*; indeed I think *both Sexes* had a fhare in it, but which was *uppermoft*, I know not: I pretend not to determine the exact method of this *Witty Fornication:* and, if I call it *Yours*, my Lord, 'tis only becaufe, whoever *got it*, you *brought it forth.*

Here, my Lord, allow me to obferve the different proceeding of the *Ignoble Poet*, and his *Noble Enemies.* What he has written of *Fanny, Adonis, Sappho*, or who you will, he own'd, he publifh'd, he fet his name to: What they have *publifh'd* of him, they have deny'd to have *written*; and what they have *written* of him, they have denied to have *publifh'd.* One of thefe was the cafe in the paft Libel, and the other in the prefent. For tho' the parent has owned it to a few choice friends, it is fuch as he has been obliged to deny in the moft particular terms, to the great Perfon whofe opinion *concern'd him moft.*

Yet, my Lord, this Epiftle was a piece not written in *hafte*, or in a *paffion*, but many months after all pretended provocation; when you was at *full leifure* at Hampton-Court, and I the object *fingled*, like a *Deer cut of Seafon*, for fo ill-timed, and ill-placed a diverfion. It was a *deliberate* work, directed to a *Reverend Perfon †*, of the moft *ferious* and *facred* character, with whom you are known to cultivate a *ftrict correfpondence*, and to whom it will not be doubted, but you open your *fecret Sentiments*, and deliver

* From furious Sappho fcarce a milder fate,
Pox'd by her love, or libell'd by her hate.
2 Sat. B. ii. Hor.

† Dr. S.   your

your *real judgment* of men and things. This, I say, my
Lord, with submission, could not but awaken all my *Reflection* and *Attention.* Your Lordship's opinion of me as a
Poet, I cannot help; it is yours, my Lord, and that were
enought to mortify a poor man; but it is not yours *alone,*
you must be content to share it with the *Gentlemen* of the
Dunciad, and (it may be) with many *more innocent* and ingenious *men.* If your Lordship destroys my *poetical* character,
they will claim their part in the glory; but, give me leave
to say, if my *moral* character be ruin'd, it must be *wholly*
the work of *your Lordship;* and will be hard even for you
to do, unless I *myself co-operate.*

How can you talk (my most worthy Lord) of all *Pope's*
Works as so many *Libels,* affirm, that *he has no invention* but
in *Defamation* *, and charge him with *selling another man's
labours printed with his own name* † ? Fye, my Lord, you
forget yourself. He printed not his name before a line of
the person's you mention; that person himself has told
you and all the world in the book itself, what part he had
in it, as may be seen at the conclusion of his notes to the
Odyssey. I can only suppose your Lordship (not having
at that time *forgot your Greek*) despis'd to look upon the
Translati n; and ever since entertain'd too mean an Opinion of the Translator to cast an eye upon it. Besides, my
Lord, when you said he *said* another man's works, you
ought in justice to have added that he *bought* them, which
very much *alters the Case.* What he gave him was five
hundred pounds; his receipt can be produced to your Lordship. I dare not affirm he was as *well paid* as *some Writers*
(much his inferiors) have been since; but your Lordship
will reflect that I am no man of Quality, either to *buy* or
sell scribling so high: and that I have neither *Place, Pen-
sion,* nor Power to reward for *secret Services.* It cannot be,
that one of your rank can have the least *Envy* to such an
author as I; but were that *possible,* it were much better
gratify'd by employing *not your own,* but some of *those low
and ignoble pens* to do you this *mean office.* I dare engage
you'll have them for less than I gave Mr. Broom, if your
friends have not rais'd the market: Let them drive the bargain for you, my Lord; and you may depend on seeing,
every day in the week, as many (and now and then as pretty) Verses, as these of your Lordship.

* *to his eternal shame,*
Proud he can ne'er want but to defame.
† *And sold Broom's labours printed with Pope's Name.* p. 7.

And

And would it not be full as well, that my poor perfon
fhould be abus'd by them, as by one of your rank and
quality ? Cannot *Curl* do the fame ? nay has he not done
it before your Lordfhip, in the fame *kind of Language*, and
almoft the *fame words* ? I cannot but think, the worthy and
difcreet Clergyman himfelf will agree, it is *improper*, nay *un-
chriftian*, to expofe the *perfonal* defects of our brother : that
both fuch perfect forms as yours, and fuch unfortunate
ones as mine, proceed from the hand of the fame *Maker* ;
who *fafhioneth his Veffels* as he pleafeth, and that it is not
from their *fhape* we can tell whether they were made for
honour or *difhonour*. In a word, he would teach you Charity to your greateft enemies ; of which number, my Lord,
I cannot be reckon'd, fince, tho' a Poet, I was never
your flatterer.

Next, my Lord, as to the *Obfcurity* [*] *of my Birth*, (a reflection copy'd alfo from Mr. *Curl* and his brethren) I am
forry to be obliged to fuch a prefumption as to name my
Family in the fame leaf with your Lordfhip's : but my Father had the honour in one inftance to refemble you, for
he was a *younger Broth r*. He did not indeed think it a Happinefs to bury his *elder Brother*, tho' he had one, who
wanted fome of thofe good qualities which *yours* poffeft.
How fincerely glad could I be, to pay to that young Nobleman's memory the debt I owed to his friendfhip, whofe
early death depriv'd your family of as much *Wit* and *Honour* as he left behind him in any branch of it. But as to
my Father, I could affure you, my Lord, that he was no
Mechanic (neither a hatter, nor, which might pleafe your
Lordfhip yet better, a Cobler) but in truth, of a very tolerable family : And my Mother of an ancient one, as well
born and educated as that *Lady*, whom your Lordfhip
made choice of to be the *Mother of your own Children* ; whofe
merit, beauty, and vivacity (if tranfmitted to your pofterity) will be a *better prefent* than even the noble blood
they derive *only* from *you*. A Mother, on whom I was
never oblig'd fo far to reflect, as to fay, fhe *fpoiled me* [†].
And a Father, who never found himfelf obliged to fay of
me, that he *difapprov'd my Conduct*. In a word, my Lord,
I think it enough, that my Parents, fuch as they were,
never coft me a *blufh* ; and that their Son, fuch as he is,
never coft them a *Tear*.

[*] *Hard as thy Heart, and hateful thy Birth of Fame.*
[†] *Noble Lord's' fuppofed character.*
his Lordfhip's account of himfelf, p. 7.

I have purpofely omitted to confider your Lordfhip's Criticifms on my *Poetry*. As they are exactly the fame with thofe of the *forementioned Authors*, I apprehend they would juftly charge me with partiality, if I gave to *you* what belongs to *them*; or paid more diftinction to the *fame things* when they are in your mouth, than when they were in theirs. It will be fhewing both them and you (my Lord) a *more particular refpect*, to obferve how much they are honour'd by *your Imitation of them*, which indeed is carried thro' your whole Epiftle. I have read fomewhere at *School* (tho' I make it no *Vanity* to have forgot where) that *Tully* naturaliz'd a few phrafes at the inftance of fome of his friends. Your Lordfhip has done more in honour of thefe Gentlemen; you have authoriz'd not only their *Affertions*, but their *Style*. For example, *A* Flow *that* wants fkill to *reftrain its* ardour,— *a* Dictionary *that gives us nothing at* its own expence.— *As luxurious branches* bear *but little fruit*, *fo Wit unprun'd is but raw fruit*—*While you* rehearfe ignorance, *you ftill* know enough *to do it in Verfe*—*Wits* are *but glittering* ignorance.—The *account of* how we pafs our time—and, *The weight on Sir R. W——'s* brain. *You can* ever *receive from* no *head more than fuch a head* (as no head) *has to give*: Your Lordfhip would have faid *never* receive inftead of *ever*, and *any head* inftead of *no head*: but all this is perfectly new, and has greatly enrich'd our language.

You are merry, my Lord, when you fay, *Latin* and *Greek*

> *Have quite deferted your poor* John Trot-head,
> *And left plain native Englifh in their ftead;*

for (to do you juftice) this is nothing lefs than *plain Englifh*. And as for your *John Trot-head*, I can't conceive why you fhould give it that name; for by fome * papers I have feen fign'd with that name, it is certainly a head *very different* from that of your Lordfhip's.

Your Lordfhip feems determined to fall out with every thing you have learn'd at fchool: you complain next of a *dull Dictionary*,

> *That gives us nothing at his own expence,*
> *But a few modern words for ancient Senfe.*

Your Lordfhip is the firft man that ever carried the love of Wit fo far, as to expect a *witty Dictionary*. A Dictionary

---

* See fome Treatifes printed in the Appendix to the Graftfman, about that time.

that

that gives us *any thing but words*, muſt not only be an *expenſive*, but a very *extravagant Dictionary*. But what does your Lordſhip mean by its giving us but a *few modern words for ancient ſenſe ?* If by *Senſe* (as I ſuſpect) you mean *words* (*a miſtake not unuſual)* I muſt do the Dictionary the juſtice to ſay, that it gives us *juſt as many modern words as ancient ones*. Indeed, my Lord, you have more need to complain of a bad Grammar, than of a dull Dictionary.

Doctor *Freind*, I dare anſwer for him, never taught you to talk

of Sapphic, Lyric, and Iambic Odes.

Your Lordſhip might as well bid your preſent Tutor, your Taylor, make you a *Coat, Suit of Cloaths,* and *Breeches ;* for you muſt have forgot your Logic, as well as Grammar, not to know, that Sapphic and Iambic are both included in Lyric : that being the *Genus,* and thoſe the *Species.*

For all cannot invent *who can* tranſlate,
No more than thoſe who cloathe *us, can* create.

Here your Lordſhip ſeems in labour for a meaning. Is it that you would have Tranſlations, *Originals ?* for 'tis the common opinion, that the *buſineſs* of a Tranſlator is to *tranſlate,* and not to *invent,* and of a Taylor to *clothe,* and not to *create.* But why ſhould you, my Lord, of all mankind, abuſe a Taylor ? not to ſay *blaſpheme* him ; if he can (as ſome think) at leaſt go halves with God Almighty in the formation of a *Beau.* Might not Doctor *Sherwin* rebuke you for this, and bid you *Remember your* Creator *in the days of your Youth ?*

From a *Taylor,* your Lordſhip proceeds (by a beautiful gradation) to a *Silkman.*

*Thus P—pe we find
The gaudy* Hinchcliff *of a beauteous mind.*

Here too is ſome ambiguity. Does your Lordſhip uſe *Hinchcliff* as a *proper name ?* or, as the Ladies ſay, a *Hinchcliff* or a *Colmar,* for a *Silk* or a *Fan ?* I will venture to affirm, no Critic can have a perfect taſte of your Lordſhip's works, who does not underſtand both your *Male Phraſe* and your *Female Phraſe.*

Your Lordſhip, to finiſh your Climax, advances up to a *Hatter* ; a Mechanic, whoſe Employment, you inform us, is not (as was generally imagined) to *cover people's heads,*

but *to dress their brains* *.   A moft ufeful Mechanic indeed !
I can't help wifhing to have been one for fome people's
fake.—But this too may be only another *Lady-Phrafe* :
Your Lordfhip and the Ladies may take a *Head-drefs* for a
Head, and underftand, that to *adorn the Head* is the fame
thing as to *drefs the Brains*.

Upon the whole, I may thank your Lordfhip for this
high Panegyric : For if I have but *drefs'd* up *Homer*, as
your *Taylor*, *Silkman*, and *Hatter* have *equipp'd your Lordfhip*,
I muft be own'd to have drefs'd him *marvelloufly indeed*, and
no wonder if he is *admir'd by the Ladies* †.

After all, my Lord, I really wifh you would learn your
Grammar. What if you put yourfelf awhile under the
Tuition of your Friend *W—m?* May not I with all refpect fay to you, what was faid to *another Noble Poet* by
Mr. Cowley, *Pray, Mr.* Howard ‡, *if you did read your
Grammar, what harm would it do you ?* You yourfelf wifh
all Lords would *learn to write* § ; tho' I don't fee of what
ufe it could be, if their whole bufinefs is to *give their Votes* ‖ :
It could only be ferviceable in *figning their Protefts*. Yet
furely this fmall portion of learning might be indulged to
your Lordfhip, without any Breach of that *Privilege* +
you fo generoufly affert to all thofe of your rank, or too
great an Infringement of that *Right* ** which you claim as
Hereditary, and for which, no doubt, your noble Father
will thank you. Surely, my Lord, no man was ever fo
bent upon depreciating himfelf !

All your readers have obferved the following Lines :

> *How oft we hear fome Witling pert and dull,*
> *By fafhion Coxcomb, and by nature Fool,*
> *With hackney Maxims, in dogmatic ftrain,*
> *Scoffing Religion and the Marriage chain ?*
> *Then from his Common-place book he repeats,*
> *The Lawyers all are rogues, and Parfons cheats,*

---

* *For this Mechanic's, like the Hatter's paint,*
  Are but for dreffing other people's brains.

† *by Girls admir'd. p. 6.*

‡ The Honourable Mr. Edward Howard, celebrated for his poetry.

§ *And when you fee me fairly write my name ;*
  For England's fake wifh all Lords did the fame.

‖ *All our bufinefs is to drefs and vote. p. 4.*

+ *The want of brains. ibid.*

** *To be fools. ibid.*

That

> *That Vice and Virtue's nothing but a jeſt,*
> *And all Morality Deceit well dreſt ;*
> *That Life itſelf is like a wrangling game,* etc.

The whole Town and Court (my good Lord) have heard *this Writing* ; who is ſo much every body's acquaintance but his own, that I'll engage *they all name* the *ſame perſon*. But to hear *you* ſay, that this is only —*of whipt Cream a fro-thy Store,* is a ſufficient proof, that never mortal was en-dued with ſo humble an opinion both of himſelf and his own Wit, as your Lordſhip : For, I do aſſure you, theſe are by much the beſt Verſes in your whole Poem.

How unhappy is it for me, that a perſon of your Lord-ſhip's *Modeſty* and *Virtue,* who manifeſts ſo tender a regard to *Religion,* *Matrimony,* and *Morality* ; who, tho' an Orna-ment to the Court, cultivate an exemplary Correſpondence with the *Clergy* ; nay, who diſdain not charitably to con-verſe with, and even aſſiſt, ſome of the very worſt of Writers (ſo far as to caſt a few *Conceits,* or drop a few *Antitheſes* even among the *Dear Joys* of the *Courant*) that you, I ſay, ſhould look upon Me alone as reprobate and un-amendable ! Reflect what I *was,* and what *I am.* I am even *annihilated* by your Anger : For in theſe Verſes you have robbed me of *all power to think* *, and in your others, of the very *name* of a *Man !* Nay, to ſhew that this is wholly your own doing, you have told us that before I wrote my *laſt Epiſtles* (that is before I unluckily mentioned *Fanny* and *Adonis,* whom, I proteſt, I knew not to be your Lord-ſhip's Relations) *I might have lived and died in glory* †.

What would I not do to be well with your Lordſhip ? Tho', you obſerve, I am a mere *Imitator* of *Homer, Horace, Boileau, Garth,* etc. (which I have the leſs cauſe to be aſham'd of, ſince they were *Imitators of one another)* yet what if I ſhould ſolemnly engage never to imitate *your* Lordſhip ? May it not be one ſtep towards an accommo-dation, that while you remark my *Ignorance in Greek,* you are ſo good as to ſay, you have *forgot your own ?* What if I ſhould confeſs I tranſlated from *D'Acier ?* That ſurely could not but oblige your Lordſhip, who are known to prefer *French* to all the learned languages. But allowing that in the ſpace of *twelve years* acquaintance with *Homer,* I might unhappily contract as much *Greek,* as your Lord-

---

* P—e, *who ne'er cou'd think.* p. 7.

† *In glory then he might have liv'd and dy'd.* ibid.

fhip did in *Two* at the Univerfity, why may I not forget it again, as happily ?

Till fuch a reconciliation take effect, I have but one thing to intreat of your Lordfhip. It is that you will not decide of my *Principles* on the fame grounds as you have done of my *Learning* : Nor give the fame account of my *Want of Grace*, after you have loft all acquaintance with my *Perfon*, as you do of my *Want of Greek*, after you have confeffedly loft all acquaintance with the *Language*. You are too generous, my Lord, to follow the *Gentlemen* of the *Dunciad* quite fo far, as to feek my *utter Perdition* : as *Nero* once did *Lucan's*, merely for prefuming to be a *Poet*, while one of fo much greater quality was a *Writer*. I therefore make this humble requeft to your Lordfhip, that the next time you pleafe *to write of me, fpeak of me*, or even *whifper of me* *, you will recollect it is full *eight Years* fince I had the honour of *any converfation* or *correfpondence* with your Lordfhip, except *juft half an hour* in a Lady's Lodgings at Court, and then I had the happinefs of her being prefent all the time. It would therefore be difficult even for your Lordfhip's penetration to tell, to what or from what *Principles*, *Parties*, or *Sentiments*, Moral, Political, or Theological, I may have been converted, or perverted, in all that time. I befeech your Lordfhip to confider, the Injury a Man of your *high Rank* and *Credit* may do to a *private Perfon*, under *Penal Laws* and many other difadvantages, not for want of *honefty* or *confcience*, but merely perhaps for having too *weak a head*, or too *tender a heart* †. It is by *thefe alone* I have hitherto liv'd excluded from all *pofts* of *Profit* or *Truft* : As I can interfere with the *Views* of *no man*, do not deny me, my Lord, *all that is left*, a little *Praife*, or the common Encouragement due, if not to my *Genius*, at leaft to my *Induftry*.

Above all, your Lordfhip will be careful not to wrong my *Moral Character*, with THOSE ‡ under whofe *Protection* I live, and thro' whofe *Lenity* alone I can live with Comfort. Your Lordfhip, I am confident, upon confideration will think, you inadvertently went a little *too far* when you recommended to THEIR perufal, and ftrengthened by the weight of your Approbation, a *Libel*, mean in its reflections upon my poor *figure*, and fcandalous in thofe on

---

* The *whifper*, that, to greatnefs ftill too near,
  Perhap· yet vibrates on his Sovereign's ear.

                                   Epift. to Dr. Arbuthnot.

† See Letters to Bifhop Atterbury, Lett. iv.
‡ The K. and Q.

my

my *Honour* and *Integrity* : wherein I was reprefented as " *an*
" *Enemy* to Human Race, a *Murderer* of Reputations,
" and a *Monfter* marked by God like *Cain*, deferving to
" wander accurs'd thro' the World."

A ftrange Picture of a man, who had the good fortune
to enjoy many friends, who will be always remember'd as
the firft Ornaments of their Age and Country : and no
Enemies that ever contriv'd to be heard of, except Mr.
John Dennis, and your Lordfhip : A Man, who never
wrote a Line in which the *Religion* or *Government* of his
Country, the *Royal Family*, or their *Miniftry*, were difre-
fpectfully mentioned ; the Animofity of any one Party
gratify'd at the expence of another ; or any Cenfure paft,
but upon *known Vice*, *acknowledg'd Folly*, or *aggreffing Impertinence*. It is with infinite pleafure he finds, that *fome Men*
who feem *afham'd* and *afraid* of *nothing elfe*, are fo very fenfible of *his Ridicule* : And 'tis for that very reafon he refolves (by the grace of God, and your Lordfhip's good
leave)

> *That, while he breathes, no rich or noble knave*
> *Shall walk the world in credit to his grave.*

This, he thinks, is rendering the beft Service he can to
the Public, and even to the good Government of his
Country ; and for this, at leaft, he may deferve fome
Countenance, even from the GREATEST PERSONS in
it. Your Lordfhip knows of WHOM I fpeak. Their
NAMES I fhould be as forry, and as much afham'd, to place
near *yours*, on fuch an occafion, as I fhould be to fee *You*,
my Lord, placed fo near *their* PERSONS, if you could ever
make fo ill an Ufe of their Ear * as to afperfe or mifreprefent any one innocent Man.

This is all I fhall ever afk of your Lordfhip, except
your pardon for this tedious Letter. I have the honour to
be, with equal *Refpect* and *Concern*,

My Lord,

Your truly devoted Servant,

A. POPE.

* " Clofe at the ear of Eve."—Ep. to Dr. Arbuthnot.

LETTERS

TO AND FROM

Dr. JONATHAN SWIFT, etc.

From the Year 1714 to 1737.

LETTER I.

Mr. POPE to Dr. SWIFT.

June 18, 1714.

WHATEVER Apologies it might become me to make at any other time for writing to you, I shall use none now, to a man who has own'd himself as splenetic as a Cat in the Country. In that circumstance, I know by experience a letter is a very useful, as well as amusing thing: If you are too busied in State affairs to read it, yet you may find entertainment in folding it into divers figures, either doubling it into a pyramidical, or twisting it into a serpentine form: or, if your disposition should not be so mathematical, in taking it with you to that place where men of studious minds are apt to sit longer than or-dinary; where, after an abrupt division of the paper, it may not be unpleasant to try to fit and rejoin the broken lines together. All these amusements I am no stranger to in the Country, and doubt not but (by this time) you begin to relish them, in your present contemplative situation.

I remember a man, who was thought to have some know-ledge in the world, used to affirm, that no people in town ever complained they were forgotten by their Friends in the country; but my increasing experience convinces me he was mistaken, for I find a great many here grievously com-

complaining of you, upon this fcore. I am told further, that you treat the few you correfpond with in a very arrogant ftyle, and tell them you admire at their infolence in difturbing your meditations, or even enquiring of your * retreat : but this I will not pofitively affert, becaufe I never received any fuch infulting Epiftle from you. My Lord Oxford fays you have not written to him once fince you went : but this perhaps may be only policy, in him or you ; and I, who am half a Whig, muft not entirely credit any thing he affirms. At Button's it is reported you are gone to Hanover, and that Gay goes only on an Embaffy to you. Others apprehend fome dangerous State treatife from your retirement ; and a Wit, who affects to imitate Balfac, fays, that the Miniftry now are like thofe Heathens of old, who received their Oracles from the Woods. The Gentlemen of the Roman Catholic perfuafion are not unwilling to credit me, when I whifper, that you are gone to meet fome Jefuits commiffioned from the Court of Rome, in order to fettle the moft convenient methods to be taken for the coming of the Pretender. Dr. Arbuthnot is fingular in his opinion, and imagines your only defign is to attend at full leifure to the life and adventures of Scriblerus. This indeed muft be granted of greater importance than all the reft ; and I wifh I could promife fo well of you. The top of my own ambition is to contribute to that great work, and I fhall tranflate Homer by the by. Mr. Gay has acquainted you what progrefs I have made in it. I can't name Mr. Gay, without all the acknowledgments which I fhall ever owe you, on his account. If I writ this in verfe, I would tell you, you are like the fun, and while men imagine you to be retir'd or abfent, are hourly exerting your indulgence, and bringing things to maturity for their advantage. Of all the world, you are the man (without flattery) who ferve your friends with the leaft oftentation ; it is almoft ingratitude to thank you, confidering your temper ; and this is the period of all my letter which I fear you will think the moft impertinent. I am, with the trueft affection,

Your, etc.

---

* Some time before the Death of Queen *Anne*, when her mini lers were quarrelli g, and the Dean could not reconcile them, he retired to a Friend's Houfe in Berkfhire, and never faw them after.

LETTER II.

From Dr. Swift to Mr. Pope.

Dublin, June 28, 1715.

MY* Lord Bishop of Clogher gave me your kind letter full of reproaches for my not writing. I am naturally no very exact correspondent, and when I leave a country without probability of returning, I think as seldom as I can of what I loved or esteemed in it, to avoid the *Desiderium* which of all things makes life most uneasy. But you must give me leave to add one thing, that you talk at your ease, being wholly unconcerned in public events : For, if your friends the Whigs continue, you may hope for some favour; if the Tories return, you are at least sure of quiet. You know how well I loved both Lord Oxford and Bolingbroke, and how dear the Duke of Ormond is to me : Do you imagine I can be easy while their enemies are endeavouring to take off their heads ? *I nunc, et verfus tecum meditare canoros—* Do you imagine I can be easy, when I think of the probable consequences of these proceedings, perhaps upon the very peace of the nation, but certainly of the minds of so many hundred thousand good subjects ? Upon the whole, you may truly attribute my silence to the Eclipse, but it was that Eclipse which happened on the first of August.

I borrowed your Homer from the Bishop (mine is not yet landed) and read it out in two evenings. If it pleaseth others as well as me, you have got your end in profit and reputation : Yet I am angry at some bad Rhymes and Triplets, and pray in your next do not let me have so many unjustifiable Rhymes to *war* and *gods*. I tell you all the faults I know, only in one or two places you are a little obscure ; but I expected you to be so in one or two and twenty. I have heard no foul talk of it here, for indeed it is not come over : nor do we very much abound in Judges, at least I have not the honour to be acquainted with them. Your notes are perfectly good, and so are your Preface and Essay. You were pretty bold in mentioning Lord Bolingbroke in that Preface. I saw the Key to the Lock but yesterday ; I think you have changed it a good deal, to adapt it to the present times †.

---

* Dr. *St. George Ash*, formerly a fellow of *Trinity College, Dublin*, (to whom the Dean was a Pupil) afterwards Bishop of Clogher, and translated to the See of Derry in 1716-17

† Put these two last obfervations together, and it will appear that Mr.
                                                                    Pope

God be thanked I have yet no Parliamentary bufinefs, and if they have none with me, I fhall never feek their acquaintance. I have not been very fond of them for fome years paft, not when I thought them tolerably good, and therefore if I can get leave to be abfent, I fhall be much inclined to be on that fide, when there is a parliament on this; but truly I muft be a little eafy in my mind before I can think of Scriblerus.

You are to underftand that I live in the corner of a vaft unfurnifhed houfe; my family confifts of a fteward, a groom, a helper in the ftable, a footman, and an old maid, who are all at board-wages, and when I do not dine abroad, or make an entertainment (which laft is very rare) I eat a mutton-pye, and drink half a pint of wine: My amufe-ments are defending my fmall dominions againft the Archbifhop, and endeavouring to reduce my rebellious Choir. *Perditur haec inter mifero lux.* I defire you will prefent my humble fervice to Mr. Addifon, Mr. Congreve, and Mr. Rowe, and Gay. I am, and will be always, extremely yours, etc.

LETTER III.

Mr. POPE to Dr. SWIFT.

June 20, 1716.

I Cannot fuffer a friend to crofs the Irifh feas without bearing a teftimony from me of the conftant efteem and affection I am both obliged and inclined to have for you. It is better he fhould tell you than I, how often you are in our thoughts and in our cups, and how I learn to fleep lefs and drink more, whenever you are named among us. I look upon a friend in Ireland as upon a friend in the other world, whom (popifhly fpeaking) I believe conftantly well-difpofed towards me, and ready to do me all the good he can, in that ftate of feparation, though I hear nothing from him, and make addreffes to him but very rarely. A Proteftant divine cannot take it amifs that I treat him in the fame manner with my patron Saint.

I can tell you no news, but what you will not fuffi-ciently wonder at, that I fuffer many things as an author

Pope was neither wanting to his friends for fear of party, nor would infult a miniftry to humour his friends. He fa'd of himfelf, and I believe h ia d t uly, that *be never wrote a line to gratify the animofity of any one party at the ex-fience of another.* See the *Letter to a noble Lord.*

militant:

militant: whereof, in your days of probation, you have been a fharer, or you had not arrived to that triumphant ftate you now defervedly enjoy in the Church. As for me, I have not the leaft hopes of the Cardinalate, tho' I fuffer for my Religion in almoft every weekly paper. I have begun to take a pique at the Pfalms of David (if the wicked may be credited, who have printed a fcandalous one * in my name.) This report I dare not difcourage too much, in a profpect I have at prefent of a poft under the Marquis de Langallerie †, wherein if I can but do fome fignal fervice againft the Pope, I may be confiderably advanced by the Turks, the only religious people I dare confide in. If it fhould happen hereafter that I fhould write for the holy law of Mahomet, I hope it may make no breach between you and me; every one muft live, and I beg you will not be the man to manage the controverfy againft me. The Church of Rome I judge (from many modern fymptoms, as well as ancient prophecies) to be in a declining condition: that of England will in a fhort time be fcarce able to maintain her own family: fo Churches fink as generally as Banks in Europe, and for the fame reafon; that Religion and Trade, which at firft were open and free, have been reduced into the Management of Companies, and the Roguery of Directors.

I don't know why I tell you all this, but that I always loved to talk to you; but this is not a time for any man to talk to the purpofe. Truth is a kind of contraband commodity, which I would not venture to export, and therefore the only thing tending that dangerous way which I fhall fay, is, that I am, and always will be, with the utmoft fincerity,   Yours, etc.

LETTER IV.

From Dr. SWIFT to Mr. POPE.

Aug. 30, 1716.

I Had the favour of yours by Mr. F. of whom before any other queftion relating to your health or fortune, or fuccefs as a Poet, I enquired your principles in the common form, " Is he a Whig or a Tory?" I am forry to find they are not fo well tallied to the prefent juncture as I could

---

* In Curl's Collection.
† One who made a noife then, as Count Bonnival has done fince.

wifh.

wiſh. I always thought the terms of *Facto* and *Jure* had
been introduced by the Poets, and that Poſſeſſion of any ·
fort in Kings was held an unexceptionable title in the courts
of Parnaſſus.   If you do not grow a perfect good ſubject
in all its preſent latitudes, I ſhall conclude you are become
rich, and able to live without dedications to men in power,
whereby one great inconvenience will follow, that you
and the world and poſterity will be utterly ignorant of their
Virtues.   For, either your brethren have miſerably deceived us theſe hundred years paſt, or Power confers Virtue, as naturally as five of your Popiſh ſacraments do
Grace.—You ſleep leſs and drink more.—But your maſter
Horace was *Vini ſomnique benignus:* and, as I take it, both are
proper for your trade.   As to mine, there are a thouſand
poetical texts to confirm the one ; and as to the other, I
know it was anciently the cuſtom to ſleep in temples for
thoſe who would conſult the Oracles, " Who dictates to
" me ſlumbering,"* etc.

   You are an ill Catholic, or worſe Geographer, for I can
aſſure you, Ireland is not Paradiſe, and I appeal even to
any Spaniſh divine, whether Addreſſes were ever made to
a friend in Hell, or Purgatory ? And who are all theſe
enemies you hint at ? I can only think of Curl, Gildon,
Squire Burnet, Blackmore, and a few others whoſe fame
I have forgot ; Tools, in my opinion, as neceſſary for a
good writer, as pen, ink, and paper. And beſides, I would
fain know whether every Draper doth not ſhew you three
or four damn'd pieces of ſtuff to ſet off his good one ?
However, I will grant, that one thorough Bookſelling-
Rogue is better qualified to vex an author, than all his
cotemporary ſcriblers in Critic or Satire, not only by
ſtolen Copies of what was incorrect or unfit for the public,
but by downright laying other men's dulneſs at your door.
I had a long deſign upon the Ears of that Curl, when I
was in credit, but the Rogue would never allow me a fair
ſtroke at them, although my penknife was ready drawn
and ſharp. I can hardly believe the relation of his being
poiſoned, although the Hiſtorian pretends to have been an
eye-witneſs : But I beg pardon, Sack might do it, although
Rats-bane would not. I never ſaw the thing you mention
as falſely imputed to you ; but I think the frolicks of merry hours, even when we are guilty, ſhould not be left to
the mercy of our beſt friends, until Curl and his reſem-
blers are hang'd.

* Milton.

With fubmiffion to the better judgment of you and your friends, I take your project of an employment under the Turks to be idle and unneceffary. Have a little patience, and you will find more merit and encouragement at home by the fame methods. You are ungrateful to your country; quit but your own Religion, and ridicule ours, and that will allow you a free choice for any other, or for none at all, and pay you well into the bargain. Therefore pray do not run and difgrace us among the Turks, by telling them you were forced to leave your native home, becaufe we would oblige you to be a Chriftian; whereas we will make it appear to all the world, that we only compelled you to be a Whig.

There is a young ingenious Quaker in this town who writes verfes to his miftrefs, not very correct, but in a ftrain purely what a poetical Quaker fhould do, commending her look and habit, etc. It gave me a hint that a fet of Quaker paftorals might fucceed, if our friend Gay * could fancy it, and I think it a fruitful fubject; pray hear what he fays. I believe further, the paftoral ridicule is not yet exhaufted; and that a porter, footman †, or chairman's paftoral might do well. Or what think you of a Newgate paftoral, among the whores and thieves there?

Laftly, to conclude, I love you never the worfe for feldom writing to you. I am in an obfcure fcene, where you know neither thing nor perfon. I can only anfwer yours, which I promife to do after a fort whenever you think fit to employ me. But I can affure you, the fcene and the times have depreffed me wonderfully, for I will impute no defect to thofe two paltry years which have flipt by fince I had the happinefs to fee you. I am, with the trueft efteem,   Yours, etc.

---

§ L E T T E R V.

From Dr. SWIFT to Mr. POPE.

Dublin, Jan. 10. 1721.

A Thoufand things have vexed me of late years, upon which I am determined to lay open my mind to you. I rather chufe to appeal to you than to my Lord Chief Juftice Whitfhed, under the fituation I am in. For, I take

* Gay did write a paftoral of this kind, which is publifhed in his works.
† Swift himfelf wrote one of this kind, intitled *Dermot and Sheelah*.
§ This Letter Mr. Pope never received, nor did he believe it was ever fent.

this

this caufe properly to lie before you : You are a much
fitter Judge of what concerns the credit of a Writer, the
injuries that are done him, and the reparations he ought
to receive. Befides, I doubt whether the Arguments I
could fuggeft to prove my own innocence would be of much
weight from the gentlemen of the Long-robe to thofe in
Furs, upon whofe decifion about the difference of Style or
Sentiments, I fhould be very unwilling to leave the merits
of my Caufe.

Give me leave then to put you 'in mind (although you
cannot eafily forget it) that about ten weeks before the
Queen's death, I left the town, upon occafion of that in-
curable breach among the great men at Court, and went
down to Berkfhire, where you may remember that you
gave me the favour of a vifit. While I was in that retirement, I writ a Difcourfe which I thought might be ufeful
in fuch a junéture of affairs, and fent it up to London ;
but, upon fome difference in opinion between me and a
certain great minifter now abroad, the publifhing of it
was deferred fo long that the Queen died, and I recalled
my copy, which hath been ever fince in fafe hands. In a
few weeks after the lofs of that excellent Princefs I came
to my ftation here ; where I have continued ever fince in
the greateft privacy, and utter ignorance of thofe events,
which are moft commonly talked of in the world. I neither know the names nor number of the Royal Family
which now reigns, further than the Prayer-book informs
me. I cannot tell who is Chancellor, who are Secretaries,
nor with what nations we are in peace or war. And this
manner of life was not taken up out of any fort of Affeéta-
tion, but merely to avoid giving offence, and for fear of
provoking Party-zeal.

I had indeed written fome Memorials of the four laft
years of the Queen's reign, with fome other informations,
which I received, as neceffary materials to qualify me for
doing fomething in an employment then defign'd me* :
But, as it was at the difpofal of a perfon, who had not the
fmalleft fhare of fteadinefs or fincerity, I difdain'd to accept it.

Thefe papers, at my few hours of health and leifure, I
have been digefting † into order by one fheet at a time,

* Hiftoriographer.
† Thefe papers fome years after were brought finifhed by the Dean into
England, with an intention to publifh them. But a friend on whofe judgment
he relied (the fame I fuppofe whom he mentions above, as being abroad at the
time of writing this letter) diffuaded him from that defign. He told the Dean
here were feveral facts he knew to be falfe, and that the whole was fo much
in

for I dare not venture any further, left the humour of
fearching and feizing papers fhould revive : not that I am
in pain of any danger to myfelf (for they contain nothing
of prefent Times or Perfons, upon which I fhall never lofe
a thought while there is a Cat or a Spaniel in the houfe)
but to preferve them from being loft among Meffengers
and Clerks.

I have written in this kingdom, a * difcourfe to perfuade
the wretched people to wear their own Manufactures inftead of thofe from England. This Treatife foon fpread
very faft, being agreeable to the fentiments of the whole
nation, except of thofe gentlemen who had Employments,
or were Expectants. Upon which a perfon in great office
here immediately took the alarm : he fent in hafte for the
Chief Juftice, and informed him of a feditious, factious,
and virulent Pamphlet, lately publifhed, with a defign of
fetting the two kingdoms at variance ; directing at the fame
time that the Printer fhould be profecuted with the utmoft
rigour of law. The Chief Juftice had fo quick an underftanding, that he refolved, if poffible, to out-do his orders.
The Grand-Juries of the county and city were practifed
effectually with to reprefent the faid Pamphlet with all ag-
gravating Epithets, for which they had thanks fent them
from England, and their Prefentments publifhed for feveral weeks in all the news-papers. The Printer was feized, and forced to give great bail : after his trial the Jury
brought him in Not Guilty, although they had been cull-
ed with the utmoft induftry : The Chief Juftice fent them
back nine times, and kept them eleven hours, until being
perfectly tired out, they were forced to leave the matter
to the mercy of the Judge, by what they call a fpecial
Verdict. During the trial, the Chief Juftice, among o-
ther fingularities, laid his hand on his breaft, and protefted
folemnly that the Author's defign was to bring in the Pretender ; although there was not a fingle fyllable of party
in the whole Treatife, and although it was known, that
the moft eminent of thofe who profeffed his own principles, publickly difallowed his proceedings. But the caufe
being fo very odious and unpopular, the trial of the Ver-

in the fpirit of party-writing, that, though it might have made a feafonable
pamphlet in the time of their adminiftration, it was a difhonour to juft hiftory.
The Dean would do nothing againft his Friend's judgment, yet it extremely
concerned him. And he told a common friend, that fince ** d'd not approve
his hiftory, he would caft it into the fire, though it was the beft work he had
ever written. However, it did not undergo this fate, and is faid to be yet in
being —It has been fince publifhed.
* A propofal for the univerfal ufe of Irifh Manufactures.

diⅽt

dict was deferred from one Term to another, until upon the Duke of G—ft-n the Lord Lieutenant's arrival, his Grace after mature advice, and permission from England, was pleased to grant a *noli profequi*.

This is the more remarkable, becaufe it is faid that the man is no ill decider in common cafes of property, where party is out of queftion ; but when that intervenes, with ambition at heels to pufh it forward, it muft needs confound any man of little fpirit, and low birth, who hath no other endowment than that fort of Knowledge, which, however poffeffed in the higheft degree, can poffibly give no one good quality to the mind.

It is true, I have been much concerned, for feveral years paft, upon account of the public as well as for my-felf, to fee how ill a tafte for wit and fenfe prevails in the world, which Politics, and South-fea, and Party, and Operas, and Mafquerades, have introduced. For, befides many infipid papers which the malice of fome have enti-tled me to, there are many perfons appearing to wifh me well, and pretending to be judges of my ftyle and man-ner, who have yet afcribed fome writings to me, of which any man of common fenfe and literature would be hearti-ly afhamed. I cannot forbear inftancing a Treatife called a *Dedication upon Dedications*, which many would have to be mine, although it be as empty, dry, and fervile a compofition, as I remember at any time to have read. But, above all, there is one Circumftance which makes it im-poffible for me to have been author of a Treatife, wherein there are feveral pages containing a Panegyric on King George, of whofe character and perfon I am utterly igno-rant, nor ever had once the curiofity to enquire into either, living at fo great a diftance as I do, and having long done with whatever can relate to public matters.

Indeed I have formerly delivered my thoughts very freely, whether I were afked or no ; but never affected to be a Counfellor, to which I had no manner of call. I was humbled enough to fee myfelf fo far out-done by the Earl of Oxford in my own trade as a Scholar, and too good a Courtier not to difcover his contempt of thofe who would be men of importance out of their fphere. Befides, to fay the truth, although I have known many great Minifters ready enough to hear Opinions, yet I have hardly feen one that would ever defcend to take Advice ; and this pe-dantry arifeth from a Maxim themfelves do not believe at the fame time they practife by it, that there is fomething profound

profound in Politics, which men of plain honeft fenfe cannot arrive to.

I only wifh my endeavours had fucceeded better in the great point I had at heart, which was that of reconciling the Minifters to each other. This might have been done, if others, who had more concern and more influence, would have acted their parts; and, if this had fucceeded, the public intereft both of Church and State would not have been the worfe, nor the Proteftant Succeffion endangered.

But, whatever opportunities a conftant attendance of four years might have given me for endeavouring to do good offices to particular perfons, I deferve at leaft to find tolerable quarter from thofe of the other Party; for many of which I was a conftant advocate with the Earl of Oxford, and for this I appeal to his Lordfhip: He knows how often I prefied him in favour of Mr. Addifon, Mr. Congreve, Mr. Rowe, and Mr. Steel; although I freely confefs that his Lordfhip's kindnefs to them was altogether owing to his generous notions, and the efteem he had for their wit and parts, of which I could only pretend to be a remembrancer. For I can never forget the anfwer he gave to the late Lord Hallifax, who upon the firft change of the Miniftry interceded with him to fpare Mr. Congreve: It was by repeating thefe two lines of Virgil,

Non obtufa adeo geftamus pectora Poeni,
Nec tam averfus equos Tyria Sol jungit ab urbe.

Purfuant to which, he always treated Mr. Congreve with the greateft perfonal civilities, affuring him of his conftant favour and protection, and adding that he would ftudy to do fomething better for him.

I remember it was in thofe times a ufual fubject of raillery towards me among the Minifters, that I never came to them without a Whig in my fleeve; which I do not fay with any view towards making my Court: For the new Principles * fixed to thofe of that denomination, I did then, and do now from my heart abhor, deteft and abjure, as wholly degenerate from their predeceffors. I have converfed in fome freedom with more minifters of State of all parties than ufually happens to men of my level, and, I confefs, in their capacity as Minifters, I look upon them

---

* He means particularly the principle at that time charged upon them, by their Enemies, of an intention *to profcribe the Tories.*

as a race of people whose acquaintance no man would
court, otherwise than upon the score of Vanity or Ambition.   The first quickly wears off (and is the Vice of low
minds, for a man of spirit is too proud to be vain) and
the other was not my case. Besides, having never received more than one small favour, I was under no necessity
of being a slave to men in power, but chose my friends by
their personal merit, without examining how far their notions agreed with the politics then in vogue. I frequently
conversed with Mr. Addison, and the others I named (except Mr. Steel) during all my Lord Oxford's Ministry, and
Mr. Addison's friendship to me continued inviolable, with
as much kindness as when we used to meet at My Lord
Sommers * or Hallifax, who were leaders of the opposite
Party.

I would infer from all this, that it is with great injustice
I have these many years been pelted by your Pamphle-
teers, merely upon account of some regard which the
Queen's last ministers were pleased to have for me : and
yet in my conscience I think I am a partaker in every ill
design they had against the Protestant Succession, or the
Liberties and Religion of their Country ; and can say with
Cicero, " that I should be proud to be included with
" them in all their actions *tanquam in æquo Trojano*."   But
if I have never discovered by my words, writings, or actions, any Party virulence, or dangerous designs against
the present powers ; if my friendship and conversation
were equally shewn among those who liked or disapproved
the proceedings then at Court, and that I was known to
be a common Friend of all deserving persons of the latter
sort, when they were in distress ; I cannot but think it
hard, that I am not suffered to run quietly among the
common herd of people, whose opinions unfortunately
differ from those which lead to favour and preferment.

I ought to let you know, that the Thing we called a
Whig in England is a creature altogether different from
those of the same denomination here ; at least it was so
during the reign of her late Majesty. Whether those on
your side have changed or no, it hath not been my business to enquire. I remember my excellent friend Mr.
Addison, when he first came over hither Secretary to
the Earl of Wharton, then Lord Lieutenant, was ex-

---

* Lord Sommers had very warmly recommended Dr. Swift to the favour
of Lord Wharton, when he went the Queen's Lieutenant into Ireland in the
year 1709.

tremely offended at the conduct and difcourfe of the Chief
Managers here : He told me they were a fort of people
who feemed to think, that the principles of a Whig con-
fifted in nothing elfe but damning the Church, reviling the
Clergy, abetting the Diffenters, and fpeaking contempti-
bly of revealed Religion.

I was difcourfing fome years ago with a certain Minifter about that whiggifh or fanatical Genius, fo prevalent
among the Englifh of this kingdom ; his Lordfhip accounted for it by that number of Cromwell's Soldiers, adven-
turers eftablifhed here, who were all of the foureft leven,
and the meaneft birth, and whofe pofterity are now in poffeffion of their lands and their principles. However, it
muft be confeffed, that of late fome people in this country
are grown weary of quarrelling, becaufe intereft, the great
motive of quarrelling, is at an end ; for, it is hardly worth
contending who fhall be an Excifeman, a Country-Vicar,
a Cryer in the Courts, or an Under-Clerk.

You will perhaps be inclined to think, that a perfon fo
ill treated as I have been, muft at fome time or other have
difcovered very dangerous opinions in government ; in anfwer to which, I will tell you what my political principles
were in the time of her late glorious Majefty, which I never contradicted by any action, writing, or difcourfe.

Firft, I always declared myfelf againft a Popifh Succeffor to the crown, whatever title he might have by the
proximity of blood : Neither did I ever regard the right
line, except upon two accounts : firft, as it was eftablifhed by law ; and fecondly, as it hath much weight in the
opinions of the people. For neceffity may abolifh any
law, but cannot alter the fentiments of the vulgar ; right
of inheritance being perhaps the moft popular of all topics ;
and therefore in great changes when that is broke, there
will remain much heart-burning and difcontent among the
meaner people ; which (under a weak Prince and corrupt
adminiftration) may have the worft confequences upon
the peace of any ftate.

As to what is called a Revolution principle, my opinion
was this : That whenever thofe evils, which ufually attend
and follow a violent change of Government, were not in
probability fo pernicious as the grievance we fuffer under
a prefent power, then the public good will juftify fuch a
Revolution. And this I took to have been the cafe in the
Prince of Orange's expedition, although in the confequences it produced fome very bad effects, which are likely
to ftick long enough by us.

I had

I had likewife in thofe days a mortal antipathy againft Standing Armies in times of Peace : Becaufe I always took Standing Armies to be only fervants hired by the Mafter of the family for keeping his own children in flavery ; and becaufe I conceived, that a Prince who could not think himfelf fecure without Mercenary Troops, muft needs have a feparate intereft from that of his Subjects. Although I am not ignorant of thofe artificial Neceffities which a corrupted Miniftry can create, for keeping up forces to fupport a Faction againft the publick Intereft.

As to Parliaments, I adored the wifdom of that Gothic inftitution, which made them annual : and I was confident our Liberty could never be placed upon a firm foundation until that ancient law were reftored among us. For, who fees not, that, while fuch Affemblies are permitted to have a longer duration, there grows up a commerce of corruption between the Miniftry and the Deputies, wherein they both find their accounts, to the manifeft danger of Liberty ? which Traffic would neither anfwer the defign nor expence, if Parliaments met once a year.

I ever abominated that fcheme of Politics (now about thirty years old) of fetting up a monied Intereft in oppofition to the landed. For I conceived, there could not be a truer maxim in our Government than this, That the Poffeffors of the foil are the beft judges of what is for the advantage of the kingdom. If others had thought the fame way, Funds of Credit and South-Sea Projects would neither have been felt nor heard of.

I could never difcover the neceffity of fufpending any Law upon which the Liberty of the moft innocent Perfons depended ; neither do I think this Practice hath made the tafte of Arbitrary Power fo agreeable, as that we fhould defire to fee it repeated. Every Rebellion fubdued and Plot difcovered, contribute to the firmer eftablifhment of the prince : In the latter cafe, the knot of Confpirators is entirely broke, and they are to begin their work anew under a thoufand difadvantages ; fo that thofe diligent enquiries into remote and problematical guilt, with a new power of enforcing them by chains and dungeons to every perfon whofe face a Minifter thinks fit to diflike, are not only oppofite to that Maxim, which declareth it better that ten guilty men fhould efcape, than one innocent fuffer ; but likewife leave a gate wide open to the whole Tribe of Informers, the moft accurfed, and proftitute, and abandoned race, that God ever permitted to plague mankind.

It

It is true the Romans had a cuftom of chufing a Dictator, during whofe adminiftration the Power of other Ma-
giftrates was fufpended; but this was done upon the greateft emergencies; a War near their doors, or fome civil
Diffention : For Armies muft be governed by arbitrary
power. But when the Virtue of that Common-wealth
gave place to luxury and ambition, this very office of
Dictator became perpetual in the perfons of the Cæfars and
their Succeffors, the moft infamous Tyrants that have any
where appeared in ftory.

Thefe are fome of the fentiments I had, relating to public affairs, while I was in the world : what they are at
prefent, is of little importance either to that or myfelf;
neither can I truly fay I have any at all, or, if I had, I
dare not venture to publifh them : For however orthodox
they may be while I am now writing, they may become
criminal enough to bring me into trouble before Midfummer. And indeed I have often wifhed for fome time paft,
that a political Catechifm might be publifhed by authority four times a year, in order to inftruct us how we are to
fpeak, write, and act during the current quarter. I have
by experience felt the want of fuch an inftructor : For,
intending to make my court to fome people on the prevailing fide, by advancing certain old whiggifh principles,
which, it feems, had been exploded about a month before,
I have paffed for a difaffected perfon. I am not ignorant
how idle a thing it is, for a man in obfcurity to attempt
defending his reputation as a Writer, while the fpirit of
Faction hath fo univerfally poffeffed the minds of men, that
they are not at leifure to attend to any thing elfe. They
will juft give themfelves time to libel and accufe me, but
cannot fpare a minute to hear my defence. So in a plot-
difcovering age, I have often known an innocent man feized and imprifoned, and forced to lie feveral months in
chains, while the Minifters were not at leifure to hear his
petition, until they had profecuted and hanged the number they propofed.

All I can reafonably hope for by this letter, is to convince my friends, and others who are pleafed to wifh me
well, that I have neither been fo ill a Subject nor fo ftupid an Author, as I have been reprefented by the virulence
of Libellers, whofe malice hath taken the fame train in
both, by fathering dangerous Principles in government
upon me, which I never mantained, and infipid Productions which I am not capable of writing. For, however
I may have been foured by perfonal ill-treatment, or by
                                                    melancholy

melancholy profpects for the public, I am too much a politician to expofe my own fafety by offenfive words. And,
if my genius and fpirit be funk by increafing years, I have
at leaft enough of difcretion left, not to miftake the meafure of my own abilities, by attempting fubjects where
thofe Talents are neceffary, which perhaps I may have loft
with my youth.

LETTER VI.

Dr. SWIFT to Mr. GAY.

Dublin, Jan. 8, 1722-3.

COming home after a fhort Chriftmas ramble, I found
a letter upon my table, and little expected when I
opened it to read your name at the bottom. The beft and
greateft part of my life, until thefe laft eight years, I fpent
in England ; there I made my friendfhips, and there I left
my defires. I am condemned for ever to another country : what is in prudence to be done ? I think to be *obli-
tu que meorum, oblivifcendus et illis*. What can be the defign
of your letter but malice, to wake me out of a fcurvy fleep,
which however is better than none ? I am towards nine
years older fince I left you, yet that is the leaft of my alterations ; my bufinefs, my diverfions, my converfations,
are all entirely changed for the worfe, and fo are my ftudies and my amufements in writing ; yet, after all, this
humdrum way of life might be pallable enough, if you
would let me alone. I fhall not be able to relifh my wine,
my parfons, my horfes, nor my garden for three months,
until the fpirit you have raifed fhall be difpoffeffed. I have
fometimes wondered that I have not vifited you, but I have
been ftopt by too many reafons, befides years and lazinefs,
and yet thefe are very good ones. Upon my return after
half a year amongft you, there would be to me *Defineris nec
pudor nec modus*. I was three years reconciling myfelf to the
fcene, and the bufinefs, to which fortune hath condemned
me, and ftupidity was what I had recourfe to. —Befides,
what a figure fhould I make in London, while my friends
are in poverty, exile, diftrefs, or imprifonment, and my
enemies with rods of iron ? Yet I often threaten myfelf
with the journey, and am every fummer practifing to get
health to bear it : The only inconvenience is, that I grow
old in the experiment. Although I care not to talk to you
as a Divine, yet I hope you have not been author of your
colic :

colic : do you drink bad wine, or keep bad company ? Are
you not as many years older as I ? it will not be always
Et tibi quos mihi dempferit Apponet annus. I am heartily forry
you have any dealings with that ugly diftemper, and I
believe our friend Arbuthnot will recommend you to temperance and exercife. I wifh they could have as good an
effect upon the giddinefs I am fubject to, and which this
moment I am not free from. I fhould have been glad if
you had lengthened your letter by telling me the prefent
condition of many of my old acquaintance, Congreve, Arbuthnot, Lewis, etc. but you mention only Mr. Pope,
who I believe is lazy, or elfe he might have added three
lines of his own. I am extremely glad he is not in your
cafe of needing great men's favour, and could heartily
wifh that you were in his. I have been confidering why
Poets have fuch ill fuccefs in making their Court, fince
they are allowed to be the greateft and beft of all flatterers : The defect is, that they flatter only in print or in
writing; but not by word of mouth : They will give
things under their hand which they make a confcience of
fpeaking. Befides, they are too libertine to haunt anti-
chambers, too poor to bribe porters and footmen, and too
proud to cringe to fecond-hand favourites in a great family. Tell me, are you not under Original fin, by the dedication of your Eclogues to Lord Bolingbroke ? I am an
ill judge at this diftance ; and befides am, for my eafe,
utterly ignorant of the commoneft things that pafs in the
world ; but if all Courts have a famenefs in them (as the
Parfons phrafe it) things may be as they were in my time,
when all employments went to Parliament-men's Friends,
who had been ufeful in Elections, and there was always a
huge Lift of names in arrears at the Treafury, which would
at leaft take up your feven years expedient to difcharge
even one half. I am of opinion, if you will not be offended, that the fureft courfe would be to get your Friend
who lodgeth in your houfe, to recommend you to the next
chief Governor who comes over here for a good civil employment, or to be one of his Secretaries, which your
Parliament-men are fond enough of, when there is no
room at home. The wine is good and reafonable ; you
may dine twice a week at the Deanry-houfe ; there is a
fet of company in this town fufficient for one man ; folks
will admire you, becaufe they have read you, and read of
you ; and a good employment will make you live tolerably in London, or fumptuoufly here ; or if you divide between both places, it will be for your health.

I wifh

I wifh I could do more than fay I love you. I left you in a good way both for the late Court, and the fucceffors ; and by the force of too much honefty, or too little fublunary wifdom, you fell between two ftools. Take care of your health and money ; be lefs modeft and more active ; or elfe turn Parfon and get a Bifhopric here : Would to God they would fend us as good ones from your fide !

I am ever, etc.

LETTER VII.

Mr. POPE to Dr. SWIFT.

Jan. 12, 1723.

I Find a rebuke in a late letter of yours, that both ftings and pleafeth me extremely. Your faying that I ought to have writ a Poftfcript to my friend Gay's, makes me not content to write lefs than a whole Letter ; and your feeming to take his kindly, gives me hopes you will look upon this as a fincere effect of Friendfhip. Indeed as I cannot but own the Lazinefs with which you tax me, and with which I may equally charge you, for both of us have had (and one of us hath both had and given *) a Surfeit of writing ; fo I really thought you would know yourfelf to be fo certainly intitled to my Friendfhip, that it was a poffeffion you could not imagine ftood in need of any further Deeds or Writings to affure you of it.

Whatever you feem to think of your withdrawn and feparate ftate at this diftance, and in this Abfence, Dean Swift lives ftill in England, in every place and company where he would chufe to live, and I find him in all the Converfations I keep, and in all the Hearts in which I defire any fhare.

We have never met thefe many years without mention of you. Befides my old Acquaintance, I have found that all my friends of a later date are fuch as were yours before : Lord Oxford, Lord Harcourt, and Lord Harley may look upon me as one entailed upon them by you : Lord Bolingbroke is now returned (as I hope) to take me with all his other Hereditary Rights : and, indeed, he feems grown fo much a Philofopher, as to fet his heart upon fome of them as little, as upon the Poet you gave him. It is fure my ill fate, that all thofe I moft loved, and with whom I moft

* Alluding to his large work on Homer.

lived

lived, muſt be baniſhed : After both of you left England, my conſtant Hoſt was the Biſhop of * Rocheſter. Sure this is a nation that is curſedly afraid of being over-run with too much Politeneſs, and cannot regain one great Genius, but at the expence of another. I tremble for my Lord Peterborow (whom I now lodge with) he has too much Wit, as well as Courage, to make a ſolid General : and if he eſcapes being baniſhed by others, I fear he will baniſh himſelf. This leads me to give you ſome account of the manner of my life and converſation, which has been infinitely more various and diſſipated, than when you knew me and cared for me ; and among all Sexes, Parties, and Profeſſions. A Glut of Study and Retirement in the firſt part of my life caſt me into this ; and this, I begin to ſee, will throw me again into Study and Retirement.

The civilities I have met with from oppoſite Setts of people, have hinder'd me from being violent or four to any Party ; but at the ſame time the Obſervations and Ex-periences I cannot but have collected, have made me leſs fond of, and leſs ſurprized at, any : I am therefore the more afflicted and the more angry at the Violences and Hardſhips I ſee practiſed by either. The merry Vein you knew me in, is ſunk into a Turn of Reflection, that has made the world pretty indifferent to me ; and yet I have acquired a Quietneſs of mind which by fits improves into a certain degree of Chearfulneſs, enough to make me juſt ſo good humoured as to wiſh that world well. My Friend-ſhips are increaſed by new ones, yet no part of the warmth I felt for the old is diminiſhed. Averſions I have none, but to Knaves (for Fools I have learned to bear with) and ſuch I cannot be commonly civil to ; for I think thoſe men are next to Knaves who converſe with them. The greateſt Man in power of this ſort ſhall hardly make me bow to him, unleſs I had a perſonal obligation, and that I will take care not to have. The top pleaſure of my life is one I learned from you both how to gain and how to uſe the Freedom of Friendſhip with men much my Superiors. To have pleaſed great men, according to Ho-race, is a praiſe ; but not to have flattered them, and yet not to have diſpleaſed them, is a greater. I have carefully avoided all Intercourſe with Poets and Scriblers, unleſs where by great chance I have found a modeſt one. By theſe means I have had no quarrels with any perſonally ;

* Dr. Atterbury.

none have been Enemies, who but were alfo Strangers to
me; and as there is no great need of an Eclairciffement
with fuch, whatever they writ or faid I never retaliated,
not only never feeming to know, but often really never
knowing, any thing of the matter. There are very few
things that give me the Anxiety of a Wifh; the ftrongeft
I have would be to pafs my days with you, and a few fuch
as you : But Fate has difperfed them all about the world ;
and I find to wifh it is as vain, as to wifh to fee the Millennium and the Kingdom of the Juft upon earth.

If I have finned in my long filence, confider there is one
to whom you yourfelf have been as great a finner. As foon
as you fee his hand, you will learn to do me juftice, and
feel in your heart how long a man may be filent to thofe he
truly loves and refpects.

LETTER VIII. *

Lord BOLINGBROKE to Dr. SWIFT.

I Am not fo lazy as Pope, and therefore you muft not expect from me the fame indulgence to Lazinefs; in defending his own caufe he pleads yours, and becomes your
Advocate while he appeals to you as his Judge : You will
do the fame on your part ; and I, and the reft of your common Friends, fhall have great Juftice to expect from two
fuch righteous Tribunals : You refemble perfectly the two
Alehoufe-keepers in Holland, who were at the fame time
Burgomafters of the Town, and taxed one another's Bills
alternately. I declare before hand I will not ftand to the
award ; my Title to your Friendfhip is good, and wants
neither Deeds nor Writings to confirm it : but annual Acknowledgments at leaft are neceffary to preferve it : and I
begin to fufpect by your defrauding me of them, that you
hope in time to difpute it, and to urge Prefcription a-
gainft me. I would not fay one word to you about myfelf
(fince it is a fubject on which you appear to have no curiofity) was it not to try how far the contraft between
Pope's fortune and manner of life, and mine, may be carried.

I have been, then, infinitely more uniform and lefs diffipated, than when you knew me and cared for me. That
Love which I ufed to fcatter with fuch profufion among
the female kind, has been thefe many years devoted to one
object. A great many misfortunes (for fo they are called,

though fometimes very improperly) and a retirement from
the world, have made that juft and nice difcrimination between my Acquaintance and my Friends, which we have
feldom fagacity enough to make for ourfelves; thofe infects of various hues, which ufed to hum and buz about
me, while I ftood in the funfhine, have difappeared fince
I lived in the fhade. No man comes to a Hermitage but
for the fake of the Hermit; a few philofophical Friends
come often to mine, and they are fuch as you would be glad
to live with, if a dull climate and duller company have
not altered you extremely from what you was nine years
ago.

The hoarfe voice of Party was never heard in this quiet
place; Gazettes and Pamphlets are banifhed from it, and
if the Lucubrations of Ifaac Bickerftaff be admitted, this
diftinction is owing to fome ftrokes by which it is judged
that this illuftrious Philofopher had (like the Indian Fohu,
the Grecian Pythagoras, the Perfian Zoroafter, and others
his Precurfors among the Zabians, Magians, and the
Egyptian Seers) both his outward and his inward Doctrine, and that he was of no fide at the bottom. When
I am there, I forget I ever was of any party myfelf;
nay, I am often fo happily abforbed by the abftracted
reafon of things, that I am ready to imagine there never was any fuch monfter as Party. Alas, I am foon
awakened from that pleafing dream by the Greek and
Roman Hiftorians, by Guicciardine, by Machiavel, and
Thuanus; for I have vowed to read no Hiftory of our own
country, till that body of it which you promife to finifh
appears.

I am under no apprehenfion that a glut of Study and Retirement fhould caft me back into the hurry of the world;
on the contrary, the fingle regret which I ever feel, is that
I fell fo late into this courfe of life; my Philofophy grows
confirmed by habit, and if you and I meet again, I
will extort this approbation from you: *Jam non confilio bo-
nus, fed more eo perductus, ut non tantum recte facere peffim,
fed nifi recte facere non poffim.* The little incivilities I have
met with from oppofite fetts of people, have been fo far
from rendering me violent or four to any, that I think myfelf obliged to them all; fome have cured me of my fears,
by fhewing me how impotent the malice of the world is;
others have cured me of my hopes, by fhewing how precarious popular friendfhips are; all have cured me of furprize: in driving me out of party, they have driven me out
of curfed company; and in ftripping me of Titles and Rank,
and

and Eftate, and fuch trinkets, which every man that will may fpare, they have given me that which no man can be happy without.

Reflection and habit have rendered the world fo indifferent to me, that I am neither afflicted nor rejoiced, angry nor pleafed at what happens in it, any further than perfonal friendfhips intereft me in the affairs of it, and this principle extends my cares but a little way. Perfect Tranquillity is the general tenour of my life : good digeftions, ferene weather, and fome other mechanic fprings, wind me above it now and then, but I never fall below it ; I am fometimes gay, but I am never fad. I have gained new friends, and have loft fome old ones ; my acquifitions of this kind give me a good deal of pleafure, becaufe they have not been made lightly : I know no vows fo folemn as thofe of friendfhip, and therefore a pretty long noviciate of acquaintance fhould methinks precede them : My loffes of this kind give me but little trouble, I contributed nothing to them, and a friend who breaks with me unjuftly, is not worth preferving. As foon as I leave this Town (which will be in a few days) I fhall fall back into that courfe of life, which keeps knaves and fools at a great diftance from me : I have an averfion to them both, but in the ordinary courfe of life, I think I can bear the fenfible knave better than the fool. One muft indeed with the former be in fome or other of the attitudes of thofe wooden men whom I have feen before a fword-cntler's fhop in Germany ; but even in thefe conftrained poftures the witty Rafcal will divert me ; and he that diverts me does me a great deal of good, and lays me under an obligation to him, which I am not obliged to pay him in another coin : The Fool obliges me to be almoft as much upon my guard as the knave, and he makes me no amends; he numbs me like the Torpor, or he teazes me like the Fly. This is the Picture of an old Friend, and more like him than that will be which you once afked, and which he will fend you, if you continue ftill to defire it.—Adieu, dear Swift, with all thy faults I love thee intirely ; make an effort, and love me on with all mine.

LETTER IX.

From Dr. Swift.

Dublin, Sept. 20, 1723.

REturning from a summer expedition of four months on account of my health, I found a letter from you, with an appendix longer than yours from Lord Boling-broke. I believe there is not a more miserable malady than an unwillingness to write letters to our best friends, and a man might be philosopher enough in finding out reasons for it. One thing is clear, that it shews a mighty difference betwixt Friendship and Love, for a lover (as I have heard) is always scribling to his mistress. If I could permit myself to believe what your civility makes you say, that I am still remembered by my friends in England, I am in the right to keep myself here—*Non sum qualis eram.* I left you in a period of life when one year does more execution than three at yours, to which if you add the dulness of the air, and of the people, it will make a terrible sum. I have no very strong faith in your pretenders to Retirement; you are not of an age for it, nor have gone through either good or bad fortune enough to go into a corner, and form conclusions *de contemptu mundi & fuga saeculi,* unless a poet grows weary of too much applause, as Ministers do of too much weight of business.

Your happiness is greater than your merit, in chusing your favourites so indifferently among either Party : this you owe partly to your Education, and partly to your Genius employing you in an Art in which Faction has nothing to do, for I suppose Virgil and Horace are equally read by Whigs and Tories. You have no more to do with the Constitution of Church and State, than a Christian at Constantinople ; and you are so much the wiser and the happier, because both Parties will approve your Poetry as long as you are known to be of neither, : . ; the

Your notions of friendship are new to me : I believe every man is born with his *quantum,* and he cannot give to one without robbing another. I very well know to whom I would give the first places in my friendship, but they are not in the way : I am condemned to another scene, and therefore I distribute it in Pennyworths to those about me, and who displease me least; and should do the same to my fellow prisoners if I were condemned to jail. I can like-

wise

wife tolerate Knaves much better than Fools, becaufe their knavery does me no hurt in the commerce I have with them, which however I own is more dangerous, tho' not fo troublefome, as that of Fools. I have often endeavoured to eftablifh a Friendfhip among all Men of Genius, and would fain have it done : they are feldom above three or four Contemporaries, and if they could be united would drive the world before them. I think it was fo among the Poets in the time of Auguftus : but Envy, and Party, and Pride, have hindered it among us. I do not include the Subalterns, of which you are feldom without a large Tribe. Under the name of Poets and Scriblers I fuppofe you mean the Fools you are content to fee fometimes, when they happen to be modeft; which was not frequent among them while I was in the world.

I would defcribe to you my way of living, if any method could be called fo in this Country. I chufe my companions among thofe of leaft confequence and moft compliance : I read the moft trifling Books I can find, and whenever I write, it is upon the moft trifling fubjects : But riding, walking, and fleeping take up eighteen of the twenty-four hours. I procraftinate more than I did twenty years ago, and have feveral things to finifh which I put off to twenty years hence ; *Hæc eft vita Solutorum*, *&c.* I fend you the compliments of a friend of yours, who hath paffed four months this fummer with two grave acquaintance at his country-houfe, without ever once going to Dublin, which is but eight miles diftant ; yet when he returns to London, I will engage you will find him as deep in the court of Requefts, the Park, the Operas and the Coffeehoufe, as any man there. I am now with him for a few days.

You muft remember me with great affection to Dr. Arbuthnot, Mr. Congreve, and Gay.—— I think there are no more *eodem tertio's* between you and me, except Mr. Jervas, to whofe houfe I addrefs this, for want of knowing where you live : for it was not clear from your laft whether you lodge with Lord Peterborow, or he with you.

I am ever, etc.

LETTER

LETTER X.

Sept. 14, 1725.

I Need not tell you, with what real delight I fhould have done any thing you defired, and in particular any good offices in my power towards the bearer of your Letter, who is this day gone for France.   Perhaps 'tis with Poets as with Prophets, they are fo much better liked in another country than their own, that your Gentleman, upon arriving in England, loft his curiofity concerning me.   However, had he try'd, he had found me his friend ; I mean he had found me yours.   I am difappointed at not knowing better a man whom you efteem, and comfort myfelf only with having got a Letter from you, with which (after all) I fit down a gainer ; fince to my great pleafure it confirms my hope of once more feeing you.   After fo many difperfions and fo many divifions, two or three of us may yet be gathered together : not to plot, not to contrive filly fchemes of ambition, or to vex our own or others hearts with bufy vanities (fuch as perhaps at one time of life or other take their Tour in every man) but to divert ourfelves, and the world too if it pleafes ; or at worft, to laugh at others as innocently and as unhurtfully as at ourfelves. Your Travels * I hear much of ; my own, I promife you, fhall never more be in a ftrange land, but a diligent, I hope ufeful, inveftigation of my own Territories †.   I mean no more Tranflations, but fomething domeftic, fit for my own country, and for my own time.

If you come to us, I'll find you elderly Ladies enough that can halloo, and two that can nurfe, and they are too old and feeble to make too much noife ; as you will guefs, when I tell you they are my own mother, and my own nurfe.   I can alfo help you to a Lady who is as deaf, tho' not fo old as yourfelf ; you'll be pleafed with one another I'll engage, tho' you don't hear one another ; you'll converfe like fpirits by intuition.   What you'll moft wonder at is, fhe is confiderable at Court, yet no Party-woman, and lives in Court, yet would be eafy, and make you eafy.

One of thofe you mention (and I dare fay always will remember) Dr. Arbuthnot, is at this time ill of a very dangerous diftemper, an impofthume in the bowels ; which is broke, but the event is very uncertain.   Whatever that

---

* Gulliver.   † The Effay on Man.

be,

be, he bids me tell you, (and I write this by him) he lives
or dies your faithful friend; and one reason he has to
defire a little longer life, is the wifh to fee you once
more.

He is gay enough in this circumftance to tell you, he
would give you (if he cou'd) fuch advice as might cure
your deafnefs, but he would not advife you, if you were
cured, to quit the pretence of it; becaufe you may by
that means hear as much as you will, and anfwer as little
as you pleafe. Believe me

Yours, etc.

LETTER XI.

From Dr. SWIFT.

Sept. 29, 1725.

I Am now returning to the noble fcene of Dublin, into
the grand Monde, for fear of burying my parts; to fig-
nalize myfelf among Curates and Vicars, and correct all
corruptions crept in relating to the weight of bread and
butter thro' thofe dominions where I govern. I have employed my time (befides ditching) in finifhing, correcting,
amending, and tranfcribing my * Travels, in four parts
compleat, newly augmented, and intended for the prefs
when the world fhall deferve them, or rather when a Printer fhall be found brave enough to venture his ears. I
like the fcheme of our meeting after diftreffes and difperfions; but the chief end I propofe to myfelf in all my labours, is to vex the world, rather than divert it; and if
I could compafs that defign without hurting my own perfon or fortune, I would be the moft indefatigable writer
you have ever feen, without reading. I am exceedingly
pleafed that you have done with Tranflations; Lord
Treafurer Oxford often lamented that a rafcally world
fhould lay you under a neceffity of mifemploying your
genius for fo long a time. But fince you will now be fo
much better employed, when you think of the world, give
it one lafh the more at my requeft. I have ever hated all
Nations, Profeffions, and Communities; and all my love
is towards Individuals: for inftance, I hate the Tribe of
Lawyers, but I love Counfellor fuch a one, and Judge
fuch a one: 'Tis fo with Phyficians, (I will not fpeak of

* Gulliver's Travels.

my

my own Trade) Soldiers, Englifh, Scotch, French, and the reft. But principally I hate and deteft that animal called Man, although I heartily love John, Peter, Thomas, and fo forth. This is the fyftem upon which I have govern'd myfelf many years (but do not tell) and fo I fhall go on till I have done with them. I have got materials towards a Treatife, proving the falfity of that definition *Animal rationale*, and to fhew it fhould be only *rationis capax*. Upon this great foundation of Mifanthropy (though not in Timon's manner) the whole building of my Travels is erected; and I never will have peace of mind, till all honeft men are of my opinion : By confequence you are to embrace it immediately, and procure that all who deferve my efteem may do fo too. The matter is fo clear, that it
1 will admit of no difpute ; nay, I will hold a hundred pounds that you and I agree in the point.

I did not know your Odyffey was finifhed, being yet in the country, which I fhall leave in three days. I thank you kindly for the prefent, but fhall like it three fourths the lefs, for the mixture you mention of other hands : however, I am glad you fav'd yourfelf fo much drudgery — I have been long told by Mr. Ford of your great fatchievements in building and planting, and efpecially of your fubterranean paffage to your garden, whereby you turn'd a Blunder into a Beauty, which is a piece of *Ars Poetica*.

I have almoft done with Harridans, and fhall foon become old enough to fall in love with girls of fourteen. The Lady whom you defcribe to live at Court, to be deaf and no party woman, I take to be Mythology, but know not how to moralize it. She cannot be Mercy, for Mercy is neither deaf nor lives at Court : Juftice is blind, and perhaps deaf, but neither is fhe a Court-lady : Fortune is both blind and deaf, and a Court-lady, but then fhe is a moft damnable Party woman, and will never make me eafy, as you promife. It muft be Riches, which anfwers all your defcription : I am glad fhe vifits you, but my voice is fo weak, that I doubt fhe will never hear me.

Mr. Lewis fent me an account of Dr. Arbuthnot's illnefs, which is a very fenfible afflittion to me, who by living fo long out of the world, have loft that hardnefs of heart contracted by years and general converfation. I am daily lofing friends, and neither feeking nor geting others. Oh if the world had but a dozen of Arbuthnots in it, I would burn my Travels ! But however he is not without fault : There is a paffage in Bede, highly commending
the

the piety and learning of the Irish in that age, where after abundance of praises he overthrows them all, by la-
menting that, alas! they kept Easter at a wrong time of
the year. So our Doctor has every quality and virtue
that can make a man amiable or useful; but alas, he
hath a sort of a slouch in his walk! I pray God protect him, for he is an excellent Christian, though not a
Catholic.

I hear nothing of our Friend Gay, but I find the Court
keeps him at hard meat. I advised him to come over here
with a Lord Lieutenant. Philips writes little Flams (as
Lord Leicester call'd those sort of verses) on Miss Carteret.
A Dublin Blacksmith, a great Poet, hath imitated his
manner in a poem to the same Miss. Philips is a com-
plainer, and on this occasion I told Lord Carteret, that
Complainers never succeeded at Court, tho' Railers do.

Are you altogether a country gentleman? that I must
address to you out of London, to the hazard of your losing
this precious letter, which I will now conclude, altho' so
much paper is left. I have an ill Name, and therefore shall
not subscribe it, but you will guess it comes from one who
esteems and loves you about half as much as you deserve,
I mean as much as he can.

I am in great concern, at what I am just told is in some
of the news-papers, that Lord Bolingbroke is much hurt
by a fall in hunting. I am glad he has so much youth and
vigour left (of which he hath not been thrifty) but I wonder he has no more Discretion.

LETTER XII.

Oct. 15, 1725.

I Am wonderfully pleased with the suddenness of your
kind answer. It makes me hope you are coming towards
us, and that you incline more and more to your old friends,
in proportion as you draw nearer to them; and are getting into our Vortex. Here is One, who was once a powerful planet, but has now (after long experience of all that
comes of shining) learned to be content, with returning
to his first point, without the thought or ambition of
shining at all. Here is another, who thinks one of the
greatest glories of his Father was to have distinguished
and loved you, and who loves you hereditarily. Here is
Arbuthnot, recovered from the jaws of death, and more

pleafed with the hope of feeing you again, than of reviewing a world, every part of which he has long defpis'd,
but what is made up of a few men like yourfelf. He goes
abroad again, and is more chearful than even health can
make a man, for he has a good confcience into the bargain
(which is the moft Catholic of all remedies, tho' not the
moft Univerfal.) I knew it would be a pleafure to you
to hear this, and in truth that made me write fo foon to
you.

I'm forry poor P. is not promoted in this age; for certainly if his reward be of the next, he is of all Poets the
moft miferable. I'm alfo forry for another reafon; if
they don't promote him, they'll fpoil the conclufion of
one of my Satires, where, having endeavoured to correct the Tafte of the Town in wit and criticifm, I end thus,

But what avails to lay down rules for fenfe ?
In ——'s Reign thefe fruitlefs lines were writ,
When Ambrofe Philips was preferr'd for Wit !

Our friend Gay is ufed as the friends of Tories are by
Whigs (and generally by Tories too.) Becaufe he had
humour, he was fuppofed to have dealt with Dr. Swift;
in like manner as when any one had learning formerly he
was thought to have dealt with the Devil. He puts his
whole truft at Court in that Lady whom I defcribed to you,
and whom you take to be an allegorical creature of fancy:
I wifh fhe really were Riches for his fake; though as for
yours, I queftion whether (if you knew her) you would
change her for the other.

Lord Bolingbroke had not the leaft harm by his fall;
I wifh he had received no more by his other fall; Lord
Oxford had none by his. But Lord Bolingbroke is the
moft improved mind fince you faw him, that ever was improved without fhifting into a new body, or being: *paullo
minus ab angelis.* I have often imagined to myfelf, that
if ever all of us meet again, after fo many varieties and
changes, after fo much of the old world and of the old man
in each of us has been altered, that fcarce a fingle thought of
the one, any more than a fingle atom of the other, remains juft the fame; I've fancied, I fay, that we fhould
meet like the righteous in the Millennium, quite in
peace, divefted of all our former Paffions, fmiling at
our paft follies, and content to enjoy the kingdom of the
Juft in tranquillity. But I find you would rather be employed as an avenging angel of wrath, to break your vial
of indignation over the heads of the wretched creatures of
this

this world : nay would make them *Eat your Book*, which you have made (I doubt not) as bitter a pill for them as possible.

I won't tell you what designs I have in my head (besides writing a set of Maxims in opposition to all Rochefoucault's principles *) till I see you here, face to face. Then you shall have no reason to complain of me, for want of a generous disdain of his world, though I have not lost my Ears in yours and their service. Lord Oxford too (whom I have now the third time mentioned in this Letter, and he deserves to be always mentioned in every thing that is address'd to you, or comes from you) expects you : That ought to be enough to bring you hither ; 'tis a better reason than if the nation expected you. For I really enter as fully as you can desire, into your Principle of Love of Individuals : and I think the way to have a public spirit is first to have a private one ; for who can believe (said a friend of mine) that any man can care for a hundred thousand people, who never cared for one ? No ill-humoured man can ever be a Patriot, any more than a Friend.

I designed to have left the following page for Dr. Arbuthnot to fill, but he is so touch'd with the period in yours to me concerning him, that he intends to answer it by a whole letter. He too is busy about a book, which I guess he will tell you of. So adieu—what remains worth telling you ? Dean Berkley is well, and happy in the prosecution of his Scheme. Lord Oxford and Lord Bolingbroke in health, Duke Disny so also ; Sir William Wyndham better, Lord Bathurst well. These and some others, preserve their ancient honour and ancient friendship. Those who do neither, if they were d----'d, what is it to a Protestant Priest, who has nothing to do with the dead ? I answer for my own part as a Papist, I would not pray them out of Purgatory.

My name is as bad an one as yours, and hated by all bad Poets, from Hopkins and Sternhold to Gildon and Cibber. The first prayed against me with the Turk ; and a modern Imitator of theirs (whom I leave you to find out) has added the Christian to 'em, with proper definitions of each in this manner,

---

* This was only said as an oblique reproof of the horrid misanthropy in the foregoing Letter ; and which he supposed, might be chiefly occasioned by the Dean's fondness for *Rochefoucault*, whose *Maxims* are founded on the principle of an universal selfishness in human nature.

The Pope's the Whore of Babylon,
The Turk he is a Jew:
The Christian is an Infidel
That sitteth in a Pew.

LETTER XIII.

From Dr. Swift.

Nov. 26, 1725.

I Should sooner have acknowledged yours, if a feverish disorder and the relicks of it had not disabled me for a fortnight. I now begin to make excuses, because I hope I am pretty near seeing you, and therefore I would cultivate an acquaintance; because if you do not know me when we meet, you need only keep one of my letters, and compare it with my face, for my face and letters are counterparts of my heart. I fear I have not exprefs'd that right, but I mean well, and I hate blots : I look in your letter, and in my conscience you say the same thing, but in a better manner. Pray tell my Lord Bolingbroke that I wish he were banished again, for then I should hear from him, when he was full of philosophy, and talk'd *de contemptu mundi.* My Lord Oxford was so extremely kind as to write to me immediately an account of his son's birth; which I immediately acknowledg'd, but before my letter could reach him, I wished it in the sea · I hope I was more afflicted than his Lordship. 'Tis hard that Parsons and beggars should be over-run with brats, while so great and good a family wants an heir to continue it. I have received his Father's picture, but I lament (*sub sigillo confessionis*) that it is not so true a resemblance as I could wish. Drown the world ! I am not content with despising it, but I would anger it, if I could with safety. I wish there were an Hospital built for its Despisers, where one might act with safety, and it need not be a large building, only I would have it well endow'd. P * * is *fort chancellant* whether he should turn Parson or no. But all employments here are engaged, or in reversion. Cast Wits and cast Beaux have a proper sanctuary in the church : yet we think it a severe judgment, that a fine gentleman, and so much the finer for hating Ecclesiastics, should be a domestic humble retainer to an Irish Prelate. He is neither Secretary nor Gentleman-usher, yet serves in both capacities. He hath published several reasons why he never

came

came to fee me, but the beft is, that I have not waited on
his Lordfhip. We have had a Poem fent from London
in imitation of that on Mifs Carteret. It is on Mifs Harvey of a day old ; and we fay and think it is yours. I
wifh it were not, becaufe I am againft monopolies.—You
might'have fpared me a few more lines of your Satire, but I hope in a few months to fee it all. To hear
boys, like you, talk of Millenniums and tranquillity ! I
am older by thirty years, Lord Bolingbroke by twenty,
and you but by ten, than when we laft were together ;
and we fhould differ more than ever, you coquetting a
maid of honour, my Lord looking on to fee how the
gamefters play, and I railing at you both. I defire you
and all my friends will take a fpecial care that my Difaffection to the world may not be imputed to my Age, for
I have credible witneffes ready to depofe, that it hath never varied from the twenty-firft to the f—ty-cighth year
of my life (pray fill that blank charitably). I tell you
after all, that I do not hate mankind, it is *vous autres*
who hate them, becaufe you would have them reafonable
Animals, and are angry at being difappointed : I have always rejected that definition, and made another of my
own. I am no more angry with—than I was with the
Kite that laft week flew away with one of my chickens ; and
yet I was pleafed when one of my fervants fhot him two
days after. This I fay, becaufe you are fo hardy as to
tell me of your intentions to write Maxims in oppofition
to Rochefoucault, who is my favourite, becaufe I found
my whole character in him ; however I will read him
again, becaufe it is poffible I may have fince undergone
fome alterations.—Take care the bad Poets do not out-
wit you, as they have ferved the good ones in every age,
whom they have provoked to tranfmit their names to pofterity. Mœvius is as well known as Virgil, and Gildon
will be as well known as you, if his name gets into your
Verfes : and as to the difference between good and bad
fame, 'tis a perfect trifle. I afk a thoufand pardons, and
fo leave you for this time, and will write again without
concerning myfelf whether you write or no.

                     I am, etc.

I Find myself the better acquainted with you for a long
absence, as men are with themselves for a long Affliction : Abfence does but hold off a Friend, to make one fee
him the more truly. I am infinitely more pleas'd to hear
you are coming near us, than at any thing you feem to
think in my favour; an opinion which has perhaps been
aggrandized by the diftance or dulnefs of Ireland, as objects look larger through a medium of fogs : and yet I am
infinitely pleas'd with that too. I am much the happier for
finding (a better thing than our Wits) our Judgments
jump, in the notion that all Scriblers fhould be paft by in
filence. To vindicate one's felf againft fuch nafty flander,
is much as wife as it was in your countryman, when the
people imputed a ftink to him, to prove the contrary by
fhewing his backfide. So let Gildon and Philips reft in
peace ! what Virgil had to do with Mœvius, that he fhould
wear him upon his fleeve to all eternity, I don't know.
I've been the longer upon this, that I may prepare you
for the reception both you and your works may poffibly
meet in England. We your true acquaintance will look
upon you as a good man, and love you ; others will look
upon you as a Wit, and hate you. So you know the
worft ; unlefs you are as vindicative as Virgil, or the a-
forefaid Hibernian.

I wifh as warmly as you for an Hofpital in which to
lodge the Defpifers of the world ; only I fear it would be
filled wholly like Chelfea, with maimed Soldiers, and
fuch as had been difabled in its fervice. I would rather
have thofe, that, out of fuch generous principles as you
and I, defpife it, fly in its face, than retire from it. Not
that I have much anger againft the Great, my fpleen is
at the little rogues of it ; it would vex one more to be
knock'd on the head with a Pifs-pot, than by a Thunder-
bolt. As to great Oppreffors, they are like Kites or Ea-
gles, one expects mifchief from them ; but to be fquirted
to death (as poor Wycherley faid to me on his death-bed)
by Apothecaries Apprentices, by the under-ftrappers of
under-fecretaries to fecretaries who are no fecretaries—
this wou'd provoke as dull a dog as Ph—s himfelf.

So much for enemies, now for friends. Mr. L— thinks
all this indifcreet : The Dr. not fo ; he loves mifchief the
beft

beſt of any good-natur'd man in England. Lord B. is a-
bove trifling : when he writes of any thing in this world,
he is more than mortal ; *if ever he trifles, it muſt be when he
turns a Divine.* Gay is writing Tales for Prince William :
I ſuppoſe Mr. Philips will take this very ill, for two reaſons ; one that he thinks all childiſh things belong to him,
and the other becauſe he'll take it ill to be taught that one
may write things to a child without being childiſh. What
have I more to add ? but that Lord Oxford deſires earneſtly to ſee you : and that many others whom you do not
think the worſt of, will be gratified by it : none more, be
aſſured, than   Yours, etc.

    P. S. Pope and you are very great Wits, and I think
very indifferent Philoſophers : If you deſpiſed the world
as much as you pretend, and perhaps believe, you would
not be ſo angry with it. The founder of your ſeĉt, that
noble Original whom you think it ſo great an honour to
reſemble *, was a ſlave to the worſt part of the world, to
the Court ; and all his big words were the language of
a ſlighted Lover, who deſired nothing ſo much as a reconciliation, and feared nothing ſo much as a rupture. I
believe the world hath uſed me as ſcurvily as moſt people,
and yet I could never find in my heart to be thoroughly angry with the ſimple, falſe, capricious thing. I
ſhould bluſh alike, to be diſcover'd fond of the world, or
piqued at it. Your definition of *Animal Rationis capax*, inſtead of the common one *Animal Rationale*, will not bear
examination : define but Reaſon, and you will ſee why
your diſtinĉtion is no better than that of the Pontiff *Cotta* ;
between *mala ratio*, and *bona ratio.* But enough of this :
make us a viſit, and I'll ſubſcribe to any ſide of theſe important queſtions which you pleaſe. We differ leſs than
you imagine, perhaps when you wiſh'd me baniſh'd again :
but I am not leſs true to you and to philoſophy in England, than I was in France.   Yours, etc. B.

LETTER XV.

From Dr. Swift.

London, May 4, 1726.

I Had rather live in forty Irelands than under the frequent diſquiets of hearing you are out of order. I always apprehend it moſt after a great dinner, for the leaſt

* Seneca.

Tranſ-

Tranſgreſſion of yours, if it be only two bits and one ſup more than your ſtint, is a great debauch ; for which you certainly pay more than thoſe ſots who are carried dead drunk to bed. My Lord Peterborow ſpoiled every body's dinner, but eſpecially mine, with telling us that you were detained by ſickneſs. Pray let me have three lines under any hand or pot hook that will give me a better account of your health ; which concerns me more than others, becauſe I love and eſteem you for reaſons that moſt others have little to do with, and would be the ſame although you had never touched a pen, further than with writing to me.

I am gathering up my luggage, and preparing for my journey ; I will endeavour to think of you as little as I can, and when I write to you, I will ſtrive not to think of you : This I intend to return to your kindneſs ; and further, I know no body has dealt with me ſo cruelly as you, the conſequences of which uſage I fear will laſt as long as my life, for ſo long ſhall I be (in ſpite of my heart) entirely yours.

LETTER XVI.

Aug. 22, 1726.

MAny a ſhort ſigh you coſt me the day I left you, and many more you will coſt me, till the day you return. I really walk'd about like a man baniſhed, and when I came home found it no home. 'Tis a ſenſation like that of a limb lopp'd off, one is trying every minute unawares to uſe it, and finds it is not. I may ſay you have uſed me more cruelly than you have done any other man ; you have made it more impoſſible for me to live at eaſe without you : Habitude itſelf would have done that, if I had leſs friendſhip in my nature than I have. Beſides my natural memory of you, you have made a local one, which preſents you to me in every place I frequent ; I ſhall never more think of Lord Cobham's, the woods of Ciceter, or the pleaſing proſpect of Byberry, but your idea muſt be joined with 'em, nor ſee one ſeat in my own garden, or one room in my own houſe without a Phantom of you, ſitting or walking before me. I travelled with you to Cheſter, I felt the extreme! eat of the weather, the inns, the roads, the confinement and cloſeneſs of the uneaſy coach, and wiſhed a hundred times I had either a Deanry

or

or a horfe in my gift. In real truth, I have felt my foul peevifh ever fince with all about me, from a warm uneafy defire after you. I am gone out of myfelf to no purpofe, and cannot catch you. *Inhiat in pedes* was not more properly applied to a poor dog after a hare, than to me with regard to your departure. I wifh I could think no more of it, but lie down and fleep till we meet again, and let that day (how far foever off it be) be the morrow. Since I cannot, may it be my amends that every thing you wifh may attend you where you are, and that you may find every friend you have there, in the ftate you wifh him, or her; fo that your vifits to us may have no other effect, than the progrefs of a rich man to a remote eftate, which he finds greater than he expected; which knowledge only ferves to make him live happier where he is, with no difagreeable profpect if ever he fhould chufe to remove. May this be your ftate till it become what I wifh. But indeed I cannot exprefs the warmth, with which I wifh you all things, and myfelf you. Indeed you are ingraved elfewhere than on the Cups you fent me, (with fo kind an infcription) and I might throw them into the Thames without injury to the giver. I am not pleas'd with them, but take them very kindly too : And had I fufpected any fuch ufage from you, I fhould have enjoyed your company lefs than I really did, for at this rate I may fay

Nec tecum poffim vivere, nec fine te.

I will bring you over juft fuch another prefent, when I go to the Deanry of St. Patrick's : which I promife you to do, if ever I am enabled to return your kindnefs. *Donarem Pateras,* etc. 'Till then I'll drink (or Gay fhall drink) daily healths to you, and I'll add to your infcription the old Roman Vow for years to come, VOTIS X. VOTIS XX. My mother's age gives me authority to hope it for yours. Adieu.

LETTER XVII.

Sept. 3, 1726.

YOURS to Mr. Gay gave me greater fatisfaction than that to me (tho' that gave a great deal) for to hear you were fafe at your journey's end, exceeds the account of your fatigues while in the way to it : otherwife believe me, every tittle of each is important to me, which fets

any

any one thing before my eyes that happens to you. I writ
you a long letter, which I guefs reach'd you the day after
your arrival. Since then I had a conference with Sir
────── who exprefs'd his defire of having feen you again
before you left us. He faid he obferved a willingnefs in
you to live among us; which I did not deny; but at the
fame time told him, you had no fuch defign in your coming this time, which was merely to fee a few of thofe you
loved: but that indeed all thofe wifhed it, and particularly Lord Peterborow and myfelf, who wifhed you loved
Ireland lefs, had you any reafon to love England more. I
faid nothing but what I think would induce any man to be
as fond of you as I, plain Truth, did they know either it,
or you. I can't help thinking (when I confider the whole
fhort Lift of our friends) that none of them except you
and I are qualify'd for the Mountains of Wales. The Dr.
goes to Cards, Gay to Court: one lofes money, one lofes
his time: Another of our friends labours to be unambiti-
ous, but he labours in an unwilling foil. One Lady you
like has too much of France to be fit for Wales: Another
is too much a fubject to Princes and Potentates, to relifh
that wild Tafte of liberty and poverty. Mr. Congreve
is too fick to bear a thin air: and fhe that leads him too
rich to enjoy any thing. Lord Peterborow can go to any
climate, but never ftay in any. Lord Bathurft is too
great an hufbandman to like barren hills, except they are
his own to improve. Mr. Bethel indeed is too good and
too honeft to live in the world, but yet 'tis fit, for its example, he fhould. We are left to ourfelves in my opinion, and may live where we pleafe, in Wales, Dublin, or
Bermudas: And for me, I affure you, I love the world fo
well, and it loves me fo well, that I care not in what part
of it I pafs the reft of my days. I fee no funfhine but in
the face of a friend.

I had a glympfe of a letter of yours lately, by which I
find you are (like the vulgar) apter to think well of people
out of power, than of people in power; perhaps 'tis a
miftake, but however there's fomething in it generous.
Mr. ** take it extreme kindly, I can perceive, and he has
a great mind to thank you for that good opinion, for which
I believe he is only to thank his ill-fortune: if I am not in
an error, he would rather be in power than out.

To fhew you how fit I am to live in the mountains, I
will with great truth apply myfelf to an old fentence:
" Thofe that are in, may abide in; and thofe that are
" out, may abide out: yet to me, thofe that are in fhall
" be

" be as thofe that are out, and thofe that are out fhall be
" as thofe that are in."

I am indifferent as to all thofe matters, but I mifs you
as much as I did the firft day, when (with a fhort figh) I
parted. Wherever you are (on the mountains of Wales,
or on the coaft of Dublin.

Tu mihi, feu magni fuperas jam faxa Timavi,
Sive oram Illyrici legis aequoris—).

I am, and ever fhall be, Yours, etc.

LETTER XVIII.

Mr. GAY to Dr. SWIFT.

Nov. 17, 1726.

ABout ten days ago a Book was publifh'd here of the
Travels of one Gulliver, which hath been the converfation of the whole town ever fince : The whole impreffion fold in a week ; and nothing is more diverting than
to hear the different opinions people give of it, though
all agree in liking it extremely. 'Tis generally faid that
you are the Author ; but I am told, the Bookfeller declares he knows not from what hand it came. From the
higheft to the loweft it is univerfally read, from the Ca-
binet-council to the Nurfery. The Politicians to a man
agree, that it is free from particular reflections, but that
the Satire on general Societies of men is too fevere. Not
but we now and then meet with people of greater perfpi-
cuity, who are in fearch of particular applications in every
leaf ; and 'tis highly probable we fhall have keys publifh'd
to give light into Gulliver's defign. Lord —— is the perfon who leaft approves it, blaming it as a defign of evil
confequence to depreciate human nature, at which it cannot be wondered that he takes moft offence, being himfelf
the moft accomplifh'd of his fpecies, and fo lofing more
than any other of that praife which is due both to the dignity and virtue of a man *. Your friend, my Lord
Harcourt, commends it very much, though he thinks in
fome places the matter too far carried. The Duchefs

---

* It is no wonder a man of worth fhould *condemn* a fatire on his fpecies ; as
it injures Virtue and violates Truth : And, as little, that a corrupt man fhould
approve it, becaufe it juftifies his principles, and tends to excufe his practice.

Dowager of Malborough is in raptures at it; she says she can dream of nothing else since she read it, she declares that she hath now found out, that her whole life hath been lost in caressing the worst part of mankind, and treating the best as her foes; and that if she knew Gulliver, tho' he had been the worst enemy she ever had, she would give up her present acquaintance for his friendship. You may see by this, that you are not much injur'd by being suppos'd the Author of this piece. If you are, you have disoblig'd us, and two or three of your best friends, in not giving us the least hint of it while you were with us; and in particular Dr. Arbuthnot, who says it is ten thousand pities he had not known it, he could have added such abundance of things upon every subject. Among Lady-critics, some have found out that Mr. Gulliver had a particular malice to Maids of Honour. Those of them who frequent the Church, say, his design is impious, and that it is depreciating the works of the Creator. Notwith-standing, I am told the Princess hath read it with great pleasure. As to other Critics, they think the flying island is the least entertaining; and so great an opinion the town have of the impossibility of Gulliver's writing at all below himself, 'tis agreed that part was not writ by the same hand, tho' this hath its defenders too. It hath pass'd Lords and Commons *nemine contradicente*; and the whole town, men, women, and children, are quite full of it.

Perhaps I may all this time be talking to you of a Book you have never seen, and which hath not yet reached Ireland; if it hath not, I believe what we have said will be sufficient to recommend it to your reading, and that you will order me to send it to you.

But it will be much better to come over yourself, and read it here, where you will have the pleasure of variety of Commentators, to explain the difficult passages to you.

We all rejoice that you have fixed the precise time of your coming to be *cum hirundine prima*; which we modern naturalists pronounce, ought to be reckon'd, contrary to Pliny, in this northern latitude of fifty-two degrees, from the end of February, Styl. Greg. at fartheft. But to us your friends, the coming of such a black swallow as you, will make a summer in the worst of seasons. We are no less glad at your mention of Twickenham and Dawly; and in town you know you have a lodging at Court.

The Princess is cloath'd in Irish silk; pray give our service to the Weavers. We are strangely surpriz'd to hear that the bells in Ireland ring without your money. I hope

hope you do not write the thing that is not. We are afraid that B— hath been guilty of that crime, that you (like Honynhnm) have treated him as a Yahoo, and difcarded him your fervice. I fear you do not underftand thefe modifh terms, which every creature now underftands but yourfelf.

You tell us your Wine is bad, and that the Clergy do not frequent your houfe, which we look upon to be tautology. The beft advice we can give you is, to make them a prefent of your Wine, and come away to better.

You fancy we envy you, but you are miftaken ; we envy thofe you are with, for we cannot envy the man we love. Adieu.

LETTER XIX.

Nov. 16, 1726.

I Have refolved to take time ; and in fpite of all misfortunes and demurs, which ficknefs, lamenefs, or difability of any kind can throw in my way, to write you (at intervals) a long letter. My two leaft fingers of one hand hang impediments to the others, like ufelefs dependents, who only take up room, and never are active or affiftant to our wants : I fhall never be much the better for 'em— I congratulate you upon what you call your Coufin's wonderful Book, which is *publica trita manu* at prefent, and I prophefy will be hereafter the admiration of all men. That countenance with which it is received by fome ftatefmen, is delightful ; I wifh I could tell you how every fingle man looks upon it, to obferve which has been my whole diverfion this fortnight. I've never been a night in London fince you left me, till now for this very end, and indeed it has fully anfwered my expectations.

I find no confiderable man very angry at the book : fome indeed think it rather too bold, and too general a Satire : but none, that I hear of, accufe it of particular reflections (I mean no perfons of confequence, or good judgment ; the mob of Critics, you know, always are defirous to apply Satire to thofe they envy for being above them) fo that you needed not to have been fo fecret upon this head. Motte received the copy (he tells me) he knew not from whence, nor from whom, dropp'd at his houfe in the dark, from a Hackney-Coach : by computing the time I found it was after you left England, fo, for my part I fufpend my judgment.

I am

I am pleas'd with the nature and quality of your Prefent to the Princefs. The Irifh ftuff you fent to Mrs.' H.
her R. H. laid hold of, and has made up for her own ufe.
Are you determined to be national in every thing, even
in your civilities ? you are the greateft Politician in Europe at this rate ; but as you are a rational Politician,
there's no great fear of you, you will never fucceed.

Another thing in which you have pleas'd me, was what
you fay to Mr. P. by which it feems to me that you value
no man's civility above your own dignity, or your own
reafon. Surely, without flattery, you are now above all
parties of men, and it is high time to be fo, after twenty or
thirty years obfervation of the great world.

Nullius addictus jurare in verba magiftri.

I queftion not, many men would be of your intimacy,
that you might be of their intereft : But God forbid an
honeft or witty man fhould be of any, but that of his country. They have fcoundrels enough to write for their
paffions and their defigns : let us write for truth, for
honour, and for pofterity. If you muft needs write about
Politics at all (but perhaps 'tis full as wife to play the fool
any other way) furely it ought to be fo as to preferve the
dignity and integrity of your character with thofe times
to come, which will moft impartially judge of you.

I wifh you had writ to Lord Peterborow; no man is
more affectionate toward you. Don't fancy none but Tories are your friends; for at that rate I muft be, at moft,
but half your friend, and fincerely I am wholly fo. Adieu,
write often, and come foon, for many wifh you well, and
all would be glad of your company.

LETTER XX.

From Dr. SWIFT.

Dublin, Nov. 17, 1726,

I Am juft come from anfwering a Letter of Mrs. H—'s
writ in fuch myftical terms, that I fhould never have
found out the meaning, if a Book had not been fent me
called *Gulliver's Travels*, of which you fay fo much in
yours. I read the Book over, and in the fecond volume
obferve feveral paffages, which appear to be patch'd and
alter'd

alter'd *, and the ſtyle of a different ſort (unleſs I am
much miſtaken). Dr. Arbuthnot likes the Projectors
leaſt †; others, you tell me, the Flying iſland; ſome
think it wrong to be ſo hard upon whole bodies or Cor-
porations, yet the general opinion is, that reflections on
particular perſons are moſt to be blam'd : ſo that in theſe
caſes, I think the beſt method is, to let cenſure and opinion take their courſe. A Biſhop here ſaid, that book
was full of improbable lies, and for his part, he hardly
believed a word of it, and ſo much for Gulliver.

Going to England is a very good thing, if it were not
attended with an ugly circumſtance of returning to Ireland. It is a ſhame you do not perſuade your Miniſters
to keep me on that ſide, if it were but by a court expedient
of keeping me in Priſon for a Plotter : but at the ſame time
I muſt tell you, that ſuch journeys very much ſhorten my
life, for a month here is longer than ſix at Twickenham.

How comes friend Gay to be ſo tedious ! another man
can publiſh fifty thouſand Lies ſooner than he can fifty
Fables.

I am juſt going to perform a very good office, it is to
aſſiſt with the Archbiſhop, in degrading a Parſon who
couples all our beggars, by which I ſhall make one happy
man ; and decide the great queſtion of an indelible character in favour of the Principles in faſhion : this I hope you
will repreſent to the Miniſtry in my favour, as a point of
merit ; ſo farewell till I return.

I am come back, and have deprived the parſon, who by
a law here is to be hanged the next couple he marries : he
declared to us that he reſolved to be hanged, only deſired
when he was to go to the gallows, the Archbiſhop would
take off his Excommunication. Is not he a good Catholic? and yet he is but a Scotchman. This is the only
Iriſh event I ever troubled you with, and I think it deſerves notice.—Let me add, that, if I were Gulliver's
friend, I would deſire all my acquaintance to give out
that his copy was baſely mangled and abuſed, and added
to, and blotted out by the Printer ; for ſo to me it ſeems,
in the ſecond volume particularly.   Adieu.

* This was the fact, which is complained of, and redreſſed in the Dublin
Edition of the Dean's works.
† Becauſe he underſtood it to be intended as a ſatire on the Royal Society.

LETTER

LETTER XXI.

From Dr. Swift.

December 5, 1726.

I Believe the hurt in your hand affects me more than it
does yourself, and with reason, becaufe I may probably be a greater lofer by it.   What have Accidents to do
with thofe who are neither jockeys, nor fox-hunters, nor
bullies, nor drunkards? And yet a rafcally Groom fhall
gallop a foundered horfe ten miles upon a caufeway, and
get home fafe.

I am very much pleas'd that you approve what was fent,
becaufe I remember to have heard a great man fay, that
nothing required more judgment than making a prefent ;
which, when it is done to thofe of high rank, ought to be
of fomething that is not readily got for money. You oblige
me and at the fame time do me juftice in what you obferve
as to Mr. P.   Befides, it is too late in life for me to act
otherwife, and therefore I follow a very eafy road to virtue, and purchafe it cheap. If you will give me leave to
join us, is not your life and mine a ftate of power, and dependance a ftate of flavery ? We care not three-pence whether a Prince or Minifter will fee us or no : We are not a-
fraid of having ill offices done us, nor at the trouble of
guarding our words for fear of giving offence.   I do agree
that Riches are Liberty, but then we are to put into the
balance how long our apprenticefhip is to laft in acquiring
them.

Since you have receiv'd the verfes, I moft earneftly intreat you to burn thofe which you do not approve, and in
thofe few where you may not diflike fome parts, blot out
the reft, and fometimes (tho' it be againft the lazinefs of
your nature) be fo kind to make a few corrections, if the
matter will bear them.   I have fome few of thofe things I
call Thoughts moral and diverting ; if you pleafe, I will
fend the beft I can pick from them, to add to the new volume. I have reafon to chufe the method you mention of
mixing the feveral verfes, and I hope thereby among the
bad Critics to be entitled to more merit than is my due.

This moment I am fo happy to have a letter from my
Lord Peterborow, for which I intreat you will prefent
him with my humble refpects and thanks, tho' he all-to-
be-Gullivers me by very ftrong infinuations. Though
you

you defpife Riddles, I am ftrongly tempted to fend a parcel to be printed by themfelves, and make a nine-penny
jobb for the bookfeller.   There are fome of my own,
wherein I exceed mankind, *Mira Poemata!* the moft folemn that were ever feen ; and fome writ by others, admirable indeed, but far inferior to.mine ; but I will not
praife myfelf.   You approve that writer who laughs and
makes others laugh ; but why fhould I who hate the world,
or you who do not love it, make it fo happy ? therefore I
refolve from henceforth to handle only ferious fubjects,
nifi quid tu, docte Trebati diffentis.

Yours, etc.

LETTER XXII.

March 8, 1726-7.

MR. Stopford will be the bearer of this letter, for
whofe acquaintance I am, among many other favours, obliged to you : and I think the acquaintance of fo
valuable, ingenious, and unaffected a man, to be none of the
leaft obligations.

Our Mifcellany is now quite printed.   I am prodigioufly
pleafed with this joint-volume, in which methinks we look
like friends, fide by fide, ferious and merry by turns,
converfing interchangeably, and walking down hand in
hand to pofterity : not in the ftiff forms of learned Authors, flattering each other, and fetting the reft of mankind at nought ; but in a free unimportant, natural, eafy
manner ; diverting others juft as we diverted ourfelves.
The third volume confifts of Verfes, but I would chufe to
print none but fuch as have fome peculiarity, and may be
diftinguifh'd for ours, from other writers.   There's no end
of making Books, Solomon faid, and above all of making
Mifcellanies, which all men can make.   For unlefs there
be a character in every piece, like the mark of the elect,
I fhoud not care to be one of the Twelve thoufand figned.

You receiv'd, I hope, fome commendatory verfes from
a Horfe and a Lilliputian to Gulliver ; and an heroic
Epiftle of Mrs. Gulliver.   The bookfeller would fain
have printed 'em before the fecond Edition of the book,
but I would not permit it without your approbation : nor
do I much like them.   You fee how much like a Poet I
write, and yet if you were with us, you'd be deep in Politics.   People are very warm, and very angry, very
little to the purpofe, but therefore the more warm and

the more angry : *Non noſtrum eſt, Tantas componere lites.* I ſtay at Twitnam, without ſo much as reading news-papers, votes, or any other paltry Pamphlets : Mr. Stopford will carry you a whole parcel of them, which are ſent for your diverſion, but not imitation. For my own part, methinks I am at Glubdubdrib with none but ancients and ſpirits about me.

I am rather better than I uſe to be at this ſeaſon, but my hand (though, as you ſee, it has not loſt its cunning) is frequently in very aukward ſenſations, rather than pain. But to convince you it is pretty well, it has done ſome miſchief already, and juſt been ſtrong enough to cut the other hand, while it was aiming to prune a fruit-tree.

Lady Bolingbroke has writ you a long, lively letter, which will attend this ; ſhe has very bad health, he very good. Lord Peterborow has writ twice to you ; we fancy ſome letters have been intercepted, or loſt by accident. About ten thouſand things I want to tell you ; I wiſh you were as impatient to hear them, for if ſo, you would, you muſt come early this ſpring. Adieu. Let me have a line from you. I am vex'd at loſing Mr. Stopford as ſoon as I knew him : but I thank God I have known him no longer. If every man one begins to value muſt ſettle in Ireland, pray make me know no more of 'em, and I forgive you this one.

LETTER XXIII.

Oct. 2, 1727.

IT is a perfect trouble to me to write to you, and your kind letter left for me at Mr. Gay's affected me ſo much, that it made me like a girl. I can't tell what to ſay to you ; I only feel that I wiſh you well in every circumſtance of life ; that 'tis almoſt as good to be hated as to be loved, conſidering the pain it is to minds of any tender turn, to find themſelves ſo utterly impotent to do any good, or give any eaſe to thoſe who deſerve moſt from us. I would very fain know, as ſoon as you recover your complaints, or any part of them. Would to God I could eaſe any of them, or had been able even to have alleviated any ! I found I was not, and truly it grieved me. I was ſorry to find you could think yourſelf eaſier in any houſe than in mine, tho' at the ſame time I can allow for a tenderneſs in your way of thinking, even when it ſeem-

ed

ᵉd to want that tendernefs. I can't explain my meaning, Perhaps you know it : But the beft way of convincing you of my indulgence, will be, if I live, to vifit you in Ireland, and act there as much in my own way as you did here in yours. I will not leave your roof, if I am ill. To your bad health I fear there was added fome difagreeable news from Ireland, which might occafion your fo fudden departure : For the laft time I faw you, you affured me you would not leave us this whole winter, unlefs your health grew better, and I don't find it did fo. I never comply'd fo unwillingly in my life with any friend as with you, in ftaying fo entirely from you : nor could I have had the conftancy to do it, if you had not promifed that before you went, we fhould meet, and you would fend to us all to come. I have given your remembrances to thofe you mention in yours : we are quite forry for you, I mean for ourfelves. I hope, as you do, that we fhall meet in a more durable and more fatisfactory ftate ; but the lefs fure I am of that, the more I would indulge it in this. We are to believe, we fhall have fomething better than even a friend, there, but certainly here we have nothing fo good. Adieu for this time ; may you find every friend you go to as pleas'd and happy, as every friend you went from is forry and troubled.   Yours, etc.

LETTER XXIV.

From Dr. SWIFT.

Dublin, Oct. 12, 1727.

I Have been long reafoning with myfelf upon the condition I am in, and in conclufion have thought it beft to return to what fortune hath made my home ; I have there a large houfe, and fervants and conveniences about me. I may be worfe than I am, and I have no where to retire. I therefore thought it beft to return to Ireland, rather than go to any diftant place in England. Here is my maintenance, and here my convenience. If it pleafes God to reftore me to my health, I fhall readily make a third journey ; if not, we muft part as all human creatures have parted. You are the beft and kindeft friend in the world, and I know nobody alive or dead to whom I am fo much obliged ; and if ever you made me angry, it was for your too much care about me. I have often wifhed that God Almighty would be fo eafy to the weaknefs of mankind, as to let old friends be acquainted in another ftate ; and if I were to write an Utopia for heaven, that would be one of my fchemes. This wildnefs you muft allow for, be-caufe I am giddy and deaf.

I find it more convenient to be fick here without the vexation of making my friends uneafy ; yet my giddinefs alone would not have done, if that unfociable comfortlefs deafnefs had not quite tired me. And I believe I fhould have returned from the Inn, if I had not feared it was only a fhort intermiffion and the year was late, and my licence expiring. Surely befides all other faults I fhould be a very ill judge, to doubt your friendfhip and kindnefs. But it hath pleafed God that you are not in a ftate of health, to be mortified with the care and ficknefs of a friend. Two fick friends never did well together ; fuch an office is fitter for fervants and humble companions, to whom it is wholly indifferent whether we give them trouble or no. The cafe would be quite otherwife if you were with me ; you could refufe to fee any body, and here is a large houfe, where we need not hear each other if we were both fick. I have a race of orderly elderly people of both fexes at com-mand, who are of no confequence, and have gifts proper for attending us ; who can bawl when I am deaf, and tread foftly when I am only giddy and would fleep.

I had another reafon for my hafte hither, which was changing my Agent, the old one having terribly involved my little affairs : to which however I am grown fo indif-ferent, that I believe I fhall lofe two or three hundred pounds rather than plague myfelf with accounts ; fo that I am very well qualified to be a Lord, and put into Peter Walter's hands.

Pray God continue and increafe Mr. Congreve's amend-ment, though he does not deferve it like you, having been too lavifh of that health which Nature gave him.

I hope my Whitehall-landlord is nearer to a place than when I left him ; as the Preacher faid, " the day of " judgment was nearer than ever it had been before."

Pray God fend you health, *det falutem, det opes ; animam aequam tibi ipfe parabis.* You fee Horace wifhed for money, as well as health ; and I would hold a crown he kept a coach ; and I fhall never be a friend to the Court till you

Yours, etc,

LETTER

LETTER XXV.

From Dr. SWIFT.

Oct. 30, 1727.

THE firſt letter I writ after my landing was to Mr. Gay;
but it would have been wiſer to direct it to Tonſon or
Lintot, to whom I believe his Lodgings are better known
than to the runners of the Poſt-office. In that letter you
will find what a quick change I made in ſeven days from
London to the Deanry, thro' many nations and languages
unknown to the civilized world. And I have often reflect -
ed in how few hours, with a ſwift horſe or a ſtrong gale,
a man may come among a people as unknown to him as the
Antipodes. If I did not know you more by your converſation and kindneſs than by your letter, I might be baſe
enough to ſuſpect, that in point of friendſhip you acted
like ſome Philoſophers who writ much better upon virtue
than they practiſed it. In anſwer, I can only ſwear that
you have taught me to dream, which I had not done in
twelve years further than by inexpreſſible nonſenſe; but
now I can every night diſtinctly ſee Twickenham, and
the Grotto, and Dawley, and many other et cetera's, and
it is but three nights ſince I beat Mrs. Pope. I muſt
needs confeſs, that the pleaſure I take in thinking of you
is very much leſſened by the pain I am in about your health:
You pay dearly for the great talents God hath given you;
and for the conſequences of them in the eſteem and diſtinction you receive from mankind, unleſs you can provide a tolerable ſtock of health; in which purſuit I cannot much
commend your conduct, but rather intreat you would mend
it by following the advice of my Lord Bolingbroke and your
other Phyſicians. When you talk'd to me of Cups and Im-
preſſions, it came into my head to imitate you in quoting
Scripture, not to your advantage; I mean what was ſaid
to David by one of his brothers: "I knew thy pride and
"the naughtineſs of thy heart;" I remember when it
grieved your ſoul to ſee me pay a penny more than my
club at an inn, when you had maintained me three months
at bed and board; for which, if I had dealt with you in
the Smithfield way, it would have coſt me a hundred
pounds, for I live worſe here upon more. Did you ever
conſider that I am for life almoſt twice as rich as you,
and pay no rent, and drink French wine twice as cheap as
you do Port, and have neither Coach, Chair, nor Mother?

ther? As to the world, I think you ought to fay to it with St. Paul, *If we have fown unto you fpiritual things, is it a great thing if we shall reap your carnal things?* This is more proper ftill, if you confider the French word *fpiritual*, in which fenfe the world ought to pay you better than they do. If you made me a prefent of a thoufand pounds I would not allow myfelf to be in your debt; and if I made you a prefent of two, I would not allow myfelf to be out of it. But I have not half your pride: witnefs what Mr. Gay fays in his letter, that I was cenfured for begging Prefents, though I limited them to ten fhillings. I fee no reafon, (at leaft my friendfhip and vanity fee none) why you fhould not give me a vifit, when you fhall happen to be difengaged: I will fend a perfon to Chefter to take care of you, and you fhall be ufed, by the beft folks we have here, as well as civility and good natufe can contrive; I believe local motion will be no ill phyfic, and I will have your coming infcribed on my Tomb, and recorded in never-dying verfe

I thank Mrs. Pope for her prayers, but I know the myftery. A perfon of my acquaintance, who ufed to correfpond with the laft Great Duke of Tufcany, fhewing one of the Duke's letters to a friend, and profeffing great fenfe of his Highnefs's friendfhip, read this paffage out of the letters, *I would give one of my fingers to procure your real good.* The perfon to whom this was read, and who knew the Duke well, faid, the meaning of *real good* was only that the other might turn a good Catholic. Pray afk Mrs. Pope whether this ftory is applicable to her and me? I pray God blefs her, for I am fure fhe is a good Chriftian, and (which is almoft as rare) a good Woman.

Adieu.

LETTER XXVI.

Mr. GAY to Dr. SWIFT.

Oct. 22, 1727.

THE Queen's family is at laft fettled, and in the lift I was appointed Gentleman-ufher to the Princefs Louifa, the youngeft Princefs; which, upon account that I am fo far advanced in life, I have declin'd accepting; and have endeavour'd in the beft manner I could, to make my excufes by a letter to her Majefty. So now all my expectations are vanifh'd; and I have no profpect, but in depend-

ing

ing wholly upon myfelf, and my own conduct. As I am us'd to difappointments, I can bear them; but as I can have no more hopes, I can no more be difappointed, fo that I am in a bleffed condition.—You remember you were advifing me to go into Newgate to finifh my fcenes the more cor-rectly—I now think I fhall, for I have no attendance to hinder me; but my Opera is already finifh'd. I leave the reft of this paper to Mr. Pope.

Gay is a Free-man, and I writ him a long Congratula-tory Letter upon it. Do you the fame : it will mend him, and make him a better man than a Court could do. Ho-race might keep his coach in Auguftus's time, if he pleas'd; but I won't in the time of our Auguftus. My Poem (which it grieves me that I dare not fend you a copy of, for fear of the Curls and Dennis's of Ireland, and ftill more for fear of the worft of Traytors, our Friends and Admirers) my Poem, I fay, will fhew what a diftinguifhing age we lived in : Your name is in it, with fome others, under a mark of fuch ignominy as you will not much grieve to wear in that company. Adieu, and God blefs you, and give you health and fpirits,

Whether thou chufe Cervantes' ferious air,
Or laugh and fhake in Rab'lais' eafy chair,
Or in the graver Gown inftruct mankind,
Or, filent, let thy morals tell thy mind.

Thefe two verfes are over and above what I've faid of you in the Poem. Adieu.

LETTER XXVII.

Dr. SWIFT to Mr. GAY.

Dublin, Nov. 23, 1727.

I Entirely approve your refufal of that employment, and your writing to the Queen. I am perfectly confident you have a keen enemy in the Miniftry. God forgive him, but not till he puts himfelf in a ftate to be forgiven. Upon reafoning with myfelf, I fhould hope they are gone too far to difcard you quite, and that they will give you fome-thing; which, although much lefs than they ought, will be (as far as it is worth) better circumftantiated : And fince you already juft live, a middling help will make you
juft

juft tolerable. Your latenefs in life (as you fo foon call it) might be improper to begin the world with, but almoft the eldeft men may hope to fee Changes in a Court. A Minifter is always feventy : you are thirty years younger; and confider, Cromwell himfelf did not begin to appear till he was older than you. I beg you will be thrifty, and learn to value a fhilling, which Dr. Birch faid was a ferious thing. Get a ftronger fence about your 1000 *l.* and throw the inner fence into the heap, and be advifed by your Twickenham landlord and me about an annuity. You are the moft refractory, honeft, good-natur'd man I ever have known ; I could argue out this paper—I am very glad your Opera is finifhed, and hope your friends will join the reader to make it fucceed, becaufe you are ill ufed by others.

I have known Courts thefe thirty-fix years, and know they differ ; but in fome things they are extremely conftant : Firft, in the trite old maxim of a minifter's never fo giving thofe he hath injured : Secondly, in the infincerity of thofe who would be thought the beft friends : Thirdly, in the love of fawning, cringing, and tale bearing : Fourthly, in facrificing thofe whom we really wifh well, to a point of intereft, or intrigue : Fifthly, in keeping every thing worth taking, for thofe who can do fervice or dif-fervice.

Now why does not Pope publifh his Dulnefs ? the rogues he marks will die of themfelves in peace, and fo will his friends, and fo there will be neither punifhment nor reward.—Pray enquire how my Lord St. John does ? there's no man's health in England I am more concerned about than his—I wonder whether you begin to tafte the pleafure of independency ? or whether you do not fometimes leer upon the Court, *oculo retorto* ? Will you not think of an Annuity, when you are two years older, and have doubled your purchafe-money ? Have you dedicated your Opera, and got the ufual dedication-fee of twenty guineas ? How is the Doctor ? does he not chide that you never called upon him for hints ? Is my Lord Bolingbroke at the moment I am writing, a planter, a philofopher, or a writer ? Is Mr. Pultney in expectation of a fon, or my Lord Oxford of a new old Manufcript ?

I bought your Opera to-day for fix-pence, a curfed print. I find there is neither dedication nor preface, both which wants I approve ; it is in the *grand gout*.

We are as full of it *promodulo noftro* as London can be, continually acting, and houfes cram'd, and the Lord Lieutenant

tenant feveral times there laughing his heart out.   I did not underftand that the fcene of Lockit and Peachum's quarrel was an imitation of one between Brutus and Caffius, till I was told it.   I wifh Macheath, when he was going to be hang'd, had imitated Alexander the Great when he was dying : I would have had his fellow-rogues defire his commands about a Succeffor, and he to anfwer, Let it be the moft worthy, etc. We hear a million of ftories about the Opera, of the applaufe at the fong, *That was levell'd at me*, when two great Minifters were in a box together, and all the world ftaring at them.   I am heartily glad your Opera hath mended your purfe, though perhaps it may fpoil your court.

Will you defire my Lord Bolingbroke, Mr. Pultney and Mr. Pope, to command you to buy an annuity with two thoufand pounds ? that you may laugh at courts, and bid Minifters ——

Ever preferve fome fpice of the Alderman, and prepare againft Age, and Dulnefs, and Sicknefs, and Coldnefs, or Death of Friends.   A Whore has a refcurce left, that fhe can turn bawd ; but an old decay'd Poet is a creature abandon'd, and at mercy, when he can find none. Get me likewife Polly's Meffotinto.   Lord, how the fchool-boys at Weftminfter, and Univerfity-lads adore you at this juncture ! Have you made as many men laugh, as Minifters can make weep ?

I will excufe Sir —— the trouble of a letter : When Ambaffadors came from Troy to condole with Tiberius upon the death of his Nephew, after two years ; the Emperor anfwered, that he likewife condoled with them for the untimely death of Hector.   I always loved and refpected him very much, and do ftill as much as ever : and it is a return fufficient, if he pleafes to accept the offers of my moft humble fervice.

The Beggar's Opera hath knock'd down Gulliver ; hope to fee Pope's Dulnefs knock down the Beggar's Opera, but not till it hath fully done its jobb.

To expofe vice, and make people laugh with innocence, does more publick fervice than all the Minifters of ftate from Adam to Walpole, and fo adieu.

LETTER XXVIII.

Lord BOLINGBROKE to Dr. SWIFT.

POPE charges himfelf with this letter; he has been here two days, he is now hurrying to London, he will be back to Twickenham in two days more, and before the end of the week he will be, for aught I know, at Dublin. In the mean time his * Dulnefs grows and flourifhes as if he was there already. It will indeed be a noble work: the many will ftare at it, the few will fmile, and all his Patrons from Bickerftaff to Gulliver will rejoice, to fee themfelves adorn'd in that immortal piece.

I hear that you have had fome return of your illnefs which carried you fo fuddenly from us (if indeed it was your own illnefs which made you in fuch hafte to be at Dublin.) Dear Swift, take care of your health, I'll give you a receipt for it, à la Montagne, or which is better, à la Bruyère. Nourriffer bien vôtre corps; ne le fatiguer jamais: laiffer rouiller l'éfprit, meuble inutil, voire en til dangereux: Laiffer fonner vos cloches le matin pour eveiller les chanoines, et pour faire dormir le Doyen d'un fommeil doux et profond, qui luy procure de beaux fonges: Lever vous tard, et aller à l'Eglife, pour vous faire payer d'avoir bien dormi et bien dejuné. As to myfelf (a perfon about whom I concern myfelf very little) I muft fay a word or two out of complaifance to you. I am in my farm and here I fhoot ftrong and tenacious roots; I have caught hold of the earth (to ufe a Gardener's phrafe) and neither my enemies nor my friends will find it an eafy matter to tranfplant me again. Adieu. Let me hear from you, at leaft of you: I love you for a thoufand things, for none more than for the juft efteem and love which you have for all the fons of Adam.

P. S. According to Lord Bolingbroke's account I fhall be at Dublin in three days. I cannot help adding a word, to defire you to expect my foul there with you by that time; but as for the jade of a body that is tack'd to it, I fear there will be no dragging it after. I affure you I have few friends here to detain me, and no powerful one at Court abfolutely to forbid my journey. I am told the Gynocracy are of opinion, that they want no better writers than Cibber and the Britifh journalift; fo that we may live at quiet, and apply ourfelves to our more abftrufe ftudies.

* The Dunciad.

The

The only Courtiers I know, or have the honour to call my friends, are John Gay and Mr. Bowry; the former is at prefent fo employed in the elevated airs of his Opera, and the latter in the exaltation of his high dignity (that of her Majefty's Waterman) that I can fcarce obtain a categori-' cal anfwer from either to any thing I fay to 'em. But the Opera fucceeds extremely, to yours and my extreme fatis-faction, of which he promifes this poft to give you a full account. I have been in a worfe condition of health than ever, and think my immortality is very near out of my enjoyment: fo it muft be in you, and in pofterity, to make me what amends you can for dying young. Adieu. While I am, I am yours. Pray love me, and take care of yourfelf.

L E T T E R XXIX.

March 23, 1727-8.

I Send you a very odd thing, a paper printed in Bofton in New-England, wherein you'll find a real perfon, a member of their Parliament, of the name of Jonathan Gulliver. If the fame of that Traveller has travell'd thi-ther, it has travell'd very quick, to have folks chriften'd already by the name of the fuppofed Author. But if you object, that no child fo lately chriften'd could be arrived at years of maturity to be elected into Parliament, I reply (to folve the Riddle) that the perfon is an *Anabaptift*, and not chriftened till full age, which fets all right. However it be, the accident is very fingular, that thefe two names fhould be united.

Mr. Gay's Opera has been acted near forty days run-ning, and will certainly continue the whole feafon. So he has more than a fence about his thoufand pound: he'll foon be thinking of a fence about his two thoufand. Shall no one of us live as we would with each other to live? Shall he have no annuity, you no fettlement on this fide, and I no profpect of getting to you on the other? This world is made for Cæfar—as Cato faid, for ambitious, falfe, or flattering people to domineer in: Nay they would not, by their good will, leave us our very books, thoughts, or words, in quiet. I defpife the world yet, I affure you, more than either Gay or you, and the Court more than all the reft of the world. As for thofe Scriblers for whom you apprehend I would fupprefs my *Dulnefs* (which by the way, for the future, you are to call by a more pompous name,

name, *The Dunciad*) how much that neſt of Hornets are
my regard, will eaſily appear to you when you read the
Treatiſe of the Bathos.

At all adventures, yours and my name ſhall ſtand link-
ed as friends to poſterity, both in verſe and proſe, and (as
Tully calls it) in *conſuetudine Studiorum*. Would to God
our Perſons could but as well, and as ſurely be inſepara-
ble ! I find my other Tyes dropping from me : ſome worn
off, ſome torn off, others relaxing daily : My greateſt,
both by duty, gratitude, and humanity, Time is ſhaking
every moment, and it now hangs but by a thread ! I am
many years the older, for living ſo much with one ſo old ;
much the more helpleſs, for having been ſo long help'd
and tended by her : much the more conſiderate and tender, for a daily commerce with one who requir'd me juſtly to be both to her ; and conſequently the more melancholy and thoughtful ; and the leſs fit for others, who want
only in a companion or a friend, to be amuſed or entertained. My conſtitution too has had its ſhare of decay
as well as my ſpirits, and I am as much in the decline at
forty as you at ſixty. I believe we ſhall be fit to live together, could I get a little more health, which might make
me not quite inſupportable : Your Deafneſs would agree
with my Dulneſs : you would not want me to ſpeak when
you could not hear. But God forbid you ſhou'd be as de-
ſtitute of the ſocial comforts of life, as I muſt when I loſe
my mother ; or that ever you ſhou'd loſe your more uſeful acquaintance ſo utterly, as to turn your thoughts to
ſuch a broken reed as I am, who could ſo ill ſupply your
wants. I am extremely troubled at the returns of your
Deafneſs ; you cannot be too particular in the accounts
of your health to me ; every thing you do or ſay in this
kind obliges me, nay, delights me, to ſee the juſtice you
do me in thinking me concern'd in all your concerns ; ſo
that though the pleaſanteſt thing you can tell me be that
you are better or eaſier ; next to that it pleaſes me, that
you make me the perſon you would complain to.

As the obtaining the love of valuable men is the hap-
pieſt end I know of this life, ſo the next felicity is to get
rid of fools and ſcoundrels ; which I cannot but own to
you was one part of my deſign in falling upon theſe Authors, whoſe incapacity is not greater than their inſinceri-
ty, and of whom I have always found (if I may quote
myſelf)

That each bad Author is as bad a Friend.

This

This poem will rid me of thofe infeɛts,

> Cedite, Romani Scriptores, cedite, Graii;
> Nefcio quid majus nafcitur Iliade.

I mean than *my Iliad*; and I call it *Nefcio quid*, which is a degree of modefty; but however if it filence thefe fellows *, it muft be fometning greater than any Iliad in Chriftendom.   Adieu.

L E T T E R XXX.

From Dr. Swift.

Dublin, May 10, 1728.

I Have with great pleafure fhewn the New-England News-paper, with the two names Jonathan Gulliver, and I remember Mr. Fortefcue fent you an account from the aflizes, of one Lemuel Gulliver who had a Caufe there, and loft it on his ill reputation of being a liar. Thefe are not the only obfervations I have made upon odd ftrange accidents in trifles, which in things of great importance would have been matter for hiftorians. Mr. Gay's Opera hath been aɛted here twenty times, and my Lord Lieutenant tells me, it is very well perform'd; he hath feen it often, and approves it much.

You give a moft melancholy account of yourfelf, and which I do not approve. I reckon that a man, fubjeɛt like us to bodily in'irmities, fhould only occafionally converfe with great people, notwithftanding all their good qualities, eafineffes, and kindneffes. There is another race which I prefer before them, as Beef and Mutton for conftant diet before Partridges: I mean a middle kind both for underftanding and fortune, who are perfeɛtly eafy, never impertinent, complying in every thing, ready to do a hundred little offices that you and I may often want, dine and fit with me five times for once that I go to them, and whom I can tell without offence, that I am otherwife engaged at prefent. This you cannot expeɛt from any of thofe that either you or I or both are acquainted with on your fide; who are only fit for our healthy feafons, and have much bufinefs of their own. God forbid I fhould

---

* It did in a little time effeɛtually filence them.

con-

condemn you to Ireland *(Quanquam O!)* and for England
I defpair; and indeed a change of affairs would come too
late at my feafon of life, and might probably produce
nothing on my behalf. You have kept Mrs. Pope longer,
and have had her care beyond what from nature you could
expect; not but her lofs will be very fenfible, whenever
it fhall happen. I fay one thing, that both fummers and
winters are milder here than with you ; all things for life
in general better for a middling fortune : you will have an
abfolute command of your company, with whatever obfe-
quioufnefs or freedom you may expect or allow. I have
an elderly houfe-keeper, who hath been my *IV. lp-le* above
thirty years, whenever I liv'd in this kingdom. I have
the command of one or two villas near this town : You
have a warm apartment in this houfe, and two gardens
for amufement. I have faid enough, yet not half. Except abfence from friends, I confefs freely that I have no
difcontent at living here ; befides what arifes from a filly
fpirit of Liberty, which as it neither fours my drink, nor
hurts my meat, nor fpoils my ftomach farther than in imagination, fo I refolve to throw it off.

You talk of this Dunciad, but I am impatient to have
it *velare per era*—there is now a vacancy for fame ; the
Beggar's Opera hath done its tafk, *difcedit uti conviva fatur*.
Adieu.

LETTER XXXI.

From Dr. SWIFT.

June 1, 1728.

I Look upon my Lord Bolingbroke and us two as a
peculiar Triumvirate, who have nothing to expect, or
to fear; and fo far fitteft to converfe with one another :
Only he and I are a little fubject to fchemes, and one of
us (I won't fay which) upon very weak appearances, and
this you have nothing to do with. I do profefs without
affectation, that your kind opinion of me as a Patriot
(fince you call it fo) is what I do not deferve ; becaufe
what I do is owing to perfect rage and refentment, and
the mortifying fight of flavery, folly and bafenefs about
me, among which I'm forc'd to live. And I will take my
oath that you have more Virtue in an hour, than I in feven years ; for you defpife the follies, and hate the vices
of mankind, without the leaft ill effect on your temper ;
with

with regard to particular men, you are inclined always
rather to think the better, whereas with me it is always
directly contrary. I hope, however, this is not in you,
from a superior principle of virtue, but from your situation, which hath made all parties and interests indifferent
to you, who can be under no concern about high and
low-church, Whig and Tory, or who is first Minister
—Your long letter was the last I received till this by Dr.
Delany, although you mention another since. The Dr.
told me your secret about the Dunciad, which does not
please me, because it defers gratifying my vanity in the
most tender point, and perhaps may wholly disappoint it.
As to one of your enquiries, I am easy enough in great
matters, and have a thousand paltry vexations in my little
station, and the more contemptible, the more vexatious.
There might be a Lutrin writ upon the tricks used by my
Chapter to teize me. I do not converse with one creature
of Station or Title, but I have a set of easy people whom
I entertain when I have a mind ; I have formerly describ'd
them to you, but, when you come, you shall have the
honours of the country as much as you please, and I shall
on that account make a better figure as long as I live.
Pray God preserve Mrs. Pope for your sake and ease; I
love and esteem her too much to wish it for her own : If I
were five and twenty, I would wish to be of her age, to be
as secure as she is of a better life. Mrs. P. B has writ to
me, and is one of the best Letter-writers I know; very
good sense, civility and friendship, without any stiffness
or constraint. The Dunciad has taken wind here, but if
it had not, you are as much known here as in England,
and the University-lads will crowd to kiss the hem of your
garment. I am griev'd to hear that my Lord Bolingbroke's
ill health forc'd him to the Bath. Tell me, is not Temperance a necessary virtue for great men, since it is the
parent of Ease and Liberty ? so necessary for the use and
improvement of the mind, and which Philosophy allows to
be the greatest felicities of life ? I believe, had health been
given so liberally to you, it would have been better hus-
banded without shame to your parts.

LETTER XXXII.

Dawley, June 28, 1728.

I Now hold the pen for my Lord Bolingbroke, who is reading your Letter between two Hay cocks; but his attention is fomewhat diverted by cafting his eyes on the clouds, not in admiration of what you fay, but for fear of a fhower. He is pleafed with your placing him in the Triumvirate, between yourfelf and me; tho' he fays that he doubts he fhall fare like Lepidus, while one of us runs away with all the power, like Auguftus, and another with all the pleafures, like Anthony. It is upon a forefight of this, that he has fitted up his farm, and you will agree, that this fcheme of retreat at leaft is not founded upon weak appearances. Upon his return from the Bath, all peccant humours, he finds, are puig'd out of him; and his great Temperance and Oeconomy are fo fignal, that the firft is fit for my conftitution, and the latter would enable you to lay up fo much money as to buy a Bifhoprick in England. As to the return of his health and vigour, were you here, you might enquire of his Hay-makers; but as to his temperance, I can anfwer that (for one whole day) we have had nothing for dinner but mutton-broth, beans and bacon, and a barn-door fowl.

Now his Lordfhip is run after his Cart, I have a moment left to myfelf to tell you, that I over-heard him yefterday agree with a painter for 200l. to paint his country-hall with Trophies of rakes, fpades, prongs, etc. and other ornaments, merely to countenançe his calling this place a farm—now turn over a new leaf—

He bids me affure you, he fhould be forry not to have more fchemes of kindnefs for his friends, than of ambition for himfelf: There, tho' his fchemes may be weak, the motives at leaft are ftrong; and he fays further, if you could bear as great a fall, and decreafe of your revenues, as he knows by experience he can, you would not live in Ireland an hour.

The Dunciad is going to be printed in all pomp, with the infcription, which makes me proudeft. It will be attended with *Proeme, Prolegomena, Teftimonia Scriptorum, Index Authorum* and Notes *Variorum.* As to the latter, I defire you to read over the Text, and make a few in any way you like beft *, whether dry raillery, upon the ftyle,

* Dr. Swift did fo.

and

and way of commenting of trivial critics; or humourous, upon the authors in the poem; or hiftorical, of perfons, places, times; or explanatory; or collecting the parallel paffages of the Ancients. Adieu. I am pretty well, my Mother not ill, Dr. Arbuthnot vex'd with his fever by intervals; I am afraid he declines, and we fhall lofe a worthy man : I am troubled about him very much.

I am, etc.

LETTER XXXIII.

From Dr. SWIFT.

July 16, 1728.

I Have often run over the *Dunciad* in an Irifh edition (I fuppofe full of faults) which a gentleman fent me. The notes I could wifh to be very large, in what relates to the perfons concerned ; for I have long obferv'd that twenty miles from London no body underftands hints, initial letters, or town-facts and paffages; and in a few years not even thofe who live in London. I would have the names of thefe fcriblers printed indexically at the beginning or end of the Poem, with an account of their works, for the reader to refer to. I would have all the Parodies (as they are call'd) referred to the author they imitate—When I began this long paper, I thought I fhould have fill'd it with fetting down the feveral paffages I had mark'd in the edition I had; but I find it unneceffary, fo many of them falling under the fame rule. After twenty times reading the whole, I never in my opinion faw fo much good fatire, and more good fenfe, in fo many lines. How it paffes in Dublin I know not yet; but I am fure it will be a great difadvantage to the poem, that the perfons and facts will not be underftood, till an explanation comes out, and a very full one. I imagine it is not to be publifhed till towards winter, when folks begin to gather in town. Again, I infift, you muft have your Afterifks filled up with fome real names of real Dunces.

I am now reading your preceding letter, of June 28, and find that all I have advis'd above is mention'd there. I would be glad to know whether the quarto edition is to come out anonymoufly, as publifhed by the Commentator, with all his pomp of prefaces, etc. and among many complaints of fpurious editions : I am thinking whether the Editor fhould not follow the old ftyle of, This excellent author, etc. and refine in many places when you meant no refinement; and into the bargain take all the load of naming the dunces, their qualities, histories, and performances?

As to yourself, I doubt you want a spurrer-on to exercise and to amusements; but to talk of decay at your season of life is a jest. But you are not so regular as I. You are the most temperate man God-ward, and the most intemperate yourself-ward, of most I have known. I suppose Mr. Gay will return from the Bath with twenty pounds more flesh, and two hundred less in money: Providence never designed him to be above two and twenty, by his thoughtlessness and Cullibility. He hath as little foresight of age, sickness, poverty, or loss of admirers, as a girl at fifteen. By the way, I must observe, that my Lord Bolingbroke (from the effects of his kindness to me) argues most sophistically: The fall from a million to a hundred thousand pounds is not so great, as from eight hundred pounds a year to one: Besides, he is a controller of Fortune, and Poverty dares not look a great Minister in the face, under his lowest declension. I never knew him live so great and expensively as he hath done since his return from Exile; such mortals have resources that others are not able to comprehend. But God bless you, whose great genius has not so transported you as to leave you to the courtesy of mankind; for wealth is liberty, and liberty is a blessing fittest for a philosopher—and Gay is a slave just by two thousand pounds too little.——And Horace was of my mind, and let my Lord contradict him, if he dares.——

LETTER XXXIV.

Bath, Nov. 12, 1728.

I Have past six weeks in quest of health, and found it not; but I found the folly of solicitude about it in a hundred instances; the contrariety of opinions and practices, the inability of physicians, the blind obedience of some patients, and as blind rebellion of others. I believe at a certain time of life, men are either fools, or physicians for themselves, and zealots, or divines for themselves.

It was much in my hopes that you intended us a winter's visit, but last week I repented that wish, having been alarmed with a report of your lying ill on the road from Ireland; from which I am just relieved by an assurance

that

that you are ftill at Sir A—'s, planting and building; two
things that I envy you for, befides a third, which is the
fociety of a valuable Lady.   I conclude (tho' I know nothing of it) that you quarrel with her, and abufe her every
day, if fhe is fo.   I wonder I hear of no Lampoons upon
her, either made by yourfelf, or by others becaufe you
efteem her.   I think it a vaft pleafure that whenever two
people of merit regard one another, fo many fcoundrels
envy and are angry at them : 'tis bearing teftimony to a
merit they cannot reach ; and if you knew the infinite content I have receiv'd of late, at the finding yours and my
name conftantly united in any filly fcandal, I think you
would go near to fing *Io Triumphe!* and celebrate my happinefs in verfe; and, I believe, if you won't, I fhall.
The infcription to the Dunciad is now printed and inferted in the Poem.   Do you care I fhould fay any thing farther how much that Poem is yours ? fince certainly without you it had never been.   Would to God we were together for the reft of our lives !   The whole weight of
Scriblers would juft ferve to find us amufement and not
more.   I hope you are too well employed to mind them :
every ftick you plant, and every ftone you lay, is to fome
purpofe ; but the bufinefs of fuch lives as theirs is but to
die daily, to labour, and raife nothing.   I only wifh we
could comfort each other under our bodily infirmities,
and let thofe who have fo great a mind to have more Wit
than we, win it and wear it.   Give us but eafe, health,
peace, and fair weather ! I think it is the beft wifh in the
world, and you know whofe it was.   If I liv'd in Ireland,
I fear the wet climate would endanger more than my life;
my humour and health; I am fo atmofpherical a creature.

I muft not omit acquainting you, that what you heard
of the words fpoken of you in the Drawing-room, was
not true.   The fayings of Princes, are generally as ill related as the fayings of Wits.   To fuch reports little of
our regard fhould be given, and lefs of our conduct in-
fluenced by them.

LETTER XXXV.

From Dr. Swift.

Dublin, Feb. 13, 1728.

I Lived very eafily in the country : Sir A. is a man of fenfe, and a fcholar, has a good voice, and my lady a better ; fhe is perfectly well-bred, and defires to improve her underftanding, which is very good, but cultivated too much like a fine lady. She was my pupil there, and feverely chid when fhe read wrong ; with that and walking, and making twenty little amufing improvements, and writing family-verfes of mirth by way of libels on my Lady, my time paft very well and in very great order ; infinitely better than here, where I fee no creature but my fervants and my old Prefbyterian houfe-keeper, denying myfelf to every body, till I fhall recover my ears.

The account of another Lord Lieutenant was only in a common news-paper, when I was in the country ; and if it fhould have happened to be true, I would have defired to have had accefs to him, as the fituation I am in requires. But this renews the grief for the death of our friend Mr. Congreve, whom I loved from my youth, and who furely, befides his other talents, was a very agreeable companion. He had the misfortune to fquander away a very good conftitution in his younger days ; and I think a man of fenfe and merit like him, is bound in confcience to preferve his health for the fake of his friends, as well as of himfelf. Upon his own account I could not much defire the continuance of his life, under fo much pain, and fo many infirmities. Years have not yet hardened me ; and I have an addition of weight on my fpirits fince we loft him ; tho' I faw him fo feldom, and poffibly, if he had liv'd on, fhould never have feen him more. I do not only wifh as you afk me, that I was unacquainted with any deferving perfon, but almoft that I never had a friend. Here is an ingenious good-humoured Phyfician, a fine gentleman, an excellent fcholar, eafy in his fortunes, kind to every body, hath abundance of friends, entertains them often and liberally, they pafs the evening with him at cards, with plenty of good meat and wine, eight or a dozen together ; he loves them all, and they him. He has twenty of thefe at command ; if one of them dies, it is no more than poor Tom ! he gets another, or takes up with the

the reſt, and is no more mov'd than at the loſs of his eat;
he offends nobody, is eaſy with every body — Is not this
the true happy man? I was deſcribing him to my Lady
A—, who knows him too, but ſhe hates him mortally by
my character, and will not drink his health : I would give
half my fortune for the ſame temper, and yet I cannot ſay
I love it, for I do not love my lord ——, who is much of the
Doctor's nature. I hear Mr. Gay's ſecond Opera, which
you mention, is forbid ; and then he will be once more fit
to be adviſed, and reject your advice. Adieu.

LETTER XXXVI.

Dr. Swift to Lord Bolingbroke.

Dublin, March 21, 1729.

YOU tell me you have not quitted the deſign of collecting, writing, etc. This is the anſwer of every
ſinner who defers his repentance. I wiſh Mr. Pope were
as great an urger as I, who long for nothing more than to
ſee truth under your hands, laying all detraction in the
duſt——I find myſelf diſpoſed every year, or rather every
month, to be more angry and revengeful ; and my rage
is ſo ignoble, that it deſcends even to reſent the folly and
baſeneſs of the enſlaved people among whom I live. I
knew an old Lord in Leiceſterſhire, who amuſed himſelf
with mending pitchforks and ſpades for his Tenants gra-
tis. Yet I have higher ideas left, if I were nearer to objects on which I might employ them ; and contemning my
private fortune, would gladly croſs the channel and ſtand
by, while my betters were driving the Boars out of the
garden, if there be any probable expectation of ſuch an
endeavour. When I was of your age I often thought of
death, but now after a dozen years more, it is never out
of my mind, and terrifies me leſs. I conclude that Providence hath order'd our fears to decreaſe with our ſpirits;
and yet I love la bagatelle better than ever : for finding it
troubleſome to read at night, and the company here growing taſteleſs, I am always writing bad proſe, or worſe verſes,
either of rage or raillery, whereof ſome few eſcape to
give offence or mirth, and the reſt are burnt.

They print ſome Iriſh traſh in London, and charge it
on me, which you will clear me of to my friends, for all
are ſpurious except one * paper, for which Mr. Pope very

* Intituled, A Libel on Dr. Delany, and a certain great Lord.

lately

lately chid me. I remember your Lordſhip us'd to ſay,
that a few good ſpeakers would in time carry any point
that was right ; and that the common method of a majority,
by calling, To the queſtion, would never hold long when
reaſon was on the other ſide. Whether politics do not
change like gaming by the invention of new tricks, I am
ignorant ; but I believe in your time you would never,
as a Miniſter, have ſuffered an act to paſs thro' the H. of
C——s, only becauſe you were ſure of a majority in the
H. of L—ds to throw it out : becauſe it would be unpopular, and conſequently a loſs of reputation. Yet this
we are told hath been the caſe in the qualification bill relating to Penſioners. It ſhould ſeem to me that Corruption, like avarice, hath no bounds. I had opportunities
to know the proceedings of your miniſtry better than any
other man of my rank ; and having not much to do, I have
often compar'd it with theſe laſt ſixteen years of a profound peace all over Europe, and we running ſeven millions in debt. I am forc'd to play at ſmall game, to ſet the
beaſts here a madding, merely for want of better game,
Tentanda via eſt qua me quoque poſſim, etc.—The D— take thoſe
politics, where a Dunce might govern for a dozen years
together. I will come in perſon to England, if I am provok'd, and ſend for the Dictator from the plough. I diſdain to ſay, *O mihi praeteritos*—— but *cruda Deo viridiſque
ſenectus.* Pray, my Lord, how are the Gardens ? Have
you taken down the mount, and remov'd the yew hedges ?
Have you not had weather for the ſpring corn ? Has Mr.
Pope gone farther in his Ethic Poems ? and is the head-
land ſown with wheat ? and what ſays Polybius ? and how
does my Lord St. John ? which laſt queſtion is very material to me, becauſe I love Burgundy, and riding between
Twickenham and Dawley.——I built a wall five years
ago, and when the maſons play'd the knaves, nothing delighted me ſo much as to ſtand by, while my ſervants
threw down what was amiſs : I have likewiſe ſeen a Mon-
key overthrow all the diſhes and plates in a kitchen, merely
for the pleaſure of ſeeing them tumble, and hearing the
clatter they made in their fall. I wiſh you would invite
me to ſuch another entertainment ; but you think, as I
ought to think, that it is time for me to have done with
the world, and ſo I would if I could get into a better before I was called into the beſt, and not die here in a rage,
like a poiſon'd rat in a hole. I wonder you are not aſham-
ed to let me pine away in this kingdom while you are out
of power.

I come

I come from looking over the *Melange* above written, and declare it to be a true copy of my present difpofition, which muft needs pleafe you, fince nothing was ever more difpleafing to my felf. I defire you to prefent my moft humble refpects to my Lady'.

LETTER XXXVII.

Dr. SWIFT to Lord BOLINGBROKE.

Dublin, April 5, 1729.

I Do not think it could be poffible' for me to hear better news than that of your getting over your fcurvy fuit, which always hung as a dead weight on my heart; I hated it in all its circumftances, as it affected your fortune and quiet, and in a fituation of life that muft make it every way vexatious. And as I am infinitely obliged to you for the juftice you do me, in fuppofing your affairs do at leaft concern me as much as my own; fo I would never have pardoned your omitting it. But before I go on, I cannot forbear mentioning what I read laft fummer in a news paper, that you were writing the hiftory of your own times. I fuppofe fuch a report might arife from what was not fecret among your friends, of your intention to write another kind of hiftory; which you often promis'd Mr. Pope and me to do; I know he defires it very much, and I am fure I defire nothing more for the honour and love I bear you, and the perfect knowledge I have of your public virtue. My Lord, I have no other notion of Oeconomy than that it is the parent of Liberty and Eafe, and I am not the only friend you have who have 'chid you in his heart for, the neglect of it, tho' not with his mouth, as I have done. For there is a filly error in the world, even among friends otherwife very good, not to intermeddle with men's affairs in fuch nice matters. And, my Lord, I have made a maxim, that fhould be writ in letters of diamonds, That a wife man ought to have money in his head, but not in his heart. Pray, my Lord, enquire whether your prototype, my Lord Digby, after the Reftoration when he was at Briftol, did not take fome care of his fortune, notwithftanding that quotation I once fent you out of his fpeech to the H. of Commons ? In my confcience, I believe Fortune, like other drabs, values a man gradually lefs for every year he lives. I have demonftration for it; becaufe if I play at piquet for fix-pence with a man or a woman two years

younger

younger than myfelf, I always lofe; and there is a young
girl of twenty, who never fails winning my money at
Backgammon, tho' fhe is a bungler, and the game be Ec-
clefiaftic. As to the public, I confefs nothing could cure
my itch of meddling with it but thefe frequent returns of
deafnefs, which have hindered me from paffing laft winter
in London; yet I cannot but confider the perfidioufnefs
of fome people, who I thought when I was laft there, upon
a change that happened, were the moft impudent in forgetting their profeffions that I have ever known. Pray, will
you pleafe to take your pen, and blot me out that political
maxim from whatever book it is in, that *Res nolunt diu
male adminiftrari*; the commonnefs makes me not know who
is the Author, but fure he muft be fome modern.

I am forry for Lady Bolingbroke's health; but I proteft I never knew a very deferving perfon of that fex, who
had not too much reafon to complain of ill health. I never wake without finding life a more infignificant thing
than it was the day before; which is one great advantage
I get by living in this country, where there is nothing I
fhall be forry to lofe. But my greateft mifery is recollecting the fcene of twenty years paft, and then all on a fudden dropping into the prefent. I remember, when I was
a little boy, I felt a great fifh at the end of my line, which
I drew up almoft on the ground, but it dropt in, and the
difappointment vexes me at this very day, and I believe it
was the type of all my future difappointments. I fhould
be afhamed to fay this to you, if you had not a fpirit fitter
to bear your own misfortunes, than I have to think of them.
Is there patience left to reflect, by what qualities wealth
and greatnefs are got, and by what qualities they are loft?
I have read my friend Congreve's verfes to Lord Cobham,
which end with a vile and falfe moral, and I remember is
not in Horace to Tibullus, which he imitates, " that all
" times are equally virtuous and vicious," wherein he dif-
fers from all Poets, Philofophers, and Chriftians that ever
writ. It is more probable that there may be an equal
quantity of virtue always in the world, but fometimes there may be a peck of it in Afia, and hardly a thim-
ble-full in Europe. But if there be no virtue, there is a-
bundance of fincerity; for I will venture all I am worth,
that there is not one human creature in power, who will
not be modeft enough to confefs that he proceeds wholly
upon a principle of Corruption. I fay this, becaufe I have
a fcheme, in fpite of your notions, to govern England
upon the principles of Virtue; and when the nation is ripe

for

for it, I defire you will fend for me. I have learned this
by living like a Hermit, by which I am got backwards a-
bout ninetecen hundred years in the era of the world,
and begin to wonder at the wickednefs of men. I dine a-
lone upon half a difh of meat, mix water with my wine,
walk ten miles a day, and read Baronius. *Hic explicit E-
piftola ad Dom.* Bolingbroke, *et incipit ad amicum* Pope.

Having finifhed my Letter to Ariftippus, I now begin
to you. I was in great pain about Mrs. Pope, having heard
from others that fhe was in a very dangerous way, which
made me think it unfeafonable to trouble you. I am afhamed to tell you, that when I was very young I had more
defire to be famous than ever fince; and fame, like all
things elfe in this life, grows with me every day more a
trifle. But you who are fo much younger, although you
want that health you deferve, yet your fpirits are as vigorous as if your body were founder. I hate a croud, where
I have not an eafy place to fee and be feen. A gret
Library always makes me melancholy, where the beft Author is as much fqueezed, and as obfcure, as a Porter at a
Coronation. In my own little library, I value the com-
pilements of Grævius and Gronovius, which make thirty-
one volumes in folio (and were given me by my Lord Bolingbroke) more than all my books befides; becaufe whoever comes into my clofet, cafts his eyes immediately upon
them, and will not vouchfafe to look upon Plato or Xeno-
phon. I tell you it is almoft incredible how Opinions
change by the decline or decay of fpirits, and I will further tell you, that all my endeavours, from a boy, to diftinguifh myfelf, were only for want of a great Title and
Fortune, that I might be ufed like a Lord by thofe who have
an opinion of my parts; whether right or wrong, it is no
great matter; and fo the reputation of wit or great learning does the office of a blue ribband, or of a coach and
fix horfes. To be remember'd for ever on the account
of our friendfhip, is what would exceedingly pleafe me;
but yet I never lov'd to make a vifit, or be feen walking
with my betters, becaufe they get all the eyes and civilities
from me. I no fooner writ this than I corrected myfelf,
and remember'd Sir Fulk Grevil's Epitaph, " Here lies,
" etc. who was friend to Sir Philip Sidney." And therefore I moft heartily thank you for your defire that I would
record our friendfhip in verfe, which if I can fucceed in, I will never defire to write one more line in
poetry while I live. You muft prefent my humble fervice
to Mrs. Pope, and let her know I pray for her continuance

in the world, for her own reafon, that fhe may live to take care of you.

<hr>

LETTER XXXVIII.

From Dr. Swift.

Aug. 11, 1729.

I AM very fenfible that in a former letter I talked very weakly of my own affairs, and of my imperfect wifhes and defires, which however I find with fome comfort do now daily decline, very fuitable to my ftate of health for fome months paft. For my head is never perfectly free from giddinefs, and efpecially towards night. Yet my diforder is very moderate, and I have been without a fit of deafnefs this half year; fo I am like a horfe, which, though off his mettle, can trot on tolerably; and this comparifon puts me in mind to add, that I am returned to be a rider, wherein I wifh you would imitate me. As to this country, there have been three terrible years dearth of corn, and every place ftrowed with beggars; but dearths are common in better climates, and our evils here lie much deeper. Imagine a nation the two thirds of whofe revenues are fpent out of it, and who are not permitted to trade with the other third, and where the pride of women will not fuffer them to wear their own manufactures, even where they excel what come from abroad: This is the true ftate of Ireland in a very few words. Thefe evils operate more every day, and the kingdom is abfolutely undone, as I have been telling often in print thefe ten years paft.

What I have faid requires forgivenefs, but I had a mind for once to let you know the ftate of our affairs, and my reafon for being more moved than perhaps becomes a Clergyman, and a piece of a philofopher: and perhaps the increafe of years and diforders may hope for fome allowance to complaints, efpecially when I may call myfelf a ftranger in a ftrange land. As to poor Mrs. Pope (if fhe be ftill alive) I heartily pity you, and pity her: her great piety and virtue will infallibly make her happy in a better life, and her great age hath made her fully ripe for heaven and the grave, and her beft friend will moft wifh her eafed of her labours, when fhe hath fo many good works to follow them. The lofs you will feel by the want of her care and kindnefs, I know very well; but fhe has amply done her part, as you have yours. One reafon why

I would

I would have you in Ireland when you shall be at your
own disposal, is that you may be master of two or three
years revenues, *provisæ frugis in annos copia*, so as not to be
pinch'd in the least when years increase, and perhaps your
health impairs : And when this kingdom is utterly at an
end, you may support me for the few years I shall happen to live ; and who knows but you may pay me exor-
bitant interest for the spoonful of wine, and scraps of a
chicken it will cost me to feed you ? I am confident you
have so much reason to complain of ingratitude ; for I
never yet knew any person, one tenth part so heartily dif-
posed as you are, to do good offices to others, without the
least private view.

Was it a gasconade to please me, that you said your
fortune was increased 100 *l.* a year since I left you ? you
should have told me how. Those *subfidia senectuti* are extremely desirable, if they could be got with justice, and
without avarice ; of which vice tho' I cannot charge myself yet, nor feel any approaches towards it, yet no usu-
rer more wishes to be richer (or rather to be surer of his
rents.) But I am not half so moderate as you, for I declare I cannot live easily under double to what you are satisfied with.

I hope Mr. Gay will keep his 3000 *l.* and live on the interest without decreasing the principal one penny ; but I
do not like your seldom seeing him. I hope he is grown
more disengaged from his intentness on his own affairs,
which I ever disliked, and is quite the reverse to you, unless you are a very dexterous disguiser. I desire my humble service to Lord Oxford, Lord Bathurst, and particularly to Mrs. B—, but to no Lady at Court. God bless
you for being a greater Dupe than I : I love that character too myself, but I want your charity.

Adieu.

LETTER XXXIX.

Oct. 9, 1729.

IT pleases me that you received my books at last : but you
have never once told me if you approve the whole, or
disapprove not of some parts of the Commentary, etc. It
was my principal aim in the entire work to perpetuate the
friendship between us, and to shew that the friends or the
enemies of the one were the friends or enemies of the other :
If in any particular, any thing be stated or mentioned in

a dif-a different manner from what you like, pray tell me freely, that the new editions now coming out here may have it rectify'd. You'll find the octavo rather more correct than the quarto, with fome additions to the Notes and Epigrams caft in, which I wifh had been increas'd by your acquaintance in Ireland. I rejoice in hearing that Drapiers-Hill is to emulate Parnaffus ; I fear the country about it is as much impoverifhed. I truly fhare in all that troubles you, and wifh you remov'd from a fcene of diftrefs, which I know works your compaffionate temper too ftrongly. But if we are not to fee you here, I believe I fhall once in my life fee you there. You think more for me. and about me, than any friend I have and you think better for me. Perhaps you'll not be contented, tho' I am, that the additional 100*l.* a year is only for my life. My mother is yet living, and I thank God for it : fhe will never be troublefome to me, if fhe be not fo to herfelf : but a melancholy object it is, to obferve the gradual decays both of body and mind, in a perfon to whom one is tied by the links of both. I can't tell whether her death itfelf would be fo afflicting.

You are too careful of my worldly affairs ; I am rich enough, and I can afford to give away a 100*l.* a year. Don't be angry : I will not live to be very old ; I have Revelations to the contrary. I would not crawl upon the earth without doing a little good when I have a mind to do it : I will enjoy the pleafure of what I give, by giving it alive, and feeing another enjoy it. When I die I fhould be afham'd to leave enough to build me a monument, if there were a wanting friend above ground.

Mr. Gay affures me his 3000*l.* is kept entire and facred ; he feems to languifh after a line from you, and complains tenderly. Lord Bolingbroke has told me ten times over he was going to write to you. Has he, or not ? The Dr. is unalterable, both in friendfhip and Quadrille : his wife has been very near death laft week : his two brothers buried their wives within thefe fix weeks. Gay is fixty miles off, and has been fo all this fummer with the Duke and Duchefs of Queenfbury. He is the fame man : So is every one here that you know : mankind is unamendable. *Optimus ille qui minimus urgetur*—Poor Mrs. * is like the reft, fhe cries at the thorn in her foot, but will fuffer nobody to pull it out. The Court-lady I have a good opinion of, yet I have treated her more negligently than you wou'd do, becaufe you like to fee the infide of a court, which I do not. I have feen her but twice. You have a defperate

rate hand at dafhing out a character by great ftrokes, and
at the fame time a delicate one at fine touches. God forbid you fhould draw mine, if I were confcious of any
guilt : But if I were confcious only of folly, God fend it !
for as nobody can detect a great fault fo well as you, nobody would fo well hide a fmall one.   But after all, that
Lady means to do good, and does no harm, which is a
vaft deal for a Courtier.   I can affure you that Lord Peterborow always fpeaks kindly of you, and certainly has
as great a mind to be your friend as any one. I muft throw
away my pen ; it cannot, it will never tell you, what I
inwardly am to you. *Quod nequeo monſtrare, et ſentio tantum.*

LETTER XL.

Lord BOLINGBROKE to Dr. SWIFT.

Bruffels, Sept. 27, 1729.

I Have brought your French acquaintance thus far on
her way into her own country, and confiderably better
in health than fhe was when fhe went to Aix.   I begin to
entertain hopes that fhe will recover fuch a degree of health
as may render old age fupportable. Both of us have clofed
the tenth Luftre, and it is high time to determine how we
fhall play the laft act of the Farce.   Might not my life
be entituled much more properly a *What-d'ye call-it* than a
Farce? fome Comedy, a great deal of Tragedy, and the
whole interfperfed with fcenes of Harlequin, Scaramouch,
and Dr. Baloardo, the prototype of your Hero.— I ufed
to think fometimes formerly of old age and of death ; e-
nough to prepare my mind ; not enough to anticipate forrow, to dafh the joys of youth, and to be all my life a dying.   I find the benefit of this practice now, and find it
more as I proceed on my journey : little regret when I
look backwards, little apprehenfion when I look forward.
You complain grievoufly of your fituation in Ireland ; I
would complain of mine too in England : but I will not,
nay, I ought not ; for I find by long experience that I can
be unfortunate, without being unhappy. I do not approve
your jo'ning together the *figure of living*, and the *pleafure of
giving*, though your old prating friend Montagne does
fomething like it in one of his Rhapfodics.   To tell you
my reafons would be to write an Effay, and I fhall hardly
have time to write a Letter ; but if you will come over,
and

and live with Pope and me, I'll fhew you in an inftant why thofe two things 'fhould not *aller de pair*, and that forced retrenchments on both may be made, without making us even uneafy. You know that I am too expenfive, and all mankind knows that I have been cruelly plundered; and yet I feel in my mind the power of defcending without anxiety two or three ftages more. In fhort (Mr. Dean) if you will come to a certain farm in Middlefex, you fhall find that I can live frugally without growling at the world, or being peevifh with thofe whom fortune has appointed to eat my bread, inftead of appointing me to eat theirs: and yet I have naturally as little difpofition to frugality as any man alive. You fay you are no philofopher, and I think you are in the right to diflike a word which is fo often abufed; but I am fure you like to follow reafon, not cuftom, (which is fometimes the reafon and oftener the caprice of others, of the mob of the world). Now to be fure of doing this, you muft wear your philofophical fpectacles as conftantly as the Spaniards ufed to wear theirs. You muft make them part of your drefs, and fooner part with your broad-brimm'd beaver, your gown, your fcarf, or even that emblematical veftment your furplice. Thro' this medium you will fee few things to be vexed at, few perfons to be angry at; and yet there will frequently be things which we ought to wifh altered, and perfons whom we ought to wifh hanged.

In your letter to Pope, you agree that a regard for Fame becomes a man more towards his Exit, than at his entrance into life; and yet you confefs, that the longer you live, the more you grow indifferent about it. Your fentiment is true and natural; your reafoning, I am afraid, is not fo upon this occafion Prudence will make us defire Fame, becaufe it gives us many real and great advantages in all the affairs of life. Fame is the wife man's means; his ends are his own good, and the good of fociety. You Poets and Orators have inverted this order; you propofe Fame as the end, and good, or at leaft great actions, as the means. You go further: You teach our felf-love to anticipate the applaufe which we fuppofe will be paid by pofterity to our names; and with idle notions of immorta-lity you turn other heads befides your own; I am afraid this may have done fome harm in the world.

Fame is an object which men purfue · fuccefsfully by various and even contrary courfes. Your doctrine leads them to look on this end as effential, and on the means as indifferent; fo that Fabricius and Craffus, Cato and Cæ-

far

far preffed forward to the fame goal. After all perhaps
it may appear, from a confideration of the depravity of
mankind, that you could do no better, nor keep up virtue
in the world without calling this paffion or this direction
of felf-love in to your aid : *Tacitus* has crowded this excufe
for you, according to his manner, into a maxim, *Contemptu famae, contenini virtutes.* But now whether we confider
Fame as an ufeful inftrument in all the occurrences of private and public life, or whether we confider it as the caufe
of that pleafure which our felf-love is fo fond of ; methinks
our entrance into life, or (to fpeak more properly) our
youth, not our old age, is the feafon when we ought to
defire it moft, and therefore when it is moft becoming,
to defire it with ardor. If it is ufeful, it is to be defired
moft when we have, or may hope to have a long fcene of
action open before us : Towards our exit, this fcene of
action is or fhould be clofed ; and then, methinks, it is
unbecoming to grow fonder of a thing which we have no
longer occafion for. If it is pleafant, the fooner we are
in poffeffion of fame the longer we fhall enjoy this pleafure. When it is acquired early in life it may tickle us
on till old age ; but when it is acquired late, the fenfation
of pleafure will be more faint, and mingled with the regret
of our not having tafted it fooner.

From my Farm, Oct. 5.

I am here ; I have feen Pope, and one of my firft enquiries was after you. He tells me a thing I am forry to
hear : You are building, it feems, on a piece of land you
have acquired for that purpofe, in fome county of Ireland. Tho' I have built in a part of the world, which I
prefer very little to that where you have been thrown and
confined by our ill-fortune and yours, yet I am forry you
do the fame thing. I have repented a thoufand times of
my refolution, and I hope you will repent of yours before
it is executed. Adieu, my old and worthy friend ; may
the phyfical evils of life fall as eafily upon you, as ever
they did on any man who lived to be old ; and may the
moral evils which furround us, make as little impreffion
on you, as they ought to make on one who has fuch fuperior fenfe to eftimate things by, and fo much virtue to
wrap himfelf up in.

My wife defires not to be forgotten by you ; fhe's faithfully your fervant, and zealoufly your admirer. She will be
concerned and difappointed not to find you in this ifland

at

at her return, which hope both fhe and I had been made to entertain before I went abroad.

LETTER XLI.

Dr. Swift to Lord Bolingbroke.

Dublin, Oct. 31, 1729.

I Receiv'd your Lordfhip's travelling letter of feveral dates, at feveral ftages, and from different nations, languages, and religions. Neither could any thing be more obliging than your kind remembrance of me in fo many places. As to your ten Luftres, I remember, when I complained in a Letter to Prior, that I was fifty years old, he was half angry in jeft, and anfwered me out of Terence, *ifta commemoratio eft quafi exprobatio.* How then ought I to rattle you, when I have a dozen years more to anfwer for, all monaftically paffed in this Country of liberty and delight, and money, and good company ! I go on anfwering your letter : It is you were my Hero, but the other * never was ; yet if he were, it was your own fault, who taught me to love him, and often vindicated him, in the beginning of your miniftry, from my accufations. But I granted he had the greateft inequalities of any man alive, and his whole fcene was fifty times more a What-d'ye-call-it, than yours : for, I declare, yours was *unie,* and I wifh you would fo order it, that the world may be as wife as I upon that article : Mr. Pope wifhes it too, and I believe there is not a more honeft man in England, even without wit. But you regard us not.—I was † forty-feven years old, when I began to think of death, and the reflections upon it now begin when I wake in the morning, and end when I am going to fleep—I writ to Mr. Pope, and not to you. My birth, although from a family not undiftinguifh-ed in its name, is many degrees inferior to yours ; all my pretenfions from perfons and parts infinitely fo ; I a younger fon of younger fons ; you born to a great fortune : yet I fee you with all your advantages funk to a degree that you could never have been without them : But yet I fee you as much efteemed, as much beloved, as much dreaded, and perhaps more (though it be almoft impoffible) than ever you were in your higheft exaltation—only I grieve like an Alderman that you are not fo rich. And

* L. Ox.
† The Year of Queen Anne's Death.

yet

yet, my Lord, I pretend to value mon·y as little as you, and I will call five hundred witneffes (if you will take Irifh witneffes) to prove it. I renounce your whole philofophy, becaufe it is not your practice. By the *figure of living*, (if I ufed that expreffion to Mr. Pope) I do not mean the parade, but a fuitablenefs to your mind; and as for the *pleafure of giving*, I know your foul fuffers when you are debarr'd of it. Could you, when your own gencrofity and contempt of outward things (be not offended, it is no Ecclefiaftical but an Epictetian phrafe) could you, when thefe have brought you to it, come over and live with Mr. Pope and me at the Deanry ? I could almoft wifh the experiment were tried—No, God forbid, that ever fuch a fcoundrel as Want fhould dare to approach you. But, in the mean time, do not brag, Retrenchments are not your talent. But, as old Weymouth faid to me in his lordly Latin, *Philo opha verba ignava opera*; I wifh you could learn Arithmetic, that three and two make five, and will never make more. My philofophical fpectacles which you advife me to, will tell me that I can live on 50 *l.* a year (wine excluded, which my bad health forces me to) but I cannot endure that *Otium* fhould be *fine dignitate* —My Lord, what I would have faid of Fame is meant of fame which a man enjoys in his life : becaufe I cannot be a great Lord, I would acquire what is a kind of *fubfidium*, I would endeavour that my betters fhould feek me by the merit of fomething diftinguifhable, inftead of my feeking of them. The defire of enjoying it in after-times is owing to the fpirit and folly of youth : but with age we learn to know the houfe is fo full, that there is no room for above one or two at moft in an age, through the whole world. My Lord, I hate and love to write to you it gives me pleafure, and kills me with melancholy. The D— take ftupidity, that it will not come to fupply the want of philofophy.

LETTER XLII.

From Dr. SWIFT.

Oct. 31, 1729.

YOU were fo careful of fending me the Dunciad, that I have received five of them, and have pleafed four friends. I am one of every body who approve every part of it, Text and Comment ; but am one abftracted from every body, in the happinefs of being recorded your friend,

while wit, and humour, and politenefs fhall have any memorial among us. As for your octavo edition, we know
nothing of it, for we have an octavo of our own, which
hath fold wonderfully, confidering our poverty, and dulnefs the confequence of it.

I writ this poft to Lord B. and tell him in my letter,
that, with a great deal of lofs for a frolick, I will fly as foon
as build ; I have neither years, nor fpirits, nor money, nor
patience for fuch amufements. The frolick is gone off, and
I am only 100 l. the poorer. But this kingdom is grown
fo exceffively poor, that we wife men muft think of nothing but getting a little ready money. It is thought
there are not two hundred thoufand pounds of fpecie in the
whole ifland ; for we return thrice as much to our abfen-
tees, as we get by trade, and fo are all inevitably undone ;
which I have been telling them in print thefe ten years,
to as little purpofe as if it came from the pulpit. And this
is enough for Irifh politics, which I only mention, becaufe
it fo nearly touches myfelf. I muft repeat what, I believe, I have faid before, that I pity you much more
than Mrs. Pope. Such a parent and friend hourly declining before your eyes is an object very unfit for your
health, and duty, and tender difpofition ; and I pray God
it may not affect you too much. I am as much fatisfied
that your additional 100 l. per Annum is for your life, as if
it were for ever. You have enough to leave your friends :
I would not have them glad to be rid of you ; and I fhall
take care that none but my enemies will be glad to get rid
of me. You have embroiled me with Lord B—about the
figure of living, and the pleafure of giving. I am under
the neceffity of fome little paultry figure in the flation I
am ; but I make it as little as poffible. As to the other
part you are bafe, becaufe I thought myfelf as great a giver
as ever was of my ability ; and yet in proportion you exceed, and have kept it till now a fecret even from me, when
I wondered how you were able to live with your whole little revenue.

LETTER XLIII.

Lord BOLINGBROKE to Dr. SWIFT.

Nov. 19, 1729.

I Find that you have laid afide your project of building in
Ireland, and that we fhall fee you in this ifland *cum zephyris, et hirundine prima*. I know not whether the love of
fame increafes as we advance in age ; fure I am that the
force

force of friendship does. I lov'd you almost twenty years
ago, I thought of you as well as I do now, better was beyond the power of conception, or, to avoid an equivoque,
beyond the extent of my ideas. Whether you are more
obliged to me for loving you as well when I knew you
less, or for loving you as well after loving you so
many years, I shall not determine. What I would say is
this : whilst my mind grows daily more independent of the
world, and feels less need of learning on external objects,
the ideas of friendship return oftener, they busy me, they
warm me more : Is it that we grow more tender as the
moment of our great separation approaches ? or is it that
they who are to live together in another state, (for *vera
amicitia non nisi inter bonos*) begin to feel more strongly that
divine sympathy which is to be the great band of their future society ? There is no one thought which sooths my
mind like this : I encourage my imagination to pursue it,
and am heartily afflicted when another faculty * of the in-
tellect comes boisterously in, and wakes me from so pleasing a dream, if it be a dream. I will dwell no more on
Oeconomicks than I have done in my former letter. Thus
much only I will say, that *otium cum dignitate* is to be had
with 500*l*. a year as well as with 5000 : the difference will
be found in the value of the man, and not in that of the
estate. I do assure you, that I have never quitted the design of collecting, revising, improving, and extending
several materials which are still in my power ; and I hope
that the time of setting myself about this last work of my
life is not far off. Many papers of much curiosity and importance are lost, and some of them in a manner which
would surprize and anger you. However I shall be able to
convey several great truths to posterity, so clearly and so
authentically, that the Burnets and the Oldmixons of another age may rail, but not be able to deceive. Adieu, my
friend. I have taken up more of this paper than belongs
to me, since Pope is to write to you ; no matter, for, upon
recollection, the rules of proportion are not broken ; he
will say as much to you in one page, as I have said in
three. Bid him talk to you of the work he is about, I

* Viz. *Reason.* Tully (or what is much the same, his Disciple) observes
something like this on the like occasion, where speaking of Plato's famous
Book of the Soul, he says, *Nescio quomodo, dum lego, adjentior : cum posui librum,
et mecum ipse de immortalitate animorum corpi cogitare, adsensio illa omnis elabitur.*
Cicero seems to have had but a confused notion of the *cause,* which the Letter-
writer has here explained, namely, that the *imagination* is always ready to indulge so flattering an idea, but severer *reason* corrects and disclaims it. As to
RELIGION, that is out of the question ; for Tully wrote to his few philoso-
phic friends.

T t 2

hope

hope in good earneft; it is a fine one, and will be, in his
hands, an original *. His fole complaint is, that he finds
it too eafy in the execution. This flatters his lazinefs, it
flatters my judgment, who always thought that (univerfal
as his talents are) this is eminentiy and peculiarly his, a-
bove all the writers I know living or dead; I do not except Horace   .   Adieu.

<hr />

LETTER XLIV.

Nov. 28, 1729.

THis Letter (like all mine) will be a Rhapfody; it is
many years ago fince I wrote as a Wit How many
occurrences or informations muft one omit, if one deter-
min'd to fay nothing that one could not fay prettily? I
lately received from the widow of one dead correfpondent,
and the father of another, feveral of my own letters of
about fifteen and twenty years old; and it was not unentertaining to myfelf to obferve, how and by what degrees
I ceas'd to be a witty writer; as either my experience
grew on the one hand, or my affection to my correfpondents on the other. Now as I love you better than moft
I have ever met with in the world, and efteem you too
the more, the longer I have compar'd you with the reft
of the world; fo inevitably I write to you more negligently, that is, more openly, and what all but fuch as love
one another will call writing worfe. I fmile to think how
Curl would be bit, were our Epiftles to fall into his hands,
and how glorioufly they would fall fhort of every ingenious reader's expectations?

You can't imagine what a vanity it is to me, to have
fomething to rebuke you for in the way of Oeconomy. I
love the man that builds a houfe fubito ingenio, and makes
a wall for a horfe: then cries, " we wife men muft think
" of nothing but getting ready money." I am glad you
approve my annuity; all we have in this world is no more
than an annuity, as to our own enjoyment: but I will increafe your regard for my wifdom, and tell you, that this
annuity includes alfo the life of another †, whofe concern
ought to be as near me as my own, and with whom my
whole profpects ought to finifh. I throw my javelin of
Hope no farther, *Cur brevi fortes jaculamur ævo*—etc.

The fecond (as it is call'd, but indeed the eighth) edi-

* Effay on Man,   † His Mother's.

tion

tion of the Dunciad, with some additional notes and epigrams, shall be sent you, if I know any opportunity : if
they reprint it with you, let them by all means follow that
octavo edition. ——The Drapier's letters are again printed
here, very laudably as to paper, print, etc. for you know
I disapprove Irish politics, (as my Commentator tells you)
being a strong and jealous subject of England.   The Lady
you mention, you ought not complain of for not acknowledging your present; she having lately received a much
richer present from Mr. Knight of the S. Sea ; and you
are sensible she cannot ever return it to one in the condition of an out-law.   It's certain, as he can never expect
any favour *, his motive must be wholly disinterested.
Will not this reflection make you blush ? Your continual
deplorings of Ireland, make me wish you were here long
enough to forget those scenes that so afflict you : I am only
in fear if you were, you would grow such a patriot here
too, as not to be quite at ease, for your love of old England.—It is. very possible, your journey, in the time I
compute, might exactly tally with my intended one to
you ; and if you must soon again go back, you would not
be unattended.   For the poor woman decays perceptibly
every week ; and the winter may too probably put an end
to a very long, and a very irreproachable life.   My constant attendance on her does indeed affect my mind very
much, and lessen extremely my desires of long life; since
I see the best that can come of it is a miserable benedicti-
on.   I look upon myself to be many years older in two
years since you saw me : The natural imbecillity of my
body, join'd now to this acquir'd old age of the mind,
makes me at least as old as you, and we are the fitter to
crawl down the hill together : I only desire I may be able
to keep pace with you.   My first friendship at sixteen,
was contracted with a man of seventy, and I found him
not grave enough or confistent enough for me, tho' we
lived well to his death.   I speak of old Mr. Wycherley ;
some letters of whom (by the by) and of mine, the Booksellers have got and printed, not without the concurrence
of a noble friend of mine and yours †.   I don't much approve of it ; though there is nothing for me to be asham'd
of, because I will not be asham'd of any thing I do not do
myself, or of any thing that is not immoral but merely

---

* He was mistaken in this. Mr. Knight was pardoned, and came home in
the year 1742.
† See the occasion, in the second and third Paragraphs of the Preface to the
first Volume of Letters.

dull

dull (as for inftance, if they printed this letter I am now writing, which they eafily may, if the underlings at the Poft-office pleafe to take a copy of it.) I admire on this confideration, your fending your laft to me quite open, without a feal, wafer, or any clofure whatever, manifeft-ing the utter opennefs of the writer. I would do the fame by this, but fear it would look like affeåtation to fend two letters fo together.—I will fully reprefent to our friend (and, I doubt not, it will touch his heart) what you fo feelingly fet forth as to the badnefs of your Burgundy, etc. He is an extreme honeft man, and indeed ought to be fo, confidering how very indifcreet and unreferved he is: But I do not approve this part of his charaåter, and will never join with him in any of his idlenefles in the way of wit. You know my maxim to keep as clear of all of-fence, as I am clear of all intereft in either party. I was once difpleafed before at you, for complaining to Mr. — of my not having a penfion, and am fo again at your nam-ing it to a certain Lord. I have given proof in the courfe of my whole life, (from the time when I was in the friend-fhip of Lord Bolingbroke and Mr. Craggs, even to this when I am civilly treated by Sir R. Walpole) that I never thought myfelf fo warm in any Party's caufe as to deferve their money; and therefore would never have accepted it: But give me leave to tell you, that of all mankind the two perfons I would leaft have accepted any favour from, are thofe very two, to whom you have unluckily fpoken of it. I defire you to take off any impreffions which that dialogue may have left on his Lordfhip's mind, as if I ever had any thought of being beholden to him, or any other, in that way. And yet, you know I am no enemy to the prefent Conftitution; I believe, as fincere a well-wifher to it, nay even to the church eftablifh'd, as any Minifter in, or out of employment whatever; or any Bifhop of England or Ireland. Yet am I of the Religion of Erafmus, a Catholic; fo I live, fo I fhall die; and hope one day to meet you, Bifhop Atterbury, the younger Craggs, Dr. Garth, Dean Berkeley, and Mr. Hutchen-fon, in that place, To which God of his infinite mercy bring us, and every body.

Lord B's anfwer to your letter I have juft received, and join it to this packet. The work he fpeaks of with fuch abundant partiality, is a fyftem of Ethics in the Horatian way.

LETTER XLV.

April 14, 1730.

THIS is a letter extraordinary, to do and fay nothing but to recommend to you (as a Clergyman, and a charitable one) a pious and a good work, and for a good and honeft man : Moreover he is above feventy, and poor, which you might think included in the word honeft. I fhall think it a kindnefs done myfelf, if you can propagate Mr. Weftley's fubfcription for his Commentary on Job, among your Divines, (Bifhops excepted, of whom there is no hope) and among fuch as are believers, or readers of Scripture. Even the curious may find fomething to pleafe them, if they fcorn to be edified. It has been the labour of eight years of this learned man's life ; I call him what he is, a learned man, and I engage you will approve his profe more than you formerly could his poetry. Lord Bolingbroke is a favourer of it, and allows you to do your beft to ferve an old Tory, and a fufferer for the Church of England, tho' you are a Whig, as I am.

We have here fome verfes in your name, which I am angry at. Sure you wou'd not ufe me fo ill as to flatter me ? I therefore think it is fome other weak Irifhman.

P. S. I did not take the pen out of Pope's hands, I proteft to you. But fince he will not fill the remainder of the page, I think I may without offence. I feek no epiftolary fame, but am a good deal pleafed to think that it will be known hereafter that you and I lived in the moft friendly intimacy together.—Pliny writ his letters for the public, fo did Seneca, fo did Balfac, Voiture, etc. Tully did not, and therefore thefe give us more pleafure than any which have come down to us from antiquity. When we read them, we pry into a fecret which was intended to be kept from us. That is a pleafure. We fee Cato, and Brutus, and Pompey, and others, fuch as they really were, and not fuch as the gaping multitude of their own age took them to be, or as Hiftorians and Poets have reprefented them to ours. That is another pleafure. I remember to have feen a proceffion at *Aix-la-Chapelle*, wherein an image of Charlemagne is carried on the fhoulders of a man, who is hid by the long robe of the imperial Saint. Follow him into the veftry, you fee the bearer flip

from

from under the robe, and the gigantic figure dwindles into an image of the ordinary fize, and is fet by among other lumber — I agree much with Pope, that our climate is rather better than that you are in, and perhaps your public fpirit would be lefs grieved, or oftener comforted, here than there. Come to us therefore on a vifit at leaft. It will not be the fault of feveral perfons here, if you do not come to live with us. But great good-will and little power produce fuch flow and feeble effects as can be acceptable to Heaven alone, and heavenly men. — I know you will be angry with me, if I fay nothing to you of a poor woman, who is ftill on the other fide of the water in a moft languifhing ftate of health. If fhe regains ftrength enough to come over (and fhe is better within a few weeks) I fhall nurfe her in this farm with all the care and tendernefs poffible. If fhe does not, I muft pay her the laft duty of friendfhip wherever fhe is, tho' I break thro' the whole plan of life which I have form'd in my mind. Adieu. I am moft faithfully and affectionately yours.

LETTER LXVI.

Lord B. to Dr. Swift.

Jan. 1730-31.

I Begin my letter by telling you that my wife has been returned from abroad about a month, and that her health, though feeble and precarious, is better than it has been thefe two years. She is much your fervant, and as fhe has been her own phyfician with fome fuccefs, imagines fhe could be yours with the fame. Would to God you was within her reach. She would, I believe, prefcribe a great deal of the *medicina animi*, without having recourfe to the Books of Trifmegiftus. Pope and I fhould be her principal apothecaries in the courfe of the cure ; and tho' our beft Botanifts complain, that few of the herbs and fimples which go to the compofition of thefe remedies are to be found at prefent in our foil, yet there are more of them here than in Ireland; befides, by the help of a little chemiftry the moft noxious juices may become falubrious, and rank poifon a fpecific—Pope is now in my library with me, and writes to the world, to the prefent and to future ages, whilft I begin this letter which he is to finifh to you. What good he will do to mankind I know not; this comfort he may be fure of, he cannot do lefs than

you

you have done before him. I have fometimes thought,
that if preachers, hangmen, and moral-writers keep vice at
a ftand, or fo much as retard the progrefs of it, they do as
much as human nature admits : a real reformation is not to
be brought about by ordinary means ; it requires thofe extraordinary means which become punifhments as well as
leffons : National corruption muft be purged by national
calamities.—Let us hear from you. We deferve this attention becaufe we defire it, and becaufe we believe that
you defire to hear from us.

LETTER XLVII.

Lord B. to Dr. Swift.

March 29.

I Have delayed feveral pofts anfwering your letter of January laft, in hopes of being able to fpeak to you about
a project which concerns us both, but me the moft, fince
the fuccefs of it would bring us together. It has been a
good while in my head, and at my heart ; if it can be fet
agoing, you fhall hear more of it. I was ill in the beginning of the winter for near a week, but in no danger either from the nature of my diftemper, or from the attendance of three phyficians. Since that bilious intermitting
fever, I have had, as I had before, better health than the
regard I have payed to health deferves. We are both in
the decline of life, my dear Dean, and have been fome
years going down the hill ; let us make the paffage as
fmooth as we can. Let us fence againft phyfical evil by
care, and the ufe of thofe means which experience muft have
pointed out to us : Let us fence againft moral evil by philofophy, I renounce the alternative you propofe. But
we may, nay (if we will follow nature, and do not work
up imagination againft her plaineft dictates) we fhall of
courfe grow every year more indifferent to life, and to
the affairs and interefts of a fyftem out of which we are
foon to go. This is much better than ftupidity. The decay of paffion ftrengthens philofophy, for paffion may decay, and ftupidity not fucceed. *Paffions* (fays Pope, our
Divine, as you will fee one time or other) are the *Gales* of
life : Let us not complain that they do not blow a ftorm.
What hurt does age do us, in fubduing what we toil to
fubdue all our lives ? It is now fix in the morning : I recall the time (and am glad it is over) when about this hour

I ufed to be going to bed, furfeited with pleafure, or ja-
ded with bufinefs : my head often full of fchemes, and my
heart as often full of anxiety. Is it a misfortune, think
you, that I rife at this hour, refrefhed, ferene, and calm ?
that the paft, and even the prefent affairs of life ftand like
objects at a diftance from me, where I can keep off the difagreeable fo as not to be ftrongly affected by them, and
from whence I can draw the others nearer to me ? Paffions
in their force, would bring all thefe, nay even future con-
tingencies, about my ears at once, and Reafon would but
ill defend me in the fcuffle.

I leave Pope to fpeak for himfelf, but I muft tell you
how much my wife is obliged to you. She fays, fhe
would find ftrength enough to nurfe you, if you was here,
and yet, God knows, fhe is extremely weak : The flow
fever works under, and mines the conftitution ; we keep
it off fometimes, but ftill it returns, and makes new breaches
before nature can repair the old ones. I am not afhamed to fay to you, that I admire her more every hour of
my life : Death is not to her the King of Terrors ; fhe
beholds him without the leaft. When fhe fuffers much,
fhe wifhes for him as a deliverer from pain ; when life is
tolerable, fhe looks on him with diflike, becaufe he is to
feparate her from thofe friends to whom fhe is more attached than to life itfelf.—You fhall not ftay for my next,
as long as you have for this letter ; and in every one, Pope
fhall write fomething much better than the fcraps of old
Philofophers, which were the prefents, Munufcula, that
Stoical Fop Seneca ufed to fend in every Epiftle to his friend
Lucilius.

P. S. My Lord has fpoken juftly of his Lady : why
not I of my Mother ? Yefterday was her birth-day, now
entering on the ninety-firft year of her age ; her memory
much diminifh'd, but her fenfes very little hurt, her fight
and hearing good ; fhe fleeps not ill, eats moderately,
drinks water, fays her prayers ; this is all fhe does. I have
reafon to thank God for continuing fo long to me a very
good and tender parent, and for allowing me to exercife
for fome years, thofe cares which are now as neceffary to
her, as hers have been to me. An object of this fort daily
before one's eyes very much foftens the mind, but perhaps
may hinder it from the willingnefs of contracting other tyes
of the like domeftic nature, when one finds how painful it
is even to enjoy the tender pleafures. I have formerly
made fome ftrong efforts to get and to deferve a friend :

perhaps

perhaps it were wifer never to attempt it, but live extem-
pore, and look upon the world only as a place to pass thro',
juft pay your hofts their due, difperfe a little charity, and
hurry on. Yet I am juft now writing (or rather plan-
ning) a book, to make mankind look upon this life
with comfort and pleafure, and put morality in good humour.—And juft now too, I am going to fee one I love
very tenderly ; and to-morrow to entertain feveral civil
people, whom if we call friends, it is by the Courtefy of
England.—*Sic, fic juvat ire fub umbras.* While we do live,
we muft make the beft of life,

Cantantes *licet ufque (minus via lædet!) eamus*,

as the fhepherd faid in Virgil, when the road was long and
heavy. I am yours.

LETTER XLVIII.

Lord BOLINGBROKE to Dr. SWIFT.

YOU may affure yourfelf, that if you come over this
fpring, you will find me not only got back into the
habits of ftudy, but devoted to that hiftorical talk, which
you have fet me thefe many years. I am in hopes of fome
materials which will enable me to work in the whole extent of the plan I propofe to myfelf. If they are not to be
had, I muft accommodate my plan to this deficiency. In
the mean time Pope has given me more trouble than he or
I thought of ; and you will be furprized to find that I have
been partly drawn by him, and partly by myfelf, to write
a pretty large volume upon a very grave and very important fubject ; that I have ventur'd to pay no regard whatever to any authority except facred authority, and that I
have ventured to ftart a thought, which muft, if it is
pufh'd as fuccefsfully as I think it is, render all your Metaphyfical Theology both ridiculous and abominable. There
is an expreffion in one of your letters to me, which makes
me believe you will come into my way of thinking on this
fubject ; and yet I am perfuaded that Divines and Free-
thinkers would both be clamorous againft it, if it was to
be fubmitted to their cenfure, as I do not intend that it
fhall. The paffage I mean, is that where you fay that you

told

told Dr. — the Grand points of Chriſtianity ought to be taken as infallible Revelations *, etc.

It has happened, that, whilſt I was writing this to you, the Dr. came to make me a viſit from London, where I heard he was arrived ſome time ago : He was in haſte to return, and is, I perceive, in great haſte to print. He left with me eight Diſſertations †, a ſmall part, as I underſtand, of his work, and deſired me to peruſe, conſider, and obſerve upon them againſt Monday next, when he will come down again. By what I have read of the two firſt, I find myſelf unable to ſerve him. The principles he reaſons upon are begged in a diſputation of this ſort, and the manner of reaſoning is by no means cloſe and concluſive. The ſole advice I could give him in conſcience would be that which he would take ill, and not follow. I will get rid of this taſk as well as I can, for I eſteem the man, and ſhould be ſorry to diſoblige him where I cannot ſerve him.

As to retirement, and exerciſe, your notions are true : The firſt ſhould not be indulged ſo much as to render us ſavage, nor the leſt neglected ſo as to impair health. But I know men, who for fear of being ſavage, live with all who will live with them ; and who, to preſerve their health, ſaunter away half their time. Adieu. Pope calls for the paper.

P. S. I hope what goes before will be a ſtrong motive to your coming. God knows if ever I ſhall ſee Ireland ; I ſhall never deſire it, if you can be got hither, or kept here. Yet I think I ſhall be, too ſoon, a Freeman.— Your recommendations I conſtantly give to thoſe you mention ; tho' ſome of them I ſee but ſeldom, and am every day more retired. I am leſs fond of the world, and leſs curious about it : yet no way out of humour, diſappointed, or angry : tho' in my way I receive as many injuries as my betters, but I don't feel them, therefore I ought not to vex other people, nor even to return injuries. I paſs almoſt all my time at Dawley and at home ; my Lord (of which I partly take the merit to myſelf) is as much eſtranged from politics as I am. Let Philoſophy be ever ſo vain, it is leſs vain now than Politics, and not quite ſo vain at preſent as Divinity ; I know nothing that moves

---

* In this maxim all bigotted *Divines* and *free-thinking* Politicians agree ; the one, for fear of diſturbing the eſtabliſh'd Religion ; the other, leſt that diſturbance ſhould prove injurious to their adminiſtration of government.

† *Revelation examined with Candour,*

ſtrongly

ſtrongly but Satire, and thoſe who are aſham'd of nothing elſe, are ſo of being ridiculous. I fancy, if we three were together but for three years, ſome good might be done even upon this Age.

I know you'll deſire ſome account of my health : It is as uſual, but my ſpirits rather worſe. I write little or nothing. You know, I never had either a taſte or talent for politics, and the world minds nothing elſe. I have perſonal obligations which I will ever preſerve, to men of different ſides, and I wiſh nothing ſo much as public quiet, except it be my own quiet. I think it a merit, if I can take off any man from grating or ſatirical ſubjects, merely on the ſcore of Party : and it is the greateſt vanity of my life that I've contributed to turn my Lord Bolingbroke to ſubjects moral, uſeful, and more worthy his pen. Dr. ————'s Book is what I can't commend ſo much as Dean Berkley's *, tho' it has many things ingenious in it, and is not deficient in the writing part : but the whole book, tho' he meant it *ad Populum*, is, I think, purely *ad Clerum*. Adieu.

* Call'd *The Minute Philoſopher.*

L E T T E R S

O F

Dr. S W I F T to Mr. G A Y.

From the Year 1729 to 1732 *.

L E T T E R XLIX.

·Dublin, March 19, 1729.

I Deny it. I do write to you according to the old ſti-
pulation, for, when you kept your old company, when
I writ to one I writ to all. But I am ready to enter into
a new bargain ſince you are got into a new world, and
will anſwer all your letters. You are firſt to preſent my
moſt humble reſpeƈts to the Duchefs of Queenſberry, and
let her know that I never dine without thinking of her,
although it be with ſome difficulty that I can obey her
when I dine with forks that have but two prongs, and
when the ſauce is not very confiſtent. You muſt likewiſe
tell her Grace that ſhe is a general toaſt among all honeſt
folks here, and particularly at the Deanry, even in the
face of my Whig ſubjeƈts.—I will leave my money in
Lord Bathurſt's hands, and the management of it (for want
of better) in yours : and pray keep the intereſt-money in
a bag wrapt up and ſealed by itſelf, for fear of your own
fingers under your careleſſneſs. Mr. Pope talks of you as
a perfeƈt ſtranger ; but the different purſuits and manners
and intereſts of life, as fortune has pleaſed to diſpoſe them,
will never ſuffer thoſe to live together, who by their inclinations ought never to part. I hope when you are rich
enough, you will have ſome little oeconomy of your own

* Found among Mr. Gay's papers, and return'd to Dr. Swift by the Duke
of Queenſberry and Mr. Pope.

in

in town or country, and be able to give your friend a pint
of Port; for the domeſtic ſeaſon of life will come on.   I
had never much hopes of you vampt Play, although Mr.
Pope ſeem'd to have, and although it were ever ſo good:
But you ſhould have done like the Parſons, and chang'd
your Text, I mean the Title, and the names of the perſons.
After all, it was an effeƈt of idleneſs, for you are in the
prime of life, when invention and judgment go together.
I wiſh you had 100 *l.* a year more for horſes—I ride and
walk whenever good weather invites, and am reputed the
beſt walker in this town and five miles round.   I writ lately to Mr. Pope: I wiſh you had a little Villakin in his
neighbourhood; but you are yet too volatile, and any
Lady with a coach and ſix horſes would carry you to Japan.

L E T T E R L.

Dublin, Nov. 10, 1730.

WHEN my Lord Peterborow in the Queen's time
went abroad upon his Ambaſſies, the Miniſtry told
me, that he was ſuch a vagrant, they were forced to write
at him by gueſs, becauſe they knew not where to write *to*
him.   This is my caſe with you: ſometimes in Scotland,
ſometimes at Hamwalks, ſometimes God knows where.
You are a man of buſineſs, and not at leiſure for inſignifi-
cant correſpondence   It was I got you the employment of
being my Lord Duke's *premier Miniſtre:* for his Grace having heard how good a manager you were of my revenue,
thought you fit to be entruſted with ten talents.   I have
had twenty times a ſtrong inclination to ſpend a ſummer
near Saliſbury-downs, having rode over them more than
once, and with a young parſon of Saliſbury reckoned twice
the ſtones of Stone-henge, which are either ninety-two
or ninety-three.   I deſire to preſent my moſt humble acknowledgments to my Lady Ducheſs in return of her civility.   I hear an ill thing, that ſhe is *matre pulchra filia
pulchrior:* I never ſaw her ſince ſhe was a girl, and would
be angry ſhe ſhould exel her mother, who was long my
principal Goddeſs.   I deſire you will tell her Grace, that
the ill-management of forks is not to be help'd when they
are only bidental, which happens in all poor houſes, eſpecially thoſe of Poets; upon which account a knife was abſolutely neceſſary at Mr. Pope's, where it was morally impoſſible with a bidential fork to convey a morſel of beef,

with

with the incumbrance of muftard and turnips, into your
mouth at once. And her Grace hath coft me thirty pounds
to provide Tridents for fear of offending her, which fum I
defire fhe will pleafe to return me.—I am fick enough to
go to the Bath, but have not heard it will be good for my
diforder. I have a ftrong mind to fpend my 200 *l.* next
fummer in France : I am glad I have it, for there is hardly
twice that fum left in this kingdom. You want no fettlement (I call the family where you live, and the foot you
are upon, a fettlement) till you increafe your fortune to
what will fupport you with eafe and plenty, a good houfe
and a garden. The want of this I much dread for you :
For I have often known a She-coufin of a good family
and fmall fortune, paffing months among all her relations,
living in plenty, and taking her circles, till fhe grew an
old Maid, and every body weary of her. Mr. Pope complains of feldom feeing you ; but the evil is unavoidable,
for different circumftances of life have always feparated thofe
whom friendfhip would join : God hath taken care of this,
to prevent any progrefs, towards real happinefs here, which
would make life more defirable, and death too dreadful.
I hope you have now one advantage that you always wanted before, and the want of which made your friends as uneafy as it did yourfelf ; I mean the removal of that folicitude about your own affairs, which perpetually fill'd your
thoughts and difturb'd your converfation. For if it be true
what Mr. Pope ferioufly tells me, you will have opportunity of faving every groat of the intereft you receive ; and
fo by the time he and you grow weary of each other, you
will be able to pafs the reft of your winelefs life in eafe
and plenty, with the additional triumphal comfort of
never having receiv'd a penny from thofe taftelefs ungrateful people from whom you deferv'd fo much, and
who deferve no better Geniufes than thofe by whom
they are celebrated.—If you fee Mr. Cefar, prefent my
humble fervice to him, and let him know that the
fcrub Libel printed againft me here, and reprinted in
London, for which he fhewed a kind concern to a friend
of us both, was written by myfelf and fent to a Whig-
printer : It was in the ftyle and genius of fuch fcoundrels,
when the humour of libelling ran in this ftrain againft a
friend of mine whom you know.—But my paper is ended.

LETTER

LETTER LI.

Dublin, Nov. 19, 1730.

I Writ to you a long letter about a fortnight paft, concluding you were in London, from whence I underftood one of your former was dated : Nor did I imagine you were gone back to Aimfbury fo late in the year, at which feafon I take the Country to be only a fcene for thofe who have been ill-ufed by a Court on account of their Virtues ; which is a ftate of happinefs the more valuable, becaufe it is not accompanied by Envy, although nothing deferves it more. I would gladly fell a Dukedom to lofe favour in the manner their Graces have done. I believe my Lord Carteret, fince he is no longer Lieutenant, may not ufe me ill, and I have told him often that I only hated him as a Lieutenant : I confefs he had a genteeler manner of binding the chains of this kingdom than moft of his predeceffors, and I confefs at the fame time that he had, fix times a regard to my recommendation by preferring fo many of my friends in the church ; the two laft acts of his favour were to add to the dignities of Dr. Delany and Mr. Stopford, the laft of whom was by you and Mr. Pope put into Mr. Pultney's hands. I told you in my laft, that a continuance of giddinefs (though not in a violent degree) prevented my thoughts of England at prefent. For in my cafe a domeftic life is neceffary, where I can with the Centurion fay to my fervant, Go, and he goeth, and Do this, and he doeth it. I now hate all people whom I cannot command, and confequently a Duchefs is at this time the hatefulleft Lady in the world to me, one only excepted, and I beg her Grace's pardon for that exception, for, in the way I mean, her Grace is ten thoufand times more hateful. I confefs I begin to apprehend you will fquander my money, becaufe I hope you never lefs wanted it ; and if you go on with fuccefs for two years longer, I fear I fhall not have a farthing of it left. The Doctor hath ill informed me, who fays that Mr. Pope is at prefent the chief Poetical Favourite, yet Mr. Pope himfelf talks like a Philofopher and one wholly retir'd. But the vogue of our few honeft folks here is, that Duck is abfolutely to fucceed Eufden in the laurel, the contention being between Concannen or Theobald, or fome other Hero of the Dunciad. I never charged you for not talking, but the dubious ftate of your affairs in thofe days was too much the fubject, and

I wish the Duchefs had been the voucher of your amend-
ment. Nothing fo much contributed to my cafe as the
turn of affairs after the Queen's death ; by which all my
hopes being cut off, I could have no ambition left, unlefs
I would have been a greater rafcal than happened to fuit
with my temper. I therefore fat down quietly at my mor-
fel, adding only thereto a principle of hatred to all fuc-
ceeding Meafures and Miniftries by way of fauce to relifh
my meat : And I confefs one point of conduct in my Lady Duchefs's life hath added much poignancy to it. There
is a good Irifh practical bull towards the end of your letter,
where you fpend a dozen lines in telling me you muft leave
off, that you may give my Lady Duchefs room to write,
and fo you proceed to within two or three lines of the bottom ; though I would have remitted you my 200 l. to
have left place for as many more.

To the Duchefs.

Madam,

My beginning thus low is meant as a mark of refpect,
like receiving your Grace at the bottom of the ftairs. I
am glad you know your duty ; for it hath been a known
and eftablifh'd rule above twenty years in England, that
the firft advances hath been conftantly made me by all
Ladies who afpir'd to my acquaintance, and the greater
their quality, the greater were their advances. Yet, I
know not by what weaknefs, I have condefcended gracioufly to difpenfe with you upon this important article.
Though Mr. Gay will tell you that a namelefs perfon fent
me eleven meffages before I would yield to a vifit : I mean
a perfon to whom he is infinitely obliged, for being the
occafion of the happinefs he now enjoys under the protection and favour of my Lord Duke and your Grace At the
fame time, I cannot forbear telling you, Madam, that
you are a little imperious in your manner of making your
advances. You fay, perhaps you fhall not like me ; I affirm you are miftaken, which I can plainly demonftrate :
for I have certain intelligence, that another perfon diflikes
me of late, with whofe likings yours have not for fome
time paft gone together. However, if I fhall once have
the honour to attend your Grace, I will out of fear and
prudence appear as vain as I can, that I may not know
your thoughts of me. This is your own direction, but it
was needlefs : For Diogenes himfelf would be vain, to have
received the honour of being one moment of his life in the
thoughts of your Grace.

LETTER

LETTER LII.

Dublin, April 13, 1731.

YOUR situation is an odd one; the Duchefs is your Treafurer, and Mr Pope tells me you are the Duke's. And I had gone a good way in fome Verfes on that occafion, prefcribing leffons to direct your conduct, in a negative way, not to do fo and fo, etc. like other Treafurers; how to deal with Servants, Tenants, or neighbouring Squires, which I take to be Courtiers, Parliaments, and Princes in alliance, and fo the parallel goes on, but grows too long to pleafe me: I prove that Poets are the fitteft perfons to be treafurers and managers to great perfons, from their virtue, and contempt of money, etc.— Pray, why did you not get a new heel to your fhoe? unlefs you would make your court at St. James's by affecting to imitate the Prince Lilliput.—But the reft of your letter being wholly taken up in a very bad character of the Duchefs, I fhall fay no more to you, but apply myfelf to her Grace.

Madam, fince Mr. Gay affirms that you love to have your own way, and fince I have the fame perfection; I will fettle that matter immediately, to prevent thofe ill confequences he apprehends. Your Grace fhall have your own way, in all places except your own houfe, and the domains about it. There and there only, I expect to have mine, fo that you have all the world to reign in, bating only two or three hundred acres, and two or three houfes in town and country. I will likewife, out of my fpecial grace, certain knowledge, and mere motion, allow you to be in the right againft all human kind, except myfelf, and to be never in the wrong but when you differ form me. You fhall have a greater privilege in the third article of fpeaking your mind; which I fhall gracioufly allow you now and then to do even to myfelf, and only rebuke you when it does not pleafe me.

Madam, I am now got as far as your Grace's letter, which having not read this fortnight (having been out of town, and not daring to truft myfelf with the carriage of it) the prefumptuous manner in which you begin had flipt out of my memory. But I forgive you to the feventeenth line, where you begin to banifh me for ever, by demanding me to anfwer all the good character fome partial friends

have

have given me. Madam, I have lived sixteen years in Ireland, with only an intermiffion of two fummers in England; and confequently am fifty years older than I was at the Queen's death, and fifty thoufand times duller, and fifty million times more peevifh, perverfe and morofe; fo that under thefe difadvantages I can only pretend to excel all your other acquaintance about fome twenty bars length. Pray, Madam, have you a clear voice? and will you let me fit at your left hand at leaft within three of you, for of two bad ears, my right is the beft? My Groom tells me that he likes your park, but your houfe is too little. Can the parfon of the parifh play at backgammon, and hold his tongue? is any one of your Women a good nurfe, if I fhould fancy myfelf fick for four and twenty hours? How many days will you maintain me and my equipage? When thefe preliminaries are fettled, I muft be very poor, very fick, or dead, or to the laft degree unfortunate, if I do not attend you at Aimfbury. For I profefs you are the firft lady that ever I defired to fee, fince the firft of Auguft 1714, and I have forgot the date when that defire grew ftrong upon me, but I know I was not then in England, elfe I would have gone on foot for that happinefs as far as to your houfe in Scotland. But I can foon recolleft the time, by afking fome Ladies here the month, the day, and the hour when I began to endure their company? which however I think was a fign of my ill-judgment, for I do not perceive they mend in any thing but envying or admiring your Grace. I diflike nothing in your letter but an affected apology for bad writing, bad fpelling, and a bad pen, which you pretend Mr. Gay found fault with, wherein you affront Mr. Gay, you affront me, and you affront yourfelf. Falfe fpelling is only excufable in a Chambermaid, for I would not pardon it in any of your waiting-women.—Pray God preferve your Grace and family, and give me leave to expeft that you will be fo juft to remember me among thofe who have the greateft regard for virtue, goodnefs, prudence, courage, and generofity; after which you muft conclude that I am with the greateft refpeft and gratitude, Madam, your Grace's moft obedient and moft humble fervant, etc.

To Mr. GAY.

I have juft got yours of February 24, with a poftfcript by Mr. Pope. I am in great concern for him: I find Mr. Pope dictated to you the firft part, and with great difficulty

culty some days after added the rest. I see his weakness by his hand-writing. How much does his philosophy exceed mine? I could not bear to see him: I will write to him soon.

LETTER LIII.

Dublin, June 29, 1731.

EVER since I received your letter I have been upon a balance about going to England, and landing at Bristol, to pass a month at Aimsbury, as the Duchess hath given me leave. But many difficulties have interfered; first, I thought I had done with my law-suit, and so did all my lawyers, but my adversary, after being in appearance a Protestant these twenty years, hath declared he was always a Papist, and consequently by the law here, cannot buy nor (I think) sell; so that I am at sea again, for almost all I am worth. But I have still a worse evil; for the giddiness I was subject to, instead of coming seldom and violent, now constantly attends me more or less, tho' in a more peaceable manner, yet such as will not qualify me to live among the young and healthy: And the Duchess in all her youth, spirit, and grandeur, will make a very ill nurse, and her women not much better. Valetudinarians must live where they can command, and scold; I must have horses to ride, I must go to bed and rise when I please, and live where all mortals are subservient to me. I must talk nonsense when I please, and all who are present must commend it. I must ride thrice a week, and walk three or four miles besides, every day.

I always told you Mr. —— was good for nothing but to be a rank Courtier. I care not whether he ever writes to me or no. He and you may tell this to the Duchess, and I hate to see you so charitable, and such a Cully; and yet I love you for it, because I am one myself.

You are the silliest lover in Christendom: If you like Mrs. —— why do you not command her to take you? if she does not, she is not worth pursuing; you do her too much honour; she hath neither sense nor taste, if she dares to refuse you, though she had ten thousand pounds. I do not remember to have told you of thanks that you have not given, nor do I understand your meaning, and I am sure I had never the least thoughts of any myself. If I am your friend, it is for my own reputation, and from a

principle

principle of felf-love, and I do fometimes reproach you for not honouring me by letting the world know we are friends.

I fee very well how matters go with the Duchefs in regard to me. I heard her fay, Mr. Gay, fill your letter to the Dean, that there may be no room for me, the frolick is gone far enough, I have writ thrice, I will do no more; if the man has a mind to come, let him come; what a clutter is here? pofitively I will not write a fyllable more. She is an ungrateful Duchefs confidering how many adorers I have procured her here, over and above the thoufands fhe had before.——I cannot allow you rich enough till you are worth 7000 *l*. which will bring you 300 *per annum*, and this will maintain you, with the perquifite of fpunging while you are young, and when you are old will afford you a pint of port at night, two fervants, and an old maid, a little garden, and pen and ink —provided you live in the country—— Have you no fcheme either in verfe or profe? The Duchefs fhould keep you at hard meat, and by that means force you to write; and fo I have done with you.

Madam,

Since I began to grow old, I have found all ladies become inconftant, without any reproach from their confcience. If I wait on you, I declare that one of your women (which ever it is that has defigns upon a Chaplain) muft be my nurfe, if I happen to be fick or peevifh at your houfe, and in that cafe you muft fufpend your domineering Claim till I recover. Your omitting the ufual appendix to Mr. Gay's letters hath done me infinite mifchief here; for while you continued them, you would wonder how civil the Ladies here were to me, and how much they have altered fince. I dare not confefs that I have defcended fo low as to write to your Grace, after the abominable neglect you have been guilty of; for if they but fufpected it, I fhould lofe them all. One of them, who had an inkling of the matter (your Grace will hardly believe it) refufed to beg my pardon upon her knees, for once neglecting to make my rice-milk.—Pray, confider this, and do your duty, or dread the confequence. I promife you fhall have your will fix minutes every hour at Aimfbury, and feven in London, while I am in health: but if I happen to be fick, I muft govern to a fecond. Yet properly fpeaking, there is no man alive with fo much
truth

truth and refpect your Grace's moft obedient and devoted fervant.

LETTER LIV.

Aug. 28, 1731.

YOU and the Duchefs ufe me very ill, for, I profefs, I cannot diftinguifh the ftyle or the hand-writing of either. I think her Grace writes more like you than her-felf, and that you write more like her Grace than your-felf. I would fwear the beginning of your letter writ by the Duchefs, though it is to pafs for yours ; becaufe there is a curfed lie in it, that fhe is neither young nor healthy, and befides it perfectly refembles the part fhe owns. I will likewife fwear, that what I muft fuppofe is written by the Duchefs, is your hand ; and thus I am puzzled and per-plexed between you, but I will go on in the innocency of my own heart. I am got eight miles from our famous metropolis, to a country Parfon's, to whom I lately gave a City-living, fuch as an Englifh Chaplain would leap at. I retired hither for the public good, having two great works in hand : One to reduce the whole politenefs, wit, Hu-mour, and ftyle of England, into a fhort fyftem, for the ufe of all perfons of quality, and particularly the maids of honour *. The other is of almoft equal importance ; I may call it the whole duty of fervants, in about twenty feveral ftations, from the fteward and waiting-woman down to the fcullion and pantry-boy †.—I believe no mor-tal had ever fuch fair invitations, as to be happy in the beft company of England. I wifh I had liberty to print your letter with my own comments upon it. There was a fel-low in Ireland, who from a fhoe-boy grew to be feveral times one of the chief governors, wholly illiterate, and with hardly common fenfe : A Lord Lieutenant told the firft King George, that he was the greateft fubject he had in both kingdoms ; and truly this character was gotten and preferved by his never appearing in England, which was the only wife thing he ever did, except purchafing fix-teen thoufand pounds a year—Why, you need not ftare : it is eafily apply'd : I muft be abfent, in order to preferve my credit with her Grace.—Lo here comes in the Duchefs

---

* *Wagftaff's Dialogues of polite Converfation*, publifhed in his life-time.
† An imperfect thing of this kind, called *Directions to fervants in general*, has been publifhed fince his death.

again

again (I know her by her dd's; but am a fool for difcovering my Art) to defend herfelf againft my conjecture of
what fhe faid—Madam, I will imitate your Grace and
write to you upon the fame line. I own it is a bafe un-ro-
mantic fpirit in me, to fufpend the honour of waiting at
your Grace's feet, till I can finifh a paultry law-fuit. It
concerns indeed almoft my whole fortune; it is equal to'
half Mr. Pope's, and two thirds of Mr. Gay's, and about
fix weeks rent of your Grace's. This curfed accident
hath drill'd away the whole fummer. But, Madam, underftand one thing, that I take all your ironical civilities
in a literal fenfe, and whenever I have the honour to attend
you, fhall expect them to be literally perform'd : though
perhaps I fhall find it hard to prove your hand-writing in
a Court of juftice; but that will not be much for your
credit. How miferably hath your Grace been miftaken
in thinking to avoid Envy by running into exile, where
it haunts you more than ever it did even at Court ? *Non
te civitas, non regia domus in exilium miferunt, fed tu utrufque.*
So fays Cicero (as your Grace knows) or fo he might have
faid.

I am told that the Craftfman in one of his papers is offended with the publifhers of (I fuppofe) the laft edition
of the Dunciad ; and I was afked whether you and Mr.
Pope were as good friends to the new difgraced perfon
as formerly ? This I knew nothing of, but fuppofed it
was the confequence of fome miftake. As to writing,
I look on you juft in the prime of life for it, the very feafon when judgment and invention draw together. But
fchemes are perfectly accidental ; fome will appear barren
of hints and matter, but prove to be fruitful ; and others
the contrary : And what you fay, is paft doubt, that e-
very one can beft find hints for himfelf : though it is poffible that fometimes a friend may give you a lucky one
juft fuited to your own imagination. But all this is almoft
paft with me ; my invention and judgment are perpetually
at fifty-cuffs, till they have quite difabled each other :
and the meereft trifles I ever wrote are ferious philofophical lucubrations, in comparifon to what I now bufy myfelf about ; as (to fpeak in the author's phrafe) the world
may one day fee *.

* His ludicrous prediction was, fince his death, and very much to his difhonour, ferioufly fulfilled, in collecting together, and publifhing every folly
that fell from his pen, in this *difabled* ftate of his wit, as he himfelf reprefents
it to be ; and which, the productions of it amply verify. This treatment of
fo great a Genius for a little paultry lucre, well deferves the indignation of the
Public.

LETTER

LETTER LV.

Sept. 10, 1731.

IF your ramble was on horfeback, I am glad of it on account of your health ; but I know your arts of patch-
ing up a journey between ftage-coaches and friends
coaches : for you are as arrant a cockney as any hofier in
Cheapfide. One clean fhirt with two cravats, and as many
handkerchiefs, make up your equipage ; and as for a night-
gown, it is clear from Homer, that Agamemnon role
without one. I have often had it in my head to put it i 1-
to yours, that you ought to have fome great work in fcheme,
which may take up feven years to finifh, befides two or
three under ones, that may add another thoufand pound
to your ftock : and then I fhall be in lefs pain about you.
I know you can find dinners, but you love twelve-penny
coaches too well, without confidering that the intereft of
a whole thoufand pounds brings you but half a crown a
day. I find a greater longing than ever to come amongft
you ; and reafon good, when I am teazed with Dukes
and Ducheffes for a vifit, all my demands comply'd with,
and all excufes cut off. You rememember, " O happy
" Don Quixote ! Queens held his horfe, and Ducheffes
" pulled off his armour," or fomething to that purpofe.
He was a mean fpirited fellow ; I can fay ten times
more ; O happy, etc. fuch a Duchefs was defigned to
attend him, and fuch a Duke invited him to command
his palace. *Nam iftos reges ceteros memorare nolo, hominum
mendicabula :* go read your Plautus, and obferve Stro-
bilus vaporing after he had found the pot of gold.—
I will have nothing to do with that Lady : I have
long hated her on your account, and the more, becaufe
you are fo forgiving as not to hate her ; however, fhe has
good qualities enough to make her efteem'd ; but not one
grain of feeling. I only wifh fhe were a fool.—I have been
feveral months writing near five hundred lines on a pleafant
fubject, only to tell what my friends and enemies will fay
on me after I am dead *. I fhall finifh it foon, for I add
two lines every week, and blot out four, and alter eight.
I have brought in you and my other friends, as well as
enemies and detractors.—It is a great comfort to fee how
corruption and ill-conduct are inftrumental in uniting
Virtuous perfons and Lovers of their country of all deno-

* This has been publifhed, and is among the beft of his poems.

minations ;

minations : Whig and Tory, High and Low-church, as foon
as they are left to think freely, all joining in opinion. If
this be difaffection, pray God fend me always among the
difaffected ? and I heartily wifh you joy of your fcurvy treatment at Court, which hath given you leifure to cultivate
both publick and private Virtue, neither of them likely
to be foon met with within the walls of St. James's or Weftminfter.—But I muft here difmifs you, that I may pay my
acknowledgments to the Duke for the great honour he hath
done me.

My Lord,

   I could have fworn that my Pride would be always able
to preferve me from Vanity ; of which I have been in great
danger to be guilty for fome months paft, firft by the conduct of my Lady Duchefs, and now by that of your Grace,
which had like to finifh the work : and I fhould certainly
have gone about fhewing my letters under the charge of fe-
crefy to every blab of my acquaintance ; if I could have
the leaft hope of prevailing on any of them to believe that
a man in fo obfcure a corner, quite thrown out of the prefent world, and within a few fteps of the next, fhould receive fuch condefcending invitations, from two fuch perfons, to whom he is an utter ftranger, and who know no
more of him than what they have heard by the partial re-
prefentations of a friend. But in the mean time, I muft
defire your Grace not to flatter yourfelf, that I waited for
Your Confent to accept the invitation. I muft be ignorant
indeed not to know, that the Duchefs, ever fince you met,
hath been moft politically employed in increafing thofe
forces, and fharping thofe arms with which fhe fubdued you
at firft, and to which, the braver and the wifer you grow,
you will more and more fubmit. Thus I know myfelf on
the fecure fide, and it was a mere piece of good manners to
infert that claufe, of which you have taken the advantage.
But as I cannot forbear informing your Grace, that the
Duchefs's great fecret in her art of government hath been
to reduce both your wills into one ; fo I am content, in
due obfervance to the forms of the world, to return my
moft humble thanks to your Grace for fo great a favour as
you are pleafed to offer me, and which nothing but impof-
fibilities fhall prevent me from receiving, fince I am, with
the greateft reafon, truth, and refpect, my Lord, your
Grace's moft obedient, etc.

Madam,

Madam,

I have confulted all the learned in occult fciences of my acquaintance, and have fat up eleven nights to difcover the meaning of thofe two hieroglyphical lines in your Grace's hand at the bottom of the laft Aimfbury letter, but all in vain. Only 'tis agreed, that the language is Coptic, and a very profound Behmift affures me, the ftyle is poetic, containing an invitation from a very great per- fon of the female fex to a ftrange kind of man whom fhe never faw; and this is all I can find, which after fo many former invitations, will ever confirm me in that refpect, wherewith I am, Madam, your Grace's moft obedient, etc.

LETTER LVI.

Mr. GAY to Dr. SWIFT.

Decemb. 1, 1731.

YOU us'd to complain that Mr. Pope and I would not let you fpeak: you may now be even with me, and take it out in writing. If you don't fend to me now and then, the poft-office will think me of no confequence, for I have no correfpondent but you. You may keep as far from us as you pleafe, you cannot be forgotten by thofe who ever knew you, and therefore pleafe me by fometimes fhewing that I am not forgot by you. I have nothing to take me off from my friendfhip to you: I feek no new ac- quaintance, and court no favour: I fpend no fhillings in coaches or chairs to levees or great vifits, and, as I don't want the affiftance of fome that I formerly converfed with, I will not fo much as feem to feek to be a dependant. As to my ftudies, I have not been entirely idle, though I cannot fay that I have yet perfected any thing. What I have done is fomething in the way of thofe fables I have already publifhed. All the money I get is by faving, fo that by habit there may be fome hopes (if I grow richer) of my becoming a mifer. All mifers have their excufes; the motive to my parfimony is independance. If I were to be reprefented by the Duchefs (fhe is fuch a downright niggard for me) this character might not be allow'd me; but I really think I am covetous enough for any who lives at the court end of the town, and who is as poor as my- felf: for I don't pretend that I am equally faving with
Y y 2   S——k.

S——k. Mr. Lewis defired you might be told that he hath five pounds of yours in his hands, which he fancies you may have forgot, for he will hardly allow that a Verfe-man can have a juft knowledge of his own affairs. When you got rid of your law-fuit, I was in hopes that you had got your own, and was free from every vexation of the law; but Mr. Pope tells me you are not entirely out of your perplexity, tho' you have the fecurity now in your own pofleffion; but ftill your cafe is not fo bad as Captain Gulliver's, who was ruined by having a decree for him with cofts. I have had an injunction for me againft pirating bookfellers, which I am fure to get nothing by, and will, I fear, in the end, drain me of fome money. When I began this profecution, I fancy'd there would be fome end of it; but the law ftill goes on, and 'tis probable I fhall fome time or other fee an Attorney's bill as long as the Book. Poor Duke Difney is dead, and hath left what he had among his friends, among whom are Lord Bolingbroke 500 l. Mr. Pelham 500 l. Sir William Wyndham's youngeft fon 500 l. Gen. Hill 500 l. Lord Maffam's fon 500 l.

You have the good wifhes of thofe I converfe with; they know they gratify me, when they remember you; but I really think they do it purely for your own fake. I am fatisfied with the love and friendfhip of good men, and envy not the demerits of thofe who are moft confpicuoufly diftinguifh'd. Therefore as I fet a juft value upon your friendfhip, you cannot pleafe me more than letting me now and then know that you remember me (the only fatisfaction of diftant friends!)

P. S. Mr. Gay's is a good letter, mine will be a very dull one; and yet what you will think the worft of it, is what fhould be its excufe, that I write in an head-ach which has lafted three days. I am never ill but I think of your ailments, and repine that they mutually hinder our being together: tho' in one point I am apt to differ from you, for you fhun your friends when you are in thofe circumftances, and I defire them; your way is the more generous, mine the more tender. Lady —— took your letter very kindly, for I had prepared her to expect no anfwer under a twelve-month; but kindnefs perhaps is a word not applicable to courtiers. However fhe is an extraordinary woman there, who will do you common juftice. For God's fake, why all this fcruple about Lord B——'s keeping your horfes, who has a park; or about
my

my keeping you on a pint of wine a day? We are infinitely richer than you imagine: John Gay fhall help me to
entertain you, tho' you come like King Lear with fifty
knights — Tho' fuch profpects as I wifh, cannot now be
formed for fixing you with us, time may provide better
before you part again : the old Lord may die, the benefice
may drop, or, at worft, you ma carry me into Ireland.
You will fee a work of Lord B——'s and one of mine :
which, with a juft neglect of the prefent age, confult only
pofterity ; and, with a noble fcorn of politics, afpire to
philofophy. I am glad you refolve to meddle no more
with the low concerns and interefts of Parties, even of Countries (for Countries are but larger Parties) *Quid verum
atque decens curare, et rogare, noftrum fit.* I am much pleafed
with your defign upon Rochefoucault's maxim, pray
finifh it *. I am happy whenever you join our names together : fo would Dr. Arbuthnot be, but at this time he can
be pleafed with nothing ; for his darling fon is dying in all
probability, by the melancholy account I received this
morning.

The paper you afk me about is of little value. It might
have been a feafonable fatire upon the fcandalous language
and paffion with which men of condition have ftoop'd to
treat one another : furely they facrifice too much to the
people, when they facrifice their own characters, families,
etc. to the diverfion of that rabble of readers. I agree
with you in my contempt of moft popularity, fame, etc.
even as a writer I am cool in it, and whenever you fee
what I am now writing, you'll be convinced I would pleafe
but a few, and (if I could) make mankind lefs admirers,
and greater Reafoners †. I ftudy much more to render
my own portion of Being eafy, and to keep this peevifh
frame of the human body in good humour. Infirmities
have not quite unmann'd me, and it will delight you to
hear they are not increas'd, tho' not diminifh'd. I thank
God, I do not very much want people to attend me, tho'
my Mother now cannot. When I am fick, I lie down :
when I am better, I rife up : I am ufed to the head-ach,
etc. If greater pains arrive (fuch as my late rheumatifm)
the fervants bathe and plafter me, or the furgeon fcarifies
me, and I bear it, becaufe I muft. This is the evil of Nature, not of Fortune. I am juft now as well as when you
was here : I pray God you were no worfe. I fincerely wifh

* The Poem on his own death, formed upon a maxim of Rochefoucault.
It is one of the beft of his Performances : But very characteriftic.
† The Poem he means is the *Effay on Man.*

my

my life were paft near you, and, fuch as it is, I would not repine at it.—All you mention remember you, and wifh you here.

LETTER LVII.

Dr. Swift to Mr. Gay.

Dublin, May 4, 1732.

I Am now as lame as when you writ your letter, and almoft as lame as your letter itfelf, for want of that limb from my Lady Duchefs, which you promis'd, and without which I wonder how it could limp hither. I am not in a condition to make a true ftep even on Aimfbury Downs, and I declare that a corporeal falfe ftep is worfe than a political one; nay worfe than a thoufand political ones, for which I appeal to Courts and Minifters, who hobble on and profper, without the fenfe of feeling. To talk of riding and walking is infulting me, for I can as foon fly as do either. It is your pride or lazinefs, more than chair-hire, that makes the town expenfive. No honour is loft by walking in the dark; and in the day, you may beckon a black-guard boy under a gate, near your vifiting-place, (*experto crede*) fave elevenpence, and get half a crown's worth of health. The worft of my prefent misfortune is, that I eat and drink, and can digeft neither for want of exercife; and, to increafe my mifery, the knaves are fure to find me at home, and make huge void fpaces in my cellars. I congratulate with you for lofing your Great acquaintance; in fuch a cafe, philofophy teaches that we muft fubmit, and be content with Good ones. I like Lord Cornbury's refufing his penfion, but I demur at his being elected for Oxford; which, I conceive, is wholly changed, and entirely devoted to new principles: fo it appeared to me the two laft times I was there.

I find by the whole caft of your letter, that you are as giddy and as volatile as ever, juft the reverfe of Mr. Pope, who hath always loved a domeftic life from his youth. I was going to wifh you had fome little place that you could call your own, but, I profefs, I do not know you well enough to contrive any one fyftem of life that would pleafe you. You pretend to preach up riding and walking to the Duchefs, yet, from my knowledge of you after twenty years, you always joined a violent defire of perpetually

shifting

fhifting places and company, with a rooted lazinefs, and an utter impatience of fatigue. A coach and fix horfes is the utmoft exercife you can bear, and this only when you can fill it with fuch company as is beft fuited to your tafte, and how glad would you be if it could waft you in the air to avoid jolting ? while I, who am fo much later in life, can, or at leaft could, ride 500 miles on a trotting horfe. You mortally hate writing, only becaufe it is the thing you chiefly ought to do; as well to keep up the vogue you have in the world, as to make you eafy in your fortune : you are merciful to every thing but money, your beft friend, whom you treat with inhumanity. Be aſſured, I will hire people to watch all your motions, and to return me a faithful account. Tell me, have you cured your Abfence of mind ? can you attend to trifles ? can you at Aimfbury write domeſtic libels to divert the family and neighbouring fquires for five miles round ? or venture fo far on horfeback, without apprehending a ſtumble at every ſtep ? can you fet the footmen a-laughing as they wait at dinner ? and do the Duchefs's women admire your wit ? in what efteem are you with the Vicar of the parifh ? can you play with him at back-gammon ? have the farmers found out that you cannot diftinguifh rye from barley, or an oak from a crab-tree ? You are fenfible that I know the full extent of your country-fkill is in fifhing for Roaches, or Gudgeons at the higheft.

I love to do you good offices with your friends, and therefore defire you will fhow this letter to the Duchefs, to improve her Grace's good opinion of your qualifications, and convince her how ufeful you are like to be in the family. Her Grace fhall have the honour of my correfpondence again when fhe goes to Aimfbury. Hear a piece of Irifh news, I buried the famous General Meredith's father laft night in my Cathedral ; he was ninetyfix years old : fo that Mrs. Pope may live feven years longer. You faw Mr. Pope in health, pray is he generally more healthy than when I was amongft you ? I would know how your own health is, and how much wine you drink in a day ? My ftint in company is a pint at noon, and half as much at night, but I often dine at home like a hermit, and then I drink little or none at all. Yet I differ from you, for I would have fociety, if I could get what I like, people of middle underſtanding, and middle rank. Adieu.

LETTER

LETTER LVIII.

Dublin, July 10, 1732.

I Had your letter by Mr. Ryves a long time after the date, for I suppose he stayed long in the way. I am glad you determine upon something; there is no writing I esteem more than Fables, nor any thing so difficult to succeed in, which however you have done excellently well, and I have often admir'd your happiness in such kind of performances, which I have frequently endeavour'd at in vain. I remember I acted as you seem to hint; I found a Moral first and studied for a Fable, but could do nothing that pleased me, and so left off that scheme for ever. I remember one, which was to represent what scoundrels rise in Armies by a long War, wherein I suppos'd the Lion was engag'd, and having lost all his animals of worth, at last Sergeant Hog came to be Brigadier, and Corporal Ass a Colonel, etc. I agree with you likewise about getting something by the stage, which, when it succeeds, is the best crop for poetry in England: But, pray, take some new scheme, quite different from any thing you have already touched. The present humour of the players, who hardly (as I was told in London) regard any new play, and your present situation at the Court, are the difficulties to be overcome; but those circumstances may have altered (at least the former) since I left you. My scheme was to pass a month at Aimsbury, and then to go to Twickenham, and live a winter between that and Dawley, and sometimes at Riskins, without going to London, where I now can have no occasional lodgings: But I am not yet in any condition for such removals. I would fain have you get enough against you grow old, to have two or three servants about you, and a convenient house. It is hard to want those *subsidia senectuti*, when a man grows hard to please, and few people care whether he be pleased or no. I have a large house, yet I should hardly prevail to find one visiter, if I were not able to hire him with a bottle of wine: so that, when I am not abroad on horseback, I generally dine alone, and am thankful, if a friend will pass the evening with me. I am now with the remainder of my pint before me, and so here's your health—and the second and chief is to my Tunbridge acquaintance, my Lady Duchess—and I tell you that I fear my Lord Bolingbroke and Mr. Pope (a couple of Philosophers) would starve

me,

me, for even of port wine I should require half a pint a
day, and as much at night, and you are growing as bad,
unlefs your Duke and Duchefs have mended you. Your
cholic is owing to intemperance of the philofophical kind ;
you eat without care, and if you drink lefs than I, you
drink too little. But your inattention I cannot pardon,
becaufe I imagined the caufe was removed, for I thought
it lay in your forty millions of fchemes by Court-hopes
and Court-fears. Yet Mr. Pope has the fame defeft, and
it is of all others the moft mortal to converfation ; neither
is my Lord Bolingbroke untinged with it : all for want of
my rule, *Vive la bagatele !* but the Doftor is the king of inattention. What a vexatious life fhould I lead among you ?
If the Duchefs be a *reveufe*, I will never come to Aimfbury ; or, if I do, I will run away from you both, to one
of her women, and the fteward and chaplain.

Madam,

I mention'd fomething to Mr. Gay of a Tunbridge acquaintance, whom we forget of courfe when we return to
town, and yet I am affured that if they meet again next
fummer, they have a better title to refume their commerce. Thus I look on my right of correfponding with
your Grace to be better eftablifhed upon your return to
Aimfbury ; and I fhall at this time defcend to forget, or
at leaft fufpend my refentments of your negleft all the
time you were in London. I ftill keep in my heart, that
Mr. Gay had no fooner turned his back than you left the
place in his letter void which he had commanded you to
fill : though your guilt confounded you fo far, that you
wanted prefence of mind to blot out the laft line, where
that command ftared you in the face. But it is my mif-
fortune to quarrel with all my acquaintance, and always
come by the worft ; and Fortune is ever againft me, but
never fo much as by purfuing me out of mere partiality to
your Grace, for which you are to anfwer. By your con-
nivance, fhe hath pleafed, by a ftumble on the ftairs, to
give me a lamenefs that fix months have not been able per-
feftly to cure : and thus I am prevented from revenging
myfelf by continuing a month at Aimfbury, and breeding
confufion in your Grace's family. No difappointment
through my whole life hath been fo vexatious by many
degrees ; and God knows whether I fhall ever live to fee
the invifible Lady to whom I was obliged for fo many
favours, and whom I never beheld fince fhe was a bratt in

hanging fleeves. I am, and fhall be ever, with the greateft refpect and gratitude, Madam, your Grace's moft
obedient, and moft humble, etc.

LETTER LIX.

Dublin, Aug. 12, 1732.

I Know not what to fay to the account of your fteward-
fhip, and it is monftrous to me that the South-fea fhould
pay half their debts at one clap. But I will fend for the
money when you put me into the way, for I fhall want it
here, my affairs being in a bad condition by the miferies
of the kingdom, and my own private fortune being wholly embroiled, and worfe than ever; fo that I fhall foon
petition the Duchefs, as an object of charity, to lend me
three or four thoufand pounds to keep up my dignity. My
one hundred pounds will buy me fix hogheads of wine,
which will fupport me a year; *provifæ frugis in annum Copia*. Horace defired no more; for I will conftrue *frugis* to
be wine. You are young enough to get fome lucky hint,
which muft come by chance, and it fhall be a thing of
importance, *quod et hunc in annum vivat et in plures*, and you
fhall not finifh it in hafte, and it fhall be diverting, and
ufefully fatirical, and the Duchefs fhall be your critic;
and betwixt you and me, I do not find fhe will grow weary
of you till this time feven years. I had lately an offer to
change for an Englifh living, which is juft too fhort by
300l. a year; and that muft be made up out of the Duchefs's pin-money before I can confent. I want to be Minifter of Aimfbury, Dawley, Twickenham, Rifkins, and
Prebendary of Weftminfter, elfe I will not ftir a ftep, but
content myfelf with making the Duchefs miferable three
months next fummer. But I keep ill company: I mean
the Duchefs and you, who are both out of favour; and
fo I find am I, by a few verfes wherein Pope and you have
your parts. You hear Dr. D—y has got a wife with 1600l.
a year; I, who am his governor, cannot take one under
two thoufand; I wifh you would enquire of fuch a one in
your neighbourhood. See what it is to write godly books!
I profefs I envy you above all men in England; you want
nothing but three thoufand pounds more, to keep you in
plenty when your friends grow weary of you. To prevent
which laft evil at Aimfbury, you muft learn to domineer
and be peevifh, to find fault with their victuals and drink,
to chide and direct the fervants, with fome other leffons,

which

which I fhall teach you, and always practifed myfelf with fuccefs. I believe I formerly defired to know whether the Vicar of Aimfbury can play at back-gammon; pray afk him the queftion, and give him my fervice.

To the Duchefs.

Madam,

I was the moft unwary creature in the world, when, againft my old maxims, I writ firft to you upon your return to Tunbridge. I beg that this condefcenfion of mine may go no farther, and that you will not pretend to make a precedent of it. I never knew any man cured of any inattention, although the pretended caufes were removed. When I was with Mr. Gay laft in London, talking with him on fome poetical fubjects, he would anfwer; " Well " I am determined not to accept the employment of Gen- " tleman-ufher;" and of the fame difpofition were all my poetical friends, and if you cannot cure him, I utterly defpair.—As to yourfelf, I will fay to you (though comparifons be odious) what I faid to the ——, that your quality fhould be never any motive of efteem to me : My compliment was then loft, but it will not be fo to you. For I know you more by any one of your letters than I could by fix months converfing. Your pen is always more natural and fincere and unaffected than your tongue ; in writing you are too lazy to give yourfelf the trouble of acting a part, and have indeed acted fo indifcreetly that I have you at mercy : and although you fhould arrive to fuch a height of immorality as to deny your hand, yet, whenever I produce it, the world will unite in fwearing this muft come from you only.

I will anfwer your queftion. Mr. Gay is not difcreet enough to live alone, but he is too difcreet to live alone ; and yet (unlefs you mend him) he will live alone even in your Grace's company. Your quarrelling with each other upon the fubject of bread and butter, is the moft ufual thing in the world; Parliaments, Courts, Cities, and Kingdoms quarrel for no other caufe ; from hence, and from hence only, arife all the quarrels between Whig and Tory ; between thofe who are in the Miniftry, and thofe who are out ; between all pretenders to employment in the Church, the Law, and the Army : even the common proverb teaches you this, when we fay, It is none of my bread and butter, meaning it is no bufinefs of mine. Therefore I defpair of any reconcilement between you till

Z z 2

the

the affair of bread and butter be adjufted, wherein I would
gladly be a mediator. If Mahomet fhould come to the
mountain, how happy would an excellent lady be, who
lives a few miles from this town ? As I was telling of Mr.
Gay's way of living at Aimfbury, fhe offered fifty guineas
to have you both at her houfe for one hour over a
bottle of Burgundy, which we were then drinking. To
your queftion I anfwer, that your Grace fhould pull me
by the fleeve till you tore it off, and when you faid you
were weary of me, I would pretend to be deaf, and think
(acording to another proverb) that you tore my cloaths
to keep me from going. I never will believe one word you
fay of my Lord Duke, unlefs I fee three or four lines in
his own hand at the bottom of yours. I have a concern
in the whole family, and Mr. Gay muft give me a particular account of every branch, for I am not afhamed of
you tho' you be Duke and Duchefs, tho' I have been of
others who are, etc. and I do not doubt but even your
own fervants love you, even down to your poftilions; and
when I come to Aimfbury, before I fee your Grace I will
have an hour's converfation with the Vicar, who will tell
me how familiarly you talk to Goody Dobfon and all the
neighbours, as if you were their equal, and that you were
godmother to her fon Jacky.

I am, and fhall be ever, with the greateft repeft, your
Grace's moft obedient, etc.

LETTER LX.

Dublin, Oft. 3, 1731.

I Ufually write to friends after a paufe of a few weeeks,
that I may not interrupt them in better company, better thoughts, and better diverfions. I believe I have told
you of a great Man, who faid to me, that he never once
in his life receiv'd a good letter from Ireland : for which
there are reafons enough without affronting our underftandings. For there is not one perfon out of this country, who regards any events that pafs here, unlefs he hath
an eftate or employment.—I cannot tell that you or I
ever gave the leaft provocation to the prefent Miniftry,
and much lefs to the Court; and yet I am ten times more
out of favour than you. For my own part, I do not fee
the politic of opening common letters, directed to perfons
generally known ; for a man's underftanding would be very
weak to convey fecrets by the poft, if he knew any, which,

I de-

I declare, I do not; and befides I think the world is already fo well informed by plain events, that I queftion
whether the Minifters have any fecrets at all. Neither
would I be under any apprehenfion if a letter fhould be
fent me full of treafon; becaufe I cannot hinder people
from writing what they pleafe, nor fending it to me; and
altho' it fhould be difcover'd to have been open'd before
it came to my hand, I would only burn it, and think no
further. I approve of the fcheme you have to grow fome •
what richer, though, I agree, you will meet with dif-
couragements; and it is reafonable you fhould, confidering what kind of pens are at this time only employed and
encouraged. For you muft allow that the bad painter
was in the right, who, having painted a cock, drove away
all the cocks and hens, and even the chickens, for fear
thofe who paffed by his fhop might make a comparifon
with his work. And I will fay one thing in fpite of the
Poft-officers, that fince Wit and Learning began to be
made ufe of in our kingdoms, they were never profeffedly
thrown afide, contemned, and punifhed, till within your
own memory; nor Dulnefs and Ignorance ever fo openly
encouraged and promoted. In anfwer to what you fay of
my living among you, if I could do it to my eafe : perhaps you have heard of a fcheme for an exchange in Berkfhire propofed by two of our friends; but befides the difficulty of adjufting certain circumftances, it would not
anfwer. I am at a time of life that feeks eafe and inde-
pendence; you'll hear my reafons when you fee thofe
friends; and I concluded them with faying, That I would
rather be a freeman among flaves, than a flave among
freemen. The dignity of my prefent ftation damps the
pertnefs of inferior puppies and fquires, which, without
plenty and eafe on your fide the channel, would break my
heart in a month.

Madam,

See what it is to live where I do. I am utterly ignorant of that fame Strado del Poe; and yet, if that Author
be againft lending or giving money, I cannot but think
him a good Courtier; which, I am fure, your Grace is
not, no not fo much as to be a Maid of honour. For I
am certainly informed, that you are neither a free-think-
er, nor can fell bargains; that you can neither fpell, nor
talk, nor write, nor think like a Courtier; that you pretend to be refpected for qualities which have been out of
                                                    fafhion

fashion ever since you were almost in your cradle ; that your contempt for a fine petticoat is an infallible mark of disaffection ; which is further confirmed by your ill-taste for Wit, in preferring two old-fashion'd poets, before Duck or Cibber. Besides, you spell in such a manner as no court-lady can read, and write in such an old-fashion'd style as none of them can understand.— You need not be in pain about Mr Gay's stock of health. I promise you he will spend it all upon laziness, and run deep in debt by a winter's repose in town ; therefore I entreat you Grace will order him to move his chops less, and his legs more the fix cold months, else he will spend all his money in physic and coach-hire. I am in much perplexity about your Grace's declaration, of the manner in which you dispose what you call your love and respect, which, you say, are not paid to Merit but to your own Humour. Now, Madam, my misfortune is, that I have nothing to plead but abundance of Merit. and there goes an ugly observation, that the Humour of ladies is apt to change. Now, Madam, if I should go to Aimsbury with a great load of Merit, and your Grace happen to be out of humour, and will not purchase my merchandize at the price of your respect, the goods may be damaged, and nobody else will take them off my hands. Besides, you have declared Mr. Gay to hold the first part, and I but the second ; which is hard treatment, since I shall be the newest acquaintance by some years ; and I will appeal to all the rest of your sex, whether such an innovation ought to be allowed ? I should be ready to say in the common forms, that I was much oblig'd to the Lady who wish'd she could give the best living etc. if I did not vehemently suspect it was the very same Lady who spoke many things to me in the same style, and also with regard to the gentleman at your elbow when you writ, whose dupe he was as well as of her Waiting-woman ; but they were both arrant knaves, as I told him and a third friend, though they will not believe it to this day. I desire to present my most humble respects to my Lord Duke, and with my heartiest prayer for the prosperity of the whole family, remain your Grace's, etc.

LETTER LXI.

To Mr. Pope.

Dublin, June 12, 1731.

I Doubt, habit hath little power to reconcile us with ficknefs attended by pain. With me, the lownefs of fpirits hath a moft unhappy effect; I am grown lefs patient with folitude, and harder to be pleas'd with company; which I could formerly better digeft, when I could be eafier without it than at prefent. As to fending you any thing that I have written fince I left you (either verfe or profe) I can only fay, that I have order'd by my Will, that all my Papers of any kind fhall be deliver'd you to difpofe of as you pleafe. I have feveral things that I have had fchemes to finifh, or to attempt, but I very fooolifhly put off the trouble, as finners do their repentance: for I grow every day more averfe from writing, which is very natural, and, when I take a pen, fay to myfelf a thoufand times, *non eft tanti*. As to thofe papers of four or five years paft, that you are pleas'd to require foon; they confift of little accidental things writ in the country; family amufements, never intended further than to divert ourfelves and fome neighbours: or fome effects of anger on Public Grievances here, which would be infignificant out of this kingdom. Two or three of us had a fancy, three years ago, to write a weekly paper, and call it an Intelligencer. But it continued not long; for the whole Volume (it was reprinted in London, and, I find, you have feen it) was the work only of two, myfelf and Dr. Sheridan. If we could have got fome ingenious young man to have been the manager, who fhould have publifhed all that might be fent to him, it might have continued longer, for there were hints enough. But the Printer here could not afford fuch a young man one farthing for his trouble, the fale being fo fmall, and the price one halfpenny; and fo it dropt. In the Volume you faw (to anfwer your queftions) the 1, 3, 5, 7, were mine. Of the 8th I writ only the Verfes, (very uncorrect, but againft a fellow we all hated) the 9th mine, the 10th only the Verfes, and of thofe not the four laft flovenly lines; the 15th is a Pamphlet of mine printed before with Dr. Sh—'s Preface, merely for lazinefs not to difappoint the town; and fo was the 19th, which contains only a parcel of facts relating purely to the miferies of Ireland, and wholly ufelefs

and

and unentertaining.   As to other things of mine fince I
left you; there are in profe a View of the State of Ireland; a Projeft for eating Children; and a Defence of
Lord Carteret : in verfe, a Libel on Dr. D— and Lord
Carteret ; a Letter to Dr. D— on the Libels writ againft
him ; the Barrack (a ftolen Copy ;) the Lady's Journal ;
the Lady's Dreffing-room (a ftolen Copy ;) the Plea of
the Damn'd (a ftolen Copy ;) all thefe have been printed
in London.   (I forgot to tell you that the Tale of Sir
Ralph was fent from England.)   Befides thefe there are
five or fix (perhaps more) Papers of Verfes writ in the
North, but perfect Family-things, two or three of which
may be tolerable ; the reft but indifferent, and the humour only local, and fome that would give offence to the
times.   Such as they are I will bring them, tolerable or
bad, if I recover this lamenefs, and live long enough to
fee you either here or there.   I forget again to tell you,
that the Scheme of paying Debts by a Tax on Vices, is
not one fyllable mine, but of a young Clergyman whom
I countenance ; he told me it was built upon a paffage in
Gulliver, where a Projeftor hath fomething upon the fame
thought.   This young man is the moft hopeful we have ;
a book of his Poems was printed in London ; Dr. D— is
one of his patrons : he is married and has children, and
makes up about 100 *l.* a year, on which he lives decent-
ly.   The utmoft ftretch of his ambition is, to gather up
as much fuperfluous money as will give him a fight of
you, and half an hour of your prefence ; after which he
will return home in full fatisfaftion, and in proper time
die in peace.

My poetical fountain is drain'd, and I profefs, I grow
gradually fo dry, that a Rhime with me is almoft as hard
to find as a Guinea ; and even profe fpeculations tire me
almoft as much.   Yet I have a thing in profe begun about
twenty-eight years ago, and almoft finifhed. It will make
a four fhilling Volume, and is fuch a perfeftion of folly,
that you fhall never hear of it till it is printed, and then
you fhall be left to guefs *.   Nay I have another of
the fame age, which will require a long time to perfeft,
and is worfe than the former, in which I will ferve you
the fame way.   I heard lately from Mr. —— who promifes to be lefs lazy in order to mend his fortune.   But
women who live by their beauty, and men by their wit,
are feldom provident enough to confider that both Wit

* Polite Converfation,

and

and Beauty will go off with years, and there is no living upon the credit of what is paſt.

I am in great concern to hear of my Lady Bolingbroke's ill health returned upon her, and, I doubt, my Lord will find Dawley too ſolitary without her. In that, neither he nor you are companions young enough for me, and, I believe, the beſt part of the reaſon why men are ſaid to grow children when they are old, is becauſe they cannot entertain themſelves with thinking; which is the very caſe of little boys and girls, who love to be noiſy among their play-fellows. I am told Mrs. Pope is without pain, and I have not heard of a more gentle decay, without un-eaſineſs to herſelf or friends; yet I cannot but pity you, who are ten times the greater ſufferer, by having the per-ſon you moſt love, ſo long before you, and dying daily ; and I pray God it may not affect you mind or your health.

LETTER LXII.

* Mr. POPE to Dr. SWIFT.

Dec. 5, 1732.

IT is not a time to complain that you have not anſwered me two letters (in the laſt of which I was impatient un-der ſome fears :) It is not now indeed a time to think of myſelf, when one of the neareſt and longeſt ties I have ever had, is broken all on a ſudden, by the unexpected death of poor Mr. Gay. An inflammatory fever hurried him out of this life in three days. He died laſt night at nine o'clock, not depriv'd of his ſenſes entirely at laſt, and poſſeſſing them perfectly till within five hours. He aſked of you a few hours before, when in acute torment by the inflammation in his bowels and breaſt. His effects are in the Duke of Queenſbury's cuſtody. His ſiſters, we ſup-poſe, will be his heirs, who are two widows ; as yet it is not known whether or no he left a will.—Good God ! how often are we to die before we go quite off this ſtage ? In every friend we loſe a part of ourſelves, and the beſt part. God keep thoſe we have left ! few are worth pray-ing for, and one's ſelf the leaſt of all.

* " On my dear friend Mr. Gay's death : Received December 15th, but not read till the 20th, by an Impulſe, foreboding ſome Misfortune." [This note is indors'd on the original letter in Dr. Swift's hand.]

I shall never see you now, I believe; one of your principal calls to England is at an end. Indeed he was the most amiable by far, his qualities were the gentlest; but I love you as well and as firmly. Would to God the man we have lost had not been so amiable, nor so good! but that's a wish for our own sakes, not for his. Sure if Innocence and Integrity can deserve Happiness, it must be his. Adieu, I can add nothing to what you will feel, and diminish nothing from it. Yet write to me, and soon. Believe no man now living loves you better, I believe no man ever did, than   A. POPE.

Dr. Arbuthnot, whose humanity you know, heartily commends himself to you. All possible diligence and affection has been shown, and continued attendance on this melancholy occasion. Once more adieu, and write to one who is truly disconsolate.

Dear Sir,

I am sorry that the renewal of our correspondence should be upon such a melancholy occasion. Poor Mr. Gay died of an inflammation, and, I believe, at last a mortification of the bowels; it was the most precipitate case I ever knew, having cut him off in three days. He was attended by two Physicians besides myself. I believed the distemper mortal from the beginning. I have not had the pleasure of a line from you these two years; I wrote one about your health, to which I had no answer. I wish you all health and happiness, being with great affection and respect, Sir, Your, etc.

LETTER LXIII.

Dublin, 1732-3.

I Received yours with a few lines from the Doctor, and the account of our losing Mr. Gay, upon which event I shall say nothing. I am only concern'd that long-living hath not harden'd me: for even in this kingdom, and in a few days past, two persons of great merit, whom I loved very well, have died in the prime of their years, but a little above thirty. I would endeavour to comfort myself upon the loss of friends, as I do upon the loss of money; by turning to my account-book, and seeing whether I have enough left for my support; but in the former case I find I have not, any more than in the other; and I know not any

any man who is in a greater likelihood than myfelf to die
poor and friendlefs. You are a much greater lofer than
me by his death, as being a more intimate friend, and
often his companion; which latter I could never hope to
be, except perhaps once more in my life for a piece of a
fummer. I hope he hath left you the care of any writings he may have left, and I wifh, that, with thofe already extant, they could be all publifhed in a fair edition under your infpection. Your Poem on the Ufe of Riches
hath been juft printed here, and we have no objection but
the obfcurity of feveral paffages by our ignorance in facts
and perfons, which makes us lofe abundance of the Satire.
Had the printer given me notice, I would have honeftly
printed the names at length, where I happened to know
them; and writ explanatory notes, which however would
have been but few, for my long abfence hath made me ignorant of what paffes out of the fcene where I am. I never had the leaft hint from you about this work, any more
than of your former, upon Tafte. We are told here, that
you are preparing other pieces of the fame bulk to be infcribed to other friends, one (for inftance) to my Lord
Bolingbroke, another to Lord Oxford, and fo on.—Doctor Delany prefents you his moft humble fervice: he behaves himfelf very commendably, converfes only with his
former friends, makes no parade, but entertains them
conftantly at an elegant plentiful table, walks the ftreets
as ufual, by day-light, does many acts of charity and generofity, cultivates a country-houfe two miles diftant, and
is one of thofe very few within my knowledge, on whom
a great accefs of fortune hath made no manner of change.
And particulary he is often without money, as he was
before. We have got my Lord Orrery among us, being
forced to continue here on the ill condition of his eftate
by the knavery of an Agent; he is a moft worthy Gentleman, whom, I hope, you will be acquainted with. I am
very much obliged by your favour to Mr. P—, which, I
defire, may continue no longer than he fhall deferve by his
Modefty, a virtue I never knew him to want, but is hard
for young men to keep without abundance of ballaft. If
you are acquainted with the Duchefs of Queenfbury, I
defire you will prefent her my moft humble fervice: I
think fhe is a greater lofer by the death of a friend than
either of us. She feems a Lady of excellent fenfe and
fpirit. I had often poftfcripts from her in our friend's letters to me, and her part was fometimes longer than his,
and they made up great part of the little happinefs I could

have

have here. This was the more generous, becaufe I never faw her fince fhe was a girl of five years old, nor did I envy poor Mr. Gay for any thing fo much as being a domeftic friend to fuch a Lady. I defire you will never fail to fend me a particular account of your health. I dare hardly enquire about Mrs. Pope, who, I am told, is but juft among the living, and confequently a continual grief to you : fhe is fenfible of your tendernefs, which robs her of the only happinefs fhe is capable of enjoying. And yet I pity you more than her ; you cannot lengthen her days, and I beg fhe may not fhorten yours.

LETTER LXIV.

Feb. 16, 1732-3.

IT is indeed impoffible to fpeak on fuch a fubjcct as the lofs of Mr. Gay, to me an irreparable one. But I fend you what I intend for the infcription on his tomb, which the Duke of Queenfbury will fet up at Weftminfter. As to his writings, he left no Will, nor fpoke a word of them, or any thing elfe, during his fhort and precipitate illnefs, in which I attended him to his laft breath. The Duke has acted more than the part of a brother to him, and it will be ftrange if the fifters do not leave his papers totally to his difpofal, who will do the fame that I would do with them. He has managed the Comedy (which our poor friend gave to the play-houfe the week before his death) to the utmoft advantage for his relations; and propofes to do the fame with fome Fables he left finifhed.

There is nothing of late which I think of more than Mortality, and what you mention, of collecting the beft monuments we can of our friends, their own images in their writings : (for thofe are the beft, when their minds are fuch as Mr. Gay's was, and as yours is.) I am preparing alfo for my own, and having nothing fo much at heart, as to fhew the filly world that men of Wit, or even Poets, may be the moft moral of mankind. A few loofe things fometimes fall from them, by which cenforious fools judge as ill of them as poffibly they can, for their own comfort : and indeed, when fuch unguarded and trifling *Jeux d'Efprit* have once got abroad, all that prudence or repentance can do, fince they cannot be denied, is to put them fairly upon that foot; and teach the public

(as

(as we have done in the preface to the four volumes of
Miscellanies) to distinguish betwixt our studies and our
idlenesses, our works and our weaknesses. That was the
whole end of the last Vol. of Miscellanies, without which
our former declaration in that preface, "That these vo-
"lumes contained all that we have ever offended that
"way," would have been discredited. It went indeed to
my heart, to omit what you called the Libel on Dr. D—,
and the best Panegyric on myself, that either my own
times or any other could have afforded, or will ever afford
to me. The book, as you observe, was printed in great
haste; the cause whereof was, that the booksellers here
were doing the same, in collecting your pieces, the corn
with the chaff; I don't mean that any thing of yours is
chaff, but with other wit of Ireland which was so, and the
whole in your name. I meant principally to oblige them
to separate what you writ seriously from what you writ
carelesly; and thought my own weeds might pass for a
sort of wild flowers, when bundled up with them.

It was I that sent you those books into Ireland, and so I
did my Epistle to Lord Bathurst even before it was publish'd, and another thing of mine, which is a * Parody
from Horace, writ in two mornings. I never took more
care in my life of any thing than of the former of these,
nor less than of the latter : yet every friend has forced me
to print it, tho' in truth my own single motive was about
twenty lines towards the latter end, which you will find
out.

I have declined opening to you by letters the whole
scheme of my present Work, expecting still to do it in a
better manner in person : but you will see pretty soon,
that the letter to Lord Bathurst is a part of it, and you
will find a plain connection between them, if you read
them in the order just contrary to that they were publish'd
in. I imitate those cunning tradesmen, who show their
best silks last; or (to give you a truer idea, tho' it sounds
too proudly) my works will in one respect be like the works
of Nature, much more to be liked and understood when
consider'd in the relation they bear with each other, than
when ignorantly look'd upon one by one; and often, those
parts which attract most at first sight, will appear to be not
the most, but the least considerable.

I am pleas'd and flatter'd by your expression of *Orna me*.
The chief pleasure this work can give me is, that I can in it,

* Sat. i. Lib. ii.

with

with propriety, decency, and juſtice, inſert the name and
charaćter of every friend I have, and every man that deſerves to be lov'd or adorn'd. But I ſmile at your applying that phraſe to my viſiting you in Ireland; a place where
I might have ſome apprehenſion (from their extraordinary
paſſion for Poetry, and their boundleſs Hoſpitality) of
being *adorned* to death, and buried under the weight of
garlands, like one I have read of ſomewhere or other. My
Mother lives, (which is an anſwer to that point) and, I
thank God, tho' her memory be in a manner gone, is yet
awake and ſenſible to me, though ſcarce to any thing elſe;
which doubles the reaſon of my attendance, and at the
ſame time ſweetens it. I wiſh (beyond any other wiſh)
you could paſs a ſummer here; I might (too probably)
return with you, unleſs you preferr'd to ſee France firſt,
to which country, I think, you would have a ſtrong invitation. Lord Peterborow has narrowly eſcaped death,
and yet keeps his chamber: he is perpetually ſpeaking in
the moſt affećtionate manner of you: he has written you
two letters, which you never received, and by that has
been diſcouraged from writing more. I can well believe
the poſt-office may do this, when ſome letters of his to me
have met the ſame fate, and two of mine to him. Yet
let not this diſcourage you from writing to me, or to him,
incloſ'd in the common way, as I do to you; Innocent
men need fear no detećtion of their thoughts; and for my
part, I would give 'em free leave to ſend all I write to
Curl, if moſt of what I write was not too ſilly.

I deſire my ſincere ſervices to Dr. Delany, who, I a-
gree with you, is a man every way eſteemable; my Lord
Orrery is a moſt virtuous and good-natur'd Nobleman,
whom I ſhould be happy to know. Lord B. receiv'd your
letter thro' my hands; it is not to be told you how much
he wiſhes for you: the whole liſt of perſons, to whom you
ſent your ſervices, return you theirs, with proper ſenſe
of the diſtinćtion — Your Lady-friend is *Semper Eadem*,
and I have written an Epiſtle to her on that qualification
in a female charaćter: which is thought by my chief
Critic in your abſence to be my *Chef d'Oeuvre:* but it cannot be printed perfećtly, in an age ſo ſore of Satire, and
ſo willing to miſapply charaćters.

As to my own health, it is as good as uſual. I have
lain ill ſeven days of a ſlight fever (the complaint here)
but recover'd by gentle ſweats, and the care of Dr. Arbuthnot. The play Mr. Gay left ſucceeds very well; it
is another original in its kind. Adieu. God preſerve
your

your life, your health, your limbs, your spirits, and your friendships!

LETTER LXV.

April 2, 1733.

YOU say truly, that death is only terrible to us as it separates us from those we love, but I really think those have the worst of it who are left by us, if we are true friends. I have felt more (I fancy) in the loss of Mr. Gay, than I shall suffer in the thought of going away myself into a state that can feel none of this sort of losses. I wish'd vehemently to have seen him in a condition of living independent, and to have lived in perfect indolence the rest of our days together, the two most idle, most innocent, undesigning Poets of our age. I now as vehemently wish you and I might walk into the grave together, by as slow steps as you please, but contentedly and chearfully : Whether that ever can be, or in what country, I know no more, than into what country we shall walk out of the grave. But it suffices me to know it will be exactly what region or state our Maker appoints, and that whatever *h*, *is Right*. Our poor friend's papers are partly in my hands, and for as much as is so, I will take care to suppress things unworthy of him. As to the Epitaph, I'm sorry you gave a copy, for it will certainly by that means come into print, and I would correct it more, unless you will do it for me (and that I shall like as well :) Upon the whole, I earnestly wish your coming over hither, for this reason among many others, that your influence may be join'd with mine to suppress whatever we may judge proper of his papers. To be plunged in my Neighbour's and my papers, will be your inevitable fate as soon as you come. That I am an author whose characters are thought of some weight, appears from the great noise and bustle that the Court and Town make about any I give : and I will not render them less important, or less interesting, by sparing Vice and Folly, or by betraying the cause of Truth and Virtue. I will take care they shall be such, as no man can be angry at, but the persons I would have angry. You are sensible with what decency and justice I paid homage to the Royal Family, at the same time that I satirized false Courtiers and Spies, etc. about 'em. I have not the courage however to be such a Satirist as you, but I would be as much or

more

more a Philofopher. You call your fatires, Libels; I
would rather call my fatires, Epiftles : They will confift
more of Morality than of Wit, and grow graver, which
you will call duller. I fhall leave it to my Antagonifts to
be witty (if they can) and content myfelf to be ufeful,
and in the right. Tell me your opinion as to Lady——'s
or Lord——'s performance ? they are certainly the Top-
wits of the Court, and you may judge by that fingle piece
what can be done againft me ; for it was labour'd, corrected, pre-commended and poft-difapprov'd, fo far as to be
difown'd by themfelves, after each had highly cry'd it up
for the other's *. I have met with my complaints, and
heard at a diftance of fome threats, occafioned by my
verfes : I fent fair meffages to acquaint them where I was
to be found in town, and to offer to call at their houfes
to fatisfy them, and fo it dropp'd. It is very poor
in any one to rail and threaten at a diftance, and have
nothing to fay to you when they fee you. I am glad you
perfift and abide by fo good a thing as that Poem †, in
which I am immortal for my Morality : I never took any
praife fo kindly, and yet, I think, I deferve that praife
better than I do any other. When does your collection
come out, and what will it confift of ? I have but laft
week finifhed another of my Epiftles, in the order of the
fyftem ; and this week (*exercitandi gratia*) I have tranflated
(or rather parody'd) another of Horace's, in which I in-
troduce you advifing me about my expences, houfe-keeping, etc. But·thefe things fhall lie by, till you come to
carp at 'em, and alter rhymes, and grammar, and triplets,
and cacophonies of all kinds. Our Parliament will fit till
Midfummer, which, I hope, may be a motive to bring
you rather in fummer than fo late as autumn : you us'd
to love what I hate, a hurry of politics, etc. Courts I
fee not, Courtiers I know not, Kings I adore not, Queens
I compliment not ; fo I am never like to be in fafhion,
nor in dependance. I heartily join with you in pitying
our poor Lady for her unhappinefs, and fhould only pity
her more, if fhe had more of what they at Court call Happinefs. Come then, and perhaps we may go all together
into France at the end of the feafon, and compare the Liberties of both kingdoms. Adieu. Believe me, dear Sir,
(with a thoufand warm wifhes, mixed with fhort fighs)
ever yours.

* See the Epiftle written on this occafion, p. 8c, etc. of this Volume.
† The ironical libel on Dr. Delany.

LETTER

LETTER LXVI.

To Mr. POPE.

Dublin, May 1, 1733.

I Answer your Letter the sooner becaufe I have a particular reafon for doing fo. Some weeks ago came over
a Poem call'd, *The Life and Chara&er of Dr. S. written by
himfelf.* It was re-printed here, and is dedicated to you.
It is grounded upon a Maxim in Rochefoucault, and the
dedication, after a formal ftory, fays, that my manner of
writing is to be found in every line. I believe I have told
you, that I writ a year or two ago near five hundred lines
upon the fame Maxim of Rochefoucault, and was a long
time about it, as that Impoftor fays in his Dedication,
with many circumftances all pure invention. I defire you
to believe, and to tell my friends, that in this fpurious
piece there is not a fingle line, or bit of a line, or thought,
any way refembling the genuine Copy, any more than it
does Virgil's Æneis; for I never gave a Copy of mine,
nor lent it out of my fight. And although I fhew'd it to
all common acquaintance indifferently, and fome of them
(efpecially one or two females) had got many lines by
heart, here and there, and repeated them often; yet it
happens that not one fingle line or thought is contained in
this Impofture, although it appears that they who coun-
terfeited me, had heard of the true one. But even this
trick fhall not provoke me to print the true one, which
indeed is not proper to be feen, till I can be feen no more:
I therefore defire you will undeceive my friends, and I
will order an Advertifement to be printed here, and tranfmit it to England, that every body may know the delu-
fion, and acquit me, as, I am fure, you muft have done
yourfelf, if you have read any part of it, which is mean,
and trivial, and full of that Cant that I moft defpife: I would
fink to be a Vicar in Norfolk, rather than be charged with
fuch a performance. Now I come to your letter.

When I was of your age, I thought every day of death,
but now every minute: and a continual giddy diforder
more or lefs is a greater addition than that of my years.
I cannot affirm that I pity our friend Gay, but I pity his
friends, I pity you, and would at leaft equally pity myfelf, if I liv'd amongft you; becaufe I fhould have feen
him oftner than you did, who are a kind of Hermit, how
great a noife foever you make by your Ill-nature in not

letting the honeſt Villains of the times enjoy themſelves in this world, which is their only happineſs, and terrifying them with another. I ſhould have added in my libel, that of all men living you are the moſt happy in your Enemies and your Friends: and I will ſwear you have fifty times more Charity for mankind than I could ever pretend to. Whether the production you mention came from the Lady or the Lord, I did not imagine that they were at leaſt ſo bad verſifyers. Therefore *facit indignatio verſus*, is only to be apply'd when the indignation is againſt general Villainy, and never operates when ſome ſort of people write to defend themſelves. I love to hear them reproach you for dulneſs; only I would be ſatisfy'd, ſince you are ſo dull, why they are ſo angry? Give me a ſhilling, and I will enſure you, that poſterity ſhall never know that you had one ſingle enemy, excepting thoſe whoſe memory you have preſerv'd.

I am ſorry for the ſituation of Mr. Gay's papers. You do not exert yourſelf as much as I could wiſh in this affair. I had rather the two ſiſters were hang'd than ſee his works ſwell'd by any loſs of credit to his memory. I would be glad to ſee the moſt valuable printed by themſelves, thoſe which ought not to be ſeen, burn'd immediately, and the others that have gone abroad, printed ſeparately like opuſcula, or rather be ſtiſled and forgotten. I thought your Epitaph was immediately to be engrav'd, and therefore I made leſs ſcruple to give a Copy to Lord Orrery, who earneſtly deſir'd it, but to no body elſe; and, he tells me, he gave only two, which he will recall. I have a ſhort Epigram of his upon it, wherein I would correct a line or two at moſt, and then I will ſend it you (with his permiſſion.) I have nothing againſt yours, but the laſt line, *Striking their aching*: the two participles, as they are ſo near, ſeem to ſound too like. I ſhall write to the Ducheſs, who hath lately honoured me with a very friendly letter, and I will tell her my opinion freely about our friend's papers. I want health, and my affairs are enlarged: but I will break thro' the latter, if the other mends. I can uſe a courſe of medicines, lame and giddy. My chief deſign next to ſeeing you, is to be a ſevere Critic on you and your neighbour; but firſt kill his father, that he may be able to maintain me in my own way of living, and particularly my horſes. It coſt me near 600 *l.* for a wall to keep mine, and I never ride without two ſervants for fear of accidents; *hic vivimus ambitioſa paupertate*. You are both too poor for my acquaintance, but he much the poorer. With

, you

you I will find grafs and wine, and fervants, but with him
not.—The colleƈtion you fpeak of is this. A Printer
came to me, to defire he might print my works (as he
call'd them) in four volumes, by fubfcription. I faid I
would give no leave, and fhould be forry to fee them printed here. He faid " he would be glad of my permiffion,
" but as he could print them without it, and was advis'd
" that it could do me no harm, and having been affur'd
" of numerous fubfcriptions, he hoped I would not be an-
" gry at purfuing his own intereft, etc." Much of this difcourfe paft, and he goes on with the matter, wherein I
determine not to intermeddle, though it be much to my
difcontent ; and I wifh it could be done in England rather
than here, although I am grown pretty indifferent in every
thing of that kind. This is the truth of the ftory.

My Vanity turns at prefent on being perfonated in your
Quae Virtus. etc. You will obferve in this letter many
marks of an ill head and a low fpirit ; but a Heart wholly
turned to love you with the greateft Earneftnefs and
Truth.

LETTER LXVII.

May 28, 1733.

I Have begun two or three letters to you by fnatches,
and been prevented from finifhing them by a thoufand
avocations and diffipations. I muft firft acknowledge the
honour done me by Lord Orrery, whofe praifes are that
precious ointment Solomon fpeaks of, which can be given
only by men of Virtue : all other praife, whether from
Poets or Peers, is contemptible alike : and I am old enough
and experienced enough to know, that the only praifes
worth having, are thofe beftowed *by* Virtue *for* Virtue.
My Poetry I abandon to the critics, my Morals I commit to the teftimony of thofe who know me ; and therefore
I was more pleas'd with your Libel, than with any Verfes
I ever receiv'd. I wifh fuch a colleƈtion of your writings could be printed here, as you mention going on in
Ireland. I was furpriz'd to receive from the Printer that
fpurious piece, call'd The life and Charaƈter of Dr. Swift,
with a letter telling me the perfon, " who publifh'd it,
" had affur'd him the Dedication to me was what I would
" not take ill, or elfe he would not have printed it." I
can't tell who the man is, who took fo far upon him as to anfwer

fwer for my way of thinking; tho', had the thing been genuine, I fhould have been greatly difpleas'd at the publifher's part, in doing it without your knowledge.

I am as earneft as you can be, in doing my beft to prevent the publifhing of any thing unworthy of Mr. Gay; but I fear his friends partiality. I wifh you would come over. All the myfteries of my philofophical work fhall then be clear'd to you, and you will not think that I am not merry enough, nor angry enough: It will not want for Satire, but as for Anger I know it not; or at leaft only that fort of which the Apoftle fpeaks, " Be ye angry " and fin not."

My Neighbour's writings have been metaphyfical, and will next be hiftorical. It is certainly from him only that a valuable Hiftory of Europe in thefe latter times can be expected. Come, and quicken him; for age, indolence, and contempt of the world, grow upon men apace, and may often make the wifeft indifferent whether pofterity be any wifer than we. To a man in years, Health and Quiet become fuch rarities, and confequently fo valuable, that he is apt to think of nothing more than of enjoying them whenever he can, for the remainder of life; and this, I doubt not, has caufed fo many great men to die without leaving a fcrap to pofterity.

I am fincerely troubled for the bad account you give me of your own health. I wifh every day to hear a better, as much as I do to enjoy my own, I faithfully affure you.

LETTER LXVIII.

From Dr. SWIFT.

Dublin, July 8, 1733.

I Muft condole with you for the lofs of Mrs. Pope, of whofe death the papers have been full. But I would rather rejoice with you, becaufe, if any circumftances can make the death of a dear Parent and Friend a fubject for joy, you have them all. She died in an extreme old age, without pain, under the care of the moft dutiful Son that I have ever known or heard of, which is a felicity not happening to one in a million. The worft effect of her death falls upon me, and fo much the worfe, becaufe I expected *aliquis damno ufus in illo,* that it would be followed

by

by making me and this kingdom happy with your prefence. But I am told, to my great misfortune, that a
very convenient offer happening, you waved the invitation preffed on you, alledging the fear you had of being
killed here with eating and drinking. By which I find
that you have given fome credit to a notion of our great
plenty and hofpitality. It is true, our meat and wine is
cheaper here, as it is always in the pooreft countries, becaufe there is no money to pay for them : I believe there
are not in this whole city three Gentlemen out of Employment, who are able to give entertainments once a
month. Thofe who are in Employment of church or ftate,
are three parts in four from England, and amount to little more than a dozen : Thofe indeed may once or twice
invite their friends, or any perfon of diftinction that
makes a voyage hither. All my acquaintance tell me,
they know not above three families where they can occafionally dine in a whole year: Dr. Delany is the only
gentleman I know, who keeps one certain day in the week
to entertain feven or eight friends at dinner, and to pafs
the evening, where there is nothing of excefs, either in
eating or drinking. Our old friend Southern (who hath
juft left us) was invited to dinner once or twice by a
judge, a bifhop, or a commiffioner of the revenues, but
moft frequented a few particular friends, and chiefly the
Doctor, who is eafy in his fortune, and very hofpitable.
The conveniencies of taking the air, winter or fummer,
do far exceed thofe in London. For the two large ftrands
juft at two ends of the town are as firm and dry in winter as
in fummer. There are at leaft fix or eight gentlemen of
fenfe, learning, good humour and tafte, able and defirous
to pleafe you : and orderly females, fome of the better
fort, to take care of you. Thefe were the motives that I
have frequently made ufe of to entice you hither. And
there would be no failure among the beft people here, of
any honours that could be done you. As to myfelf, I declare my health is fo uncertain that I dare not venture a-
mongft you at prefent. I hate the thoughts of London,
where I am not rich enough to live otherwife than by
fhifting, which is now too late. Neither can I have conveniencies in the country for three horfes and two fervants, and many others, which I have here at hand. I
am one of the governors of all the hackney-coaches, carts,
and carriages round this town, who dare not infult me,
like your rafcally waggoners or coachmen, but give me
the way ; nor is there one Lord or Squire for a hundred

of yours, to turn me out of the road, or run over me with their coaches and fix. Thus, I make fome advantage of the public poverty, and give you the reafons for what I once writ, why I chufe to be a freeman among flaves, rather than a flave among freemen. Then, I walk the ftreets in peace without being juftled, nor ever without a thoufand bleffings from my friends the vulgar. I am Lord Mayor of 120 houfes, I am abfolute Lord of the greateft Cathedral in the kingdom, am at peace with the neighbouring Princes, the Lord Mayor of the city, and the Archbilhop of Dublin, only the latter, like the K. of France, fometimes attempts encroachments on my dominions, as old Lewis did upon Lorrain. In the midft of this raillery, I can tell you with ferioufnefs, that thefe advantages contribute to my eafe, and therefore I value them. And in one part of your letter relating to my Lord B— and yourfelf, you agree with me entirely, about the indifference, the love of quiet, the care of health, etc. that grow upon men in years. And if you difcover thofe inclinations in my Lord and yourfelf, what can you expect from me, whofe health is fo precarious? and yet at your or his time of life, I could have leap'd over the moon.

LETTER LXIX.

Sept. 1, 1733.

I Have every day wifh'd to write to you, to fay a thoufand things; and yet, I think, I fhould not have writ to you now, if I was not fick of writing any thing, fick of myfelf, and (what is worfe) fick of my friends too. The world is become too bufy for me; every body is fo concerned for the public, that all private enjoyments are loft, or difrelifh'd. I write more to fhow you I am tired of this life, than to tell you any thing relating to it. I live as I did, I think as I did, I love you as I did; but all thefe are to no purpofe: the world will not live, think, or br love, as I do. I am troubled for, and vexed at, all my friends by turns. Here are fome whom you love, and who love you: yet they receive no proofs of that affection from you, and they give none of it to you. There is a great gulph between. In earneft, I would go a thoufand miles by land to fee you, but the fea I dread. My ailments are fuch, that I really believe a fea-ficknefs (confidering

dering the oppreffion of colical pains, and the great weaknefs of my breaft) would kill me ; and if I did not die o
that, I muft of the exceffive eating and drinking of your
hofpitable town, and the exceffive flattery of your moft
poetical country. I hate to be cramm'd, either way. Let
your hungry Poets, and your rhyming Poets, digeft it, I
cannot. I like much better to be abufed and half-ftarved,
then to be fo over-praifed and over-fed. Drown Ireland !
for having caught you, and for having kept you : I only
referve a little charity for her, for knowing your value, and
efteeming you : You are the only Patriot I know, who is
not hated for ferving his country. The man who drew
your Character and printed it here, was not much in the
wrong in many things he faid of you : yet he was a very
impertinent fellow, for faying them in words quite different from thofe you had yourfelf employed before on the
fame fubject : for furely to alter your words is to prejudice
them ; and I have been told, that a man himfelf can hardly
fay the fame thing twice over with equal happinefs ; Nature is fo much a better thing than artifice.

I have written nothing this year : It is no affectation to
to tell you, my Mother's lofs has turned my frame of
thinking. The habit of a whole life is a ftronger thing
than all the reafon in the world. I know I ought to be
eafy, and to be free ; but I am dejected, I am confined :
my whole amufement is in reviewing my paft life, not in
laying plans for my future. I wifh you cared as little for
popular applaufe as I ; as little for any nation, in contra-
diftinction to others, as I : and then I fancy, you that are
not afraid of the fea, you that are a ftronger man at fixty
than ever I was at twenty, would come and fee feveral people who are (at laft) like the primitive Chriftians, of one foul and of one mind. The day is come,
which I have often wifhed, but never thought to fee;
when *every mortal, that I efteem, is of the fame fentiment in Politics and in Religion.*

Adieu. All you love, are yours; but all are bufy, except (dear Sir) your fincere friend.

LETTER LXX.

Jan. 6, 1734.

I Never think of you and can never write to you, now, without drawing many of thofe fhort fighs of which we have formerly talk'd : The reflection both of the friends we have been depriv'd of by Death, and of thofe from whom we are feparated almoft as eternally by Abfence, checks me to that degree that it takes away in a manner the plea-fure (which yet I feel very fenfibly too) of thinking I am now converfing with you. You have been filent to me as to your works ; whether thofe printed here are, or are not genuine ? but one, I am fure, is yours, and your method of concealing yourfelf puts me in mind of the Indian bird I have read of, who hides his head in a hole, while all his feathers and tail ftick out. You'll have immediately by feveral franks (even before 'tis here publifhed) my Epiftle to Lord Cobham, part of my *Opus Magnum,* and the laft Effay on Man, both which, I conclude, will be grate-ful to your bookfeller, on whom you pleafe to beftow them fo early. There is a woman's war declared againft me by a certain Lord ; his weapons are the fame which women and children ufe, a pin to fcratch, and a fquirt to befpat-ter : I writ a fort of anfwer, but was afhamed to enter the lifts with him, and after fhewing it to fome people, fup-prefs'd it : otherwife it was fuch as was worthy of him and worthy of me. I was three weeks this autumn with Lord Peterborow, who rejoices in your doings, and always fpeaks with the greateft affection of you. I need not tell you who elfe do the fame ; you may be fure almoft all thofe whom I ever fee, or defire to fee. I wonder not that B—— paid you no fort of civility while he was in Ireland : he is too much a half-wit to love a true wit, and too much half-honeft, to efteem any entire merit. I hope and think he hates me too, and I will do my beft to make him : he is fo infupportably infolent in his civility to me when he meets me at one third place, that I muft affront him to be rid of it. That ftrict neutrality as to public parties, which I have conftantly obferv'd in all my writings, I think gives me the more title to attack fuch men, as flan-der and belye my character in private, to thofe who know me not. Yet even this is a liberty I will never take, un-lefs at the fame time they are Pefts of private fociety, or mifchievous members of the public, that is to fay, unlefs

they

they are enemies to all men as well as to me.—Pray write
to me when you can : If ever I can come to you, I will : if
not, may Providence be our friend and our guard thro'
this simple world, where nothing is valuable but sense and
friendship.   Adieu, dear Sir, may health attend your
years, and then may many years be added to you.

P. S. I am just now told, a very curious Lady intends
to write to you to pump you about some poems said to be
yours.   Pray tell her, that you have not answered me on
the same question, and that I shall take it as a thing never
to be forgiven from you, if you tell another what you have
conceal'd from me.

LETTER LXXI.

Sept. 15, 1734.

I Have ever thought you as sensible as any man I knew,
of all the delicacies of friendship, and yet I fear (from
what Lord B. tells me you said in your last letter) that
you did not quite understand the reason of my late silence.
I assure you it proceeded wholly from the tender kindness
I bear you.   When the heart is full, it is angry at all
words that cannot come up to it ; and you are now the
man in all the world I am most troubled to write to, for
you are the friend I have left whom I am most grieved
about.   Death hath not done worse to me in separating
poor Gay, or any other, than disease and absence in dividing us.   I am afraid to know how you do, since most
accounts I have, give me pain for you, and I am unwilling to tell you the condition of my own health.   If it
were good, I would see you ; and yet, if I found you in
that very condition of deafness, which made you fly from
us while we were together, what comfort could we derive
from it ?   In writing often I should find great relief, could
we write freely : and yet when I have done so, you seem
by not answering in a very long time, to feel either the
same uneasiness as I do, or to abstain from some prudential reason.   Yet I am sure, nothing that you and I wou'd
say to each other (tho' our own souls were to be laid open
to the clerks of the post-office) could hurt either of us so
much, in the opinion of any honest man or good subject,
as the intervening, officious, impertinence of those Gods
between us, who in England pretend to intimacies with

you, and in Ireland to intimacies with me. I cannot bu
receive any that call upon me in your name, and in truth,
they take it in vain too often. I take all opportunities
of justifying you against these Friends, especially those
who know all you think and write, and repeat your slighter
verses. It is generally on such little scraps that Witlings
feed, and 'tis hard the world should judge of our house-
keeping from what we fling to our dogs, yet this is often
the consequence. But they treat you still worse, mix
their own with yours, print them to get money, and lay
them at your door. This I am satisfied was the case in the
Epistle to a Lady ; it was just the same hand (if I have
any judgment in style) which printed your Life and Character before, which you so strongly disavow'd in your
letters to Lord Carteret, myself, and others. I was very
well informed of another fact, which convinced me yet
more ; the same person who gave this to be printed, offer'd
to a bookseller a piece in prose as yours, and as commissi-
oned by you, which has since appear'd, and been own'd to
be his own. I think (I say once more) that I know your
hand, tho' you did not mine in the Essay on Man. I beg
your pardon for not telling you, as I should, had you been
in England : but no secret can cross your Irish Sea, and
every clerk in the post-office had known it, I fancy, tho'
you lost sight of me in the first of those Essays, you saw
me in the second. The design of concealing myself was
good, and had its full effect ; I was thought a Divine, a
Philosopher, and what not; and my doctrine had a sanc-
tion I could not have given to it. Whether I can proceed in the same grave march like Lucretius, or must de-
scend to the gayeties of Horace, I know not, or whether
I can do either ? but be the future as it will, I shall col-
lect all the past in one fair quarto this winter, and send it
you, where you will find frequent mention of yourself.
I was glad you suffer'd your writings to be collected more
completely than hitherto, in the volumes I daily expect
from Ireland : I wish'd it had been in more pomp, but
that will be done by others : yours are beauties, that can
never be too finely drest, for they will ever be young. I
have only one piece of mercy to beg of you ; do not laugh
at my gravity, but permit me to wear the beard of a Philosopher, till I pull it off, and make a jest of it myself.
'Tis just what my Lord B. is doing with Metaphysics. I
hope, you will live to see, and stare at the learned figure
he will make, on the same shelf with Locke and Mal-
branche.

You

You fee how I talk to you (for this is not writing) if
you like I fhould do fo, why not tell me fo? if it be the
leaft pleafure to you, I will write once a week moft gladly ; but can you abftraƈt the letters from the perfon who
writes them, fo far, as not to feel more vexation in the
thought of our feparation, and thofe misfortunes which
occafion it, than fatisfaƈtion in the Nothings he can exprefs?
If you can, really and from my heart I cannot. I return
again to melancholy. Pray, however, tell me, is it a fatisfaƈtion ? that will make it one to me ; and we will
think alike, as friends ought, and you fhall hear me punctually juft when you will.

P. S. Our friend, who is juft returned from a progrefs of
three months, and is fetting out in three days with me for
the Bath, where he will ftay till towards the middle of
Oƈtober, left this letter with me yefterday, and I cannot
feal and difpatch it till I have fcribbled the remainder of
this page full. He talks very pompoufly of my Metaphyfics, and places them in a very honourable ftation. It is
true, I have writ fix letters and an half to him on fubjeƈts
of that kind, and I propofe a letter and an half more,
which would fwell the whole up to a confiderable volume.
But he thinks me fonder of the Name of an Author than I
am. When he and you, and one or two other friends have
feen them, *fatis magnum Theatrum mihi eſtis*, I fhall not have
the Itch of making them more public *. I know how little regard you pay to Writings of this kind. But I imagine that if you can like any fuch, it muft be thofe that
ftrip Metaphyfics of all their bombaft, keep within the
fight of every well conftituted Eye, and never bewilder
themfelves whilft they pretend to guide the reafon of others.
I writ to you a long letter fome time ago, and fent it by
the poft. Did it come to your hands ? or did the infpec-
tors of private correfpondence ftop it to revenge themfelves of the ill faid of them in it ? *Vale et me ama.*

* His Lordfhip, as appears by his laft will, altered his mind; and they
have been fince given to the world, to the admiration and aftonifhment of all
the learned and the pious.

LETTER LXXII.

From Dr. SWIFT.

Nov. 1, 1734.

I Have yours with my Lord B ——'s Poſtſcript of September 15 : it was long on its way, and for ſome weeks after the date I was very ill with my two inveterate diſor-
ders, giddineſs and deafneſs. The latter is pretty well
off; but the other makes me totter towards evenings, and
much diſpirits me. But I continue to ride and walk, both
of which, although they be no cures, are at leaſt amuſements. I did never imagine you to be either inconſtant,
or to want right notions of friendſhip, but I apprehend
your want of health ; and it hath been a frequent wonder
to me how you have been able to entertain the world, ſo
long, ſo frequently, ſo happily, under ſo many bodily diſ-
orders. My Lord B. ſays you have been three months
rambling, which is the beſt thing you can poſſibly do in a
ſummer ſeaſon ; and when the winter recalls you, we will,
for our own intereſts, leave you to your ſpeculations.
God be thanked, I have done with every thing, and of
every kind that requires writing, except now and then a
letter, or, like a true old man, ſcribling trifles only fit
for children or ſchool-boys of the loweſt claſs at beſt,
which three or four of us read and laugh at to-day, and
burn to-morrow. Yet, what is ſingular, I never am without ſome great work in view, enough to take up forty
years of the moſt vigorous healthy man : although I am
convinced that I ſhall never be able to finiſh three Trea-
tiſes, that have lain by me ſeveral years, and want nothing but correction. My Lord B. ſaid in his poſtſcript,
that you would go to Bath in three days : we ſince heard
that you were dangerouſly ill there, and that the news-
mongers gave you over. But a gentleman of this kingdom, on his return from Bath, aſſured me he left you
well, and ſo did ſome others whom I have forgot. I am
ſorry at my heart that you are peſtered with people who
come in my name, and I profeſs to you, it is without my
knowledge. I am confident I ſhall hardly ever have occaſion again to recommend, for my friends here are
very few, and fixed to the freehold, from whence nothing but death will remove them. Surely I never doubted about your Eſſay on Man : and I would lay any odds, that
I would never fail to diſcover you in ſix lines, unleſs you
you

had a mind to write below or beside yourfelf on purpofe. I confefs I did never imagine you were fo deep in Morals, or that fo many new and excellent rules could be produced fo advantageoufly and agreeably in that fcience, from any one head. I confefs in fome few places I was forced to read twice. I believe I told you before what the Duke of D— faid to me on that occafion, How a judge here, who knows you, told him that on the firft reading thofe Effays, he was much pleafed, but found fome lines a little dark : On the fecond moft of them cleared up, and his pleafure increafed : On the third he had no doubt remained, and then he admired the whole. My Lord B——'s attempt of reducing Metaphyfics to intelligible fenfe and ufefulnefs, will be a glorious undertaking, as I never knew him fail in any thing he attempted, if he had the fole management, fo I am confident he will fucceed in this. I defire you will allow that I write to you both at prefent, and fo I fhall while I live : It faves your money, and my time ; and he being your Genius, no matter to which it is addreffed. I am happy that what you write is printed in large letters ; otherwife between the weaknefs of my eyes, and the thicknefs of my hearing, I fhould lofe the greateft pleafure that is left me. Pray command my Lord B—— to follow that example, if I live to read his Metaphyfics. Pray God blefs you both. I had a melancholy account from the Doctor of his health. I will anfwer his letter as foon as I can. I am ever entirely yours.

LETTER LXXIII.

Twickenham, Dec. 19, 1734.

I Am truly forry for any complaint you have, and it is in regard to the weaknefs of your eyes that I write (as well as print) in folio. You'll think (I think you will, for you have all the candour of a good underftanding) that the thing which men of our age feel the moft, is the friendfhip of our equals ; and that therefore whatever affects thofe who are ftept a few years before us, cannot but fenfibly affect us who are to follow. It troubles me to hear you complain of your memory, and if I am in any part of my conftitution younger than you, it will be in my remembering every thing that has pleafed me in you, longer than perhaps you will. The two fummers we pafs'd together dwell always in my mind, like a vifion which gave me a glympfe of a

better

better life and better company, than this world otherwife afforded. I am now an individual, upon whom no other depends ; and may go where I will, if the wretched car-cafe I am annex'd to did not hinder me. I rambled by very eafy journeys this year to Lord Bathurft and Lord Peterborow, who upon every occafion commemorate, love, and wifh for you. I now pafs my days between Dawley, London, and this place, not ftudious, nor idle, rather po-lifhing old works than hewing out new. I redeem now and then a paper that hath been abandon'd feveral years ; and of this fort you'll foon fee one, which I infcribe to our old friend Arbuthnot.

Thus far I had written, and thinking to finifh my letter the fame evening, was prevented by company, and the next morning found myfelf in a fever, highly diforder'd, and fo continued in bed for five days, and in my chamber till now ; but fo well recovered as to hope to go abroad to-morrow, even by the advice of Dr. Arbuthnot. He himfelf, poor man, is much broke, tho' not worfe than for thefe two laft months he has been. He took extreme-ly kind your letter. I wifh to God we could once meet again, before that feparation, which yet, I would be glad to believe, fhall reunite us; But he who made us, not for ours, but his purpofes, knows only whether it be for the better or the worfe, that the affections of this life fhould or fhould not continue into the other ; and doubtlefs it is as it fhould be. Yet I am fure that while I am here, and the thing that I am, I fhall be imperfect without the communication of fuch friends as you : you are to me like a limb loft, and buried in another country ; tho' we feem quite divided, every accident makes me feel you were once a part of me. I always confider you fo much as a friend, that I forget you are an author, perhaps too much, but 'tis as much as I would defire you would do to me. However, if I could infpirit you to beftow correction upon thofe three Treatifes, which you fay are fo near compleated, I fhould think it a better work than any I can pretend to of my own. I am almoft at the end of my Morals, as I've been, long ago, of my Wit; my fyftem is a fhort one, and my circle narrow. Imagination has no limits, and that is a fphere in which you may move on to eternity ; but where one is confined to Truth (or to fpeak more like a human creature, to the appearances of Truth) we foon find the fhortnefs of our Tether. Indeed by the help of a metaphyfical chain of Ideas, one may extend the cir-culation, go round and round for ever, without making

any

any progrefs beyond the point to which providence has
pinn'd us : But this does not fatisfy me, who would rather fay a little to no purpofe, than a great deal.   Lord
B. is voluminous, but he is voluminous only to deftroy
volumes.   I fhall not live, I fear, to fee that work printed ; he is fo taken up ftill (in fpite of the monitory hint
given in the firft line of my Eflay) with particular Men, that
he neglects mankind, and is ftill a creature of this World,
not of the Univerfe : This World, which is a name we
give to Europe, to England, to Ireland, to London, to
Dublin, to the Court, to the Caftle, and fo diminifhing till
it comes to our own affairs, and to our own perfons.   When
you write (either to him or to me, for we accept it all as
one) rebuke him for it, as a Divine, if you like it, or as
a Badineur, if you think that more effeftual.

What I write will fhow you that my head is yet weak.
I had written to you by that gentleman from the Bath, but
I did not know him, and every body that comes from Ireland pretends to be a friend of the Dean's.   I am always
glad to fee any that are truly fo, and therefore do not miftake any thing I faid, fo as to difcourage your fending
any fuch to me.   Adieu.

LETTER LXXIV.

From Dr. SWIFT.

May 12, 1735.

YOUR letter was fent me yefterday by Mr. Stopford,
who landed the fame day, but I have not yet feen
him.   As to my filence, God knows it is my great mif-
fortune.   My little domeftic affairs are in great confufion,
by the villainy of agents, and the miferies of this kingdom, where there is no money to be had : nor am I un-
concern'd to fee all things tending towards abfolute power,
in both nations * (it is here in perfection already) although
I fhall not live to fee it eftablifhed.   This condition of
things, both public and perfonal to myfelf, hath given me
fuch a kind of defpondency, that I am almoft unqualified
for any company, diverfion or amufement.   The death of
Mr. Gay and the Doftor, hath been terrible wounds near
my heart.   Their living would have been a great comfort

* The Dean was frequently troubled, he tells us, with a giddinefs in his
head.

to me, although I fhould never have feen them : like a fum of money in a bank, from which I fhould receive at leaft annual intereft, as I do from you, and have done from my Lord Bolingbroke. To fhew in how much ignorance I live, it is hardly a fortnight fince I heard of the death of my Lady Mafham, my conftant friend in all changes of times. God forbid that I fhould expcĕt you to make a voyage that would in the leaft affeĕt your health : but in the mean time how unhappy am I, that my beft friend fhould have perhaps the only kind of diforder for which a fea-voyage is not in fome degree a remedy ? The old Duke of Ormond faid, he would not change his dead fon (Offory) for the beft living fon in Europe. Neither would I change you my abfent friend for the beft prefent friend round the Globe.

I have lately read a book imputed to Lord B. called a Differtation on Parties. I think it very mafterly written.

Pray God reward you for your kind prayers : I believe your prayers will do me more good than thofe of all the Prelates in both kingdoms, or any Prelates in Europe, except the Bifhop of Marfeilles *. And God preferve you for contributing more to mend the world, than the whole pack of (modern) Parfons in a lump.

I am ever entirely yours.

LETTER LXXV.

From Dr. SWIFT.

Sept. 3, 1735

THIS letter will be delivered to you by Faulkner the printer, who goes over on his private affairs. This is an anfwer to yours of two months ago which complains of that profligate fellow Curl. I heartily wifh you were what they call difaffeĕted, as I am. I may fay, as David did, I have finned greatly, but what have thefe fheep done ? You have given no offence to the Miniftry, nor to the Lords, nor Commons, nor Queen, nor the next in power. For you are a man of virtue, and therefore muft abhor vice and all corruption, although your difcretion holds the reins. " You need not fear any confequence in the com-

---

* Who continued there with his flock all the time a dreadful peftilence defolated that city.

" merce

" merce that hath fo long paffed between us; although
" I never deftroy'd one of your letters. But my Execu-
" tors are men of honour and virtue, who have ftrict or-
" ders in my will to burn every letter left behind me."
Neither did our letters contain any Turns of Wit, or
Fancy, or Politics, or Satire, but mere innocent Friendfhip : yet I am loth that any letters, from you and a very
few other friends, fhould die before me ; I believe we neither of us ever leaned our head upon our left hand to ftudy
what we fhould write next ; yet we have held a conftant
intercourfe from your youth and my middle age, and from
your middle age it muft be continued till my death, which
my bad ftate of health makes me expect every month. I
have the ambition, and it is very earneft as well as in
hafte, to have one Epiftle infcribed to me while I am alive,
and you juft in the time when wit and wifdom are in the
height. I muft once more repeat Cicero's defire to a friend ;
Orna me. A month ago were fent me over by a friend of
mine, the works of John Hughes, Efq. They are in
verfe and profe. I never heard of the man in my life,
yet I find your name as a fubfcriber too. He is too grave
a Poet for me, and, I think, among the *mediocribus* in
profe as well as verfe. I have the honour to know Dr.
Rundle ; he is indeed worth all the reft you ever fent us,
but that is faying nothing, for he anfwers your character ;
I have dined thrice in his company. He brought over a
worthy clergyman of this kingdom as his chaplain, which
was a very wife and popular action. His only fault is,
that he drinks no wine, and I drink nothing elfe.

This kingdom is now abfolutely ftarving, by the means
of every oppreffion that can be inflicted on mankind—
Shall I not vifit for thefe things ? faith the Lord. You
advife me right, not to trouble myfelf about the world :
But oppreffion tortures me, and I cannot live without
meat and drink, nor get either without money ? and
money is not be had, except they will make me a Bifhop,
or a Judge, or a Colonel, or a Commiffioner of the Revenues. Adieu.

LETTER LXXVI.

TO anfwer your queftion as to Mr. Hughes, what he
wanted as to genius he made up as an honeft man :
but he was of the clafs you think him.

I am

I am glad you think of Dr. Rundle as I do. He will be an honour to the Bishops and a disgrace to one Bishop, two things you will like: But what you will like more particularly, he will be a friend and benefactor even to your un-friended, un-benefited Nation; he will be a friend to human race, wherever he goes. Pray tell him my best wishes for his health and long life; I wish you and he came over together, or that I were with you. I never saw a man so seldom whom I liked so much as Dr. Rundle.

Lord Peterborow I went to take a last leave of at his setting sail for Lisbon: No Body can be more wasted, no Soul can be more alive. Immediately after the severest operation of being cut into the bladder for a suppression of urine, he took coach, and got from Bristol to Southampton. This is a man that will neither live nor die like any other mortal.

Poor Lord Peterborow! there is another string lost, that wou'd have help'd to draw you hither! He order'd on his death-bed his Watch to be given me (that which had accompanied him in all his travels) with this reason, " That I might have something to put me every day in " mind of him." It was a present to him from the King of Sicily, whose arms and *Insignia* are graved on the inner case; on the outer, I have put this inscription, *Victor Amadeus, Rex Siciliae, Dux Sabaudiae, etc. etc. Carolo Mordaunt, Comiti de Peterborow, D. D. Car. Mor. Com. de Pet. Alexandro Pope moriens legavit,* 1735.

Pray write to me a little oftner; and if there be a thing left in the world that pleases you, tell it one who will partake of it. I hear with approbation and pleasure, that your present care is to relieve the most helpless of this world, those objects * which most want our compassion, tho' generally made the scorn of their fellow-creatures, such as are less innocent than they. You always think generously; and of all charities, this is the most disinterested, and least vain-glorious, done to such as never will thank you or praise you for it.

God bless you with ease, if not with pleasure; with a tolerable state of health, if not with its full enjoyment; with a resign'd temper of mind, if not a very chearful one. It is upon these terms I live myself, tho' younger than you, and I repine not at my lot, could but the presence of a few that I love be added to these. Adieu.

* Idiots.

LETTER

LETTER LXXVII.

From Dr. SWIFT.

Oct. 21, 1735.

I Anſwer'd your letter relating to Curl, etc. I believe my letters have eſcap'd being publiſh'd, becauſe I writ nothing but Nature and Friendſhip, and particular incidents which could make no figure in writing. I have obſerv'd that not only Voiture, but likewiſe Tully and Pliny wrote their letters for the public view, more than for the ſake of their correſpondents; and I am glad of it, on account of the entertainment they have given me. Balſac did the ſame thing, but with more ſtiffneſs, and conſequently leſs diverting: Now I muſt tell you, that you are to look upon me as one going very faſt out of the world; but my fleſh and bones are to be carried to Holy-head, for I will not lie in a Country of ſlaves. It pleaſeth me to find that you begin to diſlike things in ſpite of your Philoſophy; your Muſe cannot forbear her hints to that purpoſe. I cannot travel to ſee you; otherwiſe I ſolemnly proteſt I would do it. I have an intention to paſs this winter in the country with a Friend forty miles off, and to ride only ten miles a day; yet is my health ſo uncertain, that I fear it will not be in my power. I often ride a dozen miles, but come to my own bed at night: My beſt way would be to marry, for in that caſe any bed would be better than my own. I found you a very young man, and I left you a middle-aged one; you knew me a middle-aged man, and now I am an old one. Where is my Lord —— ? methinks I am enquiring after a Tulip of laſt year.—" You need not apprehend any Curls meddling with your letters to me; I will not deſtroy them, but have order'd my Executors to do that office." I have a thouſand things more to ſay, *longævitas eſt garula*, but I remember I have other letters to write if I have time, which I ſpend to tell you ſo. I am ever, deareſt Sir,

Your, etc.

LETTER

LETTER LXXVIII.

From Dr. Swift.

Feb. 9, 1735-6.

I Cannot properly call you my beſt friend, becauſe I have not another left who deſerves the name, ſuch a havock have Time, Death, Exile, and Oblivion made. Perhaps you would have fewer complaints of my ill health and low-neſs of ſpirits, if they were not ſome excuſe for my delay of writing even to you. It is perfeƈtly right what you ſay of the indifference in common friends, whether we are ſick or well, happy or miſerable. The very maid-ſervants in a family have the ſame notion : I have heard them of-ten ſay, Oh, I am very ſick, if any body cared for it ? I am vexed when my viſitors come with the compliments uſual here, Mr. Dean, I hope you are very well. My popularity that you mention, is wholly confined to the common people, who are more conſtant than thoſe we miſ-call their betters. I walk the ſtreets, and ſo do my lower friends, from whom, and from whom alone, I have a thouſand hats and bleſſings upon old ſcores, which thoſe we call the Gentry have forgot. But I have not the love, or hardly the civility of any one man in power or ſtation ; and I can boaſt that I neither viſit nor am acquainted with any Lord, Temporal or Spiritual, in the whole kingdom ; nor am able to do the leaſt good office to the moſt deſer-ving man, except what I can diſpoſe of in my own Cathe-dral upon a vacancy. What hath ſunk my ſpirits more than even years and ſickneſs, is refleƈting on the moſt ex-ecrable Corruptions that run through every branch of pub-lic management.

I heartily thank you for thoſe lines tranſlated, *Singula de nobis anni*, etc. You have them in a ſtrong and admi-rable light ; but however, I am ſo partial, as to be more delighted with thoſe which are to do me the greateſt hon-our I ſhall ever receive from poſterity, and will outweigh the malignity of ten thouſand enemies. I never ſaw them before, by which it is plain that the letter you ſent me miſ-carry'd—I do not doubt that you have choice of new ac-quaintance, and ſome of them may be deſerving : For youth is the ſeaſon of Virtue ; Corruptions grow with years, and I believe the oldeſt rogue in England is the greateſt. You have years enough before you to watch whether theſe new acquaintance will keep their Virtue,

when

when they leave you and go into the world ; how long will
their fpirit of independency laft againft the temptations
of future Minifters, and Future Kings.—As to the new
Lord Lieutenant 1 never knew any of the family ; fo that
I fhall not be able to get any jobb done by him for any
deferving friend.

LETTER LXXIX.

From Dr. Swift.

Feb. 7, 1735-6.

IT is fome time fince I dined at the Bifhop of Derry's,
where Mr. Secretary Cary told me with great concern,
that you were taken very ill. I have heard nothing fince,
only I have continued in great pain of mind, yet for my
own fake and the worlds more than for yours ; becaufe I
well know how little you value life both as a Philofopher
and a Chriftian, particularly the latter, wherein hardly
one in a million of us heretics can equal you. If you are
well recover'd, you ought to be reproached for not putting me efpecially out of pain, who could not bear the lofs
of you ; although we muft be for ever diftant as much as
if I were in the grave, for which my years and continual
indifpofition are preparing me every feafon. I have
ftaid too long from preffing you to give me fome eafe by
an account of your health : pray do not ufe me fo ill any
more. I look upon you as an eftate from which I receive
my beft annual rents, although I am never to fee it. Mr.
Tickel was at the fame meeting under the fame real concern ; and fo were a hundred others of this town who had
never feen you.

I read to the Bifhop of Derry the paragraph in your letter which concern'd him, and his Lordfhip exprefs'd his
thankfulnefs in a manner that became him. He is efteemed
here as a perfon of learning and converfation and humanity,
but he is beloved by all people.

I have nobody now left but you : Pray be fo kind to
out-live me, and then die as foon as you pleafe, but without pain ; and let us meet in a better place, if my Religion will permit, but rather my Virtue, altho' much une-
qual to yours. Pray, let my Lord Bathurft know how
much I love him ; I ftill infift on his remembering me, although he is too much in the world to honour an abfent
friend with his letters. My ftate of health is not to boaft
of ;

of; my giddinefs is more or lefs too conftant : I fleep ill, and have a poor appetite. I can as eafily write a Poem in the Chinefe-language as my own : I am as fit for Matrimony as invention ; and yet I have daily fchemes for innumerable Effays in profe, and proceed fometimes to no lefs than half a dozen lines, which the next morning become wafte paper. What vexes me moft is, that my female friends, who could bear me very well a dozen years ago, have now forfaken me, altho' I am not fo old in proportion to them, as I formerly was : which I can prove by Arithmetic, for then I was double their age, which now I am not. Pray put me out of fear as foon as you can, about that ugly report of your illnefs ; and let me know who this Chefelden is, that hath fo lately fprung up in your favour? Give me alfo fome account of your neighbour who writ to me from Bath : I hear he refolves to be ftrenuous for taking off the Teft ; which grieves me extremely, from all the unprejudiced Reafons I ever was able to form, and againft the maxims of all wife Chriftian governments *, which always had fome eftablifh'd Religion, leaving at beft a toleration to others.

Farewel, my deareft friend ! ever, and upon every account that can create friendfhip and efteem.

LETTER LXXX.
March 25, 1736.

IF ever I write more epiftles in Verfe, one of them fhall be addrefs'd to you. I have long concerted it, and begun it, but I would make what bears your name as finifhed as my laft work ought to be, that is to fay, more finifhed than any of the reft. The fubject is large, and will divide into four Epiftles, which naturally follow the Effay on Man, viz. 1. Of the Extent and Limits of Human Reafon and Science, 2. A view of the ufeful and therefore attainable, and of the un-ufeful and therefore un-attainable Arts. 3. Of the Nature, Ends, Application, and Ufe of different Capacities. 4. Of the Ufe of *Learning*, of the *Science* of the *World*, and of *Wit*. It will conclude with a Satire againft the mif-application of all, thefe exemplify'd by pictures, characters, and examples.

But alas ! the tafk is great, and *non fum qualis eram !* My underftanding indeed, fuch as it is, is extended rather

* The Author of the *Differtation on Parties* appears to have been of the fame Opinion : But the Author of the Book of *Fragments* is of another mind.

than

than diminiſh'd : I ſee things more in the whole, more
conſiſtent, and more clearly deduced from, and related to,
each other. But what I gain on the ſide of philoſophy, I
loſe on the ſide of poetry : the flowers are gone, when the
fruits begin to ripen, and the fruits perhaps will never ripen perfectly. The climate (under our Heaven of a Court)
is but cold and uncertain ; the winds riſe, and the winter
comes on. I find myſelf but little diſpos'd to build a new
houſe ; I have nothing left but to gather up the reliques of
a wreck, and look about me to ſee how few friends I have
left. Pray, whoſe eſteem or admiration ſhould I deſire
now to procure by my writings ? whoſe friendſhip or converſation to obtain by them ? I am a man of deſperate fortunes, that is, a man whoſe friends are dead : for I never
aim'd at any other fortune than in friends. As ſoon as
I had ſent my laſt letter, I receiv'd a moſt kind one from
you, expreſſing great pain for my late illneſs at Mr. Cheſelden's. I conclude you was eaſed of that friendly apprehenſion in a few days after you had diſpatched yours,
for mine muſt have reached you then. I wondered a little at your quære, who Cheſelden was ? It ſhews that the
trueſt merit does not travel ſo far any way as on the wings
of Poetry ; he is the moſt noted, and moſt deſerving man,
in the whole profeſſion of Chirurgery ; and has ſav'd the
lives of thouſands by his manner of cutting for the ſtone.
—I am now well, or what I muſt call ſo.

I have lately ſeen ſome writings of Lord B.'s ſince he
went to France. Nothing can depreſs his Genius : What
ever befals him, he will ſtill be the greateſt man in the
world, either in his own time, or with poſterity.

Every man you know or care for here, enquires of you,
and pays you the only devoir he can, that of drinking
your health. I wiſh you had any motive to ſee this kingdom. I could keep you, for I am rich, that is, I have
more than I want. I can afford room for yourſelf and
two ſervants ; I have indeed room enough, nothing but
myſelf at home ; the kind and hearty houſe-wife is dead !
the agreeable and inſtructive neighbour is gone ; yet my
houſe is enlarg'd, and the gardens extend and flouriſh, as
knowing nothing of the gueſts they have loſt. I have
more fruit-trees and kitchen-garden than you have any
thought of ; nay I have good Melons and Pine-apples of
my own growth. I am as much a better Gardener, as I
am a worſe Poet, than when you ſaw me : But Gardening is near a-kin to Philoſophy, for Tully ſays, *Agricultura proxima ſapientiae.* For God's ſake, why ſhould not
you

you (that are a ftep higher than a Philofopher, a Divine, yet have too much grace and wit to be a Bifhop) e'en give all you have to the Poor of Ireland (for whom you have already done every thing elfe) fo quit the place, and live and die with me ? And let *Tales animae concordes* be our Motto and our Epitaph.

LETTER LXXXI.

From Dr. SWIFT.

Dublin, April 22, 1736.

MY common illnefs is of that kind which utterly dif-qualifies me for all converfation ; I mean my Deaf-nefs ; and indeed it is that only which difcourageth me from all thoughts of coming to England ; becaufe I am never fure that it may not return in a week. If it were a good honeft Gout, I could catch an interval, to take a voyage, and in a warm lodging got an eafy chair, and be able to hear and roar among my friends. "As to " what you fay of your Letters, fince you have many " years of life more than I, my refolution is to direct " my Executors to fend you all your letters, well fealed " and pacqueted, along with fome legacies mentioned in " my will, and leave them entirely to your difpofal : " Thofe things are all tied up, endors'd, and locked in a " cabinet, and I have not one fervant who can properly " be faid to write or read : No mortal fhall copy them, " but you fhall furely have them when I am no more." I have a little repined at my being hitherto flipped by you in your Epiftles, not from any other ambition than the Title of a Friend, and in that fenfe I expect you fhall perform your promife, if your health and leifure and in-clination will permit. I deny your lofing on the fide of poetry ; I could reafon againft you a little from expe-rience ; you are, and will be fome years to come, at the age when Invention ftill keeps its ground, and Judgment is at full maturity ; but your fubjects are much more dif-ficult when confin'd to Verfe. I am amazed to fee you exhauft the whole fcience of Morality in fo mafterly a manner. Sir W. Temple faid, that the lofs of Friends was a Tax upon long life : It need not be very long, fince you have had fo great a fhare, but I have not above one left : and in this Country I have only a few general com-

panions

panions of good-nature and middling underftandings. How
fhould I know Chefelden ? On your fide, men of fame
ftart up and die, before we here (at leaft I) know any
thing of the matter. I am a little comforted with what
you fay of Lord B's Genius ftill keeping up and preparing
to appear by effects worthy of the author, and ufeful to the,
world.—Common reports have made me very uneafy about
your neighbour Mr. P. It is affirmed that he hath been
very near death : I love him for being a Patriot in moft
corrupted times, and highly efteem his excellent underftanding. Nothing but the preverfe nature of my diforders, as I have above defcrib'd them, and which are abfolute
difqualifications for converfe, could hinder me from waiting on you at Twickenham, and nurfing you to Paris.
In fhort, my ailments amount to a prohibition, although
I am, as you defcribe yourfelf, what *I muft call well*, yet I
have not fpirits left to ride out, which (excepting walking) was my only diverfion. And I muft expect to decline every month, like one who lives upon his principal
fum which muft leffen every day ; and indeed I am likewife literally almoft in the fame cafe, while every body
owes me, and no-body pays me. Inftead of a young race
of Patriots on your fide, which gives me fome glympfe of
joy, here we have the direct contrary, a race of young
Dunces and Atheifts, or old Villains and Monfters,
whereof four fifths are more wicked and ftupid than Char-
tres. Your wants are fo few, that you need not be rich
to fupply them ; and my wants are fo many, that a King's
feven millions of guineas would not fupport me.

LETTER LXXXII.

Aug. 17, 1736.

I Find, tho' I have lefs experience than you, the truth of
what you told me fometime ago, that increafe of years
makes men more talkative but lefs writative : to that degree, that I now write no letters but of plain bufinefs, or
plain how-d'ye's, to thofe few I am forced to correfpond
with, either out of neceffity, or love : And I grow Laconic even beyond Laconicifme ; for fometimes I return only
Yes, or No, to queftionary or petitionary epiftles of half
a yard long. You and Lord Bolingbroke are the only men
to whom I write, and always in folio. You are indeed
almoft the only men I know, who either can write in this
age, or whofe writings will reach the next : Others are here

mortals. Whatever failings fuch men may have, a refpect is due to them, as Luminaries whofe exaltation renders their motion a little irregular, or rather caufes it to feem fo to others. I am afraid to cenfure any thing I hear of Dean Swift, becaufe I hear it only from mortals, blind and dull : And you fhould be cautious of cenfuring any action or motion of Lord B. becaufe you hear it only from fhallow, envious, or malicious reporters. What you writ to me about him I find to my great fcandal repeated in one of yours to——. Whatever you might hint to me, was this for the prophane ? the thing, if true, fhould be concealed; but it is, I affure you, abfolutely untrue, in every circumftance. He has fixed in a very agreeable retirement near Fontainbleau, and makes it his whole bufinefs *vacare literis.* But tell me the truth, were you not angry at his omitting to write to you fo long ? I may, for I hear from him feldomer than from you, that is twice or thrice a year at moft. Can you poffibly think he can neglect you, or difregard you ? If you catch yourfelf at thinking fuch nonfenfe, your parts are decay'd : For, believe me, great Geniufes muft and do efteem one another, and I queftion if any others can efteem or comprehend uncommon merit. Others only guefs at that merit, or fee glimmerings of their minds : A genius has the intuitive faculty : Therefore, imagine what you will, you cannot be fo fure of any man's efteem as of his. If I can think that neither he nor you defpife me, it is a greater honour to me by far, and will be thought fo by pofterity, than if all the Houfe of Lords writ Commendatory Verfes upon me, the Commons ordered me to print my Works, the Univerfities gave me public thanks, and the King, Queen, and Prince crown'd me with Laurel. You are a very ignorant man ; you don't know the figure his name and yours will make hereafter; I do, and will preferve all the memorials I can, that I was of your intimacy ; *longo, fed proximus, intervallo.* I will not quarrel with the prefent age ; it has done enough for me, in making and keeping you two my friends. Do not you be too angry at it, and let not him be too angry at it ; it has done and can do neither of you any manner of harm, as long as it has not, and cannot burn your works : while thofe fubfift, you'll both appear the greateft men of the time, in fpite of Princes and Minifters; and the wifeft, in fpite of all the little Errors you may pleafe to commit.

Adieu. May better health attend you, than, I fear, you yourfelf; may but as good health attend you always as
mine

mine is at prefent, tolerable, when an eafy mind is join'd with it.

LETTER LXXXIII.

From Dr. Swift.

Dec. 2, 1736.

I Think you owe me a letter, but whether you do or not, I have not been in a condition to write. Years and Infirmities have quite broke me; I mean that odious continual diforder in my head. I neither read, nor write, nor remember, nor converfe. All I have left is to walk and ride; the firft I can do tolerably; but the latter, for want of good weather at this feafon, is feldom in my power; and having not an ounce of flefh about me, my fkin comes off in ten miles riding, becaufe my fkin and bone cannot agree together. But I am angry, becaufe you will not fuppofe me as fick as I am, and write to me out of perfect charity, although I fhould not be able to anfwer. I have too many vexations by my ftation and the impertinence of people, to be able to bear the mortification of not hearing from a very few diftant friends that are left; and, confidering how time and fortune have ordered matters, I have hardly one friend left but yourfelf. What Horace fays, *Singula de nobis anni praedantur*, I feel every month, at fartheft; and by this computation, if I hold out two years, I fhall think it a miracle. My comfort is, you begun to diftinguifh fo confounded early, that your acquaintance with diftinguifh'd men of all kinds was almoft as ancient as mine. I mean Wycherley, Rowe, Prior, Congreve, Addifon, Parnel, etc. and in fpite of your heart you have owned me a Cotemporary. Not to mention Lords Oxford, Bolingbroke, Harcourt, Peterborow: In fhort, I was t'other day recollecting twenty-feven great Minifters, or Men of Wit and Learning, who are all dead, and all of my acquaintance, within twenty years paft: neither have I the grace to be forry, that the prefent times are drawn to the dregs as well as my own life.—May my friends be happy in this and a better life, but I value not what becomes of Pofterity, when I confider from what Monfters they are to fpring.—My Lord Orrery writes to you to-morrow, and you fee I fend this under his cover, or at leaft franked by him. He has 3000 *l.* a year about Cork, and the neighbourhood, and

has

has more than three years rent unpaid : This is our condition, in thefe bleffed times. I writ to your neighbour
about a month ago, and fubfcribed my name : I fear he
hath not received my letter, and wifh you would afk him ;
but perhaps he is ftill rambling ; for we hear of him at
Newmarket, and that Boerhaave hath reftor'd his health.
—How my fervices are leffened of late with the number
of my friends .on your fide ! yet, my Lord Bathurft and
Lord Matham and Mr. Lewis remain, and being your
acquaintance, I defire when you fee them to deliver my
compliments : but chiefly to Mrs. P. B. and let me know
whether fhe be as young and agreeable as when I faw her
laft ? Have you got a fupply of new friends to make up for
thofe who are gone ? and are they equal to the firft ? I am
afraid it is with friends as with times ; and that the *lauda-
tor temporis acti fe pueris*, is equally applicable to both. I
am lefs grieved for living here, becaufe it is a perfect retirement, and confequently fitteft for thofe who are grown
good for nothing : for this town and kingdom are as much
out of the world as North-Wales—My head is fo ill that
I cannot write a paper full as I ufed to do; and yet I will
not forgive a blank of half an inch from you.—I had reafon to expect from fome of your letters, that we were to
hope for more Epiftles of Morality ; and, I affure you,
my acquaintance refent that they have not feen my name
at the head of one. The fubjects of fuch Epiftles are
more ufeful to the public, by your manner of handling
them, than any of all your writings : and although, in
fo profligate a world as ours, they may poffibly not much
mend our manners, yet pofterity will enjoy the benefit,
whenever a Court happens to have the leaft relifh for
Virtue and Religion.

LETTER LXXXIV.

To Dr. SWIFT.

Decemb. 30, 1736.

YOUR very kind letter has made me more melancholy, than almoft any thing in this world now can do.
For I can bear every thing in it, bad as it is, better than
the complaints of my friends. Tho' others tell me you
are in pretty good health, and in good fpirits, I find the
contrary when you open your mind to me : And indeed
it is but a prudent part, to feem not fo concern'd about
others, nor fo crazy ourfelves as we really are : for we
shall

fhall neither be beloved nor efteemed the more, by our common acquaintance, for any afflidtion or any infirmity. But to our true friend we may, we muft complain, of what ('tis a thoufand to one) he complains with us; for if we have known him long, he is old, and if he has known the world long, he is out of humour at it. If you have but as much more health than others at your age, as you have more wit and good temper, you fhall not have much of my Pity : But if you ever live to have lefs, you fhall not have lefs of my Affection. A whole people will re- joice at every year that fhall be added to you, of which you have had a late inftance in the public rejoicings on your birth-day. I can affure you fomething better and greater than high birth and quality muft go toward ac- quiring thofe demonftrations of public efteem and love. I have feen a royal birth-day uncelebrated, but by one vile Ode, and one hired bonefire. Whatever years may take away from you, they will not take away the general efteem, for your Senfe, Virtue, and Charity.

The moft melancholy effect of years is that you men- tion, the catalogue of thofe we lov'd and have loft, perpetually increafing. How much that Reflection ftruck me, you'll fee from the Motto I have prefix'd to my Book of Letters, which fo much againft my inclination has been drawn from me. It is from Catullus :

Quo defiderio veteres revocamus Amores,
Atque olim amiffas flemus Amicitias !

I detain this letter till I can find fome fafe conveyance ; in- nocent as it is, and as all letters of mine muft be, of any thing to offend my fuperiors, except the reverence I bear to true merit and virtue : " But I have much reafon to " to fear, thofe which you have too partially kept in your " hand will get out in fome very difagreeable fhape, in " cafe of our mortality : and the more reafon to fear it, " fince this laft month Curl has obtain'd from Ireland " two letters, (one of Lord Bolingbroke and one of mine, " to you, which were wrote in the year 1723) and he has " printed them, to the beft of my memory, rightly, ex- " cept one paffage concerning Dawley, which muft have " been fince inferted, fince my Lord had not that place " at that time. Your anfwer to that letter he has not got ; " it has never been out of my cuftody ; for whatever is " lent is loft (Wit as well as Money) to thefe needy poe- " tical Readers."

The

The world will certainly be the better for his change of
life. He feems, in the whole turn of his letters, to be a
fettled and principled Philofopher, thanking Fortune for
the Tranquility he has been led into by her averfion, like
a man driven by a violent wind, from the fea into a calm
harbour. You afk me, if I have got any fupply of new
Friends to make up for thofe that are gone? I think that
impoffible, for not our friends only, but fo much of ourfelves
is gone by the mere flux and courfe of years, that, were
the fame Friends to be reftored to us, we could not be reftored to ourfelves, to enjoy them. But as when the continual wafhing of a river takes away our flowers and plants,
it throws weeds and fedges in their room * ; fo the courfe
of time brings us fomething, as it deprives us of a great
deal ; and inftead of leaving us what we cultivated, and
expected to flourifh and adorn us, gives us only what is
of fome little ufe, by accident. Thus I have acquired,
without my feeking, a few chance acquaintance, of young
men, who look rather to the paft age than the prefent, and
therefore the future may have fome hopes of them. If I
love them, it is becaufe they honour fome of thofe whom
I, and the world have loft, or are lofing. Two or three
of them have diftinguifh'd themfelves in Parliament, and
you will own in a very uncommon manner, when I tell
you it is by their afferting of Independency, and contempt
of Corruption. One or two are link'd to me by their love
of the fame ftudies and the fame authors : but I will own
to you, my moral capacity has got fo much the better of
my poetical, that I have few acquaintance on the latter
fcore, and none without a cafting weight on the former.
But I find my heart harden'd and blunt to new impreffions ;
it will fcarce receive or retain affections of yefterday ; and
thofe friends who have been dead thefe twenty years, are
more prefent to me now, than thefe I fee daily. You,
dear Sir, are one of the former fort to me in all refpects,
but that we can, yet, correfpond together. I don't know
whether 'tis not more vexatious, to know we are both in
one world, without any further intercourfe. Adieu, I
can fay no more, I feel fo much : Let me drop into common things.—Lord Mafham has juft married his fon. Mr.
Lewis has juft buried his wife. Lord Oxford wept over

* There are fome ftrokes in this letter, which can be accounted for no otherwife than by the Author's extreme compaffion and tendernefs of heart, too
much aff-ct'd by the complaints of a peevifh old man. (labouring and impatient under his infirmities) and too intent in the friendly office of mollifying
them.

your

your letter in pure kindnefs. Mrs. B. fighs more for
you than the lofs of youth. She fays, fhe will be agreeable many years hence, for fhe has learn'd that fecret
from fome receipts of your writing.—Adieu.

LETTER LXXXV.

March 23, 1736-7.

THOUGH you were never to write to me, yet what
you defired in your laft, that I would write often to
you, would be a very eafy tafk ; for every day I talk with
you, and of you, in my heart ; and I need only fet down
what that is thinking of. The nearer I find myfelf verging
to that period of life which is to be labour and forrow, the
more I prop myfelf upon thofe few fupports that are left
me. People in this ftate are like props indeed, they cannot ftand alone, but two or more of them can ftand, leaning and bearing upon one another. I wifh you and I might
pafs this part of life together. My only neceffary care is
at an end. I am now my own mafter too much ; my houfe
is too large ; my gardens furnifh too much wood and pro-
vifion for my ufe. My fervants are fenfible and tender of
me ; they have intermarried, and are become rather low
friends than fervants : and to all thofe that I fee here with
pleafure, they take a pleafure in being ufeful. I conclude
this is your cafe too in your domeftic life, and I fometimes
think of your old houfe-keeper as my nurfe : tho' I trem-
ble at the fea, which only divides us. As your fears are
not fo great as mine, and, I firmly hope, your ftrength
ftill much greater, is it utterly impoffible, it might once
more be fome pleafure to you to fee England ? My fole motive in propofing France to meet in, was the narrownefs
of the paffage by fea from hence, the Phyficians having
told me the weaknefs of my breaft, etc. is fuch, as a fea-
ficknefs might endanger my life. Tho' one or two of our
friends are gone, fince you faw your native country,
there remain a few more who will laft fo till death, and
who, I cannot but hope, have an attractive power to draw
you back to a Country, which cannot quite be funk or
enflaved, while fuch fpirits remain. And let me tell you
there are a few more of the fame fpirit, who would awaken
all your old Ideas, and revive your hopes of her future recovery and Virtue. Thefe look up to you with reverence,
and would be animated by the fight of him at whofe foul

they

they have taken fire, in his writings, and deriv'd from thence as much love of their fpecies as is confiftent with a contempt for the knaves of it.

I could never be weary, except at the eyes, of writing to you ; but my real reafon (and a ftrong one it is) for doing it fo feldom, is Fear ; Fear of a very great and experienc'd evil, that of my letters being kept by the partiality of friends, and paffing into the hands, and malice of enemies ; who publifh them with all their imperfections on their head ; fo that I write not on the common terms of honeft men.

Would to God you would come over with Lord Orrery, whofe care of you in the voyage I could fo certainly depend on ; and bring with you your old houfe-keeper, and two or three fervants. I have room for all, a heart for all, and (think what you will) a fortune for all. We could, were we together, contrive to make our laft days eafy, and leave fome fort of Monument, what Friends two Wits could be in fpite of all the fools in the world. Adieu.

LETTER LXXXVI.

From Dr. SWIFT.

Dublin, May 31, 1737.

IT is true I owe you fome letters, but it has pleafed God, that I have not been in a condition to pay you. When you fhall be at my age, perhaps you may lie under the fame difability to your prefent or future friends. But my age is not my difability, for I can walk fix or feven miles, and ride a dozen. But I am deaf for two months together ; this deafnefs unqualifies me for all company, except a few friends with counter-tenor voices, whom I can call names, if they do not fpeak loud enough for my ears. It is this evil that hath hindered me from venturing to the Bath, and to Twickenham ; for deafnefs, not being a frequent diforder, hath no allowance given it ; and the fcurvy figure a man affected that way makes in company, is utterly infupportable.

It was I began with the petition to you of *Orna me*, and now you come, like an unfair merchant, to charge me with being in your debt ; which by your way of reckoning I muft always be, for yours are always guineas, and mine farthings ; and yet I have a pretence to quarrel
with

with you, becaufe I am not at the head of any one of
your epiftles. I am often wondering how you come to
excel all mortals on the fubject of Morality, even in the
poetical way; and fhould have wondered more, if Nature
and Education had not made you a profeffor of it from
your infancy. "All the letters I can find of yours. I
"have faftened in a folio cover, and the reft in bundles
"endors'd: But, by reading their dates, I find a chafin
"of fix years, of which I can find no copies; and yet I
"keep them with all poffible care: But, I have been
"forced, on three or four occafions, to fend all my pa-
"pers to fome friends; yet thofe papers were all fent
"fealed in bundles, to fome faithful friends; however,
"what I have are not much above fixty." I found nothing in any one of them to be left out: None of them
have any thing to do with Party, of which you are the
cleareft of all men by your Religion, and the whole tenour
of your life; while I am raging every moment againft the
Corruption of both kingdoms, efpecially of this; fuch is
my weaknefs.

I have read your Epiftle of Horace to Auguftus: it was
fent me in the Englifh Edition, as foon as it could come.
They are printing it in a fmall octavo. The curious are
looking out, fome for Flattery, fome for Ironies in it;
the four folks think they have found out fome: But your
admirers here, I mean every man of tafte, affect to be certain, that your profeffion of friendfhip to Me in the fame
poem, will not fuffer you to be thought a Flatterer. My
happinefs is that you are too far engaged, and in fpite of
you the ages to come will celebrate me, and know you
were a friend who loved and efteemed me, although I died
the object of Court and Party hatred.

Pray, who is that Mr. Glover, who writ the Epic Poem
call'd Leonidas, which is reprinting here, and hath great
vogue? We have frequently good Poems of late from
London. I have juft read one upon Converfation, and
two or three others. But the croud do not incumber you,
who, like the Orator or Preacher, ftand aloft, and are
feen above the reft, more than the whole affembly below.

I am able to write no more; and this is my third endeavour, which is too weak to finifh the paper. I am my deareft
eft friend, yours entirely, as long as I can write, or
fpeak, or think.

                                      J. SWIFT.

VOL. IV.   F f f   LETTER

LETTER LXXXVII.

From Dr. Swift.

Dublin, July 23, 1737.

I Sent a letter to you some weeks ago, which my Lord Orrery inclofed in one of his, to which I receiv'd as yet no anfwer, but it will be time enough when his Lordfhip goes over, which will be, as he hopes, in about ten days, and then he will take with him " all the letters I preferved " of yours, which are not above twenty-five. I find there " is a great chafm of fome years, but the dates are more " early than my two laft journeys to England, which makes " me imagine, that in one of thofe journeys I carried over " another cargo." But I cannot truft my memory half an hour; and my diforders of deafnefs and giddinefs increafe daily. So that I am declining as faft as it is eafily poffible for me, if I were a dozen years older.

We have had your volume of letters, which, I am told, are to be printed here : Some of thofe who highly efteem you, and a few who know you perfonally, are grieved to find you make no diftinction between the Englifh Gentry of this Kingdom, and the favage old Irifh (who are only the vulgar, and fome Gentlemen who live in the Irifh parts of the kingdom) but the Englifh Colonies, who are three parts in four, are much more civilized than many Counties in England, and fpeak better Englifh, and are much better bred. And they think it very hard, that an American who is of the fifth generation from England, fhould be allowed to preferve that title, only becaufe we have been told by fome of them that their names are entered in fome parifh in London. I have three or four Coufins here who were born in Portugal, whofe parents took the fame care, and they are all of them Londoners. Dr. Delany, who as I take it, is of an Irifh family, came to vifit me three days ago, on purpofe to complain of thofe paffages in your Letters; he will not allow fuch a difference between the two climates, but will affert that North-Wales, Northumberland, Yorkfhire, and the other Northern Snires, have a more cloudy ungenial air than any part of Ireland. In fhort, I am afraid your friends and admirers here will force you to make a Palinody.

As for the other parts of your volume of Letters, my opinion is, that there might be collected from them the beft Syftem that ever was wrote for the Conduct of human life, at leaft to fhame all reafonable men out of their Follies

lies and Vices. It is some recommendation of this Kingdom, and of the taste of the people, that you are at least it
as highly celebrated here as you are at home   If you will
blame us for Slavery, Corruption, Atheism, and such
trifles, do it freely, but include England, only with an
addition of every other Vice.—I wish you would give orders against the corruption of English by those Scriblers,
who send us over their trash in Prose and Verse, with a-
bominable curtailings and quaint modernisms.—I am now
daily expecting an end of life. I have lost all spirit, and
every scrap of health ; I sometimes recover a little of my
hearing, but my head is ever out of order.   While I have
any ability to hold a commerce with you, I will never be
silent, and this chancing to be a day that I can hold a pen,
I will drag it as long as I am able.   Pray let my Lord Orrery see you often : next to yourself I love no man so well ;
and tell him what I say, if he visits you. I have now done,
for it is evening, and my head grows worse.   May God
always protect you, and preserve you long for a pattern of
Piety and Virtue.

Farewel, my dearest and almost only constant friend.
I am ever, at least in my esteem, honour and affection to
you, what I hope you expect me to be,

Yours, etc.

LETTER LXXXVIII.

From Dr. SWIFT.

My dear Friend,   Dublin, Aug. 8, 1738.

I Have yours of July 25, and first I desire you will look
upon me as a man worn with years, and sunk by public as well as personal vexations. I have entirely lost my
memory, uncapable of conversation by a cruel deafness,
which has lasted almost a year, and I despair of any cure.
I say not this to increase your compassion (of which you
have already too great a part) but as an excuse for my not
being regular in my letters to you, and some few other
friends.   I have an ill name in the Post-offices of both
Kingdoms, which make the letters addressed to me not
seldom miscarry, or be opened and read, and then sealed
in a bungling manner before they come to my hands.
Our friend Mrs. B. is very often in my thoughts, and high
in my esteem ; I desire you will be the messenger of my
humble thanks and service to her.   That superior univer-

ful Genius you deicribe, whofe hand-writing I know towards the end of your Letter, hath made me both proud
and happy ; but by what he writes I fear he will be too
foon gone to his forcſt abroad. He began in the Queen's
time to be my Patron, and then deſcended to be my
Friend.

It is a great favour of Heaven, that your health grows
better by the addition of years. I have abſolutely done
with Poetry for ſeveral years paſt, and even at my beſt
times I could produce nothing but trifles : I therefore reject your compliment on that ſcore, and it is no compliment in me ; for I take your ſecond Dialogue that you
lately ſent me, to equal almoſt any thing you ever writ ;
although I live ſo much out of the world, that I am ignorant of the facts and perſons which, I preſume, are very
well known from Temple-bar to St. James's : (I mean the
Court excluſive.)

" I can faithfully affure you, that every letter you
" have favoured me with, theſe twenty years and more,
" are ſealed up in bundles and delivered to Mrs. W—,
" a very worthy, rational, and judicious Couſin of mine,
" and the only relation whoſe viſits I can ſuffer : All theſe
" Letters ſhe is directed to ſend ſafely to you upon my
" deceaſe."

My Lord Orrery is gone with his Lady to a part of her
eſtate in the North : She is a perſon of very good underſtanding as any I know of her ſex. Give me leave to write
here a ſhort anſwer to my Lord B's letter in the laſt page
of yours.

My dear Lord,

I am infinitely obliged to your Lordſhip for the honour
of your letter, and kind remembrance of me. I do here
confeſs, that I have more obligations to your Lordſhip
than to all the world beſides. You never deceived me,
even when you were a great Miniſter of State : and yet
I love you ſtill more, for your condeſcending to write to
me, when you had the honour to be an Exile. I can
hardly hope to live till you publiſh your Hiſtory, and am
vain enough to wiſh that my name could be ſqueez'd in
among the few Subalterns, *quorum pars parva fui :* If not,
I will be revenged, and contrive ſome way to be known
to futurity, that I had the honour to have your Lordſhip
for my beſt Patron ; and I will live and die, with the
higheſt veneration and gratitude, your moſt obedient, etc.

P. S. I

P. S. I will here in a Poftfcript correct (if it be poffible) the blunders I have made in my letter. I fhewed
my Coufin the above letter, and fhe affures me, that a
great Collection of * your letters to me, are put up and
my you,
fealed, and in fome very fafe hand † I am, my moft dear and
honoured Friend, entirely yours,

J. SWIFT.

It is now Aug. 24,
1738.

* 'Tis written juft thus in the Original. The Book that is now printed
feems to be part of the Collection here fpoken of, as it contains not only the
Letters of Mr Pope but of Dr. Swift, both to him and Mr Gay, which were
return'd him after Mr Gay's death : tho' any mention made by Mr. P. of the
Return or Exchange of Letters has been induftriously fuppreft in the Publication, and only appears by fome of the Anfwers.

† The Earl of ORRERY to Mr. POPE,

"SIR,

"I am more and more convinced
"that your letters are neither loft nor
"burnt, but who the Dean means by
"a fafe hand in Ireland is beyond my
"power of gueffing, tho' I am parti-
"cularly acquainted with moft, if not
"all, of his friends. As I know you
"had the recovery of thofe letters at
"heart, I took more than ordinary
"pains to find out where they were :
"but my enquiries were to no purpofe,
"and if I ar whoever has them is too
"ten acious of them to difcover where
"they lie 'Mrs. — did affure me
"fhe had not one of them and feem'd
"to be under great uneafinefs that you
"fhould imagine they were left with
"her. She likewife told me fhe had
"ftop'd the D an's letter which gave
"you that information; but believed
"he would write fuch another ; and
"therefore defir'd me to affure you,
"from her, that fhe was totaly ig-
"norant where they were.'

"You may make what ufe you
"pleafe, either to the Dean or
"any other perfon, of what I have
"told you I am ready to teftify it ;
"and I think it ought to be known,
"That the Dean fays they are deliver'd
"into a fafe hand, and † Mrs. W— de-
"clares fhe has them not. The Con-
"fequence of their being hereafter
"publifh'd may give uneafinefs to fome
"of your Friends, and of courfe to you :
"fo I would do all in my power to
"make you entirely eafy in that point.'
"This is the firft time I have put
"pen to paper fince my late misfor-
"tune, and I fhould fay (as an ex-
"cufe for this letter) that it has coft
"me fome pain, did it not allow me
"an opportunity to affure you, that
"I am,

"Dear Sir,

"With the trueft efteem,

"Your very faithful and obedient Servant,

Marfton, Oct. 4, 1738.   "ORRERY."

‡ This Lady fince gave Mr Pope the ftrongeft Affurances that fhe had ufed
her utmoft Endeavours to prevent the Publication ; nay, went fo far as to fecrete
the Book, till it was commanded from her, and delivered to the Dublin Printer : Whereupon her Son in-law, D. Swift, Efq; infifting upon writing a
Preface, to juftify Mr. P from having any Knowledge of it, and to lay it upon the corrupt Practices of the Printers in London; but this he would not
agree to, as not knowing the Truth of the Fact.

LETTERS

LETTERS

T O

RALPH ALLEN, Efq.

LETTER I.

Mr. Pope to Mr. Allen.

Twitnam, April 30, 1736.

I Saw Mr. M. yefterday, who has readily allowed Mr. V. to copy the Picture. I have enquired for the beft Originals of thefe two fubjects, which, I found, were favourite ones with you, and well deferve to be fo, the Difcovery of Jofeph to his Brethren, and the Refignation of the Captive by Scipio. Of the latter, my Lord Burlington has a fine one done by Ricci, and I am promifed the other in a good Print from one of the chief Italian Painters. That of Scipio is of the exact fize one would wifh for a Baffo Relievo, in which manner, in my opinion, you would beft ornament your Hall, done in Chiaro obfcuro.

A man not only fhews his Tafte, but his Virtue, in the choice of fuch ornaments: And whatever example moft ftrikes us, we may reafonably imagine, may have an influence upon others. So that the Hiftory itfelf, if well chofen, upon a rich man's walls, is very often a better leffon than any he could teach by his converfation. In this fenfe, the Stones may be faid to fpeak when Men cannot, or will not. I can't help thinking (and I know you'll join with me, you who have been making an Altar-piece) that the zeal of the firft reformers was ill-placed, in removing *Pictures* (that is to fay, examples) out of Churches; and yet fuffering *Epitaphs* (that is to fay, flatteries and falfe hiftory) to be the burthen of Church-walls, and the fhame, as well as derifion, of all honeft men.

I have

I have heard little yet of the fubfcription *. I intend to make a vifit for a fortnight from home to Lady Peterborow at Southampton, about the middle of May. After my return I will enquire what has been done ; and I really believe, what I told you will prove true, and I fhall be honourably acquitted of a talk I am not fond of †. I have run out my leaf, and will only add my fincere wifhes for your happinefs of all kinds. I am, etc.

L E T T E R II.

Mr. POPE to Mr. ALLEN.

Southampton, June 5, 1736.

I Need not fay I thank you for a Letter, which proves fo much friendfhip for me. I have much more to fay upon it than I can, till we meet. But, in a word, I think your notion of the value of thofe things ‡ is greatly too high, as to any fervice they can do to the public ; and, as to any advantage they may do to my own character, I ought to be content with what they have done already. I affure you I do not think it the leaft of thofe advantages that they have occafioned me the good-will (in fo great a degree) of fo worthy a man ||. I fear (as I muft rather retrench than add to their number, unlefs I would publifh my own commendations) that the common run of Subfcribers would think themfelves injured by not having every thing, which difcretion muft fupprefs ; and' this, they (without any other confideration than as buyers of a book) would call giving them an imperfect collection : whereas the only ufe to my own character, as an Author, of fuch a publication, would be the fupprefsion of many things : and as to my character as a Man, it would be but juft where it is ; unlefs I could be fo vain, for it could not be virtuous, to add more and more honeft fentiments ; which, when done to be printed, would furely be wrong and weak alfo.

I do grant it would be fome pleafure to me to expunge

* For his own Edit. of the 1ft Vol. of his Letters ; undertaken at Mr. Allen's requeft

† The printing his Letters by Subfcription.

‡ His Letters.

|| Mr. Allen's friendfhip with the Author was contracted on the reading his Vol. of Letters, which gave the former the higheft opinion of the other's general benevolence and goodnefs of heart.

.   feveral

feveral idle paffages, which will otherwife, if not go down to the next age, pafs at leaft, in this, for mine; although many of them were not, and, God knows, none of them are my prefent fentiments, but, on the contrary, wholly difapproved by me.

And I do not flatter you when I fay, that pleafure would be increafed to me, in knowing I fhould do what would pleafe *you*. But I cannot perfuade myfelf to let the whole burden, even tho' it were a public good, lie upon you, much lefs to ferve my private fame entirely at another's expence †.

But, underftand me rightly: Did I believe half fo well of them as you do, I would not fcruple your affiftance; becaufe I am fure, that to occafion you to contribute to a real good would be the greateft benefit I could oblige you in. And I hereby promife you, if ever I am fo happy as to find any juft occafion where you generofity and goodnefs may unite for fuch a worthy end, I will not fcruple to draw upon you for any fum to effect it.

As to the prefent affair; that you may be convinced what weight your opinions and your defires have with me, I will do what I have not yet done: I will tell my Friends I am as willing to publifh this book as to let it alone. And, rather than fuffer you to be taxed at your own rate, will publifh, in the News, next winter, the Propofals, etc.

I tell you all thefe particulars to fhew you how willing I am to follow your advice, nay, to accept your affift-ance in any moderate degree. But I think you fhould re-ferve fo great a proof of your benevolence to a better oc-cafion.

Since I wrote laft, I have found, on further inquiry, that there is another fine picture on the fubject of Scipio and the Captive, by Pietro da Cortona, which Sir Paul Methuen has a fketch of: and, I believe, is more expreffive than that of Ricci, as Pietro is famous for expreffion. I have alfo met with a Print of the Difcovery of Jofeph to his Brethren, a defign, which, I fancy, is of La Sueur, and will do perfectly well.

I am, etc.

† Mr. A. offered to print the Letters at his own expence.

LETTER

LETTER III.

Nov. 6, 1736.

I Do not write too often to you for many reasons; but one, which I think a good one, is, that Friends should be left to think of one another for certain intervals without too frequent memorandums : it is an exercise of their friendship, and a trial of their memory : and moreover to be perpetually repeating assurances, is both a needless and suspicious kind of treatment with such as are sincere : not to add the tautology one must be guilty of, who can make out so many idle words as to fill pages with saying one thing. For all is said in this word, *I am truly yours.*

I am now as busy in planting for myself, as I was lately in planting for another. And I thank God for every wet Day and for every Fog, that gives me the head-ach, but prospers my works. They will indeed outlive me (if they do not die in their Travels from place to place ; for my Garden, like my Life, seems, to me, every day to want correction, I hope at least, for the better) but I am pleased to think my Trees will afford shade and fruit to others, when I shall want them no more. And it is no sort of grief to me, that those others will not be Things of my own poor body : But it is enough, they are Creatures of the same Species, and made by the same hand that made me. I wish (if a wish would transport me) to see you in the same employment : and it is no partiality even to you, to say it would be as pleasing to the full to me, if I could improve your works as my own.

Talking of works, mine in prose are above three quarters printed, and will be a book of fifty and more sheets in quarto. As I find, what I imagined, the slowness of subscribers, I will do all I can to disappoint *you* in particular, and intend to publish in January, when the Town fills, an Advertisement, that the book will be delivered by Lady-day, to oblige all that will subscribe, to do it. In the mean time, I have printed Receipts, which put an end to any person's delaying upon pretence of *doubt*, by determining that time. I send you a few that you may see I am in earnest, endeavouring all I can to save your money, at the same time that nothing can lessen the obligation to me.

I thank God for your health and for my own, which is better than ufual.

I am, etc.

L E T T E R IV.

Mr. Pope to Mr. Allen.

June 8, 1737.

I Was very forry to hear how much concern your humanity and friendfhip betrayed you into upon the falfe
report which occafioned your grief. I am now fo well, that
I ought not to conceal it from you, as the juft reward of
your goodnefs which made you fuffer for me. Perhaps
when a Friend is really dead (if he knows our concern
for him) he knows us to be as much miftaken in our forrow as you now were: fo that what we think a real evil
is, to fuch fpirits as fee things truly, no more of moment
than a mere imaginary one. It is equally as God pleafes;
let us think or call it good or evil.

I wifh the world would let me give myfelf more to fuch
people in it as I like, and difcharge me of half the honours
which perfons of higher rank beftow on me; and for which
one generally pays a little too much of what they cannot
beftow, Time and Life. Were I arrived to that happier
circumftance, you would fee me at Widcombe, and not
at Bath. But whether it will be as much in my power as
in my wifh, God knows. I can only fay, I think of it
with the pleafure and fincerity becoming one who is, etc.

L E T T E R V.

Mr. Pope to Mr. Allen.

Nov. 24, 1737.

THE event * of this week or fortnight has filled every
body's mind, and mine fo much that I could not get
done what you defired as to Dr. P. but as foon as I can
get home, where my books lie, I will fend them to Mr. K.
The death of great perfons is fuch a fort of furprife to *all*,
as every one's death is to himfelf, tho' both fhould equally

---

* The Queen's death.

be

be expected and prepared for. We begin to esteem and
commend our superiors, at the time that we pity them,
because then they seem not above ourselves. The Queen
shewed, by the confession of all about her, the utmost
firmness and temper to her last moments, and thro' the
course of great torments. What character historians will
allow her, I do not know; but all her domestic servants,
and those nearest her, give her the best testimony, that of
sincere tears. But the public is always hard; rigid at best,
even when just, in its opinion of any one. The only
pleasure which any one, either of high or low rank, must
depend upon receiving, is in the candour or partiality of
friends, and that small circle we are conversant in : and
it is therefore the greatest satisfaction to such as wish us
well, to know we enjoy that. I therefore thank you particularly for telling me of the continuance, or rather increase of those blessings which make your domestic life
happy. I have nothing so good to add, as to assure you I
pray for it, and am always faithfully and affectionately,
etc.

LETTER VI.

Mr. POPE to Mr. ALLEN.

Twickenham, April 28, 1738.

IT is a pain to me to hear your old complaint is so trou-
blesome to you ; and the share I have borne and still
bear too often, in the same complaint, gives me a very
feeling sense of it. I hope we agree in every other sensa-
tion besides this ; for your *heart* is always right, whatever
your body may be. I will venture too to say, my body
is the worst part of me, or God have mercy on my soul. I
can't help telling you the rapture you accidentally gave the
poor woman (for whom you left a Guinea, on what I told
you of my finding her at the end of my garden) I had no
notion of her want being so great, as I then told you, when
I gave her half a one. But I find I have a pleasure to
come, for I will allow her something yearly, and that
may be but one year, for, I think, by her looks, she is
not less than eighty. I am determined to take this charity out of your hands, which, I know, you'll think hard
upon you, but so it shall be.

Pray tell me if you have any objection to my putting
your

your name into a poem of mine (incidentally, not at all going out of the way for it) provided I say fomething of you which moft people would take ill, for example, that you are no man of high birth or quality? You muft be perfectly free with me on this, as on any, nay, on every other occafion.

I have nothing to add but my wifhes for your health: every other enjoyment you will provide for yourfelf, which becomes a reafonable man. Adieu.

I am, etc.

LETTER VII.

Mr. POPE to Mr. ALLEN.

Jan. 20.

I Ought fooner to have acknowledged yours; but I have been feverely handled by my afthma, and at the fame time, hurried by bufinefs that gave an increafe to it by catching cold. I am truly forry to find that neither yours nor Mrs. A's diforder is totally removed: but God forbid your pain fhould continue to return every day, which is worfe by much than I expected to hear. I hope your next will give me a better account. Poor Mr. Bethel too is very ill in Yorkfhire. And, I do affure you, there are no two men I wifh better to. I have known and efteemed him for every moral virtue thefe twenty years and more. He has all the charity, without any of the weaknefs of —— ; and, I firmly believe, never faid a thing he did not think, nor did a thing he could not tell. I am concerned he is in fo cold and remote a place, as in the Wolds of Yorkfhire, at a hunting-feat. If he lives till fpring, he talks of returning to London, and, if I poffibly can, I would get him to lie out of it at Twickenham, tho' we went backward and forward every day in a warm coach, which would be the propereft exercife for both of us, fince he is become fo weak as to be deprived of riding a horfe.

L. Bolingbroke ftays a month yet, and I hope Mr. Warburton will come to town before he goes. They will both be pleafed to meet each other; and nothing in all my life, has been fo great a pleafure to my nature, as to bring deferving and knowing men together. It is the greateft favour that can be done, either to great geniufes or ufeful men. I wifh too, he were a while in town, if it

were

were only to lie a little in the way of some proud and powerful persons, to see if they have any of the best sort of pride left, namely, to serve learning and merit, and by that means distinguish themselves from their predecessors.

I am, etc.

LETTER VIII.

Mr. POPE to Mr. ALLEN.

March 6.

I Thank you very kindly for yours. I am sure we shall meet with the same hearts we ever met ; and I could wish it were at Twickenham, tho' only to see you and Mrs. Allen twice there instead of once. But, as matters have turned out, a decent obedience to the government has since obliged me to reside here, ten miles out of the capital ; and therefore I must see you here or no where. Let that be an additional reason for your coming and staying what time you can.

The utmost I can do, I will venture to tell you in your ear. I may slide along the Surrey side (where no Middlesex justice can pretend any cognizance) to Battersea, and thence cross the water for an hour or two, in a close chair, to dine with you or so. But to be in town, I fear, will be imprudent and thought insolent. At least, hitherto, all comply with the proclamation *.

I write thus early, that you may let me know if your day continues, and I will have every room in my house as warm for you as the owner always would be. It may possibly be that I shall be taking the secret flight I speak of to Battersea, before you come, with Mr. Warburton, whom I have promised to make known to the only great man in Europe, who knows as much as He. And from thence we may return the 16th, or any day, hither, and meet you, without fail if you fix your day.

I would not make ill health come into the scale, as to keeping me here (tho', in truth, it now bears very hard upon me again, and the least accident of cold, or motion, almost throws me into a very dangerous and suffering condition.) God send you long life, and an easier enjoyment of your breath than I now can expect, I fear, etc.

* On the Invasion, at that time threatened from France and the Pretender.

LETTERS

OF

Mr. POPE

TO

Mr. WARBURTON,

LETTER I.

April 11, 1739.

I Have juft received from Mr. R. two more of your *Letters* *. It is in the greateft hurry imaginable that I write this, but I cannot help thanking you in particular for your Third *Letter*, which is fo extremely clear, fhort, and full, that I think Mr. Crouzaz † ought never to have another anfwer, and deferved not fo good an one. I can only fay, you do him too much honour, and me too much right, fo odd as the expreffion feems, for you have made my fyftem as clear as I ought to have done and could not. It is indeed the fame fyftem as mine, but illuftrated with a ray of your own, as they fay our natural body is the fame ftill when it is glorified. I am fure I like it better than I did before, and fo will every man elfe. I know I meant juft what you explain, but I did not explain my own meaning fo well as you. You underftand me as well as I do myfelf, but you exprefs me better than I could

---

* Commentaries on the *Effay on Man.*

† A German profeffor, who wrote remarks upon the philofophy of that *Effay.*

exprefs

exprefs myfelf. Pray accept the finecreft acknowledgments. I cannot but wifh thefe letters were put together in one book, and intend (with your leave) to procure a tranflation of part, at leaft, or of all of them into French * ; but I fhall not proceed a ftep without your confent and opinion, etc.

LETTER II.

May 26, 1739.

THE diffipation in which I am obliged to live through many degrees of civil obligation, which ought not to rob a man of himfelf who paffes for an independent one, and yet make me every body's fervant more than my own : This, Sir, is the occafion of my filence to you, to whom I really have more obligation than to almoft any man. By writing, indeed, I propofed no more than to tell you my fenfe of it : As to any corrections of your *Letters* I could make none, but what refulted from inverting the Order of them, and thofe expreffions relating to myfelf which I thought exaggerated. I could not find a word to alter in the laft letter, which I returned immediately to the bookfeller. I muft particularly thank you for the mention you have made of me in your Poftfcript to the laft Edition of the *Legation of Mofes*. I am much more pleafed with a compliment that links me to a virtuous Man, and by the beft fimilitude, that of a good mind (even a better and ftronger tye than the fimilitude of ftudies) than I could be proud of any other whatfoever. May that independency, charity, and competency attend you, which fets a good prieft above a bifhop, and truly makes his Fortune; that is, his happinefs in this life as well as in the other.

LETTER III.

Twitenham, Sept. 20, 1739.

I Received with great pleafure the paper you fent me; and yet with greater, the profpect you gave me of a nearer acquaintance with you when you come to Town. I fhall hope what part of your time you can afford me,

* They were all tranflated into that language by a French gentleman of erudition, who is now in an eminent ftation in his own country.

amongft

amongſt the number of thoſe who eſteem you; will be paſt rather in this place than in London; ſince it is here only I live as I ought, *mihi et amicis.* I therefore depend on your promiſe; and ſo much as my conſtitution ſuffers by the winter, I yet aſſure you ſuch an acquiſition will make the ſpring much the more welcome to me, when it is to bring you hither, *cum zephyris et hirundine prima*

As ſoon as Mr. R. can tranſmit to me an entire copy of your *Letters*, I wiſh he had your leave ſo to do; that I may put the book into the hands of a French gentleman to tranſlate, who, I hope, will not ſubjeĉt your work to as much ill-grounded criticiſm, as my French tranſlator * has ſubjeĉted mine. In earneſt, I am extremely obliged to you, for thus eſpouſing the cauſe of a ſtranger whom you judged to be injured; but my part in this ſentiment, is the leaſt. The generoſity of your conduĉt deſerves eſteem, your zeal for truth deſerves affeĉtion from every candid man : And as ſuch, where I wholly out of the caſe, I ſhould eſteem and love you for it. I will not therefore uſe you ſo ill as to write in the general ſtyle of compliment; it is below the dignity of the occaſion : and I can only ſay (which I ſay with ſincerity and warmth) that you have made me, etc.

LETTER IV.

Jan 4, 1739.

IT is a real truth that I ſhould have written to you oftener, if I had not a great reſpeĉt for you, and owed not a great debt to you. But it may be no unneceſſary thing to let you know that moſt of my friends alſo pay you their thanks; and ſome of the moſt knowing, as well as moſt candid judges, think me as much beholden to you as I think myſelf. Your *Letters* ‡ meet from ſuch with the Approbation they merit, and I have been able to find but two or three very ſlight Inaccuracies in the whole book, which I have, upon their obſervation, altered in an examplar which I keep againſt a ſecond Edition. My very uncertain ſtate of health, which is ſhaken more and more every

---

* *Reſnel*, on whoſe very faulty and abſurd tranſlation Crouzaz founded his only plauſible objeĉtions.
‡ On the *Eſſay on Man*.

winter,

winter, drove to Bath and Briftol two months fince; and I fhall not return towards London till February. But I have received nine or ten Letters from thence on the fuccefs of your book *, which they are earneft to have tranflated. One of them is begun in France. A French gentleman, about Monfieur Cambis the Ambaffador, hath done the greateft part of it here. But I will retard the Impreffion till I have your directions, or till I can have a pleafure I earneftly wifh for, to meet you in town, where you gave me fome hopes you fometimes pafs'd a part of the fpring, for the beft reafon, I know, of ever vifiting it, the converfation of a few Friends. Pray, fuffer me to be what you have made me, one of them, and let my houfe have its fhare of you; or, if I can any way be inftrumental in accomodating you in town during your ftay, I have lodgings and a library or two in my difpofal; which, I believe, I need not offer to a man to whom all libraries ought to be open, or to one who wants them fo little, but that 'tis poffible you may be as much a ftranger to this town, as I wifh with all my heart I was. I fee by certain fquibs in the *Mifcellanies* † that you have as much of the uncharitable fpirit pour'd out upon you, as the Author you defended from Crouzaz. I only wifh you gave them no other anfwer than that of the fun to the frogs, fhining out, in your fecond book, and the completion of your argument. No man is, as he ought to be, more, or fo much a friend to your merit and character, as, Sir,

Your, etc.

LETTER V.

Jan. 17, 1739-40.

THough I writ to you two pofts ago, I ought to acknowledge now a new and unexpected favour of the Remarks on the fourth epiftle ‡; which (though I find by yours, attending them, they were fent laft month) I received but this morning. This was occafioned by no fault of Mr. R. but the neglect, I believe, of the perfon to whofe care he configned them. I have been full three months about Bath and Briftol, endeavouring to amend a

* The Commentary on the *Effay on Man*.
* The Weekly Mifcellany, by Dr. Webfter, Dr. Waterland, Dr. Stebbing. Mr. Venn, and others.
† Of the *Effay on Man*.

complaint which more or lefs has troubled me all my life :
I hope the regimen this has obliged me to, will make the
remainder of it more philofophical, and improve my refignation to part with it at laft.   I am preparing to return
home, and fhall then revife what my French gentleman
has done, and add *this* to it.   He is the fame perfon who
tranflated the *Effay* into profe, which Mr. Crouzaz fhould
have profited by, who, I am really afraid, when I lay the
circumftances all together, was moved to his proceeding
in fo very unreafonable a way, by fome malice either of
his own, or fome other's : tho' I was very willing, at firft,
to impute it to ignorance or prejudice.   I fee nothing to
be added to your work ; only fome commendatory Devia-
tions from the Argument itfelf, in my favour, I ought to
think might be omitted.

I muft repeat my urgent defire to be previoufly acquainted with the precife time of your vifit to London ;
that I may have the pleafure to meet a man in the manner I would, whom I muft efteem one of the greateft of
my Benefactors.   I am, with the moft grateful and affectionate regard, etc.

LETTER VI.

April 16, 1740.

YOU could not give me more pleafure than by your
fhort letter, which acquaints me that I may hope to
fee you fo foon. Let us meet like men who have been
many years acquainted with each other, and whofe friendfhip is not to begin, but continue. All forms fhould be
paft, when people know each other's mind fo well : I flatter myfelf you are a man after my own heart, who feeks
content only from within, and fays to greatnefs *Tuas habeto tibi res, egomet habebo meas.* But as it is but juft your
other friends fhould have fome part of you, I infift on my
making you the firft vifit in London ; and thence, after a
few days, to carry you to Twitenham, for as many as
you can afford me. If the prefs be to take up any part of
your time, the fheets may be brought you hourly thither
by my waterman : and you will have more leifure to attend to any thing of that fort than in town. I believe alfo
I have moft of the Books you can want, or can eafily borrow them. I earneftly defire a line may be left at Mr.
R's, where and when I fhall call upon you, which I will
daily

daily enquire for, whether I chance to be here, or in the country. Believe me, Sir, with the trueſt regard, and the ſincereſt wiſh to deſerve

Yours, etc.

LETTER VII.

Twitenham, June 24, 1740.

IT is true that I am a very unpunctual correſpondent, tho' no unpunctual agent or friend; and that in the commerce of words, I am both poor and lazy. Civility and Compliment generally are the goods that letter-writers exchange, which, with honeſt men, ſeems a kind of illicit trade, by having been for the moſt part, carried on, and carried furtheſt by deſigning men. I am therefore reduced to plain enquiries, how my friend does, and what he does? and to repetitions, which I am afraid to tire him with, *how much I love him.* Your two kind letters gave me real ſatisfaction, in hearing you were ſafe and well ; and in ſhewing me you took kindly my unaffected endeavours to prove my eſteem for you, and delight in your converſation. Indeed my languid ſtate of health, and frequent deficiency of ſpirits, together with a number of diſſipations, *et aliena negotia centum,* all conſpire to throw a faintneſs and cool appearance over my conduct to thoſe I beſt love ; which I perpetually feel, and grieve at : But in earneſt, no man is more deeply touched with merit in general, or with particular merit towards me, in any one. You ought therefore in both views to hold yourſelf what you are to me in my opinion and affection ; ſo high in each, that I may perhaps ſeldom attempt to tell it you. The greateſt Juſtice, and favour too that you can do me, is to take it for granted.

Do not therefore commend my talents, but inſtruct me by your own. I am not really learned enough to be a judge in works of the nature and depth of yours. But I travel thro' your book as thro' an amazing ſcene of ancient Egypt or Greece ; ſtruck with veneration and wonder ; but at every ſtep wanting an inſtructor to tell me all I wiſh to know. Such you prove to me in the walks of antiquity ; and ſuch you will prove to all mankind : but with this additional character, more than any other ſearcher into antiquities, that of a genius equal to your pains, and of a taſte equal to your learning.

I am

I am obliged greatly to you, for what you have pro-
jeɛted at Cambridge, in relation to my Effay * ; but more
for the motive which did originally, and does confequen-
tially in a manner, animate all your goodnefs to me, the
opinion you entertain of my honeft intention in that
piece, and your zeal to domonftrate me no irreligious
man. I was very fincere with you in what I told you of
my own opinion of my own charaɛter as a poet +, and, I
think, I may confcientioufly fay, I fhall die in it. I have
nothing to add, but that I hope fometimes to hear you are
well, as you certainly fhall now and then hear the beft I
can tell you of myfelf.

LETTER VIII.

Oɛt. 27, 1740.

I Am grown fo bad a correfpondent, partly thro' the
weaknefs of my eyes, which has much increafed of late,
and partly thro' other difagreeable accidents (almoft peculiar to me) that my oldeft as well as beft friends are reafonable enough to excufe me. I know you are of the number who deferve all the teftimonies of any fort, which I
can give you of efteem and friendfhip; and I confide in
you, as a man of candour enough, to know it cannot be
otherwife, if I am an honeft one. So I will fay no more
on this head, but proceed to thank you for your conftant
memory of whatever may be ferviceable or reputable to
me. The tranflation ‡ you are a much better judge of
than I, not only becaufe you underftand my work better
than I do myfelf, but as your continued familiarity with
the learned languages, makes you infinitely more a mafter of them. I would only recommend that the Tranflator's attention to Tully's Latinity may not preclude his
ufage of fome *Terms* which may be more *precife* in modern
philofophy than fuch as he could ferve himfelf of, efpecially in matters metaphyfical. I think this fpecimen clofe
enough, and clear alfo, as far as the claffical phrafes allow ; from which yet I would rather he fometimes devi-
ated, than fuffered the fenfe to be either dubious or clouded
too much. You know my mind perfeɛtly as to the intent

---

* Mr. P pe defired the editor to procure a good tranflation of the *Effay on
Man* into Latin profe.
+ See his Life.
‡ Of his *Effay on Man* into Latin profe.

                                                         of

of fuch a verfion, and I would have it accompanied with your own remarks tranflated, fuch only I mean as are ge-neral, or explanatory of thofe paffages, which are concife to any degree of obfcurity, or which demand perhaps too minute an attention in the reader.

I have been unable to make the Journey I defigned to Oxford, and Lord Bathurft's, where I hoped to have made you of the party. I am going to Bath for near two months. Yet pray let nothing hinder me fometimes from hearing you are well. I have had that contentment from time to time from Mr. G.

Scriblerus * will or will not be publifhed, according to the event of fome other papers coming, or not coming out, which it will be my utmoft endeavour to hinder †. I will not give you the pain of acquainting you what they are. Your fimile of B. and his nephew, would make an excellent epigram. But all Satire is become fo ineffectu-al (when the laft ftep that Virtue can ftand upon, *fhame*, is taken away) that Epigram muft expect to do nothing even in its own little province, and upon its own little fubject. Adieu. Believe I wifh you nearer us; the only power I wifh is that of attaching, and at the fame time fupporting, fuch congenial bodies as you are to, dear Sir,

Your, etc.

LETTER IX.

Bath, Feb. 4, 1740-1.

IF I had not been made by many accidents fo fick of letter-writing, as to be almoft afraid of the fhadow of my own pen, you would be the perfon I fhould oftencft pour myfelf out to: indeed for a good reafon, for you have given me the ftrongeft proofs of underftanding, and accepting my meaning in the beft manner; and of the candour of your heart, as well as the clearnefs of your head. My vexations I would not trouble you with, but I muft juft mention the two greateft I now have. They have printed in Ireland, my letters to Dr. Swift, and (which is the ftrangeft circumftance) by his own confent and direction, without acquainting me till it was done. The other is one that will continue with me till fome prof-

* The *Memo'rs of Scriblerus.*
† The letters publifhed by Dr. Swift.

perous

perous event to your fervice fhall bring us nearer to each
other. I am not content with thofe glympfes of you, which
a fhort fpring vifit affords; and from which you carry
nothing away with you but my fighs and wifhes, without
any real benefit.

I am heartily glad of the advancement of your *fecond Volume* *; and particularly of the *Digreffions*, for they are *fo*
much more of you; and I can truft your judgment enough to
depend upon their being pertinent. You will, I queftion
not, verify the good proverb, that the furtheft way about,
is the neareft way home : and much better than plunging
thro' thick and thin *more Theologorum*; and perfifting in the
fame old track, where fo many have either broken their
necks, or come off very lamely.

This leads me to thank you for that very entertaining,
and I think, inftructive ftory of Dr. W***, who was, in
this, the image of ***, who never admit of any remedy
from a hand they diflike. But I am forry he had fo much
of the modern Chriftian rancour, as, I believe, he may be
convinced by this time, that the kingdom of Heaven is not
for fuch.

I am juft returning to London, and fhall the more im-
patiently expect your book's appearance, as I hope you will
follow it; and that I may have as happy a month thro' your
means as I had the laft fpring.

I am, etc.

LETTER X.

April 14, 1741.

YOU are every way kind to me; in your partiality to
what is tolerable in me; and in your freedom where
you find me in an error. Such, I own, is the inftance given of — You owe me much friendfhip of this latter fort,
having been too profufe of the former.

I think every day a week till you come to town, which
Mr. G. tells me, will be in the beginning of the next
month : When I expect, you will contrive to be as beneficial to me as you can, by paffing with me as much time as
you can : every day of which it will be my fault if I do not
make of fome ufe to me, as well as pleafure. This is all I
have to tell you, and, be affured, my fincereft efteem and
affection are yours.

* Of the *Div. Leg.*

LETTER

LETTER XI.

Twitenham, Aug. 12, 1741.

THE general indifpofition I have to writing, unlefs upon a belief of the neceffity or ufe of it, muft plead my excufe in not doing it to you. I know it is not (I feel it is not) needful to repeat affurances of the true and con-ftant friendfhip and efteem I bear you. Honeft and ingenuous minds are fure of each other's ; the tye is mutual and folid. The ufe of writing letters refolves wholly into the gratification given and received in the knowledge of each other's welfare : unlefs I ever fhould be fo fortunate (and rare fortune it would be) to be able to procure, and acquaint you of, fome real benefit done you by my means. But fortune feldom fuffers one difinterefted man to ferve another. 'Tis too much an infult upon her to let two of thofe who moft defpife her favours, be happy in them at the fame time, and in the fame inftance. I wifh for nothing fo much at her hands, as that fhe would permit fome great perfon or other to remove you nearer the banks of the Thames ; tho' very lately a nobleman, whom you efteem much more than you know, had deftined, etc.—

I thank you heartily for your hints, and am afraid if I had more of them, not on this only, but on other fubjects, I fhould break my refolution, and become an author a-new : nay a new author, and a better than I yet have been ; or God forbid I fhould go on jingling only the fame bells !

I have received fome chagrin at the delay of your Degree at Oxon. As for mine, I will die before I receive one, in an art I am ignorant of, at a place where there remains any fcruple of beftowing one on you, in a fcience of which you are fo great a mafter. In fhort, I will be doctor'd with you, or not at all. I am fure, wherever honour is not conferred on the deferving there can be none given to the underferving ; no more from the hands of Priefts than of Princes. Adieu. God give you all *true blessings*.

L E T T E R XII.

Sept. 20, 1741.

IT is not my friendſhip, but the diſcernment of that
nobleman * I mentioned, which you are to thank for
his intention to ſerve you. And his judgment is ſo un-
controverted, that it would really be a pleaſure to you to
owe him any thing; inſtead of a ſhame, which is often
the caſe in the favours of men of that rank. I am ſorry I
can only wiſh you well, and not do myſelf honour in doing you any good. But I comfort myſelf when I reflect,
few men could make you happier, none more deſerving
than you have made yourſelf.

I don't know how I have been betray'd into a paragraph
of this kind. I aſk you pardon, though it be truth, for
ſaying ſo much.——

If I can prevail on myſelf to complete † the Dunciad,
it will be publiſhed at the ſame time with a general edition of all my Verſes (for poems I will not call them) and;
I hope, your Friendſhip to me will be then as well known,
as my being an Author; and go down together to Poſterity. I mean to as much of Poſterity as poor moderns can
reach to; where the Commentator (as uſual) will lend a
crutch to the weak Poet to help him to limp a little further, than he could on his own feet. We ſhall take our
degree together in Fame, whatever we do at the Univerſi-
ty : And I tell you once more, I will not have it there
without you.——

L E T T E R XIII.

Bath, Nov. 12, 1741.

I Am always naturally ſparing of my letters to my
Friends; for a reaſon I think a great one; that it is need-
leſs after experience, to repeat aſſurances of Friendſhip;
and no leſs irkſome to be ſearching for words, to expreſs
it over and over. But I have more calls than one for
this letter. Firſt, to expreſs a ſatisfaction at your reſolution not to keep up the ball of diſpute with Dr. M. tho',
I am ſatisfied, you could have done it; and to tell you

* Lord Cheſterfield.
† He had then communicated his intention to the Editor, of adding a
fourth book to it, in purſuance of the Editor's advice.

that

that Mr. L. is pleafed at it too, who writes me word upon
this occafion, that he muft infinitely efteem a Divine, and
an Author, who loves Peace better than Victory. Secondly, I am to recommend to you as an author, a bookfeller in the room of the honeft one you have loft, Mr.
G. and I know none who is fo worthy, and has fo good a
title in that character to fucceed him as Mr. Knapton.
But my third motive of now troubling you is my own proper intereft and pleafure. I am here in more leifure than
I can poffibly enjoy even in my own houfe, *vacare literis*.
It is at this place, that your exhortations may be moft effectual, to make me refume the ftudies I have almoft laid
afide, by perpetual avocations and diffipations. If it were
practicable for you to pafs a month or fix weeks from home,
it is here I could wifh to be with you: And if you would
attend to the continuation of your own noble work, or un-
bend to the idle amufement of commenting upon a poet,
who has no other merit, than that of aiming by his moral
ftrokes to merit fome regard from fuch men as advance
Truth and Virtue in a more effectual way; in either cafe,
this place and this houfe would be an inviolable afylum to
you, from all you would defire to avoid, in fo public a
fcene as Bath. The worthy man, who is the mafter of it,
invites you in the ftrongeft terms; and is one who would
treat you with love and veneration, rather than what the
world call civility and regard. He is fincerer and plainer
than almoft any man now in this world, *antiquis moribus*.
If the waters of the Bath may be ferviceable to your complaints (as I believe from what you have told me of them)
no opportunity can ever be better. It is juft the befi feafon. We are told the Bifhop of Salifbury is expected here
daily, who I know is your friend: at leaft, tho' a Bifhop,
is too much a man of learning to be your enemy. You
fee I omit nothing to add to the weight in the balance, in
which, however, I will not think myfelf light, fince I
have known your partiality. You will want no fervant
here. Your room will be next to mine, and one man
will ferve us. Here is a Library and a Gallery ninety
feet long to walk in, and a coach whenever you would
take the air with me. Mr. ALLEN tells me, you might
on horfeback be here in three days; it is lefs than 100 miles
from Newarke, the road through Leicefter, Stow in the
Wolde in Gloncefterfhire, and Cirencefter by Lord Bathurft's. I could engage to carry you to London from
hence, and I would accommodate my time and journey to
your conveniency.

Is all this a dream ? or can you make it a reality ! can you give ear to me ?

> *Audiſtin' ? an me ludit amabilis*
> *Inſania ?*

Dear Sir, adieu ; and give me a line to Mr. Allen's at Bath. God preſerve you ever.

LETTER XIV.

Nov. 12, 1741.

YOURS is very full and very kind, it is a friendly and fatisfactory anſwer, and all I can defire. Do but inſtantly fulfil it.—Only I hope this will find you before you ſet out. For I think (on all conſiderations) your beſt way will be to take London in your way. It will ſecure you from accidents of weather to travel in the coach, both thither and from thence hither. But in particular, I think you ſhould take ſome care as to Mr. G's executors. And I am of opinion, no man will be more ſerviceable in ſettling any ſuch accounts than Mr. Knapton, who ſo well knows the trade, and is of ſo acknowledged a credit in it. If you can ſtay but a few days there, I ſhould be glad ; tho' I would not have you omit any neceſſary thing to yourſelf. I wiſh too you would juſt ſee ***, though when you have paſs'd a month here, it will be time enough, for all we have to do in town, and they will be leſs buſy, probably, than juſt before the Seſſion opens, to think of men of letters.

When you are in London I beg a line from you, in which pray tell us what day you ſhall arrive at Bath by the coach, that we may ſend to meet you, and bring you hither.

You will owe me a real obligation by being made acquainted with the maſter of this houſe ; and by ſharing with me, what I think one of the chief ſatisfactions of my life, his Friendſhip. But whether I ſhall owe you any in contributing to make me a ſcribler again *, I know not.

---

* He had concerted the plan of the fourth book of the Dunciad with the Editor the ſummer before ; and had now written a great part of it ; which he was willing the Editor ſhould ſee.

LETTER

LETTER XV.

April 23, 1742.

MY letters are fo fhort, partly becaufe I could by no length of *writings* (not even by fuch as lawyers write) *convey* to you more than you have already of my heart and efteem ; and partly becaufe I want time and eyes. I can't fufficiently tell you both my pleafure and my gratefulnefs, in and for your two laft letters, which fhew your zeal fo ftrong for that piece of my idlenefs, which was literally written only to keep *me* from fleeping in a dull winter, and perhaps to make others fleep unlefs awaken'd by my Commentator ; no uncommon cafe among the learned. I am every day in expectation of Lord Bolingbroke's arrival : with whom I fhall feize all the hours I can ; for his ftay (I fear by what he writes) will be very fhort.—I do not think it impoffible but he may go to Bath for a few weeks, to fee (if he be then alive, as yet he is) his old fervant.—In that cafe I think to go with him, and if it fhould be at a feafon when the waters are beneficial (which agree particularly with him too) would it be an impoffibility to meet you at Mr. Allen's ? whofe houfe, you know, and heart are yours. Though this is a mere chance, I fhould not be forry you faw fo great a genius, though he and you were never to meet again.—Adieu. The world is not what I wifh it ; but I will not repent being in it while two or three live.

I am, etc.

LETTER XVI.

Bath, Nov. 27, 1742.

THIS will fhew you I am ftill with our friend, but it is the laft day ; and I would rather you heard of me pleafed, as yet I am, than chagrin'd as I fhall be in a few hours. We are both pretty well. I wifh you had been more explicit if your leg be quite well. You fay no more than that you got home well. I expect a more particular account of you when you have repofed yourfelf a while at your own fire-fide. I fhall inquire as foon as I am in London, which of my friends have feen you ? There are two or three who know how to value you : I wifh I were as

fure

fure they would ſtudy to ſerve you.—A project has ariſen
in my head to make you, in ſome meaſure, the Editor of
this new edition of the Dunciad *, if you have no ſcruple
of owning ſome of the graver notes, which are now added † to thoſe of Dr. Arbuthnot.   I mean it as a kind of
prelude, or advertiſement to the public, of your Commentaries on the *Eſſays on Man*, and on *Criticiſm*, which I
propoſe to print next in another volume proportioned to
this.   I only doubt whether an avowal of theſe notes to ſo
ludicrous a poem be ſuitable to a character ſo eſtabliſhed as
yours for more ſerious ſtudies.   It was a ſudden thought
ſince we parted ; and I would have you treat it as no more;
and tell me if it is not better to be ſuppreſs'd ; freely and
friendly.   I have a particular reaſon to make you intereſt
yourſelf in me and my writings.   It will cauſe both them
and me to make the better figure to poſterity.   A very
mediocre poet, one Drayton, is yet taken ſome notice of,
becauſe Selden writ a few notes on one of his poems.—

   Adieu.   May every domeſtic happineſs make you unwilling to remove from home ; and may every friend you
do that kindneſs for, treat you ſo as to make you forget
you are not at home.

I am, etc.

LETTER XVII.

Dec. 28, 1742.

I Have always ſo many things to take kindly of you,
that I don't know which to begin to thank you for.   I
was willing to concjude our whole account of the Dunciad, at leaſt, and therefore ſtaid till it was finiſhed.   The
encouragement you gave me to add the fourth book firſt
determined me to do ſo ; and the approbation you ſeem'd
to give it was what ſingly determined me to print it.
Since that, your Notes and your Diſcourſe in the name
of Ariſtarchus, have given its laſt finiſhings and ornaments.—I am glad you will refreſh the *memory* of ſuch
readers as have no other faculty to be readers, eſpecially
of ſuch works as the *Divine Legation*.   But I hope you
will not take too much notice of another and duller

---

* That is, of the four books complete.
† Added in the three firſt books, and diſtinguiſhed in this edition of his
works.

and

fort; thofe who become writers thro' malice, and muſt die whenever you pleaſe to ſhine out in the completion of the Work; which I wiſh were now your only anſwer to any of them: except you will make uſe of that ſhort and excellent one you gave me in the ſtory of the *reading giaſs*.

The world here grows very buſy About what time is it you think of being among't us? My health, I fear, will conſine me, whether in town or here, ſo that I may expect more of your company as one good reſulting out of evil.

I write, you know, very laconically. I have but one formula which ſays every thing to a Friend, " I am " yours, and beg you to continue mine." Let me not be ignorant (you can prevent my being ſo of *any thing*, but firſt and principally) of your health and well-being; and depend on my ſenſe of all the *Kindneſs* over and above all the *Juſtice* you ſhall ever do me.

I never read a thing with more pleaſure than an additional ſheet to * Jervas's preface to Don Quixote. Before I got over two paragraphs I cried out, *en profeſus aut Diabolus!* I knew you as certainly as the ancients did the Gods by the firſt pace and the very gait. I have not a moment to expreſs myſelf in, but could not omit this which delighted me ſo greatly.

My Law-ſuit with L. is at an end.—Adieu! Believe no man can be more yours. Call me by any title you will but a *Doctor of Oxford; Sit tibi cura mei, ſi tibi cura tui.*

LETTER XVIII.

Jan. 18, 1742.

I Am forced to grow every day more laconic in my let-ters, for my eye ſight grows every day ſhorter and dimmer. Forgive me then that I anſwer you ſummarily. I can even leſs bear an equal part in a correſpondence than in a converſation with you. But be aſſured once for all, the more I read of you, as the more I hear from you, the better I am inſtructed and pleaſed. And this misfortune of my own dulneſs, and my own abſence, only quickens my ardent wiſh that ſome good fortune would draw you nearer, and enable me to enjoy both, for a greater part of our lives in this neighbourhood; and in ſuch a ſituation as

* On the origin of the books of Chivalry.

might

might make more beneficial friends, than I, efteem and
enjoy you equally. I have again heard from Lord — and
another hand, that the Lord * I write to you of, declares an intention to ferve you. My anfwer (which they
related to him) was, that he would be fure of your acquaintance for life, if once he ferved or obliged you ; but
that, I was certain, you would never trouble him with
your expectation, tho' he would never get rid of your
gratitude.—Dear Sir, adieu ! and let me be fometimes
certified of your health. My own is as ufual ; and my affection the fame, always yours.

L E T T E R XIX.

Twitenham, March 24, 1743.

I Write to you amongft the very few I now defire to have
my Friends, merely, *Si valeas, valeo.* 'Tis in effect
all I fay but it is very literally true, for I place all that
makes my life defirable in their welfare. I may truly affirm, that vanity or intereft have not the leaft fhare in
any friendfhip I have ; or caufe me now to cultivate that
of any one man by any one letter. But if any motive
fhould draw me to flatter a great man, it would be to fave
the friend I would have him ferve from doing it. Rather
than lay a deferving perfon under the neceffity of it, I
would hazard my own character and keep his in dignity.
Tho', in truth, I live in a time when no meafures of conduct influence the fuccefs of one's applications, and the
beft thing to truft to is chance and opportunity.

I only meant to tell you, I am wholly yours, how few
words fo ever I make of it. – A greater pleafure to me is,
that I chanc'd to make Mr. Allen fo, who is not only worth
more than — intrinfically ; but, I forefee, will be effectually more a comfort and glory to you every year you live.
My confidence in any man lefs truly great than an honeft
one is but fmall.——

I have lived much by myfelf of late, partly thro' ill
health, and partly to amufe myfelf with little improvements in my garden and houfe, to which poffibly I fhall
(if I live) be foon more confined. When the Dunciad
may be publifhed I know not. I am more defirous of carrying on the beft, that is, your edition of the reft of the
Epiftles and *Effay on Criticifm*, etc. I know it is there I

* L. Granville.

fhall

shall be seen most to advantage.   But I insist on one condition, that you never think of this when you can employ
yourself in finishing that noble work of the *Divine Lega-*
tion (which is what, above all, *iterum, iterunque monebo*) or
any other useful scheme of your own.   It would be a satisfaction to me at present only to hear that you have sup-
ported your health among these epidemical disorders,
which, tho' not mortal to any of my friends, have afflicted almost every one.

LETTER XX.

June 5.

I Wish that, instead of writing to you once in two
months, I could do you some service as often ; for I am
arrived to an age when I am as sparing of words as most old
men are of money, though I daily find less occasion for
any.   But I live in a time when benefits are not in the
power of an honest man to bestow ; nor indeed of an honest man to receive, considering on what terms they are
generally to be had.   It is certain you have a full right to
any I could do you, who not only monthly, but weekly
of late have loaded me with favours of that kind which
are most acceptable to veteran Authors ; those garlands
which a Commentator weaves to hang about his Poet,
and which are flowers both of his own gathering and
painting too ; not blossoms springing from the dry Author.

It is very unreasonable after this, to give you a second
trouble in revising the * *Essay on Homer.*   But I look upon you as one sworn to suffer no errors in me : and tho'
the common way with a Commentator be to erect them
into beauties, the best office of a Critic is to correct and
amend them.   There being a new edition coming out of
Homer, I would willingly render it a little less defective,
and the bookseller will not allow me time to do so myself.—

Lord B. returns to France very speedily, and it is possible I may go for three weeks or a month to Mr. Allen's
in the summer ; of which I will not fail to advertise you,
if it suits your conveniency to be there, and drink the wa-
t.   beneficially.

* ...vise and correct it as it now stands, in the last edition.

Forgive

Forgive my fcribling fo haftily and fo ill. My eyes are at leaft as bad as my head : and it is with my heart only that I can pretend to be, to any real purpofe,

Your, etc.

LETTER XXI.

July 18.

YOU may well expect letters from me of thanks : but the kind attention you fhew to every thing that concerns me is fo manifeft, and fo repeated, that you cannot but tell yourfelf how neceffarily I muft pay them in my heart, which makes it almoft impertinent to fay fo. Your alterations to the Preface and Effay * are juft ; and none more obliging to me than where you prove your concern that my notions in my firft writings fhould not be repugnant to thofe in my laft. And you will have the charity to think when I was then in an error, it was not fo much that I thought wrong or perverfely, as that I had not thought fufficiently. What I could correct in the diffipated life I am forced to lead here, I have : and fome there are which ftill want your help to be made as they fhould be.— Mr. Allen depends on you at the end of the next month or in September, and I will join him as foon as I can return from the other party. I believe not till September, at fooneft.— You will pardon me (dear Sir) for writing to you but juft like an attorney or agent. I am more concerned for your Finances † than your Fame ; becaufe the firft, I fear, you will never be concerned about yourfelf ; the fecond is fecure to you already, and (whether you will or not) will follow you.

I have never faid one word to you of the public. I have known the greater world too long to be very fanguine. But accidents and occafions may do what virtue would not ; and God fend they may ! Adieu. What becomes of public Virtue, let us preferve our own poor fhare of the private. Be affured, if I have any, I am with a true fenfe of your merit and friendfhip, etc.

---

* Prefix'd to his Homer's Iliad.
† His debt from the Executor of Mr. G.

LETTER XXII.

Octob. 7.

I Heartily thank you for yours, from which I learn'd your safe arrival. And that you found all yours in health, was a kind addition to the account; as I truly am interested in whatever is, and deserves to be dear to you, and to make a part of your happiness. I have many reasons and experiences to convince me, how much you wish health to me, as well as long life to my writings. Could you make as much a better man of me as you can make a better author, I were secure of Immortality both here and hereafter by your means. The Dunciad I have ordered to be advertised in quarto. Pray order as many of them as you will; and know that whatever is mine is yours.

LETTER XXIII.

Jan. 12, 1743.

AN unwillingness to write nothing to you, whom I respect, and worse than nothing (which would afflict you) to one who wishes me so well, has hitherto kept me silent. Of the Public I can tell you nothing worthy the reflection of a reasonable man; and of myself only an account that would give you pain; for my asthma has increased every week since you last heard from me, to the degree of confining me totally to the fire-side; so that I have hardly seen any of my friends but two, who happen to be divided from the world as much as myself, and are constantly retired at Battersea. There I have past most of my time, and often wish'd you of the company, as the best I know to make me not regret the loss of all others, and to prepare me for a nobler scene than any mortal greatness can open to us. I fear by the account you gave me of the time you design to come this way, one of them (whom I much wish you had a glympse of) will be gone again, unless you pass some weeks in London before Mr. Allen arrives there in March. My present indisposition takes up almost all my hours, to render a very few of them supportable: yet I go on softly to prepare the great Edition of my Things with your Notes, and as fast as I receive any from you, I add others in order.—

I am told the Laureat is going to publish a very abufive pamphlet. This is all I can defire; it is enough if it
be abufive and if it be his. He threatens you; but, I
think, you will not fear or love him fo much as to anfwer
him, though you have anfwered one or two as dull. He
will be more to me than a dofe of hartfhorn : and as a ftink
revives one who has been oppreffed with perfumes, his
railing will cure me of a courfe of flatteries.

I am much more concerned to hear that fome of your
Clergy are offended at a verfe or two of mine *, becaufe
I have a refpect for *your* Clergy, (though the verfes are
harder upon *ours*.) But if they do not blame *you* for defending thofe verfes, I will wrap myfelf up in the layman's
cloak, and fleep under your fhield.

I am forry to find by a letter two pofts fince from Mr.
Allen, that he is not quite recovered yet of all remains of
his indifpofition, nor Mrs. Allen quite well. Don't be
difcouraged from telling me how you are; for no man is
more yours than, etc.

LETTER XXIV.

IF I was not afhamed to be fo behind hand with you, that
I can never pretend to fetch it up (any more than I
could in my prefent ftate to overtake you in a race) I
would particularize which of your letters I fhould have
anfwered firft. It muft fuffice to fay I have received them
all ; and whatever very little refpites I have had, from the
daily care of my malady, have been employed in revifing
the papers *on the ufe of Riches*, which I would have ready
for your laft revife, againft you come to town, that they
may be begun with while you are here.—I own the late
encroachments upon my conftitution make me willing to
fee the end of all further care about me or my works. I
would reft for the one, in a full refignation of my being
to be difpofed of by the Father of all mercy ; and for the
other (though indeed a trifle, yet a trifle may be fome
example) I would commit them to the candour of a fenfible and reflecting judge, rather than to the malice of every
fhort-fighted and malevolent critic, or inadvertent and
cenforious reader. And no hand can fet them in fo good
a light, or fo well turn their beft fide to the day as your
own. This obliges me to confefs I have for fome months

* Ver. 355 to 358 fecond Book of the Dunciad.

thought

thought myfelf going, and that not flowly, down the hill.
The rather as every attempt of the phyficians, and ftill the
laft medicines more forceable in their nature, have utterly
fail'd to ferve me.   I was at laft, about feven days ago,
taken with fo violent a fit at Batterfea, that my friends
Lord M. and Lord B. fent for prefent help to the furgeon ;
whofe bleeding me, I am perfuaded, faved my-life, by the
inftantaneous effect it had ; and which has continued fo much
to amend me, that I have pafs'd five days without oppreffion, and recovered, what I have three months wanted, fome
degree of expectoration, and fome hours together of fleep.
I am now got to Twitenham, to try if the air will not take
fome part in reviving me, if I can avoid colds ; and between that place and Batterfea with my Lord B. I will
pafs what I have of life, while he ftays (which I can tell
you, to my great fatisfaction, will be this fortnight or
three weeks yet.)   What if you came before Mr. Allen,
and ftaid till then, inftead of poftponing your journey longer ?   Pray, if you write, juft tell him how ill I have been,
or I had wrote again to him : But that I will do, the firft
day I find myfelf alone with pen, ink, and paper, which
I can hardly be even here, or in any fpirits yet to hold a
pen.   You fee I fay nothing, and yet this writing is labour to me.

I am, etc.

LETTER XXV.

April 1744.

I Am forry to meet you with fo bad an account of myfelf, who would otherwife with joy have flown to the
interview.   I am too ill to be in town ; and within this
week fo much worfe, as to make my journey thither, at
prefent, impracticable, even if there was no Proclamation
in my way.   I left the Town in a decent compliance to
that ; but this additional prohibition from the higheft of
all powers I muft bow to without murmuring.   I wifh to
fee you here.   Mr. Allen comes not till the 16th, and you
will probably chufe to be in town chiefly while he is there.
I received yours juft now, and I writ to hinder — from
printing the Comment on the *Ufe of Riches* too haftily,
fince what you write me, intending to have forwarded it
otherwife, that you might revife it during your ftay. Indeed my prefent weaknefs will make me lefs and lefs capable

of any thing. I hope at leaſt, now at firſt, to ſee you
for a day or two here at Twitenham, and concert mea-
ſures how to enjoy for the future what I can of your
friendſhip *.

I am, etc.

* He died May 30, following.

THE

LAST WILL and TESTAMENT

OF

ALEXANDER POPE, Efq:

IN THE NAME OF GOD AMEN. I Alexander
Pope, of Twickenham, in the county of Middlefex,
make this my laft Will and Teftament. I refign my Soul
to its Creator in all humble hope of its future happinefs, as
in the difpofal of a Being infinitely good. As to my Body,
my will is, that it be buried near the monument of my
dear Parents at Twickenham, with the addition, after
the words *filius fecit*—of thefe only, *et fibi : Qui obiit anno*
17—aetatis—and that it be carried to the grave by fix of
the pooreft men of the parifh, to each of whom I order a
fuit of grey coarfe cloth, as mourning. If I happen to
die at any inconvenient diftance, let the fame be done in any
other parifh, and the Infcription be added on the monument at Twickenham. I hereby make and appoint my
particular friends, Allen Lord Bathurft, Hugh Earl of
Marchmont, the honourable William Murray his Majefty's
folicitor-general, and George Arbuthnot, of the court of
Exchequer, Efq; the furvivors or furvivor of them, Executors of this my laft Will and Teftament.

But all the manufcripts and unprinted papers which I
fhall leave at my deceafe, I defire may be delivered to
my noble friend, Henry St. John, Lord Bolingbroke, to
whofe fole care and judgment I commit them, either to be
preferved or deftroyed; or, in cafe he fhall not furvive
me, to the abovefaid Earl of Marchmont. Thefe, two
in the courfe of my life have done me all other good t-

1 ,

fices, will not refuſe me this laſt after my death : I leave them therefore this trouble, as a mark of my truſt and friendſhip ; only deſiring them each to accept of ſome ſmall memorial of me : That my Lord Bolingbroke will add to* his library all the volumes of my Works and Tranſlations of Homer, bound in red Morocco, and the eleven volumes of thoſe of Eraſmus : That my Lord Marchmont will take the large paper edition of Thuanus, by Buckley, and that portrait of Lord Bolingbroke, by Richardſon, which he ſhail prefer : That my Lord Bathurſt will find a place for the three ſtatues of the Hercules of Farneſe, the Venus of Medicis, and the Apollo in chiaro oſcuro, done by Kneller : That Mr. Murray will accept of the marble head of Homer, by Bernini : and of Sir Iſaac Newton, by Guelfi : and that Mr. Arbuthnot will take the watch I commonly wore, which the King of Sardinia gave to the late Earl of Peterborow, and he to me on his death-bed ; together with one of the pictures of Lord Bolingbroke.

Item, I deſire Mr. Lyttelton to accept of the buſts of Spencer, Shakeſpear, Milton, and Dryden, in marble, which his royal maſter the Prince was pleaſed to give me. I give and deviſe my library of printed books to Ralph Allen of Widcombe, Eſq; and to the Reverend Mr. William Warburton, or to the ſurvivor of them (when thoſe belonging to Lord Bolingbroke are taken out, and when Mrs. Martha Blount has choſen Threeſcore out of the number.) I alſo give and bequeath to the ſaid Mr. Warburton, the property of all ſuch of my Works already printed, as he hath written, or ſhall write Commentaries or Notes upon, and which I have not otherwiſe diſpoſed of, or alienated ; and all the profits which ſhall ariſe after my death from ſuch editions as he ſhall publiſh without future alterations.

Item, In caſe Ralph Allen, Eſq; aboveſaid ſhall ſurvive me, I order my Executors to pay him the ſum of One hundred and fifty pounds, being, to the beſt of my calculation, the account of what I have received from him ; partly for my own, and partly for charitable uſes. If he refuſe to take this himſelf, I deſire him to employ it in a way, I am perſuaded, he will not diſlike, to the benefit of the Bath-hoſpital.

I give and deviſe to my ſiſter-in-law, Mrs. Magdalen Racket, the ſum of Three hundred pounds ; and to her ſons, Henry, and Robert Racket, One hunderd pounds each.

each. I alfo releafe, and give to her all my right and intereft in and upon a bond of Five hundred pounds due to
me from her fon Michael. I alfo give her the family
pictures of my Father, Mother, and Aunts, and the dia-
mond ring my Mother wore, and her golden watch. I
give to Erafmus Lewis, Gilbert Weft, Sir Clement Cot-
terell, William Rollinfon, Nathaniel Hook, Efqrs. and
to Mrs. Anne Arbuthnot, to each the fum of Five pounds,
to be laid out in a ring, or any memorial of me ; and to
my fervant, John Searl, who has faithfully and ably
ferved me many years, I give and devife the fum of One
hundred pounds over and and above a year's wages to himfelf, and his wife ; and to the poor of the parifh of Twitenham, Twenty pounds, to be divided among them by
the faid John Searl : And it is my Will, if the faid John
Searl die before me, that the faid fum of One hundred
pounds go to his wife or children.

Item, I give and devife to Mrs. Martha Blount, younger
daughter of Mrs. Martha Blount, late of Welbeck-
Street, Cavendifh-Square, the fum of One thoufand
pounds immediately on my deceafe : and all the furniture
of my grotto, urns in my garden, houfehold goods,
chattels, plate, or whatever is not otherwife difpofed of
in this my Will, I give and devife to the faid Mrs. Martha
Blount, out of a fincere regard, and long friendfhip for
her. And it is my will, that my abovefaid Executors, the
furvivors or furvivor of them, fhall take an account of all
my eftate, money, or bonds, etc. and after paying my
debts and legacies, fhall place out all the refidue upon government, or other fecurities, according to their beft
judgment ; and pay the produce thereof, half yearly, to
the faid Mrs. Martha Blount, during her natural life : and
after her deceafe, I give the fum of One thoufand pounds
to Mrs. Magdalen Racket, and her fons Robert, Henry,
and John, to be divided equally among them, or to the
furvivors or furvivor of them ; and after the deceafe of the
faid Mrs. Martha Blount, I give the fum of Two hundred
pounds to the abovefaid Gilbert Weft ; Two hundred to
Mr. George Arbuthnot ; Two hundred to his fifter, Mrs.
Anne Arbuthnot ; and One hundred to my fervant, John
Searl, to which foever of thefe fhall be then living : and all
the refidue and remainder to be confidered as undifpofed
of, and go to my next of kin.

This is my laft Will and Teftament, written with my
own Hand, and fealed with my Seal, this Twelfth day

of December, in the year of our Lord, One thousand seven hundred and forty-three.

ALEX. POPE.

Signed, Sealed, and Declared
  by the Testator, as his last
  Will and Testament, in Presence of us,

RADNOR.
STEPHEN HALES, Minister of Teddington.
JOSEPH SPENCE, Professor of History in the University
  of Oxford.

F I N I S.